THE FORSAKEN

THE SURVIVOR CHRONICLES, BOOK 3

ERICA STEVENS

ALSO FROM THE AUTHOR

Books written under the pen name

Erica Stevens

The Coven Series

Nightmares (Book 1)

The Maze (Book 2)

Dream Walker (Book 3)

The Captive Series

Captured (Book 1)

Renegade (Book 2)

Refugee (Book 3)

Salvation (Book 4)

Redemption (Book 5)

Broken (The Captive Series Prequel)

Vengeance (Book 6)

Unbound (Book 7)

The Kindred Series

Kindred (Book 1)

Ashes (Book 2)

Kindled (Book 3)

Inferno (Book 4)

Phoenix Rising (Book 5)

The Fire & Ice Series

Frost Burn (Book 1)

Arctic Fire (Book 2)

Scorched Ice (Book 3)

The Ravening Series

The Ravening (Book 1)

Taken Over (Book 2)

Reclamation (Book 3)

The Survivor Chronicles

The Upheaval (Book 1)

The Divide (Book 2)

The Forsaken (Book 3)

The Risen (Book 4)

Books written under the pen name
Brenda K. Davies

The Vampire Awakenings Series

Awakened (Book 1)

Destined (Book 2)

Untamed (Book 3)

Enraptured (Book 4)

Undone (Book 5)

Fractured (Book 6)

Ravaged (Book 7)

Consumed (Book 8)

Unforeseen (Book 9)

Forsaken (Book 10)

Relentless (Book 11)

Coming Fall 2020

The Alliance Series

Eternally Bound (Book 1)

Bound by Vengeance (Book 2)

Bound by Darkness (Book 3)

Bound by Passion (Book 4)

Bound by Torment (Book 5)

The Road to Hell Series

Good Intentions (Book 1)

Carved (Book 2)

The Road (Book 3)

Into Hell (Book 4)

Hell on Earth Series

Hell on Earth (Book 1)

Into the Abyss (Book 2)

Kiss of Death (Book 3)

The Edge of the Darkness

Coming Summer 2020

Historical Romance

A Stolen Heart

*This book is dedicated to Eric and Steve.
Thank you for bringing so much joy and laughter into my life. You
are still loved and missed every day.*

*Special thanks to my husband for being my best friend and making
me laugh, to my parents for always being there, my siblings, nieces
and nephews who make life more interesting and fun. To my friends
for helping to keep me sane. To Leslie Mitchell for being such a
good friend and amazing help, and to all the fans who make
everyday such a wonderful adventure!*

CHAPTER 1

John

HE TILTED his head back and released a small sigh as the sun heated his skin and warmed him from the outside in. It was perfect out today, and though he was looking forward to tonight, this was just what he needed as he adjusted the sunglasses on his face and reached for the glass of ice water sitting beside him.

His hand fumbled with air before a cool bottle was thrust into it. He reluctantly cracked open one of his eyes as curiosity got the best of him. The grinning face of his father greeted him as he nodded toward the bottle. "Happy birthday."

John frowned as his gaze finally turned toward the bottle. Beads of water slid down the longneck and were already beginning to gather on his hand. An eyebrow lifted as he stared at the beer label. *Was this some kind of trap?*

"I know it's not your first, but I think you're old enough for us to share one together." He almost opened his mouth to deny his father's statements, but what was the point? "It's not a trap." John returned his father's easy smile as he seemed to read his mind. "I shared my first beer with my father on my eighteenth birthday, and I thought we should do the same."

"Mom?"

"She doesn't have to know about this," his father said with a laugh and tipped his bottle back to his mouth.

John nodded his agreement as he took his first tentative sip. It wasn't his first beer, not even his first of this brand, but it was the best he'd ever tasted as it slid down his throat. His father placed a small cooler with a six pack in between them and settled into the lawn chair beside him.

John studied the trees lining the backyard and smiled as two birds flew through the oaks in a flirting dance as they squawked loudly. "What are your plans for the night?"

He turned from the birds back to his father. "Going to The Pit with Corey and Elliot."

His father nodded. The Pit had been there ever since his father was a kid; it was where everyone went to hang out and party from the time they were in high school to their early twenties. John knew his friends were planning a party for him there tonight.

"I spent my eighteenth down there." His father leaned over and pulled another beer from the cooler. "That was the night I met your mom."

"*Mom* went to The Pit?"

His father's smile widened as he twisted the cap off. "Don't let her motherly demeanor fool you; she was once a little crazy."

John wasn't entirely sure he wanted to think about his mom any less mom-like; he certainly didn't like thinking about her at The

Pit. They were his parents, and he liked to keep them in that box. His father handed him another beer, as he twisted the cap off he realized perhaps he liked them out of the box just a little bit.

"Hard to picture," he commented.

"You'll get to see it one day."

"I hope so," John said as he tossed the cap into the cooler.

His father smiled at him and tapped his glass against John's. "You will. Happy birthday son, the best ones are yet to come. Maybe you'll meet someone tonight."

"I hope not."

His dad snorted as he chugged down his beer and leaned back in the chair. "I felt the same exact way, believe me."

The sun moved lower in the sky as they drank their beer in amicable silence. He should get up and start getting ready, but he was loath to tear himself away. Though he was only eighteen, he knew he'd never have this moment again. They may share more drinks together, but once he stood up *this* moment would be over.

His phone began to vibrate against his leg as the default ringer played. "You going to answer that?" his father asked.

"There are two beers left, I'll call them back."

His father nodded as the sun reached the horizon. "It won't always be like this you know," his father said.

"Like what?" John asked.

"Simple. Easy. It only gets tougher with age."

He didn't think his life was simple and easy now, but he wasn't in the mood to argue with his dad, not today. "I believe it. There was no recess in high school after all."

His dad chuckled as he reached into the cooler again. The ice water sloshed against the side as he pulled out the last two beers and handed one to John. "No, there wasn't."

Pink and orange spread across the sky in a growing wave that made it seem as if a giant hand reached toward him. The thought caused a shudder to ripple through him as he became unreasonably chilled. He couldn't shake the image of someone, or some*thing*, reaching out of the sky to grab hold of him and put an end to his simple life.

"You're not really here you know."

John had to tear his attention away from the sky to focus on his father again. "Excuse me?"

"Here, you're not here, I'm not here. You realize that don't you?" John frowned as his father swung his legs over the side of the chair and leaned toward him. "This, *none* of this exists anymore. *I* don't exist anymore."

"Don't say that."

The bottle dangled from his father's fingertips as he held it between his middle and index fingers. There was a look in his eyes John would have associated with someone looking for their next drug fix. He was tempted to lean away from his father, but this was his *dad*, there was no reason to feel any unease around him.

A whisper of wind blew across the nape of his neck as the trees to the left of him flickered oddly. "Look around you John, it's gone."

He didn't want to look around him, if he did he would *see* things, and he didn't want to see anything. He preferred to sit here and enjoy these beers with his dad. He tipped the bottle back to his lips, but where there had been plenty of liquid in it before, nothing dripped into his throat now.

Pulling it away from his mouth, he went to shake it, but as he held it before him it turned to sand and pooled onto the midnight blue lawn chair he was sitting on. A small sound escaped him as he stared at the pile of sand between his legs. The urge to scoop it up and save it seized him as he began to frantically brush it into the palm of his hand. If he could only save it, then he could...

He could what? What could he possibly do with sand?

"John." He couldn't look. "John." He kept his head bowed as he continued to try and brush the sand into his palm, but it kept running through his fingers and falling back to the lawn chair that had faded to a more ocean blue in hue. "Son *look* at me."

He felt like a petulant child being denied a candy bar. "No."

His father rested a hand upon his forearm. He couldn't deny it anymore, he had to look. His father's face seemed to be fading as rapidly as the blue in the chair. It had a ghostlike quality to it that he was half-tempted to stick his hand through, if it wouldn't be so morbid and awful to do so.

The features blurred before snapping briefly back into acute focus. "It's coming you know."

John frowned and sat back as the sand continued to trickle through his fingers. "What's coming?" he asked.

"*It* is." He didn't think he'd ever been more confused in his life. His father's eyes, so similar to his own, seemed to burn out of his head like some kind of freaky human jack-o-lantern. "Be prepared."

"Be prepared for what, I don't understand. I don't..."

His words broke off as he finally took in the world around him now. The trees that had lined the backyard he'd played in as a child, and the trail leading to the pond he'd gone swimming in often, had vanished. Before him was a barren landscape that was somehow strangely desert, and sickly forest, all rolled into one. Gone were the pines and oaks, left were scraggly and twisted looking trees the likes of which he'd never seen before. A few curled and browned leaves clung stubbornly to the hooked branches bent toward the earth.

Where the hell was he?

"Dad?"

The hand on his arm tightened. He was frightened he would find a skeletal hand when he looked down, but he did so anyway. Thankfully the hand grabbing him was still fleshy, but it faded in and out like a bad hologram at a crappy carnival.

"Dad?"

"Be prepared John, it's only just beginning."

In the distance a dull thud began to sound, he didn't know what it was as he couldn't bring himself to look away from his father, and it wasn't a sound he was overly familiar with. He was tempted to look, but he was certain if he looked away he would never see his father again. Certain this was the last time he'd ever talk to him, but that made absolutely no sense.

"Dad…"

"Be strong son. Be strong."

The thudding was getting closer, and he found he couldn't resist the incessant pull to turn his head. The last of the sand slipped through his fingers as he realized the incessant thudding was the approaching sound of hoof beats. Through the foggy terrain and broken trees, he spotted a lone man on a horse.

A gurgled noise escaped him; he started and abruptly sat up. He moved so quickly he almost tumbled off the incredibly uncomfortable old blue couch. Blinking, he looked around to find Carl staring at him with a questioning expression on his face that made John feel like an idiot. A hammer dangled from Carl's fingers; he removed a few nails from where they'd been clamped between his lips. Xander stood on the other side of the board holding it up against the window as he studied John.

It took John a minute to register it had only been a dream. He struggled to assimilate the memory of his eighteenth birthday from the haunting dream, and the reality facing him now. He didn't know what was worse, the realization it had only been a dream or the awful image at the end of it. Those beers, and that birthday, really had been one of the best days of his life. He cursed the idiot by the church for ruining his dream with his talk of the apocalypse, and Carl for his nonsense about the four horsemen. He tried to shake off the renewed grief the dream had brought him, but he had to take a few deep breaths in order to get himself under control again.

"Look who finally woke up. Bad dream?"

John flipped Carl the finger and winced as he pulled himself up straighter on the couch. It really was the most uncomfortable piece of furniture he'd ever had the misfortune of sleeping on as every one of his muscles protested the movement.

"Yeah," he muttered. Carl's gray eyes narrowed upon him as he swung the hammer idly in his fingers. The beaten and faded Red Sox cap he always wore had been pushed back to reveal his light brown hair. The stress of these past few days had caused his weathered face to appear older than his forty-one years. John couldn't hold Carl's gaze; he was still half afraid he might shed a few tears as he focused on the board between them. "We're staying here?"

"Only for a day, maybe two. We'd like to try and scrounge up some more gas before hitting the road again, and I think we could all use a brief break from the vehicles."

"Is it safe to stay here?"

"Is anywhere safe anymore?" Riley inquired. He looked over as she stepped into the doorway and leaned against the frame. The freckles on her nose stood out against a complexion made paler by stress and lack of sleep. Her cornflower blue eyes were shadowed by dark circles as she glanced at Xander before looking away.

Xander's frown deepened; he went to release the board but snagged hold of it when it slid to the side.

"The windows will be boarded up for the short time we're here," Carl said. "And continuing on without a good gas supply won't be any less dangerous."

John nodded and then winced as he rubbed the back of his neck. He was dreading rising to his feet, but he forced himself up. Though none of them had gotten drunk last night, the taste of whiskey filled his mouth as he tried to stretch his aching muscles. Carl finished hammering the nail in and stepped back as John made his way out of the room. Riley stepped aside to let him pass and then followed him down the hall toward the kitchen. John watched her retreating back before going into the bathroom. He dug out some mouthwash and gurgled with it for a few minutes before spitting it out again.

He barely recognized the man staring back at him as he looked in the mirror. There were lines marking his face and shadows under his eyes that made him seem far older than his twenty-four... No, if he was right, it was July sixteenth, and he was now twenty-five. It would be the first birthday in seven years he wouldn't be sharing a beer with his father.

He pulled at his cheeks as he washed his face and tried to shake the memories and misery the dream had elicited and the uneasy feeling it had created within him. *Just a dream,* he told himself. *There were no hoof beats, only nails.*

The dream lingered as badly as the whiskey. He gargled once more and dried his hands on the hideously cheerful flower printed towel before leaving the pink bathroom. He could hear Carl and Xander working on the other window, but he didn't really feel like listening to the pounding of the hammer right now.

Riley and Al were sitting at the table with their heads bent close together. Riley's hand was enfolded in Al's as he patted it soothingly and said something John couldn't hear. They both looked up at him and managed listless smiles as he leaned against the wall. The windows in the kitchen, and on the back door, had already been covered by what he could only assume was broken pieces of furniture.

"Where are the others?" he inquired.

"Mary Ellen, Rochelle, Josh and Bobby are upstairs. I think Peter is with Carl and Xander now," Riley answered.

He grabbed hold of a chair and glanced questioningly at them. Riley nodded as she unfolded her hands from Al's. "You guys are ok with staying here?" John asked as he settled in across from them.

"We won't be getting far without any gas, so I don't think we have a choice," Riley answered.

John leaned back in his chair; he glanced down the hall toward where he could hear the others talking discreetly. "We've been going this entire time, it feels so weird to stop and sit; I don't like it."

"Neither do I," Al admitted. "But we don't have a choice, not right now."

Riley leaned back in the chair and folded her arms over her chest. "That stadium was awful, but I have to admit I am a little curious to see if something has been established in this town."

"So am I," John agreed.

"I'm really not all that thrilled by the prospect," Al said. "The last thing I want to do is see or be around any more people."

"Have you seen anymore of *those* people?" John inquired.

"Not since yesterday," Riley glanced nervously over his shoulder as the hammering stopped, but she relaxed when it began again seconds later. He frowned at her in confusion, she'd been so happy last night, but now her hands were shaking as she tore small pieces off a napkin. "I don't want to know what they're thinking, plotting."

"You think they're capable of that?" John asked as Al eased the napkin from Riley's hand and placed it on the table.

Color filtered across Riley's cheeks as she fisted her hands before her. "Don't you?" she asked.

He didn't really like thinking about it. When he did, he had to admit all he could picture was them getting together and plotting in some way only their disease-infested brains would understand. The hair on his neck stood on end as he glanced at the covered windows.

"Don't you think they'll notice the boards?" he asked.

"I do," Riley said. "But the curtains and blinds have been placed in front of the boards so it looks like someone simply closed the blinds. It doesn't mean it will keep them out, but neither will not boarding up the windows."

"Mary Ellen and Xander said some of them don't like bright lights and noise, so that's helpful," Al told him.

John nodded as he leaned back in his chair. "Are we going to try and make it to your cabin?" he asked Al.

Al nodded. "If you plan to stay with us, I think that's our next step."

They had talked about Al's cabin last night, but they hadn't made any real plans. He had no intention of splitting off and going a different way if he and Carl were welcome amongst them. These people had become his friends, they were the only family he had left, and he didn't want to lose them.

"As long as you're still willing to put up with Carl, I'm in," he said with a grin.

Riley chuckled as she unclenched her hands and began to pick at the napkin pieces again. "I think that's possible," she told him.

"So do I," Al agreed.

The hammering stopped, and he leaned back to watch Carl walk down the hall with Xander limping behind him. Peter remained in the living room watching out the small window in the door. "We're going to go in search of supplies; who wants to go with us?" Xander asked.

"Your leg," Riley protested.

Xander rolled his shoulders. "It's feeling better, and a lot of the swelling has gone down."

Her fingers curled around the napkin pieces as she nodded. "I'm coming with you then."

"Ok," Carl agreed.

"Wait…" Xander started.

"I'm good with a gun, and I'm faster than you are now," she briskly interrupted Xander.

"She's right on both counts," Carl said. Xander frowned at them both, but didn't protest further as Riley stood up.

"I'll go too." It was the last thing John felt like doing, but he also didn't feel like sitting here and waiting for them to return.

"That should be enough; we have to leave some people here too," Carl said.

"Are we taking the truck?" John asked.

Carl shook his head. "The car. It has more gas left in it, and if something should happen it's the vehicle we can stand to lose."

John nodded and took the gun from Carl he'd been using, but had placed on the coffee table last night. "Happy birthday," Carl told him.

John was surprised he had remembered, but it felt good to have someone else acknowledge it. "Thanks."

"Oh, happy birthday," Riley said as she slapped him on the shoulder. "Maybe we can find you a cake or something."

"I would prefer a beer," John told her as Carl cautiously opened the backdoor and peeped out.

"We can do that," Carl promised as he stepped into the overly vivid day beyond. John took a deep breath before following him out the door.

CHAPTER 2

Mary Ellen

IT WAS hours before Mary Ellen could pry herself away from Rochelle's slumbering form. She'd gotten little sleep as she hadn't been able to stop watching her daughter. She couldn't believe the miracle that had been granted to her, couldn't believe Al and the others had managed to find Rochelle in this crazy messed up world. She was scared it was all just a dream, and she would wake up to discover her daughter gone. She was scared if she looked away for just a second Rochelle would disappear.

Hunger eventually won out as she climbed off the bed and left the room they had shared. She placed her feet carefully around Bobby as he slept on the floor in the hall. He'd started out lying against the wall, but sometime during the night he'd sprawled across the entire hallway. The three bedroom house wasn't big enough for all of them, and more than a couple of them had ended up sleeping on the floor. She dodged a flopping arm as Bobby released a muted snore and turned back over. His shaggy brown hair was plastered against his face.

She spotted Josh sleeping in the room at the end of the hall before she crept down the stairs. She nodded to Peter standing by the small window in the front door. He nodded back but didn't take his eyes off the outside world. She didn't know much about the good looking teacher, but she did know the bags under his eyes hadn't been there yesterday.

She'd heard the hammer but the amount of wood covering the lower windows and the shadows enshrouding the room surprised her. It was night again down here and for a disconcerting second she felt as if the world had ceased to exist outside of those boards. She shook her head to clear it of her thoughts.

"If you want to get some sleep I can keep watch," she offered.

He gave her a wan smile as he shook his head and rubbed at the thickening hair lining his jaw before running his fingers over his mustache. His brown eyes were bloodshot, his short brown hair stood on end from running his fingers through it. "I'm fine right now, maybe in a couple of hours."

"I'll be here," she assured him.

She turned away from him and made her way into the kitchen. Al sat at the table with a mug clutched between his hands and a bowl of fruit already starting to brown. She couldn't help but smile as she took him in. The lines in his face were deeper than the last time she'd seen him and his hand was bandaged, but he was a welcome sight for sore eyes.

"Where is everyone?" she asked.

"They went to look for more supplies."

"*Xander* went with them?" she blurted.

Al frowned at her as he placed his mug on the table and sat back in his chair. "He'll be fine."

"He almost died. I was certain he *was* going to die, or become one of *them*. He shouldn't be out there right now."

Al's forehead furrowed over the bridge of his nose as he studied her. "What happened to him?"

Mary Ellen sighed as she pulled out her chair and sat down. She picked through the bowl of fruit before pulling out an apple not as badly bruised as the others. "He was bitten by some of those sick people and his leg became badly infected. He was incredibly sick for a while and just regained full consciousness yesterday morning."

Al frowned as he studied the back door. "Are you sure it was because his leg became infected he was so sick?"

"What else could it have been?"

"You said he was bitten. What if he was actually infected by one of those people? What if he was sick with whatever is making these people something less than human?"

"He's fine Al. He hasn't tried to eat any of us, and he hasn't started aimlessly wandering into things. If he'd been infected I'm pretty sure his brain would have been fried by now and we would know."

"Maybe, maybe not," he muttered. He glanced up as Peter appeared in the doorway and leaned against it. "Everything ok?"

"It's fine," Peter assured him. "There's nothing out there right now."

Mary Ellen focused her attention back on Al. "What do you mean maybe, maybe not?"

Al pushed the bowl aside as he leaned across the table toward her. "I mean when I was a kid my siblings and I all contracted influenza. Though they were older and stronger they both died but I somehow managed to survive. Xander may have contracted whatever it is those people have, but unlike them, and Lee, his body was able to fight it off."

Mary Ellen remembered the handsome surfer looking guy from their brief time at the stadium. They'd been informed last night Lee hadn't made it, but no other details about the young man's untimely death had been given.

"Lee became infected?" she asked.

Al gave a brisk nod. "He did."

"And it killed him?"

"It did." There was a flicker in Al's eyes and though he never looked away from her, she sensed something more behind his words.

She didn't press him further though; they'd all seen and done things none of them were proud of. She imagined that whatever had happened to Lee, one of them had been the person to intervene, like Xander had with Molly. "I've seen what the sickness does to people, I'm not sure anyone can survive it," she muttered.

"We have no idea what is going on, no idea what is causing this sickness, but odds are there would be people who could survive it," Peter said. "If Xander is one of those people then that presents us with two interesting possibilities."

"Which are?" Mary Ellen asked.

"One, Xander could possibly help to beat whatever this sickness is. If we could get him to a doctor or an immunologist they may be able to find a cure or a vaccine derived from his blood. Two, if it was the sickness he beat, then the rest of us could still become infected by a bite and become one of *those* things."

A shiver slid down her spine as her mouth went dry. "It does kind of remind me of rabies," Al said.

"They should know about this. They're out there…"

"They know getting bit by one of those things isn't good," Peter said. "Even if Xander never contracted the sickness that was a nasty infection, and he was lucky to survive it. We might not be so lucky if it were to happen to someone else. The combination of antibiotics and steroids we used on Xander could have pulled him through, so we should try and remember exactly what we gave him."

"I know what he took," Mary Ellen said. "We'll have to find some more of it, if we can."

"Medical supplies are on their list of things to try and find," Al assured her.

"But they're out there, and they don't know it could possibly start with a bite…"

"They know to stay away," Al assured her. "Believe me Mary Ellen we've had more than a few close encounters with those things. Carl and Riley have been nearly torn open by them. The last thing any of them want to be is within a hundred feet of those sick people if they can help it. I wish we could tell them to be extra careful, but I don't think it's necessary, and I wouldn't know where to start looking for them."

Mary Ellen glanced nervously at the kitchen door again. It took everything she had not to go after them, but Al was right, she didn't know where to begin to look. They could be anywhere in this town, and running out there after them would probably only get someone killed.

She rose from the table and paced over to the backdoor. Her fingers rested against the board as she bowed her head and took a deep breath. "Though we still don't know if it can be spread by a bite, it definitely isn't spread by a scratch," Al said. "Carl and Riley have both sustained a fair amount of scratches and scrapes at the hands of those people… things?"

Mary Ellen wasn't entirely sure what they were anymore either.

"But they're both healthy and never got sick. Their wounds didn't even get infected," Al continued.

Mary Ellen shuddered. She wished she could see through the boards to the strange world beyond. At the same time she was grateful to have this brief reprieve from the destruction and violence that had been waged upon the earth.

"The human mouth is full of bacteria and germs under the best of circumstances, and I highly doubt those things are brushing and flossing," Peter said.

Mary Ellen couldn't help but release a small snort of laughter. "I doubt they are too."

"I'm going to go check the window again." Peter turned and hurried back down the hall to the front door.

Al smiled at her as she took a bite of her apple and walked over to take her seat again. "It's good to see you," he said.

"You too. Thank you for keeping Rochelle safe."

He reached over and squeezed her hand. "It was my pleasure. She's a good kid, tough, and very capable of taking care of herself."

"I still can't believe all of you found each other." Mary Ellen wiped a tear from her eye as her thoughts returned to her amazingly good fortune. "I thought I'd lost her."

"I thought we were all lost for a little while there," he admitted.

"And now?"

"Now I realize the world is a large and crazy place, but I think we can make it through. We've made it this far, knock on wood." He tapped his knuckles on the table as he pushed his mug aside. "But we're going to have to be tougher, and we're going to have to get some place safer, with less people."

She nodded as she glanced around the kitchen. "I could almost

believe we are safe here, almost believe we could stay, and that someone will come to save us, but no one's coming."

"No, they're not," he agreed.

"The only people capable of saving us are us. It does feel good to just sit for a bit."

"It does."

Mary Ellen couldn't help but recall the kindly neighbor who had been her only companion before all of this had started as he smiled at her, but behind the sparkle in his blue eyes she sensed something different about her neighbor. Something harder and more resilient, but then Al had proven tougher than she'd ever thought he could be when they'd been fleeing Newport in search of Rochelle.

What had he gone through out there?

Her daughter had said very little about their journey to get here. Rochelle had been more focused on talking about the friendships she'd forged over the past few days, the people she had come to care for and had helped her when she'd needed them most. Though, Mary Ellen hadn't shared any of *her* stories with her daughter either as she'd prefer to protect her daughter. However, looking and listening to Al she began to realize there wasn't much left to protect her daughter from.

"She's seen it all already hasn't she?"

"Not all, but enough. She's tough Mary Ellen, there was more I tried to protect her from but in the end we can't, not anymore, and she can handle it."

"She's always been older than her years."

"No matter how we try to protect our children they always see things we don't want them too," he said kindly.

Heat crept into her cheeks as she bowed her head. She hadn't thought of Larry in a while, she hadn't wanted to give her dead

husband any more time in her life, but Al's words reminded her that she hadn't kept her daughter as protected as she'd tried to from his abuse.

"He wasn't a good man," she whispered.

"I didn't think he was."

"But he gave me an amazing daughter."

"He really did," Al agreed as he drank from his mug again.

"What do you have in there?" she asked.

"Tea. It's cold, but the caffeine boost is amazing."

Cold or not, she wanted some too. Rising, she dug through the cabinets and pulled down the box of tea. Filling a mug with water she dropped the teabag in and turned back to the table. She found herself looking forward to the cup of cold tea as she placed it on the table and sat back down in her chair.

Peter appeared in the doorway again. "You should come see this."

Mary Ellen glanced wistfully at her tea mug but left it on the table as she followed him into the living room. He stepped aside to let her look out the small window. She frowned as she searched the broken front yards before her, but she saw nothing different from yesterday. Then she saw what had caught Peter's attention as she spotted the dogs creeping through the backyard across the street. Except, they weren't the domestic dogs she was used to, she couldn't quite identify the breed.

"What are they?" she asked as she stepped aside.

Al peered out the window before dropping back down. "Coyotes," he muttered as he walked over and picked up the gun sitting on the table.

"They won't bother us, will they?" she asked nervously.

Al shook his head. "I doubt it, but they're probably just as

disrupted, out of sorts, and hungry as we are. I'm not taking any chances."

"There *are* still animals out there," she breathed as a sense of relief filled her. They may be dangerous animals, but they were the first animals she'd seen in a while.

"Let's hope the zoos held up; I really don't feel like encountering a tiger," Peter said.

"Or a hyena," Mary Ellen said with a shudder.

Those hideous animals had always creeped her out. She stepped back to the window as another coyote stalked across the front yard. The hair on her neck stood on end as shadows slipped through the forest at the edge of the woods across the street. These shadows were too tall to be coyotes, and as much as she hated them, they were too ominous to be hyenas.

A smaller coyote, one that didn't appear as old as the others, paused to sit on the lawn across the street. She knew it was impossible, but she was certain it realized they were in the house as its head tilted to the side, and it studied the house with a raised ear. She'd never seen a coyote, but it wasn't as ugly or frightening as she'd pictured after some of the stories she'd heard about them. She found it kind of cute as it yawned to reveal a mouthful of razor sharp teeth.

A shadow fell across the coyote and before she could blink, or issue a sound of warning, something that would have been exceptionally foolhardy for her to do, some of the larger shadows from the woods were upon the animal. Knowledge of what was happening coursed through her mind, and she slapped her hands over her mouth to silence her cry. The animal's neck was broken and the two men, and what she could only tell was a woman because of her long hair, pounced upon the coyote with the savagery of a hyena.

Mary Ellen dropped away from the door and took a step back. Al stared questioningly at her before returning to the window. "I guess we're not their only source of food," he said so quietly she could barely hear him.

"For some reason I don't find that comforting." She glanced at the window again but there was no way she was looking out there again. "They just took down a wild, deadly animal."

"Humans are the most dangerous animal there is," Peter said.

"I can't wait to get out of this town and find somewhere with a lot less people," she muttered.

Peter stepped up to the window again. His upper lip curled in a sneer as he shook his head. "Disgusting."

"We'll get out of here as soon as we can," Al assured her.

She felt a lot better when he walked over and pulled a rifle and another gun from the bag they had placed in the hall closet last night. "Can you use a rifle?" Al asked Peter.

The teacher shook his head as he stepped away from the door. "I've never shot a gun before."

Al nodded as he pulled out a smaller rifle and hastily showed him how to use it. "There's not as much kick to this one, it won't dislocate your shoulder, but it might not stop them with one shot either."

"It's better than nothing," Peter told him as he took the gun.

Mary Ellen's eyes went to the ceiling above her. "I'll be back."

"Here."

Al pressed a gun into her hand before she fled the room. She tried to be as noiseless as possible as she hurried up the stairs, but every step seemed as loud as a gunshot in her ears. Bobby was still sprawled out in the hall, but he was on his back now with his mouth open and a trail of drool on his chin. Mary Ellen shook her head but stepped over him in order to enter the room she'd left Rochelle in.

Her daughter wasn't much more elegant than Bobby as she snored loudly. It never failed to amaze her how much Rochelle looked like her with her dark hair, freckles, and eyes she knew were a warm brown color and sparkled when she was happy. Mary Ellen was tempted to cover Rochelle's mouth, but she doubted the snores were as loud as they seemed to her right now. She crept toward the window and pulled a slat in the blinds down a little. Taking a deep breath, she braced herself before moving closer to the window and peering out.

The three who had taken down the coyote were still feasting on their meal. Behind them though, in the shadows of the forest, more people were creeping forth and spreading out as they walked through the backyards. Mary Ellen's breath froze in her chest; she'd never been so hot and yet so cold in her life. She almost instinctively jerked down on the blind but managed to stop herself in time. She couldn't have been more frightened if she had come face to face with a full on poltergeist.

She glanced over her shoulder, but thankfully Rochelle remained sleeping soundly as the first person stepped onto their front yard. They could all know how to use the guns downstairs, and they still wouldn't be able to stop the tide spilling out of the woods and coming toward them. She couldn't take her eyes off of her daughter as she was gripped with the certainty she'd just gotten Rochelle back, only to lose her again.

CHAPTER 3

Riley

FOLLOWING XANDER'S DIRECTIONS, Riley navigated through the broken roads of the town. The car creaked and groaned as it bounced over a pothole. "I hate this car," John stated from the back. His knees were practically in his chest as he glowered out the window. His brown hair curled around his ears and the nape of his neck; his brown eyes were narrowed as he watched the scenery passing by. His pointed chin was covered in stubble, and a bruise marred one of his high cheekbones.

Riley ignored him as she made a left onto another road and navigated through the ditches, cars, and debris littering the road. "Where is everyone?" Carl asked.

She'd been wondering the same thing as they crept through empty neighborhood after empty neighborhood. She couldn't take her eyes off the road for more than a second at a time as this area of the town had taken a pounding during the quakes. She'd be astounded if the grocery store remained standing. She turned onto another road to discover the destruction leveled out, and by the time she was three blocks farther down, it seemed as if the town hadn't been touched at all.

"Freaking twilight zone around here, I swear," John muttered.

She couldn't help but agree with John as they passed standing house after standing house. Some of the homes still had potted plants sitting prettily on the banisters of their porches. Just an hour ago she'd been glad they were going to get a chance to stay in one place for a little bit, to have some time to recuperate and plan for the next step in their journey, now she wanted out of this town in the worst possible way.

"Take the next left," Xander instructed.

Riley made the turn, and the sign for the grocery store came into view. There were half a dozen cars in the parking lot; she assumed they belonged to the employees and shoppers who had been taken off guard by the quakes and fled the mayhem on foot. They rolled by the large glass windows, but the dim interior gave no hint as to what may be inside.

She stopped the car outside of the front door. "It doesn't look as if it's been looted yet, maybe we should have brought the truck."

"If it's safe, and there is more stuff in there than we'd expected, we'll bring the truck back before we leave. For now let's just see what we have going on in there," Carl said.

Riley shifted the car into park and turned to Xander. Though she wasn't looking forward to having to tell him about Lee, he was still the most wonderful thing she'd seen since all of this had started. There were shadows under his gold-flecked hazel eyes, and stubble lining his normally clean-shaven jaw and cheeks, but he was still handsome. Especially when he smiled at her in the crooked little way that revealed the dimple in his left cheek. His disheveled, dark blonde hair made her fingers itch to run through it.

"Maybe you should stay in the car," she suggested as her gaze traveled to his bandaged leg.

"I'm fine, really." He took hold of her hand and squeezed it between both of his.

"You may feel fine, but if this is anything like the last time we entered a store, you're going to need two good legs," John said as he opened the back passenger door. John's eyes widened; he leapt from the car as Carl shot him a look that would have scared off a grizzly bear. Riley felt the color drain from her face.

"What happened last time?" Xander inquired.

"A trigger happy lunatic with a fully functioning brain, or at least it wasn't a rotting cannibalistic brain like those sick people. John nearly shit his pants," Carl informed Xander when words failed her.

John was scowling as he reappeared in the door. "I saved both *your* asses," he retorted.

"You just keep telling yourself that," Carl said as he opened his door.

Riley could feel Xander's eyes burning into her as she turned back to him. "It wasn't fun," she managed to choke out. "But we survived because we could move fast."

"I can still move fast, and you're going to need more arms and eyes in there than just the three of you," he replied.

"Someone should watch the car."

"It's not like it's a fortified building; we can keep watch well enough from inside."

She started to protest more, but Carl intervened, "He's right and we're wasting time, let's go."

Cursing, Riley pulled the keys from the ignition and climbed out after Xander. Carl held his hand up, and she tossed him the keys. He snatched them out of the air, unlocked the trunk, and pulled the empty gas cans and tubing from inside. "Let's see if there's still gas in these cars before we go in."

She knew Carl had intended to make sure the others had something sturdy to drive and enough supplies to get them through in case they didn't return when he'd left the rack body dump truck behind, but it really would have come in handy now.

"Are you going to tell me what happened in that store?" Xander asked as he stepped beside her.

She found herself barely able to meet his gaze again as she took the can from him. "Yes."

"I did some things I'm not proud of too Ri, we all have."

"I know." She wondered if what he'd done could possibly have been worse than putting a bullet in Lee's head, but she wasn't about to get into it now. She took the can from his hands and turned away as Carl began to draw gas from the first car.

Twenty minutes later, Carl had the gas cans filled off of two cars and tucked back into the trunk of their car. Riley's palms were sweating as she shifted the gun between her hands and eyed the dark grocery store warily. She'd seen nothing to indicate there were people inside, nothing to make her suspect someone waited to open fire on them, but she couldn't shake the feeling of impending doom as they approached the building.

John put his gun down on the brick sill under the window and cupped his hands around his face as he pressed them to the glass. "Do you see anything?" Carl asked.

"Registers and lanes, some shelves," John answered.

Riley placed her gun down on the bricks also, and looking much like John, she pressed her face to the glass and peered inside.

It was difficult to discern anything, but she saw no movement amongst the lanes and the first few feet of the shelves.

"It doesn't look like anything has been touched?" She hadn't meant for it to be a question, but it came out sounding like one.

"No, it doesn't," John agreed.

"How is that possible?" Xander asked as he stepped away from the window. "I figured this would be one of the first places people would come."

Riley stepped away from the glass and looked toward Carl who was leaning against the wall as he smoked a cigarette. "This whole fucking town doesn't make sense," he said. "But there could be gas in there keeping people out."

"What kind of gas?" Xander asked.

Riley informed him of the pockets of gas they'd encountered that could turn a human body into something resembling gooey soup with bone and sinew. Xander rubbed at his chin as he nodded. "We ran across something like that after we escaped the stadium. You think it could be what happened in there?"

"Only one way to find out," Carl said as he walked over to the first door.

Riley stepped to the other side of the door as he stuck his foot out and pushed the door open with it. The door only moved an inch before sliding closed again. "Get me the trashcan," he said.

John grabbed hold of the trashcan at the end of the metal divider between the entrance and exit doors and handed it to Carl. Xander stepped forward to help him push the door open and wedged the can in to keep it open. Xander and Carl's faces were both red from holding their breaths as they stepped away from the door. Riley held her breath as she stepped closer and strained to see if anything moved within.

"I think it's safe to go in," Riley said.

Carl nodded, pulled the can out, and pushed his way into the store. John followed behind him, and she and Xander took up the rear. She pulled her shirt over her nose as the rancid smell of rotting meat and spoiled milk caused her to take a step back. She had to force herself not to gag as the odor assaulted her senses. Breathing through her mouth only made her taste it too, so she snapped her mouth closed.

"We'll sweep through and make sure it's safe before we start gathering supplies. From the looks of things we can at least bag stuff up and set it aside to make it quicker for us when we come back." Carl spoke with assurance, but he was starting to look a little green around the gills by the time he was done.

Riley glanced out the window passed the car and to the town beyond. The street remained just as serene as it had when they'd driven through it. From here, it almost seemed as if it had all been a dream, and the world was just the same as it had been Monday morning. A shiver slid down her spine and despite the sauna-like heat of the day, she couldn't suppress a shudder as an ominous feeling settled over her.

"What about the car?" she asked.

"It will be ok, they're not going to get far without the keys," Carl reminded her.

She still felt uncomfortable leaving it unguarded. She couldn't shake the feeling someone would be in there waiting to pounce on them when they returned. "Nobody would want to steal that hunk of junk anyway," John said.

"It's gotten us this far," she reminded him.

John shrugged and glanced out the window at it. "True, but it won't get us much further if we don't have something other than chips and jerky to fuel *us*."

Riley nodded and turned away from the window. If someone

was waiting for them, then they had better be faster and stronger than a bullet. She winced as John's sneaker squeaked on the linoleum; it was gratingly loud in the hushed store. Walking to the first row they split off as Carl and John went all the way to the end while she and Xander stayed at the top. Keeping pace with each other they walked down the rows as they searched for someone hiding amongst the aisles.

A few of the rows had goods lying in the middle of them and dark stains on the floor, but in the dim illumination she couldn't tell what the stains were. There were carriages discarded amongst the aisles like old relics of a time forgotten. She wondered if in a thousand years, if there was even something of the human race left, if they would uncover these artifacts and put them in a museum like humans did with lost civilizations now.

One carriage still had a purse in the front of it, its owner having run out in a panic after the initial quakes started. *Why hadn't they taken their cars?* Her step faltered as the thought blazed through her mind. There were no people in here, no bodies so far, but there had been cars in the parking lot outside.

Maybe they all hopped into a vehicle or two together. It wasn't the best answer, but it was the only one she could come up with. Staying together, being with people they knew, would have been a natural instinct for the people leaving here and one she would have shared.

She could feel every beat of her heart in her ears as on each new row she kept expecting to find some hideous creature, but the store remained strangely empty up until the last row. Her hands fell back to her sides as she lowered the gun. A small tremor shook her hand as unreasonable dread held her firmly within its relentless grasp.

"I don't like this," she said to Xander.

"Neither do I."

Carl held up his hand and gestured toward something they couldn't see in between the deli counter and the back row of refrigerated goods now stinking up the air. "Bathroom," he called in a hushed whisper.

He gestured to John and then disappeared down the hall they couldn't see. John glanced nervously at them before focusing his attention on wherever Carl had gone. Riley didn't have to go to the bathroom, but she felt like she was doing the pee-pee dance as she shifted from foot to foot.

She heaved an audible breath of relief when Carl reemerged from the bathroom. He gave them a thumbs up sign before heading down the back aisle again. John hurried after him. Riley and Xander followed them along the front of the rows until they spotted Carl standing in the middle of the store by a set of black swinging doors.

Riley's heart plummeted and then shot into her throat. Those doors seemed like a yawning abyss straight into the devil's belly. *God has forsaken us,* ran through her mind as she flashed back to the man outside of the church.

"Carl," the name came out of her in a croak that didn't travel past her or Xander as Carl cautiously pushed the door open. Her shoulders hunched as she braced herself for demons, hell hounds, or Satan himself to come bursting through the door.

The store remained so still she could hear the faint drop of something dripping onto the floor. She wasn't breathing as Carl stepped through the door and disappeared. John grabbed the door before it could swing completely shut and poked his head inside.

Riley had to force her head to turn as she looked toward the fifteen-foot high glass windows at the front. The glare of the sun gleamed on the glass and made it difficult to see the car from this angle. She didn't care about the car right now; she was simply looking for a distraction from the fact Carl hadn't reemerged yet.

Movement in her peripheral vision drew her attention back to the doors as Carl reappeared. Relief filled her as the doors swung shut, and John and Carl made their way down the aisle toward them. "There are a lot of boxes and supplies back there, but it looks pretty clear. I couldn't get the back door open though."

"Why not?" Riley asked.

"I don't know. This area is in relatively good shape, but it still sustained some shocks. The door could be warped from the quakes or something may be blocking it."

"Would it be faster if we just took the boxes from the back?" John asked.

"I don't know what's in any of them; it would probably take more time to go through them than to just grab stuff," Carl answered.

Riley grabbed one of the carts at the end of the self-checkout aisle and an armload of the cloth bags displayed by the front door. "Good to see you're doing your part to save the environment," John said.

She couldn't help but grin at him. "What's left of it anyway."

He smiled as he turned away. Xander slid his cart over beside hers and grabbed some bags for himself. Without a word they split off, and she and Xander went toward the bread aisle on one end, while John and Carl headed toward the fruit and deli aisle.

"You've become good friends with them," Xander commented.

Riley nodded as she began to shove loaves of bread into one of her bags. "They're really good guys. The first time we met them was right after the stadium, and they were protecting Rochelle from three men trying to take her." Riley finished stuffing the bag and turned to put it in the cart. "I was only trying to scare them away, but I shot one of the men. It was the first time I killed someone."

Now wasn't exactly the time to discuss what had happened with Lee, but those words had popped out of her mouth before she could stop them. Xander froze in the act of filling his bag and lifted his head to meet her gaze head on. "I killed a teenage girl when she turned into whatever those people are out there and tried to attack us. Her name was Molly; I helped rescue her from the school with Peter and Josh, and then I bashed her head in with a metal pole."

Riley winced and placed another bag in the cart. The words were blunt, but she sensed the anguish behind them in the terseness of his tone, the pinched corners of his mouth, and the abject look in his eyes. "That must have been awful," she whispered.

"It was." Riley couldn't meet his gaze again as she began to pull more rolls from the shelves. "We've all done things Ri, that girl, she was just a child, but it had to be done. What you did to that man *had* to be done. Whatever else you've done…"

"I killed Lee." The words were a whisper so bare she wasn't sure she'd said them until she heard his abrupt intake of breath. She shoved another thing of rolls into her bag and dumped it in the cart. "He turned into one of those things, he tried to kill us, and I shot him in the head."

She grabbed her cart and moved down the aisle before she could see the condemnation or hatred in his eyes. There was only so much bread they could eat and it would go bad soon enough anyway. She skipped over the frozen food aisle and the cleaning supplies aisle. She was grabbing toilet paper when Xander caught up to her. The calluses on his palm brushed against her skin as he grabbed hold of her arm. Though she tried to look everywhere but at him she finally met his gaze.

She was terrified of what he would say or do, but she was so unbelievably relieved to finally have it out between them that tears burned her eyes. Even if he couldn't forgive her, she knew she would move on, she would continue to live and fight and survive. He may hate her, but Lee's death wasn't hanging over her head, and there wasn't an invisible wall between them anymore. She could *breathe* again.

She had braced herself for his anger; she was stunned by the love she saw in his eyes instead, and she understood now it had always been love with him. He didn't ask her what had happened, didn't tell her she'd done what had to be done. He simply cupped her cheeks and kissed her with a tenderness that made her heart swell and her toes curl.

"When you're ready to talk about it, I'll be here," he whispered against her mouth.

She grabbed hold of his hands and pressed them against her cheeks. Emotion swelled through her, and it took all she had not to start sobbing. Forgiveness, he wasn't the one who would be able to give it to her. She had to be the one to forgive herself, but he'd given her something almost as good with his acceptance of her and the choices she'd had to make.

"We should get moving," she told him as she heard John and Carl bickering just a few aisles over.

He smiled as he brushed away the single tear sliding free before kissing her nose and releasing her. "Yes ma'am."

Riley wiped at her nose and shoved another bunch of toilet paper into the cart. For a minute she was so happy, she almost forgot where she was and what was going on around them. The next aisle doused any sense of elation she felt as they stepped around the dried puddle in the middle of the chips and dip aisle. A few bags had tumbled onto the floor, but none of them could explain the dark stain.

"Is that blood?" she asked as Xander knelt beside it.

"It is."

A stone settled into the pit of her stomach as she recalled too late her conversation with John, *"I don't want to know what they're thinking, plotting,"* she'd said.

"You think they're capable of that?" John had asked.

"Don't you?"

She cursed herself a fool as she tilted her head back to look into the darkened rafters. They were enshrouded in shadows, but she could see enough to make out no one hid above. She still knew, with absolute certainty they were in here, somewhere.

"We have to go."

"What?" Xander asked as she seized hold of his arm.

"We have to find Carl and John and get out of here."

She left the carts behind as she pulled him out of the aisle in search of Carl and John.

CHAPTER 4

Carl

"Don't you think we have enough junk food?" Carl demanded as John began to shove bags of chocolate into the shopping cart.

"There's never enough junk food," John retorted.

"We should focus on trying to find healthier things like canned peas and beans, maybe broccoli. You know, things that will actually keep our bodies going without giving us diabetes."

"Well, you can have your broccoli and beans, but don't come complaining to me when you're craving a Kit Kat and have gas."

"John..."

"Hey I didn't complain when you were stocking up on cowboy killers; let me have my sugar fix, I'm not getting my coffee one."

Carl wanted to argue further, but as much as he hated to admit it, John *did* have a point. "Fine, just hurry up."

He pushed his cart further down the row to grab some cans of peanuts and drop them into the cart. For every can he took he pushed another aside in case someone else finally stumbled across the grocery store. He was grabbing for a bag of pistachios when movement at the front of the aisle caught his attention. Carl brought his gun up to fire before he realized it was Riley skidding around the corner. She didn't blink when she spotted the gun, but the look in her eyes made him forget all about the nuts. Her nearly black hair, straggling around her face, did little to ease her harried appearance.

"We have to go," she said bluntly.

"What? Why?" John didn't pause in the act of sweeping more candy into his cart.

"Something is *not* right here," Riley said.

"You're being paranoid," John said as he dropped another bag in and pushed his cart toward them. "We searched every square inch of this store..."

"We didn't search the outside," she inserted.

John frowned; he clamped his mouth shut as he glanced toward the back of the store. Carl followed the direction of his stare, but from what he could see it remained clear of any movement. A shudder rippled down his back as his thoughts turned to the swinging black doors leading to the storage room.

"Let's go up front for a minute," he suggested.

"We're perfectly fine; you're just not used to having something go our way, because it's all gone wrong lately, but..." John's voice trailed off as he glanced behind him. "Yeah ok, let's go up front."

John didn't relinquish his cart as he pushed it forward. One of the wheels made a small clicking noise; Carl wanted to grab it and heave it toward the back of the store as a distraction. He pushed his cart to the side and followed Riley toward the front of the building.

He was stepping out of the aisle when he heard the squeak of rubber on tile. His hand went to the gun at his waist as he froze.

Riley took an abrupt step back into the aisle and brought her gun up before her. Carl motioned for the three of them to stay back before poking his head warily out from behind the shelf.

He glanced around but saw nothing by the front of the store. Carl nodded toward them before creeping out of the aisle. The others were so close on his heels he could feel Riley's breath against his back and hear the whistle of John's breath as it coursed out of his nostrils. Another squeak caused Carl to stop as he realized it was coming from the row just in front of them.

The others pressed closer against his back. He was tempted to shoo them away, but he found he didn't have the heart to, and he actually liked knowing they were there as he took the next step around the row of shelves. Two young men and a young woman lifted their heads to look at them as they all stepped into the cereal aisle. The men threw their hands in the air and jumped back when they spotted Carl, but the girl continued to shove handfuls of cereal into her mouth.

Carl's hand wavered on the gun as he took them in. They didn't appear to be much older than John, or that's what he guessed from what he could see of them beneath the layers of dirt and grime caking their skin and clothes. The girl's shirt was so torn she may as well have been wearing only her bra, but the men weren't much better off as their clothes were nothing more than tatters. Carl's eyes ran over them, but he saw no cuts on any of them.

"We… we mean you no harm," one of the men stuttered. "We're just so hungry."

Carl could see that as the girl continued to stuff handfuls of cereal into her mouth. She eyed the gun with a look of part dread and part hope. It was the hope part scaring him most as he recognized the desperate look in her eyes, a look partway between wanting to continue on and wanting it to end. He wasn't about to help her take door number two and moved his gun away from her.

"Where did you come from?" Xander demanded.

"We've been hiding in the hardware store across the street for three days," the other man answered.

"You've been across from the grocery store all this time, and you're just coming in here now?" John asked incredulously. "Why?"

"Because we saw you come in." Maybe that answer would have made sense to someone else, but it made absolutely none to him as his gaze ran over them again, and he waited for the other shoe to drop. "And we didn't hear you screaming."

He could almost hear the shoe plopping onto the floor. Riley was right, they had to get out of here. They never should have come inside in the first place.

"How many people have come in here?" John asked.

"We've seen at least twenty," the other man said. "Most came on foot but a few drove their cars."

"And how many left the store?" Riley asked in a choked voice.

"None."

Carl's breath exploded out of him. "Let's go," he said.

"But the screams usually come within the first five minutes; you've been here for at least twenty." Bits of cereal sprayed from the girl's mouth as she rushed to get the words out.

"That's twenty minutes too long in my book," John informed her.

Carl was turning away when he heard a small swishing sound from the rear of the store. A sound he instantly associated with the black swinging doors closing again. The exit was blocked back there, he knew that, but he was beginning to realize it had been blocked to keep them *in*. To allow their enemies to enter when their prey had been lulled into a sense of false security, like a Venus fly trap waiting for its victim.

His heart plummeted as his gaze ran rapidly over the store. The black swinging doors were two aisles ahead of them, in between them and their only exit. Even if they bolted forward and ran as fast as they could, they would be taken down before they ever made it to those doors. To go forward now was suicide, he was certain of it.

"What was that?" one of the men asked.

Xander held his finger to his lips and shook his head. "But what was that?" the other guy demanded.

"Shh," John hissed in a low whisper.

The girl reluctantly released her handfuls of cereal and climbed to her feet. Carl didn't have to see them; he could clearly picture those sick people emerging from the storage room and creeping through aisles around them. Picture those people stalking *them* as they moved throughout the store.

"Is it them?" the girl asked.

Carl's finger twitched on the trigger. Didn't they understand the concept of being discreet? They were going to get them all killed before they had a chance to try and figure out an escape route. His mind stumbled through the possibilities of an escape plan.

Every primal instinct he'd ever had was surging to the forefront as his body screamed at him to run. He could picture the sick people, just out of view, moving as stealthily as a hawk through the shadows toward its prey. "Was there another way out?" Xander asked in a low whisper.

Carl shook his head. "Only the backdoor," he barely spoke the words.

Xander frowned as he glanced down the aisle toward the back of the store. Carl noticed Riley's attention was focused on the rafters and couldn't help but drop his own head back to search the beams of the ceiling. He wasn't in the mood to deal with people hanging from the rafters like some sort of demented bat again. There was nothing up there now, but the more time they remained standing here, the more likely it would be they would take to the beams in an effort to make their move.

Xander frowned as he followed their gazes. "Really?" he mouthed.

Riley nodded in response.

"We need to get out of here; you have to get us out of here," the girl's voice held a tinge of hysteria that troubled Carl almost as much as the people lurking just beyond his sight. Carl lifted his finger to his mouth and shook his head. "Do you know what they do to people?" she demanded.

Xander stepped closer to her. "You're going to get us all killed if you don't shut up," he growled in a low voice.

Her large brown eyes rolled in her head as they spun around the store. One of the men rested his hand on her arm and pulled her back a step. The girl seemed to calm a little, but not much as her chest continued to heave and her eyes rolled. Riley stepped closer to all of them and lowered her head. "They're expecting us to go for the front door, but what if we circle around and go for the back-door?" she whispered.

"Are you crazy?" John demanded in a low voice.

"It's a possibility," she admitted.

John was shaking his head as Carl began to ponder her sugges-tion. "They'll all be up here looking for us. None of them will stay back there. They'll be too eager for our meat," Carl said.

"They're smart Carl," John said. They *were* smart, far smarter than Carl had been willing to give them credit for, but they were also hungry animals that had established a good setup here. One they didn't think could go wrong. No, Riley was right; going for the backdoor was their best chance. "We don't know how many there are, maybe we can fight through them."

"They'll be on us before we can put up much of a fight. We have to go now, before they realize we're not going for the front door and they come for us."

John looked about to protest more, but his shoulders sagged as he looked helplessly toward the tempting front doors. The three strangers watched them, and for a moment, Carl thought they might go for the front door anyway. "It's your choice," Carl told them. "But stay quiet if you follow us."

The girl hesitated, but the men were close on his heels as they moved swiftly down the aisle. Carl kept his attention focused forward as Riley continued to study the ceiling and tops of the shelves. Reaching the end of the aisle he stopped and took a deep breath to gather his courage. This was it, if he stuck his head out now and there was someone out there, their cover was blown. There would be no turning back. They'd never make it to the front of the store in time.

Riley's breath exploded from her at the same time Xander and John released muffled curses. He felt the blood turn to ice in his veins as he glanced over his shoulder. There, at the end of the aisle, perched on top of the shelf like some hideous gargoyle was a single human. The dim light from the large front windows illuminated it against the shadows. It was hunched over with both hands resting on the shelf and its chin thrust forward. Though its features were hidden in shadow, he could see the glimmer of its eyes as the orbs focused upon them.

For one fraction of a second, he thought his heart ceased to beat as those eyes seemed to latch upon him. It was almost as if a demon from Hell was staring at him, seeing straight into his soul, judging him and finding him lacking. He wasn't about to stand there and be judged by one of those things.

"Run," he breathed.

Carl gave up all attempts at trying to be subtle as he burst into motion. The doors were only fifteen feet away, but it seemed more like fifty as he rushed toward them. From the corner of his eye he saw movement amongst the aisles as the gargoyle released a distorted cry and started racing toward them. Gargoyle's new direction alerted his companions they weren't trying to escape out the front door.

He chanced a glance down the aisle across from the swinging doors. His heart sank as he took in the spectacle before him. Like owls scenting a mouse, at least ten heads swiveled in their direction, and their eyes narrowed with lethal intent. There was another one on top of the shelves moving toward the other side of the grocery store, but it froze when it heard the commotion.

They'd sent out scouts, he realized in horror. Scouts most people wouldn't have thought to look for.

He hit the doors at a dead run and shoved them open with his shoulder. He didn't expect any of the sick people to still be back here, but then he hadn't expected them to set such an elaborate trap either. With his gun raised, he searched the shadows as he ran toward the exit.

"They're coming!" Riley cried.

"Please don't let the door be blocked!" John panted as he ran beside Carl. Carl crashed into the bar on the exit door as the swishing sound of the doors swinging open behind them reached him. For a second he didn't think the door was going to open as he shoved his shoulder into it and pushed forcefully against the bar.

He practically fell on his face as the door gave way beneath him, and he plummeted outside. Someone grabbed hold of the back of his shirt, causing him to gag as the collar tightened against his neck and briefly cut off his air supply. John yanked him back to his feet as Xander spun and slammed the door shut.

"Get me the dumpster!" Xander gasped. His face was florid as he pressed his back against the door and braced his legs on the ground.

A loud bang echoed from behind Xander as the sick people inside the store crashed into the door. John released him and lurched awkwardly for the dumpster. "Help me," John grunted to the three strangers standing near him as Riley threw herself against the door with Xander.

One of the men bolted away from them and ran toward the woods bordering the back of the store. Carl cursed as the resounding thudding against the back door began to grow. The girl moved to help John as Carl got behind him and started pushing the dumpster. Carl's nose wrinkled at the ripe smell of the garbage, but the dumpster started to groan as its wheels began to turn. The other man joined Xander and Riley as a strange howling erupted from inside the store.

John's eyes widened as he shot Carl a look. "Almost sounds like werewolves."

"Screw you," Carl returned breathlessly as Xander, Riley, and the man got out of the way in time for them to wedge the dumpster against the door.

Carl wiped the sweat from his brow with the back of his arm as he surveyed the area around them. From the sounds of it, he thought all of the ones inside were beating against the door, but he wasn't about to fall for that. Going back for the car was out of the question. The woods behind the store offered some protection, but he couldn't shake the feeling the woods belonged to *those* people now.

"This way," the girl said and started running toward the right.

Carl glanced at the others, but there was little choice right now as the howling at the back door had ceased. "Hurry," the man encouraged.

Carl didn't have to be told twice as he broke into a brisk run behind them. His lungs began to burn before they made it to the end of the supermarket, and he was laboring to breathe in the stale air. He was beginning to rethink his thoughts on not quitting smoking as they sprinted across the back of the stores bordering the grocery store.

They grabbed at the doors of the other buildings as they ran, but none of the doors gave way to their grasp. Carl chanced a look over his shoulder; he didn't see anything pursuing them but that meant nothing. He fell back when Xander and Riley began to lag. Though Xander wasn't complaining, he was beginning to sweat excessively, and his limp had become more pronounced by the time they got to the end of the street.

The businesses fell away and homes started to replace them. Xander wasn't going to make it much farther if they didn't find somewhere to hide soon. The man ran up the back steps of one of the houses and twisted the handle. The door opened with a groan of hinges that almost made Carl balk against the idea of going in there. A glimpse over his shoulder changed his mind as John now had Xander's arm wrapped around his shoulders and was helping him forward. Carl hurried up the porch steps and into the house. There was no time to search it thoroughly as John assisted Xander into the house. Carl closed and locked the door and nodded to Riley. "Help me with the table."

They turned the small rectangular kitchen table onto its side and pinned it against the door. "The front door," she whispered.

He nodded and hurried out of the room with Riley close on his heels. She studied the stairwell down to the basement of the split level ranch as he threw the locks on the front door and pushed the curtain aside. The street remained clear, but he had no doubt they were out there, somewhere. He looked up as John and Xander stepped into the doorway between the kitchen and living room.

John moved away from the door and walked toward him as Riley hurried to Xander's side. She took hold of Xander's arm and helped him away from the door to the couch. The man and girl appeared in the doorway. The girl nervously rang her hands before her as she repeatedly glanced behind her.

"What do we do now?" John asked.

"We get ready," Carl answered.

"Ready for what?"

"For when they find us."

CHAPTER 5

Al

Al placed his hand on Bobby's shoulder and gently shook the snoring boy. Brown eyes blinked up at him, there was a flash of confusion and then Bobby started upright. Al placed his hand over his own lips in a gesture to silence him as Bobby's gaze darted around the hall. Bobby's eyebrows drew together as he looked at him and then at Josh, who Al had woken first. Bobby's shoulders slumped; he heaved a sigh as he focused on Al again.

"What is it?" he whispered.

Al nodded toward the room where Mary Ellen and Rochelle had slept. "I'll show you."

Al heard the subtle groan Bobby released as he shoved himself to his feet. Al stepped into the doorway of the bedroom and spotted Mary Ellen kneeling beside Rochelle on the bed. The young girl was sitting on the bed; her coffee colored hair a tumbled mess around her shoulders as she stared at them from red-rimmed eyes.

Mary Ellen looked to them and climbed quickly to her feet. She gestured toward the window, and Al walked over to meet her at it. Ever so slowly, Al moved a corner of the curtain aside to peer out. His breath caught in his chest; a small tremor shook his hand as the horde of people spilled out of the woods, across the street, and into the yard. He hadn't seen so many people since the stadium, and he hadn't ever wanted to see so many in one place again.

Especially ones that looked and moved like these people did. He could instantly tell the difference between the mindless wanderers, or The Lost Souls as he was beginning to think of them, and the angrier more rabid individuals. The Lost Souls weren't focused on anything, if there was a tree before them they walked into it and often remained there until someone or something else knocked them away. The ones who didn't get caught up on something walked aimlessly around, sometimes in circles, and they were usually staring at their own feet. More often than not, The Lost Souls picked at their own skin and hair. His stomach turned at the sight of their tortured and brutalized flesh.

There was nothing left to them, there simply couldn't be. No human, no matter how sick, would pick off their skin to the bone if there was any reasonable thought left within their brains.

The angrier ones left The Lost Souls alone for the most part, but weren't above pushing them out of their way, knocking them to the ground or stepping on them when they fell.

All of the faces of the sick ones bore some sort of rot; perhaps it was leprosy, perhaps it was simply their bodies deteriorating from whatever illness ravaged them. Bodies he believed couldn't hold up for much longer, but then he'd also been certain a tsunami would never hit Rhode Island.

Life was funny about certainty; he knew it liked to prove people wrong. It most certainly had proven him wrong more times than he could count.

Though the horde had chased most of the coyotes off, he spotted a coyote at the edge of the woods dragging one of The Lost Souls into the shadows. Though their legs were still limply kicking on the ground, the person did little to try and fight the animal off. *"Shit,"* was the only coherent thought he could form as he watched the disturbing display.

Bobby's breath hissed out beside him as more people filtered from the woods. More of them fell upon the remains of the coyote, tearing into it as if it were a leg from a Thanksgiving turkey.

"The creepy bastards remind me of birds," Bobby muttered. "Like they're flocking or something."

"Lost Souls," Al murmured. "They've been forgotten. They don't know where to go anymore."

"I don't know where to go either, and I really don't want to know where *they're* going. Not even a little bit," Bobby said.

"Nowhere good," Rochelle whispered.

"Get away from the window," Mary Ellen told her as she gently nudged Rochelle back.

More people spilled out of the woods and flowed unerringly around the houses, truck, and Cadillac. Thankfully they paid little attention to the vehicle loaded down with all of their supplies. Apparently normal food was not what they craved anymore as more of them fell upon the downed coyote. Meat, all they seemed to crave was meat or flesh, or perhaps it was blood they scented and that drove them onward, who really knew?

He was more than a little curious as to where they were going, what was drawing them onward, but he wasn't about to step foot out there in order to find out. There had to be some food source out there only they knew about or could sense. Food and killing seemed to be all they cared about as the ones surrounding the coyote rose and began to move onward. Though he fought against looking, his gaze was inescapably drawn to the bones littering the front yard across from them. If he hadn't known any better he would have thought the skeleton had been there for years it was so picked clean. All that remained was the blood streaking the scattered pile of bones and lawn around them.

"Now that's just plain wrong," Josh said and shook his head. The young Asian boy's once spiked black hair now hung around his face. His almond shaped black eyes were puffy from lack of sleep. "They're worse than vultures."

"Birds," Bobby said again and shook his head. He stepped away from the window. "I've seen enough; let me know if they head this way so I can start shooting."

There was no way they would be able to fend off this many people, but he would still put up one hell of a fight. His finger tightened on the trigger of his gun; he wasn't going to allow them to take him alive. He would take as many of them as he could out with him, but he wasn't going to be alive when they tore into him.

"I think we should all get away from the window," Mary Ellen suggested and turned away from the window. She'd pulled her brown hair into a ponytail that emphasized the beauty of her broad cheekbones and the freckles speckling her face. Her deep brown eyes were troubled as she focused on him. "Peter can watch from downstairs, but the less of us gathered around the window the better off we are."

"Who is watching the back of the house?" Rochelle asked.

"I'll go," Al volunteered.

He wanted a few minutes alone to gather his thoughts and try to formulate some kind of a plan anyway. Turning away from the others, he made his way to the master bedroom at the back of the house. There was a single bathrobe still laid out on the bed, seemingly waiting for its owner after a shower. Stopping beside the bed he was briefly caught up in the memory of Nellie humming as she stepped out of a shower and put her robe on. He could see her smile as she knotted the belt before her and dried her hair. He was so entangled in the memory, he briefly lost touch with reality and was transported to a different time and place. She was so real he could almost touch her as her scent engulfed him.

A small bang shattered the memory and lurched him back into the present. He held his breath as he strained to hear anything else. The bang echoed again from somewhere outside. Shaking away the lingering memory, he removed his hand from the cotton robe, he didn't remember touching it in the first place. Striding over to the window, he pulled the curtain back and peered out, but he couldn't see the source of the bang as it sounded again from somewhere in the woods behind the house. A horde of people had gathered back there too, though not in the droves they'd been in the front yard.

He watched them for a moment before letting the curtain slide back into place. He wasn't going to do any good up here if they did decide to come at the house anyway. Moving out of the room, he crept down the stairs and found everyone gathered within the living room. He was about to ask if there was anything new outside when gunshots reverberated through the air.

Al instinctively ducked as more shots rang out and shouts rang out all around him. "What the…"

Al didn't hear the rest of Peter's words as he turned and hurried back up the stairs to the window. He nudged the curtain aside, but though he saw scattered corpses at the end of the street, he couldn't see the source of the shots. *Those things didn't use guns too, did they?*

That made absolutely no sense; they had some intelligence, unfortunately that much had become obvious, but this whole time they'd been using themselves as weapons and not guns. No, it hadn't been the sick ones firing the guns but then... who?

More shots erupted, he leaned closer to the window and strained to see further down the road, but the houses obstructed his view. A few more bodies toppled over in the street, but more were drawn forward by the gunfire. They were pulled in like the tide during a full moon as they rolled relentlessly forth, some falling over each other in their rush to get to a house he couldn't see.

"What's going on?"

He turned toward Mary Ellen and shook his head. "I don't know."

A sound, one that made something inside of him quiver and long to cry, filled the air. His heart lurched as it went out to what-ever was making the sound, yet he knew the noise came from a human. Not one of the sick humans either, he felt the sick ones were beyond the pain and distress encompassed within the cry echoing through the air.

He stepped away from the window and inhaled a shaky breath as he tried to block out the sound but failed to do so. They were sitting ducks if they stayed in this house, and yet they couldn't leave either. His gaze slid to the truck and then around the street again. Even if they could make it through all of those people to the truck, he didn't know where the others were, and they couldn't just take everything and leave them in this town.

The haunting wail abruptly cut off; he found the ensuing silence worse than the sound had been. Mary Ellen's chest heaved as her eyes met his. Another sound rent the air, but this one was easily recognizable as a tortured scream. Taking a deep breath, Al turned back to the window and pulled the curtain aside again. There were more bodies in the street, but most of them remained standing as they moved persistently toward the house he couldn't see.

"What do we do?" Mary Ellen breathed.

He observed the street as he took a step back. He didn't think it was going to get any clearer than it was right now as all of the people were making their way toward the end of the road. He didn't know what had drawn them to that house in the first place. They had been in this house for a day now, and he'd never suspected there were other people on the street with them.

If they left this house now they could probably make it to the truck and the Cadillac, but then what? They drive aimlessly through the town in search of the others? That was if they could get away from these sick humans. The sick ones were fast, not faster than a vehicle when it got going, but that was the problem, they couldn't get the vehicles to any kind of real speed. The potholes and debris littering the road made it nearly impossible.

His mind spun; in seventy-two years he didn't think he'd ever been rendered completely speechless, but he didn't know what to say or do.

They could take the vehicles and escape the town. Everything in him screamed against doing that. They couldn't just abandon their friends; they couldn't abandon the people who had saved his life and had been there for him. He'd had his faults over the years. It was rare, but he could have a temper, his patience was known to fray, but he had pride in the fact he considered himself a decent and honorable man. A man who wouldn't abandon his friends in order to save himself.

Taking those vehicles would shatter all of the beliefs he'd ever had about himself. It would be the cowardly way to go, and he was far too old to go out as a coward. The others weren't old though. Rochelle and Josh were just children; they'd barely had a chance to live. It was complete crap out there now, but the world may not stay that way forever. Man had come through some horrible things before, maybe not *this* bad, but they had persevered in times when the odds hadn't been in their favor.

In order to persevere during those times, he knew those men had done many things they hadn't wanted to do and had been ashamed of. They'd done them though in order to ensure the species survived, and for the species to carry on the young had to live. Riley, Carl, John, and Xander were tough, they were smart and gritty; they were fighters and wouldn't give up. He was determined to believe they were still alive out there, but they had to stay alive *here* too. There was a good chance the others wouldn't be able to make it back to this street.

He was going to hate himself for the words he was about to say. He would spend the rest of his days with them hanging over his head, but say them he did, "We have to go."

Mary Ellen rang her hands before her as her eyes flitted toward the window. "The others?" she breathed.

"We'll leave them a note, and we'll see if we can find them, but to stay here… we just can't," he managed to get out.

He moved away from the window and walked by her before he could change his mind. It felt as if he was walking through quicksand; his legs moved, but they did so reluctantly as he climbed down the steps and into the living room. It felt like he was someone else, as if he stood outside of himself as he continued to speak the words that would condemn him for the rest of his life.

"We have to go, while they're distracted. We have to get out of this house," he stated.

Peter's face was pale as he turned away from the window. His gaze fell to Josh and Rochelle before he looked helplessly back at Al. He read the understanding in the teacher's gaze, but the man shook his head. "They're not distracted," he said in a low whisper. "Not anymore."

Al frowned at him before hurrying to the window. Rising up on his toes he peered out of the small pane of glass. On the right, he could see the mob clustered by the house at the end of the road. From this angle though, on the left, he could also see a new mass of them spilling out of the woods and onto the road. A low curse escaped him as he dropped away from the window and backed away.

"Get the keys for the vehicles," he instructed.

"We can't go out there," Peter said at the same time Rochelle blurted, "We can't leave the others behind!"

"Shh," Mary Ellen said as she wrapped her arm around her daughter and pulled Rochelle against her chest.

"She's right, I'm not leaving my friends," Bobby stated.

Al glanced back at the door and then at them. "Right now we don't have a choice, we're stuck here, but we're going to need those keys if we get the opportunity to escape."

"We can't leave," Rochelle said firmly.

"Absolutely not," Bobby agreed.

Al took a deep breath, he wasn't irritated with them, he completely understood where they were coming from, but their words only served to remind him of the people he was opting to leave behind. People he would have sacrificed himself for, but he couldn't sacrifice the children. Although Riley, Xander, and John weren't much older than Josh and Rochelle. They would understand, he knew they would, and he knew Carl would have made the same decision had he been the one still standing in this house.

"They could be dead already, and if they're not, do you think they're going to make it down this street with those people out there?" he asked. "We need the keys, and we need to start preparing ourselves for those things in case they come in here. The most important thing is keeping you kids safe, the others are extremely capable of taking care of themselves."

Mary Ellen hurried from the room and returned with the two sets of keys, a notepad, and a pen. Peter took the car keys and slid them into his pocket as Mary Ellen handed Al the pad, pen, and truck keys. "You know how to get to the cabin in New York," she said.

Al nodded and began to scribble down instructions for how to get to the cabin. "Mr. Dade…" Josh started to protest.

"They're right, we can't stay here," Peter interjected.

The reassurance didn't make Al feel any better as he jotted a sorry at the end of the note. He knew it completely failed to convey the true depth of how sorry he was. *Forgive me*, he added and placed the pad on the coffee table.

With a heavy heart and a much heavier gate, he returned to the front door. He'd made many difficult decisions in his life, some he hadn't been proud of, but this was by far the worst. "We will look for them," he vowed.

He was about to rise up to look back out the window again, when he heard the distinct thud of a boot hitting the porch. For a second his heart soared as he recalled the heavy work boots Carl and John had been wearing the last time he'd seen them, but he knew he was wrong. They wouldn't be strolling up to the front door amongst that crowd out there.

Gesturing the others back, he moved away from the door and plastered his back against the wall next to it. The dull thud of the boots sounded across the porch to the bordered up window where they paused before turning away and walking back across the porch. Al held his breath as he heard the distinct thud of more footsteps climbing the stairs. Mary Ellen pushed Rochelle further behind her and toward the kitchen.

Peter closed his eyes as he remained next to the door. Bobby pushed Josh behind him as he nodded toward the kitchen and Rochelle. The boots sounded over the porch again, stopping outside the front door. Al wasn't so sure his old ticker could take much more. It hit his ribcage with a thud so forceful he was certain they could hear it outside as the knob began to rattle.

CHAPTER 6

Xander

HE TRIED to push Riley's hands away, but she was as persistent as a dog digging for a bone as she tugged at the bandages wrapped around his leg. The fresh blood staining the inside of the wrap didn't startle him as he'd already felt it seeping from the injury. Tossing the bandages aside, she sat back on her heels and focused on the two strangers still hovering in the doorway.

"You," she said and thrust her index finger at the girl. "Go to the bathroom and see if you can find me some clean bandages, if not I need towels and tape. Antiseptic of some kind would be good too."

A wolf with a bone, he decided over her protective and commanding attitude. Though the girl had begun to silently cry, she didn't question the command as she turned on her heel and rushed from the room.

"I'll be fine," he assured her.

Her eyes narrowed upon him, and for a second he thought she might actually punch him again. "You're a stubborn ass."

She didn't seem at all pleased or calmed by the smile he gave her, one that had made other girls melt but only made her glower more fiercely. "It takes one to know one," he replied.

"John, give me a hand with the chair," Carl commanded from the door.

John placed his gun down on the end table by the couch and hurried to help Carl. They lifted the recliner from the corner by the fireplace and carried it down the stairs to block the front door. They both hurried back up the stairs.

"Is there another way out of here?" the man inquired from the doorway to the kitchen.

"Do we look like the family in the picture?" John retorted as he gestured to the family portrait of a mother, father, and two boys over the mantle.

"John," Carl said in a low tone and shook his head.

John pulled the curtains framing the picture window aside and peered out. "It's calm out there; maybe they won't come after us."

"They'll come," the girl whispered in a forlorn voice. Xander hadn't realized she'd returned until she spoke. In one hand she was holding a towel, a box of cloth bandages and an ace ankle wrap. In the other she possessed a bottle of rubbing alcohol and one of peroxide. "They always come, they will always *keep* coming."

"Yeah well, they're in for a fight when they get here," Riley said as she snatched the supplies out of the girl's hand.

The girl didn't seem to notice Riley though as her gaze remained focused on the window. "There is no escape," she whispered.

The blank look about her concerned him, but his attention was torn from the girl as Riley knelt before him. She twisted the cap off the alcohol and unceremoniously began to pour it on his leg. His hands clenched on the couch, and his breath hissed in through his teeth. She didn't give him a chance to protest before she began to pour some of the peroxide onto the wound too. Foaming bubbles enveloped his leg and slid down toward his sock.

"Kitchen table," Carl said and nodded for John to follow him from the room.

Riley opened the box and pulled the bandage free. "This looks awful," she muttered as she gently dabbed at the cut with the towel and wiped the excess liquid from his leg.

He took hold of her hands before she could start to wrap his leg again. He was shocked to find her hands trembling within his. "It will be fine," he assured her.

She took a steadying breath and nodded. He squeezed her hands, briefly savoring their warmth before releasing her. Her shoulders stiffened as she bowed her head and approached the injury with a lot more care and caution. He heard the thud of the kitchen table being placed against the backdoor.

"They're going to just keep coming and coming and…"

"No, they won't," Riley interrupted the girl briskly.

"Debra," the man said calmingly and rested his hand on the girl's shoulder.

"We should check out the basement," Carl said as he and John reentered the living room.

Riley finished taping the bandage and sat back on her heels. She rested her hands on her knees before rising to her feet and grabbing her gun from where she'd left it on the coffee table. He'd always known she was tough, always known there was a steel rod within her, but staring at her now she reminded him of an Amazon woman. Her chin jutted proudly out. She held the gun with far more comfort than she had the one he'd handed her in the den of the police officer's house. His heart skipped a beat as her eyes slid to him. He was struck by just how beautiful she was and just how much she had changed since he'd last seen her.

I killed Lee, the words, spoken so bluntly by her in the grocery store had rendered him speechless, but it had been the look in her eyes that had robbed the breath from his lungs when she'd said them. She had killed one of his best friends, and as she stared at him now, he knew it had broken a piece of her. It had damaged her, but the damage could be repaired and healed given enough time and understanding.

He rose awkwardly to his feet and balanced on his good leg as Carl and John thumped down the stairs to the basement. "You should rest," Riley protested. "We might have to run again, soon."

He grabbed hold of her arm and pulled her against him. "I love you Riley Lennox," he whispered in her ear. "I always have, I always will."

She remained unmoving in his embrace before her arms wrapped around him, and she hugged him back. The feel of her was better than the smell of freshly cut grass or a cold beer on a hot August day. It was better than anything he'd ever experienced before. He hadn't realized just how broken and fractured he was until now, and she helped to fix those broken pieces.

"I love you too Xander Noland." His heart soared with joy as he pressed her closer. Her fingers dug into his back; she turned her mouth into his neck and kissed him. "But I'm not dying in this damn house, and I'm not carrying you so sit down, please."

He laughed as he hugged her against him once more and released her. Though she was right, he wasn't willing to sit on the couch again. He felt much too vulnerable when he was sitting down. Riley moved to the curtain and used the tip of her gun to pull it back so she could look out. Resting his hand on her shoulder, he stared at the silent street over the top of her head.

He looked over the half wall separating the living room from the double stairway of the split level ranch. Carl leaned over the recliner pressed against the front door to peer out the window. "What's downstairs?" Xander asked.

"Just the basement," Carl answered. "There's a way out through the bulkhead if we have to take it and a door into the garage. No vehicle though."

"Of course not," Xander muttered.

He looked back to the window as a small shiver ran through Riley. "The back door," she said and spun away from him.

She pushed by the man and woman still standing in the doorway of the kitchen. Xander hurried forward as the man turned to go with her. The girl was still silently weeping; her head was bowed over her hands, and her shoulders shook from the force of her sobs. Xander wanted to stop and comfort her, but he didn't like the idea of Riley out of his view with a stranger.

The man was standing by the window over the kitchen sink as Riley peered out of the glass in the backdoor. "I don't see anything," Riley murmured.

Xander stepped into the kitchen and glanced down the hall. The door at the end was open to reveal the posters covering one of the walls. The irresistible urge to shut the door seized him. He hurried down the hall to the room with rock bands and women lining the walls. The room reminded him of his own when he'd been fourteen, and he couldn't help but smile a little as he shut the door on the memory.

He closed the other doors along the hall as he made his way back toward the others. Carl and John had climbed the stairs and were standing by the front window. The young woman was still crying, but now she also murmured words he couldn't quite make out due to her bowed head and broken voice.

Apprehension gnawed at him; he glanced at the others, but none of them seemed to have noticed this new development. He didn't think they could hear her words, but she made the hair on the nape of his neck rise as she continued to talk to herself. He rested his hand on the young woman's shoulder and squeezed it.

"Everything will be all right, Debra," he assured her.

She lifted her head and looked up at him from under strands of straggling brown hair. His hand fell limply back to his side as she pinned him with her green eyes, but though she was looking at him, he felt as if she stared right through him. There were panes of glass not as transparent as he felt right now.

Cuckoo, ran through his mind, and he couldn't help but take a step away from her as tears continued to spill down her face and words tumbled more stridently from her lips.

"I looked and there before me was a pale horse," she stated.

His skin began to crawl with the sensation of a thousand spiders creeping over him as he stared at her in complete confusion. "Excuse me?" he asked.

Over Debra's shoulder he could see Riley frowning as she turned away from the door and the man took a step away from the window. "Debra?" the man inquired.

"Its rider was named Death," Debra said.

"Isn't that a song?" John asked. Xander felt a small spurt of hope. It was still weird, but if she was trying to comfort herself by recalling a song then he could live with that, maybe.

Debra continued on as if none of them were present. "And Hades was following close behind him."

"No seriously, didn't someone sing that?" John demanded.

"Not quite that version of it," Carl answered. Xander didn't think Carl realized he had an unlit cigarette dangling between his lips.

"They were given power over a fourth of the earth to kill by sword, famine and plague and by the wild beasts of the earth," Debra continued.

Carl was ashen as he stepped away from the window. The look on his face caused Xander to take another step away from Debra and more to the side. He met Riley's gaze as she and the man guardedly approached Debra from behind.

"What does that mean? What is she talking about?" Riley whispered.

"Revelation," Carl answered. "It's about the four horsemen of the apocalypse."

The color drained so fast from John's face; it amazed Xander he remained standing afterward. John took a step back and rested his hand against the wall behind him as his shoulders slumped. "Horses again," John whispered.

Again? Xander thought as Carl shot John a look that clearly said he thought the kid might have lost his mind. "Again?" Carl asked.

John shook his head in response and held up his hand. "Nothing," he said.

"There's no war," Riley whispered. "There is *no war*."

"This whole event has been nothing but a battle for survival," Carl responded.

Xander became increasingly convinced John was going to pass out as he rested his shoulder against the wall now. Riley shook her head, but her eyes were pleading as they met his. He wasn't sure what they were talking about. "What's going on?" he asked.

"There was this guy before we entered Sturbridge..." Carl started to explain. "Whoa!"

Xander fell back as Debra lifted her hands to reveal the gun within them. It took him only a second to realize she had no intention of shooting any of them. He lurched toward her, but it was already too late, as she turned the gun on herself. The world seemed to slow as he reached forward to try and stop her. His hand was almost to her arm when the gunshot reverberated through the house. Blood splattered over Riley and the other man when Debra's head snapped back. A piercing scream escaped Riley as Debra's body slumped to the ground. Debra's fingers continued to twitch due to the last bit of neurons still firing within her body.

Riley slapped her hands over her mouth, her nostrils flared over top of her hands as she continued to scream against her palms. The gunshot seemed to still be echoing through the house, but he knew it was just the ringing in his ears creating the noise. He could barely breathe; his mind spun in revulsion as his gaze remained riveted upon the lifeless body. He'd seen people die, he'd even been the cause of it, but he had never expected to see anything like *this*.

Edging his way around Debra's body he moved over to Riley. Her eyes were crazed as they settled upon him; she had stopped screaming, but she almost sobbed against her palm. He wrapped his arms around her and pulled her head into his shoulder. Muted cries continued to escape her as she shook against him.

John was plastered against the wall, his mouth gaping. Carl's mouth had dropped; the cigarette was barely dangling at the edge of his bottom lip as his stunned eyes came up to meet Xander's.

The man took a step back and spun toward the sink. Turning the water on, he pushed the sleeves of his shirt up before frantically washing his face and arms. Xander nudged Riley toward the sink as the man's skin began to take on the shade of a lobster from the scrub part of the sponge he was running over his arms and face.

Xander grabbed hold of the man's hand to stop him before he

began to rip the flesh from his own bones. The man stared at him before releasing the sponge and stepping aside. His chest heaved, and his eyes rolled, but he seemed to be regaining control of himself. "Is it still on my face?" he choked out.

Xander shook his head as Riley stuck her hands beneath the faucet. With his chest pressed against her back, he stretched around to help her wash the blood from her arms. She still shook, but she had finally stopped gasping for breath. Xander stepped out from behind her, grabbed a dishtowel, and wet it in the water. Her lower lip trembled as he gently washed the blood from her face and neck.

"Why?" she whispered.

He shook his head. "There's no answer for that Riley. Unfortunately, there never is."

The sound of a boot falling on the kitchen floor brought his head up as Carl stepped around Debra's body. At least the hideous twitching had finally stopped. "Where did she get the gun?" Carl asked as he stuck his foot on top of the weapon and pulled it away from the growing puddle of blood.

"It…" John broke off as he swallowed. "It was mine. I put it on the table when I went to help you move the chair."

Carl thrust his gun at him and bent to pick up the one on the floor. "We have to get out of this house, that gunshot is going to bring them here," Carl said.

Xander nodded, but it was Riley who turned the water off. She inhaled a shuddery breath and grabbed another dishtowel from the cabinet in front of her. She dried her arms and face before turning away from the sink.

The young man remained where he was as Carl and John pulled aside the curtain over the back window. "I'm sorry about your friend," he said to the man. "But we have to go."

The man's gaze moved from Debra's motionless figure to him. "I didn't know her before three days ago."

"That's almost a lifetime," Riley whispered.

The man's rust brown eyes studied her before he nodded and took a step away from the sink. "It is a lifetime," he agreed.

Carl and John lifted the table away from the door. "You ok?" John asked Riley.

"Not really, you?"

"Not particularly."

Carl shoved the curtain aside and peered out the window again before flipping the locks and opening the door. Xander took hold of Riley's hand as they stepped out the door and into the open. He didn't like feeling so exposed, but as he ran alongside Riley, he found he was grateful to be away from that house. The hideous memory of what had just occurred would forever haunt him, but at least he was free of the smell.

His leg had been rewrapped, but it still throbbed like a son of a bitch as they ran through backyards. He tried to keep his gait as steady as possible so Riley wouldn't worry, but by the time they made it to the next street, he was beginning to limp again. He knew they were making their way in the general direction of the McDougal's house, but it would take them forever to get there by foot.

"A car," Carl said and nodded toward a silver Toyota sitting in a driveway.

"Let's just get it and get out of this godforsaken town," John said.

Xander seconded that notion as they moved in on the car. John got to it first and pulled the driver's side door open. He slid into the seat and searched for the keys to the car but came up with nothing. "Inside," Riley said and ran up the porch steps of the home.

Thoughts of the last time he'd entered a house in search of keys propelled him up the steps far faster than he would have thought possible a minute ago. Riley had gone through enough today; she didn't need to see more bodies if they were in there. Xander stepped to the side as she thrust the door open and moved hastily out of the way.

Carl went in first, his gun raised as he hurried through the kitchen and into the dining room. Xander and Riley followed him into the house with John and the other guy close on their heels. Riley found the keys hanging from a hook on a cabinet in the kitchen. They jingled as she held them up.

"We've got wheels again," she said with a strained smile.

Xander kissed her forehead. "Good, let's get out of here. It's time to move on from this town."

"We can't," the man said from the backdoor.

Xander lifted his head and spotted the group of people moving across the backyard as the man silently closed the door. The click of the lock sliding into place sounded like a nail in a coffin to him.

CHAPTER 7

John

THE CLICK of the lock stopped him in mid-stride in the dining room behind Carl. He strained to hear anything, but after the click the house had a tomb-like silence enshrouding it. He shuddered at the thought, and he couldn't help but feel as if this house may just become his crypt.

He turned to look behind him, but from here he couldn't see the kitchen or Riley, Xander, or the stranger anymore. A thousand awful scenarios crashed through his mind as his heart beat loudly in his ears, making it more difficult to hear anything within the home. They didn't know that man; they *never* should have left Riley and Xander alone with him.

Then he realized, they may not know him, he may be dangerous, but Xander and Riley could handle themselves. That man couldn't have gotten the upper hand on them both, and Riley wouldn't hesitate to shoot if it became necessary.

No, the heavy hush after the lock had nothing to do with the stranger amongst them. John took a step back toward the doorway as Riley slid around the corner with Xander right behind her. "What's...?"

"They're coming," Riley whispered. That was *not* at all what he wanted to hear. His gaze shifted to the window across the way. There was little he could see of the street beyond the curtains, but it appeared to be deserted. "I have the keys," Riley held them up before slipping them into her pocket. "If we can get out..."

The sound of glass shattering cut her off. He adjusted the gun in his hand as Carl moved around the dining room table and into the front hall. A thud resounded through the house followed by some loud bangs as the backdoor began to rattle in its frame. It didn't matter what was outside the front door, what was outside the backdoor was going to come in, and there was nothing they could do to stop it.

Wood splintered as the backdoor gave way with a crash that rocked the house and shook the windows in their frames. Carl threw the front door open and ran out onto the porch and down the steps. The street still appeared to be empty, but John knew it wouldn't last as feet thudded heavily on the floor and reverberated through the house.

His legs were moving faster than he'd thought possible as he darted across the porch and down the steps. He was about to jump off of the stairs when a heavy weight fell upon his back and shoved him forward. A startled cry escaped him as his knees hit the ground and hands curled into the back of his shirt. The collar of his shirt dug into his neck and cut into his windpipe as his air supply was choked off. The force of the impact would have knocked the gun from his hand if he hadn't been holding it as firmly as a safe held money. After what had happened in the other house he didn't think he'd ever put the weapon down again.

His fingers tugged the collar at his neck as he tried to ease the choking. He beat at whoever held him with the gun as he tried and failed to knock them off. Stars burst before his eyes; he gagged loudly before the sound was effectively cut off. Carl spun back toward him as Xander's shoes appeared beside him and a gunshot fired.

Xander seized hold of his arm and pulled him out from under the woman who slid to the side and fell upon the ground beside him. Her eyes, staring blindly ahead, reminded him of the horror that had just occurred with Debra. Gasping for air, John grabbed at his wounded throat as he scrambled back to his feet and chanced a glance at the roof of the house. More people were crawling over the top of it toward them.

Did these people have no fear? John wondered in astonishment as they moved with the speed and assurance of a squirrel on the pitched shingles.

He got his answer as one of them leapt off the roof of the house instead of climbing down to the porch roof above them. They may not have any fear, but their bones still broke as the man's legs gave way with a loud crack. John winced at the sound and sight; he took a step away from the man still trying to come at them but failing miserably with his ruined legs.

"Car," Riley panted. "Let's get to the car."

The car was only fifteen feet away but as Carl started toward it, John could see more people flowing around from the back of the house toward them. Carl shot the woman in the lead through the head, but it did little good as three more rose up to take her place. Accuracy still wasn't something John could rely on, and it wasn't something he was striving for now as he fired uncontrollably into the crowd in an attempt to make them at least hesitate in their onward rush.

No, they had no fear at all, John decided as they kept coming despite the bullets flying at them and the other people falling around them.

Even during the worst times of his life, when he'd been fighting with his parents, when he'd been dumped and had his heart broken, he had never contemplated suicide. With the world falling apart around him now, he would fight until the bitter end. He would never understand what had driven Debra to do what she had done, but the thought of those things getting their filthy, rotten hands on him was enough to make him want to slit his own throat. Something he may just have to do, he was sure he was running out of bullets as he continued to shoot into the crowd as he ran.

Riley made it to the car first and flung open the driver's side door. Carl didn't bother to attempt to run around the car as he jumped onto the hood and ran across the top of it. Carl jumped off on the other side as the stranger threw open the door on Riley's side and scrambled across the backseat. John was right behind him. He hadn't looked to see where Xander was, but he felt Xander shoving in behind him before the door slammed shut.

Riley must have already had the car in gear as she hit the gas as soon as the door closed. The tires squealed, stones flew up against the side and pinged along the undercarriage as the car lurched out of the drive. The momentum threw him against the backseat before he was thrust forward. He didn't have time to get his hand braced before he was thrown against the seat again like a ragdoll.

His arms and legs were tangled up with Xander's and the other guy's. It was almost impossible to right himself in the seat as Riley squealed around a corner and hit a pothole that bounced them all into the air. His teeth clattered together so forcefully he was afraid he'd broken them. The stranger, taller than him and Xander, banged his head off the roof. Xander grunted beside him and tugged at his leg as he tried to pull it out from under John.

"Watch out!" Carl shouted.

John couldn't see what Carl was yelling about, but the car maneuvered sharply to the right. Pushing himself off the shoulder of Riley's seat, he finally managed to free his leg from the stranger and get his hand braced against the back of Carl's seat. "I forgot what a lunatic you were behind the wheel," he muttered as Riley took another turn. It felt as if the car's wheels were coming off the ground.

Riley didn't take her eyes off the road as she made a sharp left hand turn. He was squished up against the stranger as Xander's weight was thrust against him. He felt a little too up close and personal to someone he didn't know right now, but he couldn't push himself away from the guy as Riley was still making the turn. Just when he thought the door wouldn't be able to take their weight anymore, and they were going to sprawl out in the street, she finally straightened out the car.

John managed to sit up enough to see through the windshield in time for Riley to run over a woman with gray hair wearing a tattered red bathrobe smeared with dirt. The elderly woman reminded him of Mrs. Claus, if Mrs. Claus was from a land where zombie-like people made toys at the North Pole instead of the elves. The woman spun up over the hood of the car, but instead of going over the roof like he'd expected, she fell over the side and under the back wheels.

An enormous crater loomed before them; Riley had to leave the road in order to avoid it. She plowed through a small white picket fence and into someone's front yard. "This car can't take hitting much," Carl told her.

"Do you have a better route to take?" she demanded.

"No, you're doing good, just letting you know."

John had a brief glimpse of a tree before something slammed into the side of the car. A startled cry escaped John. Xander threw his hands over his head and ducked away from the man clinging to the window beside him. Watching the man, John was reminded of the wall crawlers he used to get from the machines at the exit of the grocery store when he was a kid. He'd spend hours throwing the crawlers at the wall and watching them walk down the surface.

"Holy shit!" the stranger shouted as yellowed eyes peered in at them. They were so yellow John could barely discern they'd once been blue. The man's face moved over the window as he appeared to be sniffing at the glass.

"Hold on," Riley grated through her clamped teeth.

Carl made a strangled sound and braced his hand against the dash as she aimed at a tree. "What are you doing?" John yelled.

His hands fell to his side, but it was too late, there was no time to get a seatbelt on, and he didn't think it would do him any good. He threw his arms up and slammed his foot against the console in front of him to brace for impact, but she veered off at the last second. The driver's side mirror slammed against her window and caused a spider web of fractures to spread through the glass.

The tree crashed into the man with a sickening thunk that made his stomach turn. John's head whipped around as the man was torn from the car and tumbled across the yard. Disbelief and amazement filled him as he turned back around to face Riley. "Who taught you how to drive?" he demanded.

Riley eased off the gas as she maneuvered the car around a large hole in the road. "My dad, but he definitely wasn't around when Carol and I went four wheeling down the power lines."

"Jesus," Xander muttered.

"You know you did it too," she said to him.

Xander just shook his head as John lowered his foot from the console. It now sported a boot-like indention where his foot had been. He glanced out the windows and noticed they had finally lost the mass of people who'd been pursuing them since they'd left the house.

"Where are we Xander?" Riley asked.

Xander took a deep breath as he studied the area around them. "We're heading back toward the grocery store."

"Let's not do that," the stranger said.

"We have to," Xander told him. "It's the only way back to my grandmother's road without taking a lot of back roads."

"Grocery store it is then," Carl said. He took his hat off and pushed the hair back from his face before shoving the brutalized hat back on.

John didn't like either one of those options, but he had to admit the grocery store was a better choice than being stuck on a back road with these things. He glanced at where the man had been hanging onto the car. "Only a honey badger should be as fearless as they are," John said.

"A honey badger would come in handy right about now as our extra bullets are in the car. We have more ammo in the truck, but that's not going to do us any good right now," Carl said.

John turned the gun over in his hand as he studied the weapon. Days ago, he never would have touched the thing. Now he didn't know what he would do without it. Images of Debra's last minutes filled his head. He'd watched Riley kill Lee, but he never thought he'd see something like what had happened with Debra or hear someone utter the words she had spoken.

There before me was a pale horse, John shuddered at the memory of his dream her words had conjured. He'd never really been around horses before or had any real desire to do so, but he'd rode the ponies at the fair as a kid, and that had been fun enough. Now he'd run in the other direction if he heard the sound of hoof beats or saw a horse in the distance.

He took a deep breath in order to try and calm himself. He'd had the dream because they had been talking about the apocalypse before he'd fallen asleep. Debra had clearly been out of her mind; no one in the right frame of mind would kill themselves. Or perhaps *they* were the crazy ones for continuing to try and fight a world he was growing increasingly convinced was seeking to destroy him. He wasn't entirely sure it was Mother Nature looking to do the destroying anymore either.

Now *that* thought was crazy.

But as he tried to reassure himself such a notion was nuts, he couldn't shake the approaching hoof beats of his dream from his mind. He really wished he had managed to find a beer from somewhere as he could really use one right now. A sinking sensation filled his stomach when he recognized the road Riley turned onto.

He'd never planned to see that grocery store again, but his gaze was pulled toward the massive front windows. "We could try and get the car," Riley said in a low voice.

"I don't think that's a good idea," John told her.

"The gas though."

"They set a trap in that store; I wouldn't be at all surprised to find one around the car somewhere too."

Her gaze remained riveted on the car though as they approached the store. "He's right Ri," Xander said. "Stopping at that place again is a *bad* idea."

Riley looked as if someone had just kicked her in the shin as she reluctantly turned her attention away from the car. John began to realize it wasn't the car she was after as her words finally sank in. "How much gas do we have?" He demanded as he leaned forward. She didn't have to answer as he spotted the yellow light flashing beneath the odometer. "How long has that been on?"

"I don't know. I wasn't looking when we first got in the car, but I feel like it's been on for a while," she replied.

He bit back a string of curses and limply slid back in his seat and dropped his head into his hands. Just once he would like for something to be easy.

"We just have to get back to the house, we'll have enough gas for that," Carl said forcefully.

"And if we don't?" the stranger asked.

"We'll cross that bridge when we get to it, but we *will* have enough."

John wanted nothing to do with that bridge, but with the way things were going he thought they were already halfway across it. He expected the car to start sputtering any second now and mentally began to brace himself for the run he knew was coming.

"My name is Donald; I just thought you should know in case we die."

John couldn't argue with the truth behind those words. Donald appeared to be in his mid-thirties at the oldest, but the tired look in his eyes made it seem as if he'd seen far more of this world than John had. Donald's eyes were the same color as the graham cracker crust on the cheesecake his mother used to make him for his birthday every year. His hair color was nearly the same as his eyes; the coloring produced a disconcerting affect that made it seem as if his whole face blended together. John blinked and shook his head to clear the strange image away; he really needed to get some sleep.

"I'm John, Mr. Optimism up front is Carl, that's Riley and Xander."

Carl turned in the seat to scowl at him. "We'll run out of gas on the next street, does that make you feel better?"

"Not really, no," John admitted.

Riley turned onto another road at Xander's instruction and drove back onto a yard. In the distance a puff of smoke drifted into the air. John leaned forward as flames shot out above the treetops. "That can't be good," Xander said before directing them down a road leading away from the smoke.

John couldn't tear his gaze away from the blinking gas light. He knew it wasn't, but the light seemed to be blinking faster the more they drove. He was so focused on it that he hadn't noticed they were getting closer to where they'd left the others until they passed another house nearly in the road. He recalled driving by it earlier because the house had been painted the ugly yellow of piss.

He finally shifted his attention away from the gas light to the road again. Riley turned onto the street and hit the brakes. John felt his mouth drop as heads swiveled in their direction, and though he knew it wasn't possible, he swore the eyes of the people on the street glimmered like cat's eyes in the rays of the sun filtering over them.

No, *now* was when they would run out of gas, he knew.

On the porch of the McDougal's house there were at least six of them clustered around the closed door. He saw no sign they'd forced their way into the house yet, but it was only a matter of time before they did.

Riley pulled a U-turn in the middle of the street. She drove away from the house as the people began to filter off the porch toward *them*. "Where do we go?" she yelled.

John was absolutely certain the gas light blinked faster now, that it mocked him as his eyes were drawn back to it. He glanced behind him as the people spilled onto the street behind them.

CHAPTER 8

Mary Ellen

Mary Ellen took a step back from the door as the knob began to rattle. She kept her hand firmly on Rochelle's shoulder to keep her daughter in place and herself grounded. Bobby shot Al a look and nodded toward the upstairs as he pointed at the ceiling. Al hesitated before giving a brisk nod. Ducking down to avoid the window in the center of the door, Bobby hurried past Al.

Mary Ellen's heart was in her throat as she watched him creep up the stairs. If those people outside happened to get in here Bobby would be trapped up there, he'd never be able to escape from them. Josh moved to go after him, but Peter grabbed his arm and shook his head admonishingly. Josh opened his mouth to protest; he closed it again when the knob began to rattle once more.

The door shook in its frame. A shadow moved across the window in the door as someone walked by it. Mary Ellen pulled Rochelle closer when a hand pressed against the glass. Peter jerked

Josh back as the hand rose away from the window and slapped back against the glass. The sound echoed in the abnormally hushed house. The hand pulled away and hit against the glass again with a solid thwack that set her teeth on edge.

Rochelle shuddered against her side as the glass rattled loudly in the window. The mottled black and red palm remained pressed against the window. Something banged against the front window as Al leaned over to peer up the stairs.

A cold trickle of apprehension slid down her spine and caused her to look behind her. She was half convinced something would be there, coming toward her with malignant resolve. There were only shadows behind her, but she sensed something more beyond the kitchen and in the yard she couldn't see. They may not be swarming on the back porch, but they were out there; they were hungry, and she couldn't shake the feeling they were watching her.

She suspected they were *always* hungry. That nothing would ever fill them up again.

The door jerked in the frame before going still again. Mary Ellen's eyebrows drew together as the hand slid away from the window and quiet ensued. Confusion swirled through her; she glanced at Al who looked just as baffled as she was. She pushed Rochelle back another step as she waited breathlessly for the door to be violently kicked in. Peter and Josh crept further away and were almost on top of her when Bobby flew down the steps.

"We have to go now," he blurted.

"What?" Mary Ellen demanded.

"Now, we have to go now. Riley and Carl were just at the end of the road. They turned around, but those things out there are following them. I don't think we'll get another chance if we don't leave now."

Mary Ellen felt her heart drop into her toes as her eyes traveled back to the now empty, dirt-streaked window. The last thing she felt like doing was stepping outside of this house and into whatever awaited them out there. Rochelle's shoulders thrust back as her chin jutted out; Mary Ellen knew there was no other option. They simply couldn't stay in this house for one minute more.

"Wait!" Josh said when Al's hand fell on the knob. "We can't go out there."

"We can't stay in here," Al told him.

Josh shook his head as he glanced warily at the door. "If you open that door you'll expose us all."

"We've already been exposed," Al told him. "It's only a matter of time before they come in here. Just as it was only a matter of time before they got into the house at the end of the street."

"The people in that house must have done something to alert those things to their presence there," Josh said.

"Those things will come back, and they *will* come in here," Mary Ellen said.

"We don't know that," Josh insisted. "We're safe here right now, we have supplies…"

"We're not safe here, and eventually those supplies will run out," Bobby said. "Besides, the others might need our help. Those things were following *them*. They weren't in the same car as before, something has already happened to them."

"Then how do you know it was them?" Josh demanded. "It could have been someone else in the car."

"I've known Riley since I was seven years old; I think I know what she looks like," Bobby retorted harshly. The normally easy-going guy was starting to lose his composure as his hands fisted, and he took a step forward. "Xander went after you in that school, even when he didn't want to, he went after you in there, and he got you *out*."

"Josh we have to go," Peter said softly. Josh shook his head. "I know you're scared Josh, but ,we have to go. I'm just looking out for you."

"No, I'm not going out there," Josh said adamantly.

"Then you stay, we're leaving," Bobby told him.

Al was grabbing for the door when Josh seized hold of his hand. "If you open the door you'll let them know we're here."

Bobby stepped off the stairs and took a threatening step toward the younger boy. "Get away from the fucking door!" Bobby exploded.

Mary Ellen knew this was escalating toward violence, and though Josh was being obstinate, she wasn't going to let the young man get hurt. Peter held up his hand to hold Bobby back as he shook his head.

"Don't make me pull you away from the door and drag you out of here Josh," Peter told him.

The color drained from Josh's face as he shook his head. Mary Ellen felt sorry for the boy but if Peter didn't pull him out of the way, she would. Her hand constricted on Rochelle's shoulder as her daughter took a step forward. "Josh, we'll be ok out there. I know we will, but we have to go now, or we *are* going to die in this house," Rochelle said gently.

Josh's eyes flickered to her, his nostrils flared as he took a deep, shuddering breath. His shoulders fell as he released the door-knob and took a step back. "Sorry," he muttered.

Peter squeezed his shoulder. "It's ok. We're all scared."

Josh's eyes slid away to focus on the wall behind Bobby. Al pulled the keys to the truck from his pocket. Peter nodded to Al, who turned the knob and poked his head out. "Looks clear," he said to them before stepping outside.

"Stay close to me," Mary Ellen said to her daughter and took hold of her hand, something Rochelle never would have let her do just a few short days ago.

Bobby and Josh followed Al out the door with Peter, Mary Ellen, and Rochelle close behind. The day seemed strange to her, too bright, surreal almost. The heat of it wasn't a shock, it hadn't been cool in the house, but the day spent in the shadows of the house had adjusted her eyes to the darkness. Now the harsh luminosity of the day caused her to take a step back. Rochelle fell against her side as she seemed to be briefly blinded by it too.

Blinking back the tears burning her eyes, Mary Ellen finally brought the others, and the porch, into focus again. Al had already stepped off the porch and onto the fissured sidewalk. She'd forgotten how fast he could move as he rushed toward the truck. Mary Ellen tugged Rochelle along behind her as she followed after Al.

Her gaze flew rapidly over the street. She spotted a few people still wandering through the backyards and a couple more down the road, but they appeared to be the sluggish, less threatening ones. The sight of them spurred her on faster though as she kept the gun down by her side. Amongst the shadows of the still standing homes she saw something shifting and moving as people stalked them from a few houses away.

Her hand tightened on Rochelle's as she moved her daughter to the other side of her, keeping her body in between Rochelle and the people hunting them. The car and truck hadn't seemed far away before, now she felt as if she would never reach them. Her lungs burned as she labored to get air into them.

Down the street, more of them began to appear as they seemed to have lost interest in Xander and the others. It was only a matter of time before they were swarming over this road again. Across the street, she spotted another handful of people as they emerged from the woods. Josh stumbled and nearly fell, but Peter managed to keep him upright with a brusque tug on his arm.

"I told you, I told you," Josh panted as Peter pulled him forward.

He *had* told them, but there were no other options, and she knew the safety they'd found within that house would have only lasted a few more hours at most. Still, she couldn't help but feel she had just led her daughter to her death as more of them emerged across the street.

Peter and Josh rushed toward the car with Bobby on their heels. She had just thrown the passenger side door of the truck open when the loud squeal of tires turned her attention to the end of the street. A Toyota she didn't recognize slid sideways around the turn. It left a trail of smoke and burning rubber behind it.

"Riley," Al muttered.

Mary Ellen pushed Rochelle ahead of her and into the truck as the car corrected itself from its sideways skid. The engine made a sound the likes of which Mary Ellen had never heard before. She turned away as Al climbed into the driver's side, and Rochelle settled into the middle of the truck. Mary Ellen hopped in behind her daughter as the first of the people appeared at the edge of the street.

A man honed in on Peter who was fumbling with the keys. "Hurry!" Bobby shouted at him.

"You're not helping!" Peter shouted back.

The engine of the car continued to race, and as it got closer Mary Ellen saw the crumpled bumper and broken radiator grill hanging in pieces from the vehicle. The hood had a body-sized dent in it, and the windshield had spider web fractures spreading throughout it. Riley's hands gripped the wheel rigidly as the car began to make a sputtering noise Mary Ellen recognized well from her teen years. Larry had never purposely run out of gas in order to pull the old make out trick on her, but they had run out a few times because they'd had nothing but hope and prayers to fill the gas tank with after Rochelle was born. Unfortunately, cars didn't run on those two things.

Al slammed his door shut and started the truck. The sick man was almost at Peter when Riley hit him at a much slower speed than the one she'd been traveling at before. The man let out a squeal that still sounded like a human in pain, but there was little human about its disfigured face and body as it rolled off the hood of the car and fell away from Peter.

Peter finally got the doors on the Cadillac open as the Toyota sputtered to a halt near the back of the truck. "Get in the back!" Mary Ellen heard Carl shout as the doors of the car were thrust open.

John leapt up and grabbed hold of the side of the truck. His feet kicked up to the side in a move she'd believed only gymnasts could pull off. He balanced precariously on the small edge of the truck bed on the outside of the metal sides of the truck. He seized hold of Riley's hand and helped to tug her up as Xander pushed at her waist and then her ass. They'd acquired more than a different car, Mary Ellen realized as she spotted the strange man amongst them.

John lifted himself up and toppled into the back of the truck with a loud bang that made her wince. Carl, Xander, and the stranger climbed onto the sides beside Riley. Mary Ellen's attention was torn away from them as the Caddy pulled away from the curb. It didn't go in the direction Riley and the others had come from, but made a turn in the middle of the street and headed off in the other direction.

A thump in the back of the truck drew her attention as Riley and Xander flipped over the five foot high side. Carl and the stranger were still holding onto the side as Al shifted awkwardly into drive with his bandaged hand. She heard the click of the truck sliding into gear before Al began to make a U-turn in the street. The stranger went over the side after the others. She met Carl's eyes briefly before he lifted himself up and disappeared over the side of the truck and into the bed.

"Hurry," Rochelle breathed as Al hit the gas.

The first rush of people hit the side of the truck as Al drove onto the broken sidewalk. Carl appeared back over the side of the boards and shot at the people trying to grasp hold of the truck. John, Riley and Xander appeared beside him and began to fire at the people rushing toward them. The people falling around them did nothing to deter the other sick humans from continuing to come at them. More sick people spilled around the corner from where the Toyota had just appeared.

The truck bounced over the ruts, jarring them in their seats as Al drove rapidly away from the street. Gunshots continued to sound from the back of the truck as more of the sick ones fell behind them. The Caddy stayed close behind them as they drove through streets she didn't know and just wanted away from. She spotted the sick, stalking them through the shadows of the woods and the edges of the yards as they tried to keep pace with the vehicle.

Xander banged on the side of the truck to get her attention. She rolled the window down, recoiling slightly as the stale, humid air blasted her in the face. "Tell him to take the next right," Xander called to her.

Al nodded and made a right onto what looked like an exit ramp. Mary Ellen's heart leapt into her throat as she spotted the toppled sign for the Mass Pike and Interstate eighty-four. It had been a while since she'd been on the highway, and she wasn't eager to return to it now. "The Pike?"

"It's ok," Al said. "It will help us get to New York faster, and maybe we can ditch some of these guys."

Mary Ellen bit her lip as she recalled how congested and difficult to traverse the highway had been before. She doubted it would get any easier on the Pike. Al eased the truck around a van parked almost in the middle of the exit ramp and onto the highway. She stared at the road unwinding before them in a seemingly endless ribbon of black stretching as far as she could see. The strangest urge to cry seized hold of her as the nothingness surrounding them engulfed her.

Some of the vehicles on the road had crashed, but others appeared to have been abandoned. Some still had their doors open, and as they drove by an SUV with its back passenger side door open, she spotted the baby seats still sitting in the back of it. A lump formed in her throat as she turned away.

She studied the broken trees and homes beside the side of the interstate, but other than the group of people growing steadily more distant behind them, she didn't see any of those creatures out there. They had found a bit of peace in the middle of a highway. Never in a million years had she thought the words peace and highway would go together, but today they did.

She wrapped her arm around Rochelle's shoulders. She'd never thought things could be good again, but right now they seemed about as close to perfect as they were going to get. Tears burned her eyes; she blinked them away before Rochelle could see her cry.

She glanced in the mirror to find the others standing at the side of the truck staring at the broken down town. Smoke rose from toppled buildings as a blaze smoldered in the distance. New holes and canyons marked the landscape, but one thing that really stood out to her was the lack of people. She didn't see anyone moving amongst the crumpled homes and businesses that had once stood alongside the highway.

"It's so peaceful, after everything, it's just so peaceful now," Rochelle whispered.

Mary Ellen silently counted her blessings as Al weaved in and out of the cars congesting the road. Carl hit the side of the vehicle with his hand as he moved toward the window and leaned in to speak. "We're going to have to see if some of these abandoned cars have gas left in them. Try finding the wrecked ones or a highway patrol vehicle. We need some new gas cans too."

She nodded and turned to Al. "I heard him," Al assured her as he pulled up next to a three car accident and put the truck in park.

Mary Ellen glanced around her before opening the door and climbing out. "Mind opening the back doors? I don't think my knees can take jumping out of this thing," Carl told her.

Hurrying around to the back of the truck, she frowned as she studied the lock on them. She pushed up one side of the latch as Carl leaned over the door and pulled the latch up. The doors gave way with a small pop. "Thanks," he muttered as he climbed out. "First things first, let's get these guns reloaded. Then see if we can find some tubing and something to hold the gas in."

Mary Ellen stood back as Carl pulled the ammunition from the truck. He reloaded his gun before loading the others. She studied the sleek Caddy as it pulled to a stop behind them. "Let's see if we can find another car too. I know I would prefer a seat, that truck is tough on my back," John said as he rubbed at his lower back.

Mary Ellen turned Rochelle away as she spotted a couple of

bodies still within the crashed vehicles. "Stay by the truck," she told her before heading toward one of the cars in search of supplies.

The highway may seem peaceful, but she didn't intend to be stranded out here tonight.

CHAPTER 9

Riley

BENDING down she pressed her hands against the glass and tried to peer into the suped-up car's driver side window. The heavy tint on the window made it impossible to see inside though. Shaking her head, she stepped back from the car. The tint was irritating, but she had to admire the sleek lines of the vehicle. She wondered how fast it would have gone if it wasn't embedded in the back of a truck.

She grabbed hold of the door handle. Before it was half a foot open, she knew she'd made the wrong decision. She slammed the door shut again before she could see whatever in there was causing her gag reflex to kick into hyper drive, her eyes to burn, and her nose to wrinkle. Her hand flew to her nose as she took an abrupt step back from the rotten smell of whoever remained in that car.

She blinked back the tears burning her eyes as she turned toward the others. Carl bit on his inner cheek to keep from laughing as he watched John from the side of a Jeep that had rolled onto its side. She could barely hear John's muffled curses as his feet kicked in the air out of one of the back windows.

Xander was watching her from the edge of the road where he stood with Bobby beside a pickup truck. She shook her head and pinched her nose as she indicated the car. He gave a brief nod and turned away. Al gave up inspecting a car with a flat tire and joined her. "This is some slim pickings," he said.

"It is," she agreed.

They walked down the road together to the next set of cars. Riley opened the door, pulled the visor down, and searched the floor and glove box for keys, but she came up empty. She retreated from the vehicle and took a step back from it. Al was standing by the hood; his hand was against his forehead as he tried to shade his eyes from the sun beating down upon them. Riley tugged at her shirt as she attempted to peel it from the sweat coating her body.

Her parents had taken her to Florida during summer break when she was twelve. They'd intended to explore the state and go to all the parks. They'd spent more time trying to get inside, and away from the oppressive heat, than they had doing anything else. She'd sworn she'd never go back there in the summer again, but now, standing on the side of this road, she knew she would have taken a hundred summers in Florida over this as steam rose from the baking asphalt.

She tried not to think about the fact there was almost no way they'd ever be able to grow anything in this hostile environment. There was no way *anything* could thrive anymore she realized as she closed the door on the car. They could attempt to figure that out later, when they weren't stranded on a highway. Besides, she was sticking to the possibility they would wake up to find the weather had stabilized again soon. It didn't seem likely, but then it hadn't seemed likely lava would run through her hometown, or she would see someone commit suicide right before her eyes either.

"There was a girl." She glanced over her shoulder to where Donald, Mary Ellen, Peter, Josh, and Rochelle had moved in the opposite direction in search of supplies. "With Donald. She ah... She killed herself Al."

Al's hand dropped to his side. The lines in his face were deeper as he turned toward her. "You saw her do it?"

Her gaze drifted toward Xander as he jogged across the road with Bobby to join Carl and John. She started walking with Al again to the next set of cars. "We all did."

"That had to have been awful."

She didn't think those words were enough to cover what it had been like, what it still felt like. She'd never be able to get the image out of her head or understand what had driven Debra to do what she did. Had Debra really believed the words she'd spoken before ending her life? Is that what had driven her to pull the trigger? Riley shuddered and wrapped her arms around her middle as her stomach began to twist. Debra had only been feet away from her when she'd killed herself, yet none of them had been able to stop it. They'd been helpless to save Debra, and she still felt helpless now, a feeling she was struggling to shake off.

"It was," she agreed as she stopped next to another car.

Peering in the windows, she was relieved to see this car was empty. She popped the trunk latch before leaning inside to search through it. She came up with a few lint balls and a couple of hairy breath mints, but nothing she would eat, or they could use. Pulling down the glove box, she sorted through the papers before slamming it closed again.

Frustration was beginning to fill her as she leaned out of the car and rested her arm on the roof of the vehicle. Her breath hissed out of her, she jerked her arm back as she swore she heard her skin sizzle from the contact. Across the street John was finally emerging from the Jeep with the help of Carl and Xander pulling at his legs. He was grinning like he'd just struck gold as he held up a gas can, a set of jumper cables, and a cooler. Riley couldn't stop the smile tugging at her lips as John continued to happily wave his finds in the air and did a dance while he turned in a circle.

Al shook his head and slammed the trunk closed. "That kid."

"He kind of grows on you," Riley said as they continued down the road.

Carl took the cooler from John and popped it open. Judging by the curl of his lip, and his recoil, there was nothing salvageable within. Carl tossed it back into the Jeep and jogged across the road to them. "Any luck?" he asked.

"Nothing so far," Riley told him as she stopped next to another car. She searched through it, but this one only offered her a bunch of coins and an overflowing ashtray that the heat of the past few days had done nothing to help the stale smell of. She withdrew from the car before the oppressive scent made her vomit.

"I was telling Al about Debra," she said as she continued down the road.

"Who's Debra?" Bobby asked from the back of a pickup he had climbed into. Shading her eyes she tilted her head back to look up at him. One hand was on his hip while a six pack of beer dangled from his fingertips. John leaned over the side of the truck and tugged one of the cans free of the ring.

"That's going to be more skunked than Pepe Le Pew," Bobby informed him.

"It is," John agreed, but he popped the top on it anyway. "But it's my birthday, and it's kind of a tradition."

"I think I'd break tradition this time," Xander said as he moved past him.

John made a face, but he chugged the beer. Riley guessed he was about halfway through it before he pulled it away, wiped his mouth, and lifted it to the sky. A pang stabbed her heart as she realized this tradition involved someone who was no longer with them. Unexpected tears burned her eyes as she ducked into another truck and pushed the bench seat forward.

John tossed the empty beer can into the back of the truck when she reemerged empty handed again. "I hate to say it, but we're most likely going to find stuff in the cars that still have bodies in them," Carl said. "Anybody with any brains would have taken everything of use they could with them."

Riley glanced back at the suped-up car and shuddered. "Some of them may have been sick and not thinking clearly when they abandoned their vehicles; maybe they wouldn't have thought to take any of their stuff with them."

"Maybe."

"So," Bobby said as he jumped out of the back of the truck and strode toward them. "Who was Debra?"

"A woman with Donald when we found him. She killed herself, but not before spouting off some crazy stuff," John informed him.

Al stopped walking as his eyes drifted back to Riley. She found she couldn't meet Al's gaze; she'd been trying to figure out how to broach the subject with him, or if she wanted to know any more answers about what Debra had been talking about. She might actually prefer the alien theory to the idea there were four horsemen riding around killing people because God had had enough.

How were they ever supposed to escape that?

"What kind of stuff?" Al asked.

Xander's arm brushed against her shoulder as he stepped beside her. She leaned into his chest, taking solace in the fact he was there to touch. Her fingers brushed briefly over his shirt and back as the simple act of touching him helped to ease some of the anguish Debra's death had inflicted upon her.

"She started talking about the apocalypse and horsemen and death riding a horse. It was... It was just one of the creepiest things I've seen, and we've seen some creepy crap recently," John answered. Riley did a double take when she saw he had another beer in his hand. "Then she blew her brains out."

"John," Carl said as he leaned out from the back door of an SUV.

John shrugged. "Well, she did. Crazy right?"

John's gaze pinned Al; he seemed to be seeking some reassurance it *was* crazy. Al's frown deepened as he tapped his chin thoughtfully. "Sounds like it was from Revelation."

"That's what I said." Carl shut the door on the vehicle and stepped away.

"Great so we've confirmed it's Revelation," John said.

Riley grimaced as he took a long swallow of what had to be piss warm beer. He crumpled the can in his hand and tossed it into the back of an empty car. "Let's just avoid horses from here on out," Bobby suggested, but though he tried to smile, it faltered as he shook his head and walked toward another vehicle.

She glanced back at where they'd left the car and truck. She'd expected the others to be far enough away she couldn't make out their features; she was startled to realize they hadn't made it nearly as far as she'd thought. Exhaustion had really started to wear on her. She rubbed at her cheeks and eyes as she attempted to revive herself a little.

A bed, or even a floor, sounded like a great thing right now, but she still turned away and forced her feet to move toward the SUV closest to her. Peering in the window, she felt her stomach drop as she spotted the man in the front seat with his head bent forward. She knew Carl was right, but she wasn't about to start searching the vehicles with people still in them unless it became absolutely necessary.

She turned away and made her way toward another pickup. Her arms shook as she placed her hands on the open tailgate. Heat radiated into her palms, and she tried to lift herself quickly into the truck to spare her skin. The events of this day had left her far more drained than she'd realized though as her muscles protested the movement, and it took all she had to pull herself into the bed of the truck.

The adrenaline that had propelled her through the grocery store and houses was fading away. The temptation to just sit and let the others continue onward gripped her, but Debra had probably felt that way in the end. Perhaps all Debra had really wanted was to sit and rest, to have just a minute of peace again. Riley didn't want to ever truly understand how Debra had felt at the end, but she knew simply sitting here was a good way to start.

With a groan, she pushed herself up and forced her feet to shuffle toward the metal toolbox taking up a good chunk of the truck bed. Kneeling down she popped the lock up on the right hand side of the box and leaned over to look in. She lifted a tarp out of the box but that was all it contained.

Tossing the tarp back inside, she moved to the other side of the box and unlocked it. A sigh of relief escaped her, and she almost let out a shout of joy as she spotted the red gas can tucked neatly within. The sight of it was better than the time Santa had brought her the bike she'd been hinting, asking, and finally begging for, for Christmas.

Two cans, they were up to at least two gas cans again now. She grabbed hold of it and went to pull it out of the box but it gave her more resistance than she'd expected. Liquid sloshed within it as she reached in with her other hand and pulled it out.

"There's gas in there?"

She turned as Xander rested his hand on the side of the truck before quickly pulling it away. "Yeah."

"Strange."

Riley leaned forward and peered through the back window into the front seat of the older model truck. The dashboard had yellow bits of stuffing sticking out of the cracks in it, the material on the ceiling was hanging down, and the awful dice hanging from the rearview mirror looked as if someone had actually tried to use them in more than a few games. She hadn't been paying much attention when she'd first climbed into the back of the truck; now she noticed the holes and flakes of rust speckling the bed.

"I'm guessing it was more than a gas problem stopping it," she said.

Xander leaned over to look in the window. "I'm going to say you're right. Nice dice." He stepped back and held his hand out. "I'll take the can."

The quaking muscles in her arms were relieved to hand it over. He met her at the end of the truck and helped her climb out of the bed. Riley spotted the others gathered around a cluster of vehicles crashed into each other and nearly barricading the entire highway. There was a strip on the right hand side they would just barely be able to drive the truck through.

"Bet you this brings back some memories for you," she heard John say as she and Xander walked up to where the others had gathered. She didn't know what John was talking about until he stepped back to reveal Carl searching through the backseat of a police car. Carl said something she couldn't make out, but she knew it hadn't been friendly as John chuckled and shook his head. "Easy killer."

"What did you find?" Bobby asked.

Xander lifted the gas can into the air. "Riley found a full can of gas."

"That may be our best find out of all of this," Carl said as he climbed out of the back of the car.

Al was smiling as he walked up to them with a four-foot piece of rubber tubing. "Looks like we're going to stay in business."

She slumped against the police car as relief filled her. "Good let's get some more gas and get back on the road."

Taking hold of Xander's hand she stayed close to his side while they walked back to the others. Mary Ellen waved at them and pointed to a small pile set up beside the truck. Riley spotted a set of jumper cables, a few granola bars and four cases of soda amongst the pile. A spare donut tire was propped against the side of the Cadillac.

"What did you guys find?" Mary Ellen asked.

"Gas cans," Riley told them with a smile. "And some tubing."

She sat on the ground next to the Cadillac and leaned against the side of it. Tilting her head back, she stared at the sky. It was still the color of blood, but on the horizon she could see a steady spiral of smoke drifting into the air. There was something almost soothing about the billowing smoke; something that made the frantic beat of her heart finally ease.

Taking a deep breath, she shoved herself to her feet as Carl began to siphon and fill the other gas can. She moved through the cars closest to them, inspecting the inside of them for keys. She found a set shoved above the visor of a Ford. Sliding the key into the ignition she turned it over enough to make sure the battery still worked and to see where the gas gage was at. The gas light instantly blazed to life, the needle didn't even give a little jump off the line.

"I don't understand why they didn't search the other vehicles before leaving here," she said to John as he stepped next to the car.

"They might have, but they might have given up when they couldn't find anything right away."

"Yeah, I guess."

"You think it was something else?"

She shook her head and sat back in the seat. "They probably thought walking was their best bet, that they could find help somewhere. We've all been there."

"You've given up on finding any help?" he asked.

"Haven't you?"

He rested his hand on the glass of the open window as he looked down at her. Normally she wouldn't have been able to smell the beer on him, but the oppressive heat seemed to magnify the smell of it on his breath. It wasn't unpleasant, not compared to the other scents in the air.

"I think I have," he admitted. "I'm not saying help's not out there somewhere; I'm just not sure it's anywhere near us, and I'm not entirely sure I want it anymore. After the gas station I don't really want to be around people."

"Neither do I. We did find Donald though."

He glanced over to where the stranger stood with Xander and Carl as they siphoned gas to fill the truck. "Yeah, I don't trust him either though, and he's only one guy. Imagine being around a bunch of people?"

"No," she said as she pulled the key from the ignition and climbed out of the car. "No I can't."

She surveyed the empty highway as they walked back to the others. Taking hold of Xander's hand again she enfolded it in both of hers. No, she absolutely did not want to be around other people anymore. She just wanted to get somewhere safe with all of the people surrounding her. It didn't seem like much to ask for, but she couldn't shake the hideous notion it would be impossible to do so.

CHAPTER 10

Carl

IT WAS JULY, but night fell early as the sky darkened to a shade of red that reminded him of the lava that had flowed through Foxboro before becoming completely black. He couldn't shake the feeling the sky was as angry and hungry as the lava had been. Tearing his gaze away from the sky, he took the exit ramp toward the Connecticut Welcome Center. The headlights splashed over the woods and picnic tables spread out around the area. Headlights bobbed like fireflies in the side mirrors of the truck from the cars following behind them.

"Connecticut," John muttered and shook his head.

"What's wrong with Connecticut?" Carl asked him.

John shrugged as he surveyed the parking area they pulled into. If it wasn't for the headlights Carl wouldn't have any idea where they were parking as he pulled up in front of the gloomy building. The pines and oaks surrounding the parking lot probably blocked the lights from the interstate on a normal night, but tonight they made it nearly impossible to see anything when he turned the truck off.

He could barely see John, but he could hear him fumbling for the flashlight on the dashboard. "Hopefully a lot less than what was wrong with Massachusetts," John said as he clicked on the flashlight.

Carl couldn't help but agree as he pushed the door of the truck open and stepped into the night. They'd made better time than he'd expected once they'd finally been able to start moving again, but the early night had forced them to stop far sooner than he would have liked. He was eager to see what Connecticut had to offer too; there just may be something better in this state.

He didn't think that was likely, but it was something to hope for.

He cupped his hand around his lighter as he lit his cigarette and surveyed the woods around them. Grabbing the gun from inside the truck, he kept it close to his side as he closed the door and shut off the bulb inside. Ever since they'd hit the highway they hadn't seen any of those sick, violent humans on the road. He'd spotted them amongst the towns they had passed, but he hadn't seen any beside the interstate. But then there had been few other people traveling on the highway, and they'd had no contact with the ones they had seen. The sick would go where the food supply was, and the supply seemed to be concentrated amongst the towns and homes.

For now.

Though the last part of the day had been a good reprieve, he knew it couldn't last forever. The sick ones would spread out further when the food source started to run low, but maybe their luck would hold up, and they could stay on the highway for a while. He turned toward the Welcome Center and studied the shadowed building. It was just a simple brick building with a few Porta Potties on the outside of it, but it looked better than a dozen cartons of his favorite cigarettes right now.

Riley stepped out of the Ford and stood beside him as she surveyed the building. He glanced at the car as Bobby and Donald climbed out of the backseat, and Xander slid out from behind the wheel. "How does the new guy seem?" he asked her discreetly.

Her gaze slid to Donald and she shrugged. "He seems harmless, and he's friendly enough."

"But?" he prompted when he sensed more behind her words.

She gave him a halfhearted smile. "But nothing, I'm just not the most trusting person anymore."

The snort of laughter he released caused his smoke to trail before him in the air. He hadn't been the most trusting person before this, now he was likely to shoot first and ask questions later. "I'll keep an eye on him."

"We all will," Riley said.

"Let's go see if there's something of use inside."

"A place to sleep would be nice."

He stepped on his butt and crushed it into the ground. "We'll have to find some blankets."

"Never thought I'd hear those words in this heat," John said as he stepped around the front of the truck.

Carl had to agree, but he didn't say so as he walked toward the front of the building with Riley and John close at his side. He heard the others behind him, but he didn't look back as he approached the glass front doors. Leaning forward he pressed his hands to the glass and peered into the windows. The wall of impenetrable darkness enshrouding the inside of the building reminded him of being buried beneath the waves of the Atlantic ocean with no way out. It had happened to him once, as a child when they had gone to the beach, but his father had been there to pull him out. There was no one to pull him out now.

"This place reminds me of the grocery store," John said.

Carl shot him a look. "Now why did you have to say that?"

John shrugged and lifted his flashlight to shine it in the windows. "Because it does."

Carl followed the beam as it bounced over metal railings leading into what he assumed was the bathrooms. He saw papers on the bulletin board across from them, but he couldn't make out what they said. He glanced over his shoulder to find Riley surveying the roof with her light. Taking a step back, he looked at the slanted roof. All he saw up there were pine needles, pinecones, and sap. Riley kept her beam focused on the roof as he stepped under the alcove once more and grabbed hold of the handle.

"Be prepared," he hissed to John.

John shot him a look that made Carl think he was about to heave the flashlight at him. Carl almost threw his arm up just in case, but John only continued to glower at him. He had expected the door to be open and wasn't surprised when it gave way beneath his hand. Raising his gun he cautiously entered the welcome center. The no pets allowed sign, scribbled on a piece of paper in marker, slipped from where it had been taped to the door.

Stepping over it, the first thing that hit him was the smell wafting from the men's room on his left. It wasn't unbearable, but there was no doubt what the room was used for as the potent odor of days old ammonia made his nose wrinkle. He kept the gun raised as he turned the corner and swept into the main room. The beam of the flashlight played over broken pieces of glass littering the floor from the empty vending machines. Both soda machines had also been kicked in, but he thought he spotted a few cans lying in the bottom of one of them.

He nodded toward the men's room. "Come with me," he said to John.

Riley moved further into the main room and stopped outside of the woman's room. Xander moved passed her to stand by the back door. He craned his neck to try and see out, but Carl doubted Xander could see anything beyond the wall of black pressing against the glass. There was something so absolute about the blackness that made it seem as if there was nothing beyond the glass, nothing beyond this building, nothing left to the world anymore.

He could almost believe the world had completely ended and only a void remained out there. A void he swore he could almost hear licking at his heels as it threatened to suck all of them into it.

A shudder rippled down his back as he turned away from the unnerving spectacle and toward the bathroom. He walked past the metal railing and stepped cautiously into the room. The potent stench of urine hung heavily in the still air. The squeak of his shoes on the linoleum floor made his hand clench on the gun as he crept forward. John's flashlight beam caused his shadow to stretch forward like some sort of demented boogeyman. The unnerving sight of that shadow caused his skin to tingle and his groin to tighten as it bounced and floated over the yellow and brown streaked floor.

He moved passed the first urinal and stopped at the door across from it. He didn't hesitate before he pushed the stall door open. He wasn't entirely sure he was breathing as he continued through the room to the last stall. John was still waiting near the front of the bathroom when he was done. In the dim glow from the flashlight,

Carl could see the sweat beading on John's forehead and trickling down his cheeks as they left the room.

Everyone was gathered in the main room when they emerged. "We'll check out the women's room," he said.

Riley fell into step behind him as he entered the pink room. It didn't smell like roses or perfume but it didn't make his nose burn like the men's room had. "It's the forbidden land." John was trying to sound light, but his voice sounded as if he had been coughing all day.

Carl didn't look back at him as he pushed open the first stall with a lot less confidence than he'd approached the doors in the men's room. He was becoming increasingly convinced he was going to open a door and find someone with a rotting face standing on the toilet seat with hooked fingers as they waited to pounce on him. In the hush of the room, he was certain he could hear the creature's nearly silent exhalations while it eagerly waited to leap on him and rip him open.

The impending feeling of doom didn't get better with each door he opened either, instead it got worse. His hand shook as he pushed open the second to last door. He took a step back, brought his gun up and aimed it into the dark. The door made a small clacking noise as it bounced against the metal partition between the stalls and creaked back toward him. He hated the tremor in his arm as he lowered the gun from the empty stall.

With a heavy heart he turned toward the last door. A cigarette would have been outstanding right now, but he wasn't going to be distracted for the one-second it would take to light it. He became aware of the muted plop of water as he continued to stare at the last door. He could walk away, just say it was good and relentlessly watch the bathroom door all night or he could open the door and get it over with. He'd never been the smartest of men, the kindest of men, or the richest of men, but he'd never considered himself a coward either. He didn't know where this cold dread was coming from, didn't understand what kept his hand from moving the six inches forward it had to go. Maybe it was instinct, maybe it was just terror, but he found himself completely immobile.

"Carl?" John asked.

Carl shook his head but didn't look back at his friend. Taking a deep breath he lifted his gun hand and forced himself to close the distance between himself and the metal door. Hundreds of horrible images of leprosy looking people waiting to eat him filled his mind while the door creaked open.

He remained immobile, his gun aimed into the stall, as he waited for something to spring out at him. The solid beat of his heart pulsed in his throat as images of the last moments of his life flooded his mind. He was so ensnared by those images it took him a minute to realize the stall was empty. No one sat there waiting to eat him.

His shoulders slumped. His hand still shook as it fell back to his side. He felt like an idiot as he turned back to the others. John and Riley were so ashen they appeared almost spectral in the dim illumination filling the room. "Clear," he managed to croak out.

Regaining his composure, he stepped away from the door and noticed his reflection in one of the mirrors over the sink. He barely recognized the scruffy, pale faced man looking back at him. His eyes hadn't been this bloodshot since the drunken benders he'd gone on in his twenties. Using the back of his arm, he wiped away the sweat trickling steadily down his brow and into his eyes.

Not liking the fevered look in his bloodshot eyes, he turned away from the mirror and made his way toward Riley and John. Light flooded the room as Xander stepped around the corner. "Everything ok?" Xander inquired.

"It's fine," Riley assured him.

Carl followed them into the main room where the others were gathered near the vending machines. He'd thought he'd looked half crazed in the mirror, but looking at the exhaustion and strain on their faces, he realized he just looked normal now. "Did anyone check that room?" he asked as he nodded toward the only other door within the building.

"It's just an office and it's safe," Al answered.

"We got a broom though," Mary Ellen said as she held it up.

Carl nodded and walked over to the map of Connecticut pinned to the wall. *You are here,* was written with black marker and a red arrow pointed to where the welcome center was located on the map.

"How do they know where I am?" John asked.

Carl frowned at him as he turned away from the map. "Huh?"

John shook his head as he ran a hand through his disheveled brown hair. "Nothing, it was just a joke I heard once."

Carl's tired mind finally tripped into place and a small snort of laughter escaped him. "Bad joke."

"I never said it was a good one."

Carl continued to study the map as John moved away. He tugged it free of the wall and handed it to Al. "In case we have to get off the highway, you'll know where we're going," he told the older man.

Al nodded and carefully folded the map up. The tinkling of glass caught his attention as Mary Ellen began to sweep the glass toward the ruined vending machines. "Let's get some supplies," he suggested. "I don't know about you guys, but I'm starving."

John nodded and stepped away from the wall he'd been leaning against. Riley said something to Xander he couldn't hear, but when she gestured toward his leg Carl got the gist of the conversation.

He hoped the kid didn't argue with her again and actually took some time to get off of the leg. Xander had been holding up well given the trials of the day, but continued abuse to his damaged limb wasn't going to do any of them any good.

Riley leaned forward and kissed Xander's cheek before hurrying over to him and John by the door. Bobby walked over to join them also. Carl pushed the door open and stepped into the still night. He strained to hear anything, but the only sound was the forlorn breeze of the wind moving through the looming trees surrounding them. The trees creaked and the leaves rustled within the boughs as they swayed back and forth.

He may have been a landscaper, but he'd always hated a lot of noise. Slapping on his earmuffs and firing up the mower was a way to lose himself, and zone out for a while, but horns blaring and people screaming in the city had always set his teeth on edge. Now he'd give anything to hear some noise, to have someone curse him out and blare a horn, to hear the loud wail of a siren. To hear a cricket chirrup would have made his whole day.

This hush only served to reinforce the strange feeling they were the only people left on this broken planet.

The lock popping on the back of the truck sounded like a gunshot, and he couldn't help but look around for something to jump out at them. His gaze searched the woods to see if anything had been drawn forward by the noise, but the woods remained as unmoving as a corpse. John and Bobby leapt into the back of the truck and began to gather food and drinks to bring back into the building with them. Riley's gaze remained riveted on the treetops as she stood beside him. Carl felt his own eyes drawn to the tops of the trees as he recalled the monkey like agility the rabid-like sick ones exhibited.

Bobby and John were moving supplies into a smaller bag when

Al appeared next to Riley. She jumped a little when she spotted him. "Shit," she hissed. "This isn't exactly the best time to be sneaking up on people when they have a gun."

Al smiled at her and looked into the back of the truck. "We still have a fair amount of supplies."

Carl eyed the mound in the truck. "It won't last eleven people for long."

"No, it won't," Al agreed.

"This cabin of yours, do you think it will be safe, and will we be able to get food?" Bobby asked as he walked over holding two jugs of water in his hands.

Al shrugged as he shook his head. "I don't know. When this all started I thought it was the perfect place to go. I still think it will be safer than many other places, but I also thought we'd be able to fish and hunt there, now I'm not so sure."

"That doesn't seem very likely now," John said as he dropped a small bag of junk food at the end of the truck bed.

"The mountains might have sustained the quakes better." Riley grabbed the bag off the truck and placed it on the ground before turning back to them. "If that's the case then it really could be safe, and we really could survive there for a while."

John handed the last bag out of the truck and jumped down. Bobby hopped out beside him. Gathering the supplies they made their way tiredly back toward the building. Even the promise of some much needed food in his grumbling stomach couldn't get his feet to move any faster. The promise of sleep seemed much more enticing right now than eating, but it was going to be awhile before he got the chance to close his eyes.

Three cans of soda had been salvaged from the vending machine and gathered in the center of the room. The glass had been pushed into a corner and most of the others were already settled onto the floor. Xander and Peter were the only ones who remained standing. Rochelle leapt to her feet and hurried over to John.

John handed the bag of food over to her. Rochelle dug into the bag and pulled out the Twizzlers. "I'm sure these are for you," she said as she thrust them at John.

He gave her a weary smile as he took the bag from her. "You know me so well."

Rochelle turned away and began to place the food in the center of the room. "We can't keep surviving on junk food," Al said from beside him.

"No, we can't," Carl agreed. "Do you think we should still try and get to your cabin or should we try something else?"

Al rubbed at his chin as he watched the others divide the food. "Unless you can think of something better, or somewhere else to go, I don't have any other ideas."

That was the problem, he didn't have any other ideas either. Perhaps Riley was right, and the mountains had withstood the quakes better. He really didn't like the idea of going anywhere near more highly populated areas, but maybe that was the wrong choice. Maybe the higher populated areas are where they would find safety, food, and stable shelter.

They'd probably find a lot more sick people too which was the last thing he wanted to do.

"I don't," he admitted. "We'll just have to keep scrounging for supplies as we go. It's all we've been able to do so far, and we're still alive. We'll ask the others what they think after they've eaten though."

Al nodded. "And if they would prefer something different?"

Carl didn't like the idea of it. They may go through supplies faster by having more people around, but there was safety in numbers. If people chose to go their own way he wasn't going to stop them. "Then we'll have to say goodbye."

Carl didn't miss the relief filling Al's face as he nodded. Apparently Carl wasn't the only one who hadn't changed his mind about not going into more populated areas. "Are you guys going to eat?" Rochelle asked around a mouthful of chips.

"Of course," Al said as he strode forward.

Carl stayed back as they eagerly dug into their dinner. His stomach rumbled, but he retreated to the door to keep watch. He glanced over at Xander, who was leaning against the other door, his eyes on Riley and the others as they ate. Carl turned away, but he couldn't see two feet beyond the glass in front of him.

CHAPTER 11

Al

"DO WE HAVE A CHOICE?" Peter asked in a harsh, challenging tone.

"Why wouldn't you?" Carl had been staring out the glass doors, but now his head turned and his brow furrowed as he looked to Peter.

Al hadn't known Carl for long, but something in his tone that caught his attention and made the sleepiness clinging to him fade away. Everyone was tired, hungry, beaten, and on edge. Though he didn't think Carl was reckless or volatile, he *was* protective. If he thought Peter might become a threat, Carl would do something about it.

Donald had gone into the office earlier and returned with a notebook and pen. The man had been writing something, but at Peter and Carl's words the pen stopped moving and his head came up. Al wiped at his eyes and sat up straighter against the closed office door as he turned toward the middle-aged teacher.

"We can't just walk out of here," Peter retorted.

"If you would prefer to go your own way, or if you have a better plan for all of us, just say so. That's why we're having this discussion," Carl told him.

Peter glanced around the room, but Al knew what he would see, a ragtag bunch of survivors who looked like they'd not only been run over by a bus, but the bus had been followed up by a Mac truck and then a train. At least that's the way his body felt, and his mind was just as brutalized. He pushed his glasses up and rubbed at his eyes to try and clear the blurriness from them, but when he dropped the glasses back into place things were still a little wavy.

There had been a time, before he'd gotten glasses as a child, he'd believed the world was a bunch of blurs and blobs. He'd been fine with it then, but he wasn't fine with it now as his tired eyes finally managed to blink the others into focus.

"I'm just saying that if some of us decided to try and go into a city or in a different direction, we can't walk there without any supplies," Peter said. "It would be a suicide mission, and I doubt any of *you* would part with anything useful."

Carl lifted an eyebrow at the teacher as a muscle in his cheek began to twitch. Slowly turning away from Peter, he glanced at the others, but it was Al who gave him a subtle nod. Carl studied him for a second before his shoulders slumped, and his eyes drifted back to Peter. "If any of you decide to leave, then we'll give you a car and two days worth of supplies. If you don't want to stay we're not going to force you to, and we're not going to turn you away with nothing."

Peter remained unmoving as he held Carl's steely stare. "Does anyone else think we should head for a city?" Peter inquired without looking away from Carl.

"I don't want to go anywhere near a place where there were a lot of people before," Riley informed him. She had retreated to Xander and was sitting on the floor by his feet as he continued to watch out the backdoor. The remaining bag of chips she'd brought him was in his hand, but he seemed to have forgotten about it as his gaze drifted down to her. "I don't care if this cabin is a pile of rubble, I don't care if we can't make it into the mountains because there are rocks in the way, or if we get there only to find the lake is lava, and there's absolutely nothing to eat. I am *not* going anywhere near higher populated areas that will..."

"The sickness may not be in the cities; we have no idea what has caused it or how it is passed," Peter finally looked away from Carl to all of them. "For all we know it could have only been in Mass. If we go to Hartford or New York City there may only be *healthy* people."

"You don't understand," Riley told him. "I'd prefer not to be around *any* other people. The healthy ones are just as dangerous, if not more so, than the sick ones. At least we know what the sick ones want, we have no idea what the healthy people are going to do."

Sadness crept through Al as Riley folded her arms over her chest. Though she tried to hide it, a vulnerable expression briefly filtered over her features. Al was tempted to hug her, or at least squeeze her hand, but she was ten feet away and if the set of her chin was any indication, she wouldn't welcome any comfort right now.

"I'm not sure I agree," Peter said.

"Then you haven't run into enough of them," Riley retorted. Al had seen darts not as pointed as Riley's gaze when it slid back to Peter. "You don't know who is sick and who isn't. One of us could be, right now, and we wouldn't know until they were curled up in the back of a car or trying to tear us open." Her hands flickered to her stomach as she relentlessly held Peter's gaze. "Do you really want to go somewhere where there are *even* more ticking time bombs just walking around waiting to go off?"

Peter didn't seem to be able to meet her gaze as he looked beyond her. "Yes, I do. This whole staying to back roads and avoiding people hasn't really gotten us anywhere. We should try something different."

"It's kept us alive, which is more than we can say for a whole lot of the population right now."

"Does no one else want to try a city or a bigger town?" Peter demanded.

"I'll go with you Mr. Dade," Josh volunteered.

"I had enough with Foxboro," Mary Ellen told him. "I'm not letting Rochelle anywhere near any of the confusion and distrust that comes from being with a large group of people. Plus, there were so many people trying to escape the stadium we barely made it out of there alive. I understand safety in numbers, but there's also a thing as *too* many numbers."

"What about you?" Peter looked to John, who was sitting with his back against the wall in between both of the bathrooms.

John stared back at him as if Peter had just started singing a show tune. "Maybe there is a lovey dovey lala land of refuge out there, but I highly doubt it with people becoming sick, people trying to eat other people, and people trying to *shoot* people for *no* reason whatsoever. There is *no* way I'm getting back on the crazy train anytime soon."

Carl met Peter's look with one of stony silence as he folded his arms over his chest. Xander simply shook his head. Peter didn't bother to look at him before turning his attention to Donald. "This is a bit of peace to me after everything else that has happened, I'm not ready to plunge back into the insanity," Donald told him.

Peter threw his hands up as he shook his head. He turned away from them and paced to the wall before coming back. There was an agitated look in his eyes as his gaze swept the room. "There could be insanity a half a mile down the road from here."

"There could, but for now, I'm staying." Donald didn't look at him again as he bent his head and put pen to paper once more.

Peter looked tempted to stomp his foot as he stared at everyone gathered in the room. "I think you're wrong."

"You can take one of the cars; we'll give you enough food for two days," Carl reminded him.

"And gas?"

Carl looked torn as Al placed his hand against the office door and used it to help him rise. "We'll fill whatever car you choose with gas, but you'll be on your own for finding more gas cans and tubing," Al informed them. He agreed with sending them with supplies, but it would be their choice to leave, and he wasn't willing to part with something they would desperately need in the future. "We can only give you so much help if you choose to do this. You'll have to learn to be on your own anyway."

Peter's face was red as his gaze drifted toward the windows. "Take the night," Al continued. "Think it over. You can't go out there now anyway. If you change your mind and stay that's fine, but if you would still like to go then so be it. You can strike out on your own in the morning."

Al moved away from the office door and into the bathroom. He didn't really have to go, he just needed some time to himself to stretch his legs and wash his face. Turning on the cold water, he stuck his hand under the faucet and let the water pool within his good hand. Splashing it up, he wiped it over his face as he sought, and failed, to rejuvenate himself a little.

Grasping hold of the sink, he looked down at the hand he had wrapped around the basin. Sometimes he still didn't recognize his own hands; sometimes he still expected to look down and see the hands of his youth. Hands that had been strong and unlined, they had at one time carved some of the finest furniture in New England. Hands that had been covered in nicks and Band-Aids, but they had been steady and competent.

Now, his knuckles were almost twice their younger size, and age spots marked the backs of hands that had once only been marked by an occasional freckle or two. Where had all the time gone, and just how much of it did he have left? He lifted his head to meet his eyes in the mirror. The man staring back at him was someone he'd gotten used to seeing over the years, but there were times he still expected to see the man of his youth. A man with wavy brown hair instead of gray, an unlined face, and who still had perfect hearing. The man Nellie had fallen in love with.

What would Nellie think about him sending a teenage kid and a teacher packing in the morning without a fight?

He could try and talk Peter out of it, and perhaps if the man still planned to leave tomorrow, he would attempt it, but he thought he'd give the teacher some time to think it over first. He seemed like a reasonable enough man; he was just frightened right now, and frightened people didn't always make the best choices.

But then maybe he was the wrong one. Maybe they would make it to the cabin and realize it had been the worst decision they could have possibly made. Meanwhile Peter and Josh would be safely ensconced in some refuge in the city with plenty of food, water, and shelter.

That thought made him look down at the water coming from the tap again. He almost laughed out loud when he realized it was clear. It smelled fresh and crisp like the water he had always known. He wasn't sure what he had been expecting, the water in

Foxboro had been fine, but he'd still been anticipating something different from this sink. Maybe he'd been anticipating lava, or perhaps sulfur straight from the depths of Hell itself.

Instead, it continued to run clear and as he stuck his hand under it again, it remained cold. He didn't know what had happened to the animals along the shore, except for the dogs, he knew what had happened to those dogs. The image of those dogs plummeting over the cliff would haunt him for the rest of his days. He didn't recall seeing any animals in Foxboro or for much of their journey, but there had been coyotes in Sturbridge.

With a trembling hand he shut the water off. The water near Newport had been hot enough to kill the fish within it, the sky offered no promise of normal daylight, but the more he thought about it the more he realized there was promise still out there. The further from the ocean they got, the more promise there was.

He was turning away from the sink, eager to talk with the others when a flash of something out of the corner of his eye caught his attention. An icy chill slid down his spine as the muted plop of water dripping into the sink sounded abnormally loud in his suddenly hypersensitive ears. At the other end of the room was a small rectangular window carved high into the yellow concrete wall. There was no way a grown man could fit through it, even a child would have a tough time of squeezing through. He didn't consider it an access point, but as he strained to see through the bits of brown and cobwebs clogging the screen, he realized it was a way for them to see out.

Or for something else to see *in*.

Two ruby red, disembodied eyes were gleaming in the dim illumination of the flashlight he'd placed on the corner of the sink. Many things had frightened him throughout his life; the loss of his siblings, Nellie's sickness, the death of too many friends, this whole awful mess they were fighting to survive through, but those eyes, floating through the dust-clogged screen evoked a whole new level of fear. His gut tightened, the hair on his arms stood on end, and a chill slid down his spine.

He grabbed hold of the sink as those eyes seemed to meet and hold his stare. The room had suddenly become a giant vacuum that all of the air had been sucked out of, making it difficult to breathe.

Not human, those eyes couldn't possibly be human.

This realization couldn't ease the accelerated beat of his heart as he grabbed the light and flashed it at the eyes. The raccoon, illuminated by the splash of light, scurried away from the beam. Al pressed his hand against his chest, over the place where his heart beat so rapidly. Good health or not, his old ticker was beating faster than a teenager on a snare drum.

He wanted to curse the animal at the same time he wanted to jump for joy at this further sign of continued life. Either way, he had to wash his face again in order to pull himself together enough to leave the room. Carl and Xander were still standing watch by the two doors. Riley had her head against Xander's leg. Her chest rose and fell in an even rhythm, but Al had the feeling she was awake. John held a gun before him, but instead of staring out the door with Carl, his gaze was focused upon where Peter had retreated to stand by one of the vending machines.

Al had never seen that look on John's face before. It wasn't callous, it wasn't cold, it was simply a look resolved to do whatever had to be done. They would let Peter and Josh go, they would give them supplies, but if they chose to leave they could also become a threat. John wasn't a fighter by nature, but for the first time Al truly saw in him the determination to do whatever it took to keep them all safe.

He just didn't want the situation to deteriorate to the point where someone got hurt.

"There was a raccoon at the window in the bathroom, damn near gave me a heart attack."

Mary Ellen paused in the act of brushing Rochelle's hair back with her fingers to look at him. "I imagine it did."

Al realized they were missing the point when Carl lifted his head off the glass door and turned it toward him. "It must have been hiding somewhere when I searched."

Al shook his head. "It was outside the window."

"Oh."

"It was *alive*, and it was outside the window," he elaborated as their exhausted brains seemed to have decided to take a vacation right now.

Riley was the first to gasp as she confirmed his doubts about her truly being asleep when she suddenly bolted upright. "Animals!" she blurted. "There's a live animal outside!"

"So, there were coyotes in Sturbridge..." Bobby's mouth parted as his eyes became round. "Oh. I wasn't thinking."

"You saw coyotes?" John asked.

"We did. Did you see anything?"

John tapped the gun against his knee as he focused on the door. "Nothing good," he muttered.

Riley moved to her knees and placed her hands in her lap as she eagerly leaned forward. "So the farther away from the coast we move, the better things seem to get."

"It would seem so," Al agreed.

"Do you think there will still be sick people out there or do you think that will also get better as we travel?" Rochelle inquired.

"Yes, but maybe they'll dwindle down the farther inland we go," Al answered.

"There could be a steady food supply in the mountains," Carl said. "If there's animals here, then there's a good chance there will be more in the mountains."

"Do you really think so?" John asked.

"I think we've been seeing signs of life we haven't really noticed until now, because of everything else going on," Al answered.

"Do you think we should just stay here?" Josh asked. "We have shelter, water and there are animals we could trap and eat. I can honestly say the idea of eating raccoon doesn't sound all that appealing."

"Better than starving," Carl told him.

Josh shrugged as he looked around the building. "There's also bathroom facilities."

"I don't think that's a good idea, it's right on the highway. Don't get me wrong the highway has been good to us so far today, but I'd prefer to be somewhere that won't attract the attention of other passersby," Al said.

"But it is safe here right *now*," Josh insisted.

The tone of his voice made Al recall the scene at the McDougal's house. A tendril of dread slid through him as the young teen looked on the verge of losing it. He wasn't proud of it, but Al found himself hoping Peter and Josh *did* decide to go their own separate way. Whereas everyone else seemed to be holding it together fairly well, Josh was becoming a little too unstable for his liking.

"It won't stay that way," Carl told him. "More people *will* stop here and they may also decide it's where they would like to stay. Riley's right, we don't want to be around them when that happens."

Josh folded his arms over his chest as he glanced nervously around the room. "I'm going to the cabin," Riley said forcefully. "I think it's the best choice we have and our best chance of surviving."

"I think so too," Al agreed.

Peter tugged at his hair as he shook his head. "We'll decide tomorrow."

Al made his way back to the office door and leaned against it as he slid down to the floor. Like John though, he pulled out a gun and rested it against his knee. He didn't look at Peter and Josh, he didn't want them to feel threatened, but he was acutely aware of their every movement. He realized there would be little sleep again tonight as he, the teacher, and student settled in against the vending machines.

CHAPTER 12

Xander

XANDER GLANCED down at Riley as she pulled off her other sneaker and wiggled her toes. He blinked and did a double take as his gaze landed on her one striped black and blue sock and one red and white one. Memories of her and his sister running through his house flooded him. He could clearly see them laughing as they slid across the hardwood floor together. Carol had always worn white socks; Riley on the other hand had always revealed a myriad of colored socks over the years, but had never worn a matching pair at the same time. He knew, because he had asked Carol about it, the socks matched when Riley's mom put them in her sock drawer, but when Riley put them on she always mismatched them.

"You still do that," he remarked.

She twisted her head to look up at him. Her eyes had circles under them big enough to rival any football player getting ready to step onto the field, but they were still beautiful. Lines creased her forehead as she frowned at him. "Do what?"

"Mismatch your socks."

For a moment she didn't seem to understand what he was talking about, and then her gaze drifted to her feet. A wistful smile curved her mouth. "Well yeah, why would I start being normal now?"

"You'll never have to worry about being normal," he assured her.

"You know just what to say to make a girl feel special."

He rested his hand on her shoulder. "I try."

His attention was drawn back to the sky as light seeped outward becoming angrier as the sun rose higher into the fiery sky. "Red sky at night, sailor's delight. Red sky in the morning, sailors take warning," Riley murmured as she pulled her shoes back on.

"I think the sky is going to be red from now on," John said.

Xander's attention was pulled away from the sky as someone's shoe squeaked on the tiled floor. Peter's eyes were swollen, his hair stood out at odd angles from his face as he made his way into the bathroom. It was time for them to start moving again, but his feet seemed to be stuck to the floor as he watched the sky brighten over Carl's shoulder. They could stay here for one more day, maybe get some rest or at least let their brains take a break. They all needed it, but he knew there would be no rest for them, not today anyway. Maybe one day in the future.

Riley held her hand up for him. His fingers slid over her skin as he wrapped her wrist within his hand and helped pull her up. She winced as she stepped onto her feet and shifted uncomfortably. "Are you hurt?" he asked.

"Just some blisters growing blisters," she informed him. "I'm going to use the bathroom. I'll take a look at your leg when I get out."

"It's fine," he assured her.

There were mom's holding a report card full of F's from their child who didn't look anywhere near as disapproving as Riley. "And we're going to keep it that way."

"She is a bossy little thing," John muttered, but Xander was aware he'd waited until Riley had moved out of hearing range first.

"She's calmed down in her old age," Bobby said with a laugh from his position near Al. Though Al had stayed up for most of the night, he'd recently nodded off and his chin was resting against his chest. Rochelle was snoring against Mary Ellen's chest; Mary Ellen was as sound asleep as her daughter was. Josh was curled into a ball beside them, his back to the room as his chest rose and fell in an even rhythm.

Bobby rose to his feet and wiped his ass off. "We didn't bring any medical supplies inside but I'll go get them."

"I'll go with you," Xander volunteered.

John squinted one eye up at him. "I could stand to get out of this place for a bit."

Carl lifted his head off the door as they walked over to join him. "A car just went by on the other side of the highway. People are starting to move again so be careful out there."

"Aye, aye, captain sir," John told him with a brief salute Carl seemed to find about as amusing as a gob of spit. John didn't seem to notice though as they stepped into the daylight.

Xander took a deep breath of the not so fresh air and leaned back to stretch. His back cracked with a loud pop that made him feel more like forty than nineteen. He didn't make it one step before the layer of sweat constantly coating his body now began to trickle down his skin again. He'd give anything for a cold shower, an icy beer, and some air conditioning, but those things all looked like distant pipe dreams, especially the air conditioning.

A low sound brought his attention back to the road as a car moved down the other side of the highway. He found his gaze riveted upon the filthy blue sedan as it maneuvered in and out of the vehicles blocking the road. "I never thought I'd experience the day when seeing another car gave me the creeps," Bobby said as he stepped off the sidewalk and into the road.

Xander followed behind him. "Let's grab the stuff and get out of this place before more people stop by."

His leg was a little stiff, and he could feel the scabs breaking as he walked, but it wasn't as on fire as it had been for the past couple of days. He wasn't about to argue with Riley over it though, she wasn't going to relent until she'd taken a look at it. Bobby went to the Cadillac and popped the trunk. He pulled out the medical supplies they had stashed there when they had stopped before.

"Do you think Peter and Josh will leave?" Bobby asked as he closed the trunk on the car.

"I don't know," Xander answered.

"I think they're crazy if they do, but to each their own," John said with a shrug.

Xander leaned back on his heels to survey the road. "I think we're all going to be a little crazy by the time this is over."

"Maybe we already are," John responded. "Maybe we're all in an insane asylum and none of this is real."

It was an absurd notion, but one Xander couldn't shrug off as he studied the hushed world around him. A low rumbling brought all of their heads up as a Mac truck crept down the highway toward the exit ramp headed for the rest area. Xander's breath froze in his chest as he waited to see what the large black truck with flames shooting out of its grill would do. It slowed as it neared the ramp, but the driver seemed to change their mind as the truck remained on the highway.

The cab of the truck was packed with people as it crept by them; he wondered how many more were piled into the trailer. "Seems like a poor choice gas wise." John shaded his eyes against the sun as he took a step toward the front of the car. "But it would hold a lot of supplies and probably go right through a good chunk of the obstacles."

"I doubt any of us know how to drive one of those, and even if we did, we would never make it far trying to keep it gassed up," Bobby said.

"I didn't know how to piss in a toilet for a couple of years either, but I eventually figured that one out," John retorted.

"And we appreciate it," Xander told him.

John was still watching the truck as it disappeared from view. "I wouldn't mind driving one though."

"I wouldn't mind a freaking shower, but we're all SOL on that for now," Bobby said.

John glanced over his shoulder and shrugged. "We are. Let's get you doctored up and hit the road."

Bobby kept the bag in hand as they retreated toward the building. "Our friend Lee, did he become sick?" Bobby asked. "When Riley was talking last night she made it seem as if you also had some experience with the sick people."

Xander took a few steps farther before he realized John wasn't with them anymore. He looked back to find John frozen in the middle of the road. The look in his eyes was so similar to the one he'd seen in Riley's in the grocery store, that for a second Xander couldn't breathe.

"He did," John confirmed after a full minute elapsed.

"Did he die from it?"

John's gaze slid past Bobby to the front door of the building. His fingers began to fiddle with each other as he shifted from foot to foot and searched for words. "No, he didn't die from the sickness," Xander finally answered. He wasn't sure what to say or how much to reveal. Bobby had known Riley for almost as long as he had, they were friends, but he'd been thrown off and uncertain of how to proceed when she'd told him what had happened with Lee. "There are some times when the best thing you can do for someone is let it end."

Bobby frowned as he glanced between the two of them. "Lee killed himself?"

John finally tore his attention away from the building. "No."

"Did you kill him?" Bobby demanded.

"No."

Bobby looked like a high school student trying to figure out quantum physics. "It was Riley, Bobby. She killed Lee," Xander said gently.

Those words didn't seem to penetrate at first, but finally the baffled look slid from Bobby's face as his mouth parted and his eyes became as round as Cheerios. "What?" he gasped.

"You didn't see him, and you don't know what we went through," John retorted defensively. "She tried everything she could to save him; she rode in that car with him for hours while he was sick and we were all nervous... No, we all *knew* what he was becoming, but none of us wanted to face it. She took care of him and stayed with him when the smartest choice might have been to leave him on the side of the road.

"And then, when we didn't think things could get any worse, we stumbled across some loony tune with a gun who tried to kill us. You have no idea what it's like to be stuck in a store with someone firing at you, no idea what it's like to be certain you were going to die, and somehow miraculously surviving. No idea what it was like to see Lee tearing into that man like a vulture on road kill, and you have no idea what it was like to be Lee's next target. No one else was able to pull the trigger, but she did."

Xander could only stand and gape at John as his face flushed the color of the sky and sweat slid steadily down his temple to his cheek. That look in his eyes was no longer haunted and tormented but full of passion as he glared at Bobby. "Don't judge us and don't judge her. Be glad she's on our side, I know I am."

Bobby still seemed to be reeling from John's tirade as no words came from him. "No one is judging," Xander said while looking over at Bobby. "*No* one."

John remained unmoving, his shoulders thrust back as he glanced between the two of them. The door opening brought all of their attention back to the building as Riley stepped out. Her hair hung in wet tendrils about her face as she studied them. "Everything ok?"

"Everything's fine," he assured her. "We'll be right in."

She hesitated for a second before retreating into the building. "I can't believe it," Bobby whispered.

"Yeah well, you just wait till you have to do something crappy, and then you'll believe it," John told him.

"We've all done crappy things," Xander said.

"Yeah, yeah we have," John muttered before brushing by them and heading for the building.

Xander turned back to Bobby. He knew him well, or at least he had before he'd gone away to college, but he had no idea what was going on in Bobby's head right now. Bobby may actually have been closer to Riley over the past year than he had been to either himself or Lee. Bobby had also always been the most tolerant, even-tempered, and easy going one of them, but there was no way to know how he was going to react.

"You knew about this?" Bobby asked.

"She told me yesterday, at the grocery store. Bobby..."

He shook his head as he turned to stare at the highway. "This is a cruel world," he muttered.

"It always has been." Xander felt like he was telling a child there was no Santa, but he didn't know what else to say. "It's just gotten a whole lot crueler and weirder."

"I feel like I fell down the rabbit hole."

"At this point I actually wouldn't be amazed to run into a talking rabbit."

"Me either." Bobby admitted. "She must feel awful."

"I don't think she's had time to process how she feels, not with everything else going on."

"I suppose she hasn't."

Xander wiped the sweat from his brow with the back of his arm. "Don't say anything to her."

Bobby's hair stood on end when he tugged at it with his fingers. "I wouldn't know where to begin."

"Neither do I," he admitted.

Bobby seemed to stare right through him before he finally focused on him once more. "We should probably get in there before she starts to yell at us."

"Yeah," Xander agreed.

There was a mountain of unspoken words between them that needed to be said, but for the life of him he couldn't think of anything right then. Maybe if things were different they would talk about the expensive therapy sessions they would all require in the future. They could ponder the lasting and damaging impact all of this would have on them, but therapy sessions didn't exist anymore, and the way things were going they might not have the time to develop any long lasting damage.

Riley gave him a quizzical look when he stepped through the door, and Bobby handed the bag over to her. "Everything ok?"

"Fine," he assured her.

Bobby squeezed her shoulder and gave her a sympathetic smile before disappearing into the bathroom. Her forehead furrowed with realization as she stared after him before turning back to Xander. "He knows," she stated flatly. "You told him."

Though the words sounded accusatory, her tone wasn't. "It's ok," Xander assured her. "He asked about Lee and…"

"And you can't lie to him," she whispered.

"I don't think there's room for lies between any of us."

"You're probably right," she agreed, but tears still shimmered in her eyes.

"It's fine, he understands Ri. Come on, you can torture me for a bit, that will probably make you feel better."

She blinked away the tears as she released a snort of laughter. "It will."

He slipped his arm around her shoulders and pulled her against his side. Despite the lack of a shower and the days old clothes she wore, he caught the hint of the soap she'd used to wash her hair with in the bathroom as she rested her head on his shoulder. Her breath tickled against his neck when she lifted her head and pressed a kiss against him.

A shiver of pleasure slid over his skin as they stepped through the door of the office. With the back of his foot, he nudged the door closed to give them at least a few minutes of privacy. He wrapped his other arm around her waist, drawing her before him to kiss her fully on the mouth. The building and people faded into the distance as everything within him became focused upon her. In those few stolen moments his whole world became centered upon everything she was and everything they could be together. *If* they were ever given a chance to see where it could all go, to see what they could become as a couple. He knew the two of them shared something so incredibly special and right.

His fingers slid into her hair as he pulled her head back to deepen the kiss. Her hands dug into his back as she clung to him. He could stay here forever, lose himself to her and briefly shut out the rest of the world, but as much as he desired to do that, he knew he couldn't.

Reluctantly, his grip on her loosened, and he tore himself away from her. Her chest rose and fell rapidly with her inhalations; color crept through her cheeks. Her lashes lowered, the playful grin she gave him melted his heart further. Damp tendrils of her hair tangled around his fingers when he slid his hand from her hair.

"Let's get you taken care of," she whispered.

She stepped away from him and gestured toward the office chair. He slumped into the seat and propped his leg out for her. With tender care, she began to unwrap the bandage from his leg. A lot of the swelling and redness had come out of the wound, and though it was still sore looking with some blood and puss, it looked a lot better than it had.

Riley's shoulders slumped; her eyes sparkled with joy as she lifted her head to him. "It looks much better."

"It's feeling a lot better."

The door creaked open and Al stuck his head in. "How's it going?"

"Really good," Riley assured him.

"Glad to hear it." He ducked back out of the office.

"I think we can start leaving it unwrapped once in a while." She said the words, but she pulled a bandage out of the bag. "When you're in the car."

He bit back a smile at her commanding attitude, it appeared she got bossier the more tired and stressed she became. She re-bandaged his leg and sat back on her heels. "That should do it."

Xander stood up and pulled the door open. The others were gathered near the front door, peering out the glass. Carl's face was strained, his mouth pursed as he glanced at them over his shoulder. "We have company."

"What is it?" Riley demanded as she pulled the gun out from where it had been tucked against her back. Xander blinked at the no nonsense attitude descending over her and the quickness with which she grabbed the weapon.

How much had they all already changed and how much more were they going to change before this was over? he wondered.

"Two cars," Carl answered.

Xander felt his spirits crash at this intrusion into their brief reprieve. Al, Carl, Riley, and John had gathered together at the front of the group by the door. He elbowed his way past Peter and Josh to join them as a small black car pulled to a stop behind the truck. Another blue car was right behind it.

Xander found he barely breathed as the doors on both vehicles opened. A man and woman stepped out of the first car and two women and one man climbed out of the second. The first man and woman hurried to the back passenger door and opened it. Xander didn't know what they were doing until they pulled a young woman from the backseat. The man wrapped her arm around his shoulder and propped her up as the woman hurried to close the door.

The young woman the man was holding winced and buried her head in the man's chest. She lifted her hand over her eyes. She nearly fell as her knees gave out, but the man was able to keep her up.

"She's sick," Riley muttered as the new arrivals started to make their way toward the building.

CHAPTER 13

John

JOHN'S GAZE was riveted upon the group of people as they made their way toward the glass doors of the building. The look on the girl's face was one he'd seen before and knew he would never forget. Lee had looked just like that, shortly before he'd decided intestines were his new favorite happy meal. John shuddered at the reminder as his stomach twisted sickly. He had to fight the urge to grab the door and hold it closed as the group of people stopped to survey the truck.

He didn't see any weapons amongst them, but he didn't like it when their gazes turned toward the front doors. With the sun behind them, John didn't think they were able to see inside the building. There was no flicker of acknowledgement on the people's faces as their gazes ran over the doors. It seemed like they couldn't see into the building, but John refused to take a small breath. The new arrivals remained standing by the truck, talking amongst themselves as they tried to decide what to do.

"I hope they don't try for the truck," Carl muttered.

John hoped for the same thing, but judging by the look of them, he didn't think they were in any condition to put up a fight, or to continue their journey. "She's not the only who's sick," Riley whispered. "The other man is sick too. Maybe more of them."

John tore his gaze away from the girl and focused on the man at the back of the group. There were etched lines around his pursed lips that Lee had also exhibited when he'd first woken again in the hotel. It was a look of bleak despair John knew immediately, and feared. There was little spark of life left within the man's shadowed eyes.

If he'd been dead, John would have been certain someone was tap dancing on his grave as shivers ran over his body. He was alive, or at least he was fairly certain he was still alive, but that was a dilemma to sort through on another day.

"We have to get out of here," Carl said, but he didn't move.

John waited impatiently, his gaze focused on Carl's unmoving hand upon the door. "Before they decide human flesh is the new chicken," he prompted.

He felt Carl's eyes slide toward him, but he didn't look at him as the people outside began to move again. The young girl's legs buckled, and another woman in the group leapt forward to help the man holding her to keep her up. They braced the girl between them as they labored toward the doors they stood behind.

John could almost feel the points of those tap shoes digging into his back as the closer they got the more he was able to recognize the signs of the sickness on their faces. "Carl..."

Carl threw his shoulders back and pushed open the door. It was too late for them to escape the building before the other group arrived. Carl stepped outside as the other group stumbled toward them. The girl almost dragged the man and woman down with her when her legs gave out. Carl reached out to help steady her; he pulled his hands away from the girl as soon as the others were able to support her again.

John had no choice but to step aside as the group staggered into the building. He caught Carl studying his hands before shrugging and dropping them back to his side. "Maybe you should wash those," John suggested.

"That may have been the cleanest thing I've done in days," he responded.

John knew he was right, but he still wanted to take Carl's hands under a hot spray of water and douse them with soap. The other sick man almost brushed against him as he entered the building, but he was able to jump back before *that* could happen.

It took all he had not to sprint into the bathroom and start scrubbing his skin as the girl collapsed onto the floor. He readjusted his hold on his gun and braced his feet as six sets of eyes swung toward them. The girl, too weak to lift her head, stared at the floor as she slumped against one of the machines.

"We just need a place to rest," the woman who had been helping to carry the girl said as her eyes drifted over the weapons they held. "My daughter she's ah…"

"Sick," Riley supplied.

"She'll be fine," the man who had helped her inside insisted.

For the first time in his life, John bit his tongue and refrained from telling them there was most likely no chance the girl would recover. What did he know? Xander had survived the infection ravaging his body, and for all he knew that may be what was wrong with the girl. She could have just caught some other bug or maybe she'd been attacked by one of those things and was battling an infection too.

And then the girl reached up to rub the back of her neck. The loud clacking of tap shoes rang in his head as her eyes remained squinted closed and her hand continued to massage her neck. He'd seen Lee do that far too often to have any further doubt about what was wrong with the girl. His gaze slid over to the other man who appeared sick as sweat beaded across the man's brow and slipped down the side of his cheek. The two of them didn't look like they could do much damage, but he'd seen the inhuman strength Lee had exhibited and knew exactly what they *could* do to a human body after they got past this stage of the sickness.

The door seemed way too far away for him right now. He hadn't been thinking about it, didn't recall having any intention of doing it, but he took an abrupt step back. He had the impulse to raise his gun and level it at the girl; he just didn't think it would be an accepted course of action right now.

"I'm sure she will," Mary Ellen said.

"We're not looking for any trouble," the woman continued, her gaze focused on the guns they held. "We only need a break. Please."

He hated the pleading tone in her voice, hated that his hand remained clenched around his gun, and he was just waiting for the girl to make a move. "We weren't staying," Carl told her and started toward the door.

"Wait!" The woman stretched a hand out to halt them. There was something in her eyes, something so frantic and desperate that for a second John forgot all about the sick people who had entered with them. "Wait please, we haven't seen or spoken with anyone else in days."

"You're probably better off," Riley muttered so softly he didn't think the words went beyond him and Xander.

"Have you seen anyone else?" the woman asked. "Any form of help?"

"Not in a while, everything's been so confused and chaotic," Carl answered.

"What little help we found turned out to be no help against Mother Nature," Mary Ellen said.

"I'm not sure there's help to be found anywhere anymore," Carl said.

"You have no idea where we can find help?" The hitch in her voice caused him to take a step forward. He was tempted to comfort her, to assure her it would be all right, but he knew he couldn't. It wasn't his place to do such a thing, and there was no way he could tell her it would be all right when he knew it most likely wouldn't.

"I'm sorry," he said simply.

The woman's watery blue eyes focused on him before her hand fell to her side. "There has to be something. There has to be medical personal, military, or some kind of police force somewhere."

"Maybe there is." John doubted that, but he couldn't take away the optimism he saw burning in her gaze.

The sweat trickling down his back had nothing to do with the heat of the day and everything to do with the woman staring at him like he had all the answers, like *he* could be her savior. The only problem was he didn't have any answers, and he was most certainly no one's savior. He almost apologized to her again, but the words lodged in his throat.

"Have you seen them, those people out there?" she choked out.

"We've seen them," Carl confirmed.

Her gaze shifted to her daughter, apprehension flickered over her features before she pushed it aside and turned back to them. "Where did you come from?"

"The Cape originally," he answered. "Most recently Sturbridge. You?"

"We were in the city." John's ears pricked at these words and the sharp inhalation of breaths filled the room.

"What was it like?" Peter demanded in a far brisker tone than normal.

The woman shook her head, but the other woman behind her began to sob quietly. The third woman knelt at her side and rested her hand on her arm reassuringly. John didn't know what to say or do as the man with the pinched mouth slumped against the machine and slid to the floor. Pity slithered through him, at the same time he found his gaze riveted upon the younger girl and the man. All he wanted was to escape from here before whatever was ravaging through their systems rotted their brains and sent them on a rampage.

"Death, there's nothing but death there," the woman before him said in a tone of voice that reminded him of a fortune teller hovering over her crystal ball as she revealed a future no one wanted to hear. "Or at least that's all we encountered there."

"There were more of us," the still healthy looking man said.

"Twenty more of us," the woman in front of him said.

Rochelle pressed in closer against his side. "What happened to them?" she inquired.

The one woman began to sob harder. The young girl continued to rub at her neck as she curled into the fetal position. John struggled against the memory of Lee doing the same thing. What had happened in that gas station wasn't something he liked to recall. He knew what had happened there would haunt him forever, but being confronted by this in his face reminder was causing the memories to churn rapidly. Judging by the pallor of Carl and Riley's faces, the haunted look in Al's eyes, and the hand Rochelle wrapped around his arm, he wasn't the only one fighting the memories of what had happened to Lee.

A tear slid from the woman's eye before she bowed her head. "There were just so many of those things; we couldn't fight them all off. We had guns..." Her voice trailed off as her gaze slid to the door beyond. "But they're so difficult to stop and there were *so* many of them. We didn't make it all the way into the city before we were overrun."

"Maybe it was just that one area," Peter suggested.

"You don't know what it was like," the healthy man said as he knelt beside the girl. The look in his eyes mirrored the look of someone who had been to Purgatory and somehow managed to walk out the other side. They'd been through Hell themselves, but there was something in these people's eyes that made him think there were worse things than what they'd endured, and these people had survived it. "No area through there is safe. There's nothing left in Boston except murder and destruction. The earthquakes made the roads nearly impassable and those *things* knew it."

"They set a trap," Riley whispered.

"They set a trap," the woman confirmed. "They were everywhere and they were on us before we realized they were there."

"And then there was just screaming," the other woman said. "Nothing but the endless screaming, and the blood."

No one moved, he didn't take a breath as he stared at the beaten and broken group before them. "They are fast," Rochelle finally said.

"We barely got out of there alive," the healthier looking man informed them.

They hadn't all gotten out of there unscathed though. They had lost more people than they had escaped with, and they hadn't escaped the sick people, not entirely. A low moan escaped the girl as she rolled over. "I'm sorry for what you endured, but we were just getting ready to leave," Carl told them.

"Do you have a plan?" the woman asked eagerly. "Somewhere to stay?"

To get the hell away from you, John thought, but he kept his mouth clamped shut. "To keep moving," Xander said. "I would suggest you do the same."

"Keep moving," the man muttered and looked toward the young girl John assumed was his daughter. "I guess that works."

"It's all we know how to do right now," Xander admitted. He nudged Riley toward the door and nodded at it. "It's safe here though; you'll be able to get some rest for a little bit."

Riley didn't move as her gaze remained riveted upon the young girl. John didn't have to be told twice though, he wanted absolutely nothing to do with the impending meltdown he sensed was about to unfold within this building. Taking hold of Rochelle's hand, he pulled her gently in front of him and toward the door. He looked toward Mary Ellen and nodded for her to go next.

Carl held the door open for Peter, Bobby, and Josh to walk outside. He turned to John and waved his hand at him as Donald slipped outside with the others. John hesitated though as he turned back to Xander and Riley.

"Riley." Xander wrapped his hand around her arm and pulled her toward him, but she remained rigid in his grasp. "Ri…"

"She'll turn on you," Riley whispered.

"Riley," Xander hissed as the woman's eyes narrowed upon her.

"You don't know what you're talking about!" the woman retorted.

John had seen snow with more color than Riley's now bleached out pallor as she lifted her head to meet the woman's relentless gaze. "Unfortunately, I do."

John winced and Xander tugged more firmly on Riley's arm as the woman took a threatening step forward. "She's just sick; she'll be fine if she has a chance to get some rest."

"I'm sure she will," Xander tried to pacify, but Riley wasn't giving in.

"Please listen to me," Riley implored. "It won't hurt for you to restrain her, for her own safety as well as yours." The woman only continued to glower at her as Xander finally succeeded in getting Riley to take a few steps. "Please."

"Riley *go*," Xander said forcefully as the healthy man rose back to his full height.

John grabbed hold of her hand and pulled her toward the door. "John…"

"I understand what you're trying to do," John told her under his breath as he succeeded in pulling her past Carl. "But they're not willing to hear it."

"They don't know what could happen," she protested.

"They know what could happen; they've had firsthand experience with it. You've told them, and that's all you can do. A fight isn't going to solve anything and we have to go," John said.

He released her hand as Carl closed the door behind them and lit a cigarette. "Do you still intend to split off?" Carl demanded of Peter.

There was no color left in Peter's face as he shook his head. "It doesn't seem like that would be a wise choice right now," he admitted.

"I didn't think so." John lifted an eyebrow at Carl's abrupt tone, but his friend was staring at the teacher. "Let's get out of here, now."

John slid into the passenger seat of the truck and shut the door. Carl didn't speak as he hopped in beside him and slammed the door with enough force to rattle the mirror. "Who pissed in your Cheerios today?" he asked as Carl started the truck.

Carl frowned at him and pulled out behind the car Al was driving. They followed it down the exit ramp and onto the highway. "I really don't want to see what is about to go down in there, and that guy is beginning to annoy me."

"What guy? Peter?"

"Yeah."

John shrugged as he grabbed some licorice and leaned back in the seat. "He seems like a nice enough guy."

Carl silently pondered John's words. "I know what he seems like, what he may have *been* before all of this went down, but I'm not so sure about him."

John stared at the Caddy following behind them with Mary Ellen, Rochelle, and Donald in the backseat and Josh in the front. "Maybe we shouldn't have let them get into the car with him then."

"We don't have many choices, and he hasn't done anything wrong. I just don't get a good vibe from him."

"I've known you for a while Carl, and the few people you haven't liked at work all turned out to be losers who didn't last. I'll trust your gut even if you don't."

Carl grabbed his pack of butts off the dashboard and sat back. "Josh doesn't seem to be holding up too well anymore either."

"He's a kid."

"So is Rochelle. So are Xander and Riley. So are *you* in all honesty."

John might have taken offense to that a few days ago, but the events of these past days had left him feeling strangely childlike and ancient all at once. He kept his gaze focused on the car behind them as a shiver of foreboding crept up his spine. "What do we do?"

"Don't let your guard down around them, at all. I don't think they'll do anything to harm any of us, but to be on the safe side keep an eye on them both."

John wanted to think Carl was overreacting, but Carl had always been a better judge of character than he was. There had been plenty of new people who had started at their work he'd thought were decent guys that ended up being complete assholes. Carl had never liked any of them, and had warned John about them, but he'd always learned the hard way that not everyone was what they seemed.

Maybe it was the years Carl had on him, maybe it was life experience, or maybe his instincts were just better. No matter what it was, John knew Carl was right. That Peter and Josh weren't to be as trusted as they had been, not anymore.

CHAPTER 14

Mary Ellen

Rochelle's head rested against her shoulder as they crested over the top of a hill and headed down into a valley crowded with cars and trucks. Peter's hands were white knuckled on the wheel as he maneuvered around a cluster of motorcycles that had skidded under a jackknifed Mac truck. Rochelle's nose wrinkled; she pulled her shirt over her face when they drove past the corpses still littering the highway. Not all of those corpses were from the motorcycles though, as more than a few cars had also hit the truck and one was completely wedged underneath it.

There may be a bunch of crazy humans running around right now, but at least the dead were staying dead, she thought as she stared at the scattered corpses. A shudder rocked through her, and she turned her eyes away from the remains scattered across the highway. There wasn't much scenery to enjoy outside the window, yet she felt her eyes repeatedly drawn back to the gory landscape.

It was already too late to cover Rochelle's eyes, but she pulled her daughter closer against her side. Donald lifted his head from the notebook he had been writing in. He blinked his eyes for a few seconds before dropping his head again. Mary Ellen looked around Rochelle as she tried to decipher what he was writing, but he was leaning against the door with the notebook tilted in a way she couldn't see it.

She sat back again as they were finally able to drive around the accident blocking the road. Her gaze was drawn back to Peter's head as he released a low curse, and the car bumped over a rut in the middle of the median. She'd spent a fair amount of time with the teacher, but he seemed a lot edgier today than he had been over the past couple of days. It was more than just the red vessels running through his swollen eyes; there was something frantic in his gaze, something that reminded her of Larry just before he was about to blow.

She'd climbed into the back of this car because she'd believed it would be safe; she liked Peter, but the more he muttered to himself, the more all she was tempted to do was throw the door open and jump out. They were fine, she assured herself. Peter was fine; he was just stressed out and overtired. Even still, she planned to try and switch vehicles the next time they all stopped, or at least offer to give Peter a break from driving. She hoped some rest would ease the crazed look in his eyes, but if not, she would get Rochelle away from him.

"What are they doing?" Peter muttered as Al pulled up next to an RV lying on its side. Carl parked the truck next to him, and John leaned out the window to speak with Al. John's hand waved in the air, and then he pulled himself half out of the window to look back at them. Though Josh and Peter rolled their windows down, she couldn't hear the words being exchanged.

John opened the door of the truck and jumped out. "What the hell are they doing?" Peter demanded again.

Mary Ellen wasn't more curious about what they were up to as she just wanted out of the car, and she especially wanted Rochelle out of the car too. Rochelle had never seen Larry at his most volatile, and she wasn't about to let her see Peter if he had a melt-down. Throwing the door open, she grabbed hold of her daughter's hand and practically tore her from the vehicle.

Rochelle staggered out of the car and sent her a look that screamed she thought her mother had lost her mind, but Mary Ellen ignored her as she tugged her daughter toward the others. They were already gathered by the massive front wheels of the RV, and as they approached John jumped up and seized hold of the wheel over his head. His shirt pulled up to reveal his belly button as he swung his legs up and pulled himself onto the wheel. Bobby followed after him.

"What are they doing?" Mary Ellen inquired.

"There might be food and supplies in there. Possibly a small barbecue or something," Carl answered.

Mary Ellen nodded as she studied the vehicle. Riley said something to Xander and gestured to his leg before grabbing hold of the wheel and climbing up after them. Xander scowled as he folded his arms over his chest, but he didn't make an attempt to follow as the three on top of the vehicle moved to the passenger side window. Xander slipped around to the front of the RV with Carl, Mary Ellen, and Rochelle close on his heels.

Mary Ellen frowned as she strained to see into the interior of the RV, but it was completely black. She placed her hands against the glass in an attempt to block out the glare from the sun, but she still couldn't see anything within. It wasn't until Riley pulled back the curtain, causing all of them to gasp and fall back, that she realized the curtain had come loose and fallen over the window when the RV had crashed.

Riley grinned at them as she bit her lip to keep from laughing and tied the curtain back. She gave them a brief wave before climbing off the side of the driver's chair she had been standing on. Grabbing hold of the wall, Riley used it to balance herself in the tilted vehicle as she bypassed the single stair leading to the rest of the large motor home.

Mary Ellen felt her head, and saw the others heads, leaning to the side to watch Riley climb onto another chair and step off next to John. Bobby's shadow blocked some of the sun's rays filtering into the RV as he stood over the passenger window to look inside. John flicked on a flashlight and shone it around the vehicle.

There were homes smaller than this monstrosity on wheels; Mary Ellen couldn't help but be impressed by the open space, cushiony couch, and gleaming faucets on the double sided sink. Tupperware and plates had spilled out of the cabinets dangling above the sink. The microwave door had also fallen open during the crash and scattered pieces of its door lay amongst the rubble piled onto the oak cabinets, right next to where John currently stood.

Riley said something and pointed downward. John nodded and took an abrupt step off the cabinet as Riley knelt to open one of them. They said something else to each other, then John turned away to begin searching for something. Opening the cabinet under the sink, he tugged out a box of garbage bags and handed them down to Riley.

"Hey Bobby," Xander called as he took a step back.

The dull thud of Bobby's sneakers sounded on the vehicle before his head popped over the side and he looked down at them. "Yeah?"

"Let them know the seat of the couch usually pulls up, my grandparents used to store a hibachi in there."

Bobby gave him a salute before returning to the window. Riley and John stopped moving as the sound of Bobby's muffled voice could be heard. John nodded and climbed carefully onto the dining room table. Stretching across the hallway, John pulled at the sofa cushion as Riley began to shove things into one of the trash bags.

John continued to tug and yank at the sofa with increased intensity. Though Mary Ellen couldn't understand what he was saying, the higher tone of his voice, and the reddening color of his face, gave her a good idea what words were coming out of his mouth. He slipped and nearly fell but managed to get his hands down on the floor before he face planted onto it.

Carl rolled his eyes as Rochelle let out a little giggle. "He's got the grace of a water buffalo," Carl muttered.

Rochelle giggled again, and Xander chuckled as John pushed himself off the floor. Riley said something to him; he pulled the cushion straight up instead of trying to pull it toward him. Mary Ellen had to smile at that one. John stood on his tiptoes as he flashed the light into the dark space beneath the sofa.

Placing the flashlight between his teeth, John used his hand to keep the seat up as he dug in and began to toss things onto the floor. Board games clattered onto the dining room table, their contents spilled across the floor in a jumble of dice, game pieces, and cards. Releasing the cushion, it fell down on top of him as he reached in with both hands to grab hold of something.

He wiggled his way back out from under the cushion and triumphantly held up the small hibachi with both hands over his head. The kid was a clumsy mess, but Mary Ellen couldn't help but grin with him as he continued to show off his newfound treasure.

"What are we going to do with that?" Peter asked.

Mary Ellen hadn't realized he was there until he spoke. She glanced over her shoulder at him, but didn't bother to respond as John finally climbed off the table and walked over to hand the grill up to Bobby. "I wouldn't mind some warm peas and beans, and maybe we'll actually be able to catch something and have some fresh meat we can cook on it," Carl answered.

"Couldn't we just build a fire?"

Mary Ellen didn't miss the anger and annoyance that flashed over Carl's face before he suppressed it. He did, however, dig into his pocket and pull out a cigarette before answering. "We can't carry a fire around with us, and I would prefer to have it than not have it."

"So would I," Al murmured.

"Who knows maybe we'll get lucky and not even need it. Maybe we'll find a place where the electricity is still on if the mountains weren't as badly affected as the coastal areas," Carl said.

"You think?" Rochelle asked eagerly.

Carl shrugged. "Anything's possible."

Mary Ellen pulled Rochelle a step closer to her as John returned to the sofa and tossed aside more items, but reemerged empty-handed. Riley had two bags full of food she handed to John. He fed the bags up to Bobby who reappeared at the front of the RV. Xander and Donald stretched up to take the bags from Bobby and then the small grill. It was meant to be a propane grill, but they could still shove wood or charcoal, if they could find some, into the bottom of it in order to cook food.

Bobby retreated to the passenger side window again. Riley and John positioned themselves on either side of the door that closed off the kitchen and living room area from the back half of the vehicle. Riley held her gun before her; her legs were spread wide as she waited for John to push the door open.

Mary Ellen released Rochelle and pressed her hands against the glass as she strained to see inside better. Beside her, Xander leaned so far forward his nose nearly touched the glass. "Maybe they shouldn't..."

John threw the door open before Xander could finish his statement. Mary Ellen saw a flash of walls, and what looked like a bed, before the door slammed shut again with enough force to rattle the windshield. Her breath hissed out of her as Carl took a step back from the windshield. He surveyed the area around them before returning to look back into the vehicle.

"Xander's right," he decided. "There's no reason for them to go in there."

"Bobby!" Xander called again. Bobby reappeared at the edge of the roof and looked down. "Tell them to get out of there, there's nothing else we need."

Mary Ellen had been looking up at Bobby and hadn't realized Riley and John were still fiddling with the door until Donald spoke. "Too late."

Her eyes flew back to the windshield as John propped the door open with what appeared to be a broom handle. The handle bowed in the middle, but held firm. Xander released a low hiss beside her. Carl brought his gun forward, though she had no idea what he was going to do with it. When nothing exploded out of the back, Riley lowered her gun and pulled out a flashlight.

Mary Ellen held her breath while John and Riley shone their beams into the backroom of the motor home. The shadows were too deep back there for Mary Ellen to see much, but she could definitely make out the foot of a bed. Xander let out an explosive curse. His hands fisted and for a second, she thought he was going to drive one of them into the glass. Riley swung her leg over the door and ducked down to avoid knocking the broom out of the way.

"They're fine," Mary Ellen assured Xander.

He didn't look at all appeased though as the muscles in his forearms stood out and his arms began to shake. John handed his light over to Riley and followed her through the door. The bob and sway of their lights over the walls was making her dizzy as she tried to follow their progress into the bedroom. It looked like some sort of macabre disco was going on in the backroom as the beams of the flashlight played over the ceiling and walls before returning to the ceiling again.

One of them put the flashlight down and focused the steady beam of light on the bed. Someone bent down and pulled the blanket off the bed; she thought it was Riley as it looked like the taller person was rifling through the closet beside the bed. Riley climbed back through the doorway; a blanket and some sheets dragged over the ground behind her as she made her way to the passenger side window.

Bobby said something to her, and she shook her head. She turned to the window and held up her hand with her fingers spread in the five-minute gesture before she gave the ok symbol and smiled at them. Xander remained silent as she disappeared into the bedroom again. This time it was John who came out with an armload of bedding and clothes.

He gave them all a brief wave before rejoining Riley. Donald and Xander took the sheets and blankets from Bobby and placed them on the ground. Another blanket was tossed out the bedroom door and onto the cabinets, but neither Riley nor John followed behind it. John moved around to the other side of the bed. Riley climbed out and tossed four pillows on the floor by the passenger window.

Riley was turning away when the flashlight that had been propped in place was suddenly knocked aside. The rapidly spinning beam made Mary Ellen's eyes cross and her heart jump into her throat. Xander leapt forward and slammed both hands against the glass, but unless he had super human vision she knew he saw the same thing she did, a blinding light twirling around a bed... no a wall... the floor... legs... wall...legs... and then a bed again. She strained to hear or see anything that could have caused the flashlight to fall, but the motor home remained eerily silent.

Where was John? She thought frantically.

Riley disappeared through the door and into the bedroom again. The flashlight stopped spiraling around. John was finally revealed again as he held it up beneath his chin. Riley reappeared and gave them the thumbs up sign again.

"I'm going to kill that kid," Carl groaned.

"Get in line," Xander muttered.

Riley climbed back through the doorway and grabbed the blanket from the floor. She shook bits of glass and plates off it before heading over and tossing it up to Bobby along with the pillows. Mary Ellen heard the muffled shout before Riley turned toward where John remained on the bedroom side of the motor home.

With his flashlight between his teeth, John knelt down and grabbed hold of another door. "What is that?" Mary Ellen asked.

"Bathroom I think," Donald answered.

John tugged at it for a few seconds before flipping a switch that must have been keeping the door locked. He didn't have a chance to try and pull the door open again as it burst upward with enough force to throw him through the doorway and into the living room area. Muffled shouts echoed from inside the RV as the broom was knocked aside, and the door swung closed with a resounding crash that blew Riley and John's hair back.

Mary Ellen took an instinctive step away before moving closer to the window again. Her mind churned rapidly as she tried to puzzle out what had just happened. John's face twisted into a grimace as he rolled to the side and attempted to get his hands underneath him. Riley was going back for him when he began to wave his hand at her to go away. She ignored him though and grabbed hold of his arm to help him to his feet. John was bent over as he limped forward; his arm was wrapped around his middle in a protective gesture.

A loud crash echoed throughout, the door in the middle of the home began to rattle and shake within its frame. "Get out!" Xander shouted as he ran as fast as he could manage toward the tires. "Bobby, get them out of there!"

Riley threw John's arm around her shoulders and propelled him forward. The door in the middle of the home became completely still before it began to open. "Hurry!" Mary Ellen screamed as she slapped her hands against the glass.

Whatever was on the other side hadn't been prepared for the weight of the door as it crashed closed again. It didn't stay closed for long. A mottled black and red hand, that brought to mind images of rotting fruit in a bowl, wrapped around the door and grasped hold of it. She knew it wasn't real, but she heard a creaking sound in her head as the door inched open again.

Bobby had knelt down; his arms were stretched into the motor home in an attempt to grab them. A head emerged from the shadows of the hall and poked around the door. For the space of a heartbeat, Mary Ellen wasn't sure the world continued to turn as a face that seemed to have emerged straight from the bowels of Hell peered out at them. There were very few features left to distinguish as most of them were obscured by some kind of reddish rot that had begun to eat away at the person's cheeks and nose. She caught a glimpse of mottled brown, shoulder length hair, before the sick human slithered like a worm through the opening it had managed to make in between the door and the frame.

As Riley stepped beneath the passenger window, Mary Ellen realized with a sinking heart there was no way they were going to get out of there in time. Riley kept her arm locked around John's waist as she grabbed for Bobby's hands. A scream rose and strangled in Mary Ellen's throat as the thing crept toward them with the agility of a stealthy predator hunting its prey.

CHAPTER 15

Riley

THE LIVE ONES *smell worse than the dead ones,* she couldn't recall where she'd heard that before, but it was screaming through her head right now as the scent of the sick person hit her.

The worst part was it was true. She had become accustomed to the stench of rotten and decomposing flesh, but these live ones smelled more potent. It was as if still being able to walk around somehow enhanced the scent, or perhaps it was because they were still breathing. Maybe these sick people were decaying from the inside out, and every breath forced the rot out of them. She felt the idea they were decomposing was a definite possibility if the look of this person's face was any indication. It was so badly disfigured she couldn't tell if it was male or female anymore.

Her eyes watered; it became difficult to breathe in the snug confines of the motor home as the thing that could *almost* still be considered a human stalked them from the shadows. John leaned to the side in an attempt to take his weight off of her, but his arm remained draped around her shoulders, his breathing heavy in her ear. She wasn't sure if John had broken any ribs, but he had at the very least bruised them pretty good.

There was no way either of them were going to be able to move quickly if that twisted human came at them, and it *was* going to come at them, of that much she was certain as she followed its stealthy movements through the shadows. The little bit of illumination filtering through the windows reflected off of its eyes and made them gleam like a cat's. It was a disconcerting picture to see the two white orbs looking back at her from the dark of the cabinets.

"Grab my hands," Bobby grunted from above.

She glanced up at her friend's hands dangling temptingly above her. "Reach for him John," she said from between teeth as she grappled to free her gun from her side.

Why did I put the damn thing away? She thought angrily.

"You first," John told her.

"You can't even stand upright on your own. Reach for his arms!" she snapped.

John hesitated before trying to stretch his arms above his head. A loud groan escaped him; he winced and grabbed hold of his ribs again. Riley took a stumbling step back and unwrapped her arm from around John's waist as she realized there was no way she was going to be able to get him out of here right now.

"I'm coming down," Bobby said.

"No!" Riley shouted at him. "Three of us down here isn't going to help any."

And it would only be feeding the animals more, she realized as she was finally able to pull her gun free. Stepping in front of John, she planted her body before his as she tried to track the motion of their stalker through the shadows. It had climbed onto the dining room table John had been standing on, but unlike John it crouched with one hand grasping the table and the other hanging before it. Its eyes continued to shine as it tilted its head to the side to study them.

Her hand didn't waver as she pointed the gun at it and pulled the trigger. Though she'd done it within an instant, the thing was already moving before the bullet left the gun. Her ears rang from the bullets being fired within the close confines. She couldn't keep up with its scurrying movements as she fired four more times in a desperate attempt to kill it.

An annoying trickle of sweat slid down the side of her face and into her eye. She didn't dare take her eyes off the person for an instant, not even to wipe the sweat away as it continued to move swiftly through the RV. Bobby released a startled cry and jerked back as it scrambled across the couch and ran over the windshield.

She caught a brief glimpse of the others gathered outside the windshield before it raced toward the cabinets again. She continued to track it through the shadows as the certainty it would kill them, and eat them, began to consume her. Her finger pulled on the trigger again; the bullet slammed into the cabinet just centimeters from the person's face.

It fell back; a startled squeal escaped it before it scurried off in a different direction. There were spiders that didn't move as rapidly, or as smoothly as it did, she realized as it hit the door in the middle of the RV and tumbled into the backroom. She wasn't fooled into thinking it had given up though as she heard its movements through the back of the vehicle.

"Riley," Bobby breathed from above her.

Her heart was in her throat when she chanced a brief glance up at him. Something banged in the backroom, causing her to jump as a small squeak escaped her. John's breathing seemed exceedingly loud in the ensuing hush overtaking the RV. She was tempted to put her hand over his mouth, but she knew it wouldn't do any good. Another loud bang sounded from the backroom. She didn't know what it was doing back there, but she knew it couldn't be anything good.

Riley took a step back with John as she frantically searched for some way to get them out of here. Bobby stretched his hands down again as the door in the middle began to creak open once more. She tried to get off another shot in an attempt to scare it away, but the empty clicking of the gun reminded her of the click of a coffin closing on them as John let out a low groan.

"In my waistband at my back is my gun," he grated.

Her hand fumbled at his back, but she didn't feel anything there. "John..." Her words trailed off as she spotted the gun lying amongst the rubble that had tumbled from the cabinets. It must have fallen out when he'd been knocked through the door. A scream of frustration welled up her throat, but she kept it trapped inside. "John."

"Shit," he muttered as the door opened further and that hideous face peered out at them again. Knowledge gleamed in those eyes; it knew they were nearly defenseless as it placed one hand onto the cabinet and then another.

"Get down! Get down!" It took a moment for Carl's shouts to penetrate her ringing ears and scattered thoughts. "Get away from the windshield!"

Riley spun and grabbed hold of John. Pulling him down with her behind the passenger seat of the RV, she threw her hands over her ears as gunshots reverberated loudly through the air. She flinched and curled closer to John. The zing of a bullet bouncing through the RV resonated as glass shattered and fell to the ground in a tinkling wave.

What little fresh air there was outside filtered into the RV. She peeked her head over top of the chair to take in the broken front window and the curtain flapping in the subtle breeze. "We have to go," she said briskly to John.

Grabbing hold of his arm, she ignored his protesting groan as she helped him back to his feet. They hadn't made it out from behind the chair before it came screaming out of the shadows at them. Either the idea of its meal escaping, or the prospect of the fresh meat outside the window had made it reckless as it charged toward the front of the vehicle.

Riley fell back with John. They pressed themselves against the wall as it raced toward the others. Three rounds from Carl's gun slammed into its chest, knocking it back into the RV. Riley's mouth dropped open; her hand grasped John's arm as it began to kick around on its back. It released a series of sounds that reminded her of a frightened pig while it continued to spin in circles. Finally, blessedly, it went silent. Its hands continued to clutch at its bleeding chest before falling limply to its side.

Though she knew they were now safe, she found herself unable to move as her gaze was riveted on what had once been a normal human being. John seemed to be feeling the same way as he remained immobile beside her. "Are you ok?" Carl demanded gruffly.

John managed a brief nod, but Riley stayed silent. Glass crunched under foot when Xander stepped carefully into the RV. He was nearly as pale as she felt as he climbed onto the passenger chair. It took all she had not to throw herself into his arms when he held his hand out to her, but they had to get John out of there before she could give herself a chance to take a few minutes to sit and breathe. She kept her arm around John as she took hold of Xander's hand and allowed him to help her navigate through the debris littering the floor.

Carl stepped forward and took hold of John's arm. Her shoulders sagged as his weight eased from her tense and aching shoulders. "Thank you," she said to Carl as they stopped beside him.

He gave her a brief nod before walking carefully around the dead body lying on the ground. "Think I broke a rib," John muttered as he cradled his side.

"Next time don't open closed doors," Carl told him.

John scowled at him. "We would all appreciate some toilet paper wouldn't we?" he retorted.

"That we would," Mary Ellen told him soothingly as she took hold of John's free arm and helped Carl lead him over to a grassy spot in the median.

"You ok?" Xander asked.

"Yeah," Riley said, but it felt really good to allow her legs to give out beside John. Her fingers dug into the ground; she took a deep breath and closed her eyes as she tried to calm the frantic beat of her heart.

"Ow!" Riley's eyes flew open at John's shout. Mary Ellen was pressing tenderly against his ribs as she tried to discern the amount of damage inflicted upon him.

"Sorry," Mary Ellen muttered.

Bobby had jumped down from the RV and was approaching them with an armload of blankets. He rested his hand on her shoulder as he stopped beside her. "Glad you're still alive."

"Me too," Riley muttered.

"I'm going to put this stuff in the truck."

"I'll help you," Donald volunteered.

"Can you bring back some tape?" Mary Ellen asked. "I don't think there are any broken ribs, but just to be on the safe side."

"Sure," Bobby said.

"There's some duct tape behind the seat in the truck, it will have to do," Carl told him.

"Got it."

"You going to be ok?" Rochelle asked nervously as she hovered by John's feet.

"I'll be fine kid," he told her.

Riley watched as Bobby and Donald headed toward the truck with their newfound supplies. She knew they should be getting ready to go, sitting still was never a good thing, but the simple feel of the grass beneath her was extremely enticing. She couldn't stay there forever though. Taking a deep breath, she held her hand up to Xander and allowed him to help her to her feet.

He wrapped his hand around the back of her neck and drew her against him. Laying her head against his chest, she listened to the steady, reassuring beat of his heart. "Here you go," Bobby said as he reappeared and held the tape out to Mary Ellen.

John lifted his shirt as she took hold of the tape and turned back to him. "This is probably going to hurt," she told him.

"I'm sure it will," he responded with a weak smile.

Riley winced as the tape made a loud, sticky noise when Mary Ellen pulled it out. Carl returned to John's side with a pillowcase. "Put this around him before you tape him, we don't want to tear his skin off when we take the tape off."

"Yes, let's not do that," John muttered.

Carl held the pillowcase in place as Mary Ellen taped John's ribs with tender care. When she was done, Mary Ellen sat back and rose to her feet. John was sweating profusely, his face was flushed, but he seemed to be holding up well enough as he took a deep breath and attempted to rise to his feet. Carl grabbed hold of John's elbow and helped him up when he almost fell back down.

"Thanks," John said. Carl nodded and released his arm. John lifted his head and pinned Riley with his gaze. "*You*, I am *never* going into anything with just *you* again."

Riley couldn't help but chuckle. "I'll agree with that."

"I thought you would."

"We should get out of here," Carl said.

Al held the map from the welcome center in his hand as he approached them. "That's something we're going to have to discuss," he said as he placed the map on the tailgate of a small pickup truck.

Riley exchanged a look with Xander; she'd thought they were making good time on the highway. "If we stay on the highway," Al said. "We're going to run into Hartford, and if by some miracle we manage to make it through there, we'd have to make it through Waterbury and Danbury afterward too. After what we heard from those people at the rest area, I don't think we'd be able to make it through one city, let alone three of them."

Riley felt her heart plummet into her toes as she stared at the squiggly lines, towns and route numbers spread out before her. She didn't recognize any of the places on the map, and it was enough to make her eyes cross. "We can stay on the highway for a little while longer, but eventually we are going to have to get off and start trying to make it through the back roads. The only problem is, the closer we get to the cities the more populated the towns around them become."

Carl uttered a curse as he began to tap his fingers on the back of the truck. "So get off the highway now is what you're saying," Xander said.

"It's our best option. The cabin is in the Catskills; we'll be heading more toward southern New York than northern."

"Can you get us there?" Bobby asked.

"I can navigate; I'm just not sure what we're going to encounter along the way."

"What else is new?" John asked with a snort.

Carl looked like he was tempted to elbow him in the ribs, but he fought the impulse as his attention returned to the map before Al. "The area of the state we'll be driving through is pretty populated," Al continued. "But then so was most of what we just came through in Mass."

"We just have to keep moving, keep surviving," Riley said.

"Let's go then, is the truck loaded?" Carl asked.

"All set," Bobby answered.

Riley turned to head back to the car, but Mary Ellen stopped her before she could take a step. "Wait," she said.

Riley looked at Mary Ellen over her shoulder and lowered her raised foot. Mary Ellen glanced over to where Peter and Josh were standing by the Cadillac. Riley hadn't realized they'd retreated to the car until now. "I'd like it if Rochelle rode with you guys in the truck."

"Wait, why?" Rochelle asked nervously.

"I just think it would be better if you are in a bigger vehicle if we're going to be entering more populated areas again," Mary Ellen played with Rochelle's hair as she answered her question.

Riley folded her arms over her chest as she glanced between Mary Ellen and the guys by the car. Though it sounded like a plausible excuse, she didn't buy it for a minute. There was something off, she wasn't sure what, but with the look Carl and John exchanged, she knew something was wrong. She didn't know Peter and Josh well, and the teacher had seemed more than a little agitated last night, but she'd thought things had been smoothed over this morning.

She was beginning to realize she'd been wrong.

"What's going on?" Rochelle demanded.

"Nothing…"

"Don't nothing me. Something's not right."

Mary Ellen sighed and stopped fiddling with her daughter's hair as her shoulders slumped. "I just think it would be best if you weren't in the car right now."

"Maybe you shouldn't be in the car either," Carl said.

"I don't think four of us are going to fit in the truck, and besides I'm hoping Peter will let me drive, some sleep will do him good."

"Maybe, but if it doesn't…"

"I'll be driving the car at least, hopefully," Mary Ellen added with a backward glance at the others.

"Am I missing something here?" Riley asked. "I thought Peter seemed like a nice enough guy."

"He is," Xander said.

"I don't trust him," Carl said flatly. "And apparently I'm not the only one. Josh has been a little on edge too."

"It's not that I don't trust him," Mary Ellen hedged. "I just think he needs some rest."

"He needs something," Donald muttered.

"And I think Josh is just frightened," Mary Ellen continued. "It might be good if Rochelle rode with you guys for a bit, if you don't mind?"

"Not at all," Carl said. "But it would probably be best if I rode in the car, and you rode with John and Rochelle."

Rochelle perked up at this suggestion, but Mary Ellen shook her head. "I'll be fine," she insisted. "I'm not afraid of him."

"I'll be there too," Donald said.

"See," Mary Ellen said. "We'll be fine."

Riley found she couldn't tear her gaze away from Peter and Josh. She still wasn't sure there was anything for them to be wary of with them, but apparently more than a few people within the group were. "If that's what you want," Al said.

"It is," she said forcefully.

Al nodded and pulled the map off the back of the truck. "Let's get going then. Maybe we can get a lot of ground covered before we're forced to stop."

Riley didn't hold out much confidence in that. Returning to the back roads and towns most likely meant they were going to be slowed down, a lot. She stopped by the truck and gathered more ammo from Carl before climbing into the backseat of the car with Xander. Bobby slid behind the wheel as Al sat in the passenger seat and opened the map again.

"Do you think there's something wrong with Peter?" she asked as Bobby started the car.

"Probably nothing some sleep can't fix," Al answered absently.

Riley turned in her seat and was relieved to see Mary Ellen behind the wheel of the car. "Let's hope so," she said.

Her concerns over Peter and Josh faded as Al directed Bobby to take the next exit off the highway. A knot began to form in her chest; her hand slid into Xander's as they returned to small town America and all the dreadful secrets she knew it was hiding.

CHAPTER 16

Carl

USING the butt end of the rifle, Carl broke out the window in the door of the sporting goods store. He put his hand inside and searched for the lock on the other side of the door. He found the one on the handle with ease, but it took a few seconds of fumbling around before he uncovered the deadbolt. Finally locating the lock, he turned it to the side and pushed the door open.

"Let's just get in and get out as fast as possible." He knew he didn't have to tell them that, but he said it anyway. The tranquility of this new town was beginning to grate on his nerves a little.

He flicked on his flashlight and shone the beam around the store. He wasn't sure if there would be any guns in the store, but he wasn't about to turn down some tents, fishing equipment, sleeping bags and coolers if it had them. It was a small little gold mine, or at least he'd thought it was going to be until his beam revealed the wreckage of the store.

"Looks like we're a little late to the party," Peter muttered.

Carl would have preferred it if Peter hadn't been invited to the party at all, but he couldn't do anything about that right now. He kicked aside a broken lantern as he walked further into the store. The gun felt reassuring in his hand, but after seeing the way that thing in the RV had moved, he knew he'd have to be fast with the weapon in order to avoid shooting up the store.

"There has to be some stuff we can still use," Riley said.

He glanced over at her as she brushed past Peter and through the door. Xander and John followed behind her. Carl nodded toward the back of the store, and though he didn't say anything, Riley seemed to understand what he was implying as she went the other way. John fell into step behind him as he began a search of the aisles. Donald and Peter remained by the front door, surveying what was left within the store. Al had stayed by the vehicles with Mary Ellen, Rochelle, Bobby, and Josh to keep watch of the serene town.

Riley and Xander were making the turn around the aisle at the end of the store when Carl discovered the broken back door. He stepped forward, nudged the door open with his toe and poked his head into the alley behind the store. Pieces of paper skittered past him and caught in the chain link fence blocking the back alley from the main street.

He glanced in the other direction, but the area behind the stores lining the street remained empty. Stepping back inside, he grabbed hold of the door and pulled it closed. His fingers slid into the hole created by the knob being busted out of the door; he held it closed. "See if you can find me some..."

John thrust a thin strand of rope into his face before Carl could finish speaking. "I think we're spending a little too much time together," he told him as he took the rope from John.

"Ouch," John retorted.

Carl chuckled as he slipped the rope through the hole and looped it around the latch side of the door. He took both ends of the rope and tied them to a stuffed black bear propped at the edge of a display campsite set up next to the door. If they didn't find any other tents in the store, there was at least a popup they could steal by the bear.

He wiped his hands off as Xander and Riley reappeared after finishing the sweep of the store. "There are definitely some things we can salvage," Xander said and tossed a bag of trail mix to John. "I'm guessing someone was allergic to peanuts."

"Good," John said as he tore open the bag and shook some out before handing it over to Carl.

Carl popped a handful into his mouth as he wandered back down the aisle toward the front of the store. Donald was standing by the cash register, searching for something under the shelves. Peter remained by the door, one foot in the store and the other outside of it. "Any bags back there?" Carl's voice was harsher than he had intended as he directed the question to Donald.

Donald glanced up at him and shook his head. "No."

"We'll search the backroom, there may be some boxes or bags back there," Xander volunteered.

"We'll go with you," Carl told him around a mouthful of dried cranberry and nuts.

He dropped the bag of trail mix on the front counter and followed them to the swinging door hiding the back of the store from the front. He got his gun ready with Riley as Xander pressed his foot against the door and pushed it open. John's light bounced off of half a dozen boxes stacked neatly against the back wall. A small kitchenette, nineteen eighties style card table, and four chairs that didn't look like they would support the weight of a five year old rounded out the rest of the room.

"I wouldn't open the fridge," Xander said as John moved toward it.

John switched direction and headed for the cabinets. The doors clanked and clicked as John began to open and close the cabinets. He pulled down a container of coffee and some filters, a box full of plastic utensils, but other than that the cabinets were bare. "Old Mother Hubbard," Carl said under his breath.

Riley glanced at him over her shoulder, but no one else gave any indication they had heard him. John grabbed the trashcan beside the fridge and turned it upside down to empty it of the couple of pizza boxes and napkins inside. He dropped the coffee and filters into the bottom and handed the trashcan over to Xander.

"Let's see what's in these boxes." John pulled out some plastic knives and gave one to each of them as he headed toward the boxes stacked in the back.

Carl knelt and slit the tape on the first box; pulling it back he discovered boxes of golf balls. He turned the box upside down and dumped the contents onto the floor before grabbing hold of the next one. When they were done, they had six empty boxes and a pile of useless goods scattered around their feet. He pushed back into the main store and began to gather whatever supplies he could find that would be of some use.

He grabbed two fishing poles, and a couple packages of hooks, from the back of the store. He tossed some bobbers and lures into his box, but there was little else of use in his area. Returning to the front of the store, he placed his box down with the others and surveyed the others supplies. There were two small popup tents still in boxes, and Donald had dismantled the one in the campsite and stuffed it into the trashcan. Carl was glad they had the tents, but he'd prefer not to have to sleep outside if they could help it; that seemed like something almost guaranteed to get someone eaten. It disheartened him to see that out of the six boxes only four of them were full, but it was more than they had come in here with.

"I found some water purification tablets," Riley said as she tossed a sleeping bag onto two of the boxes.

"Those will come in handy," Carl said.

"We should get going, we have to find a place to stay tonight," Peter said from the doorway, where he hadn't moved a foot one way or the other since Carl had last seen him.

Annoyance spurted through him, but he lifted the box and pushed by Peter to get out the door. They weren't going to make it out of this town before the early nightfall set in, but there had to be a safer place to stay than the camping store. His gaze slid up and down the street as he searched for someplace a little more protected, but there wasn't much. A pizza/bait shop across the street piqued his curiosity simply because he would have liked to have seen the people who had actually ordered pizza from there.

"I hope one of the special toppings wasn't worms," Riley murmured from beside him.

"Just minnows and anchovies," John told her.

Riley's face scrunched up as she shook her head. "Yuck."

Al's hands were in his pockets as he approached them. "How about the library?" he suggested.

"The library?" John inquired.

"It's a building that houses books," Carl informed him flatly.

John gave him a look that would have shot daggers through his heart if it could have. "I *know* what the library is, but why would we stay there?"

"I'm hoping there might be some answers there, maybe not for what caused the earthquakes but for the sickness. Maybe we can find something that will help us understand what is going on," Al explained.

"I'm all for a few answers," Xander said. "And honestly I don't see anywhere else in this town that looks or sounds any more appealing."

"Library it is then," Carl said as Bobby opened the backdoors of the truck.

They loaded the boxes and trashcan inside, retreated to their vehicles, and headed back toward the brick fronted building they had passed on their way into town. Carl drove back by the streets and deserted home fronts. There wasn't any movement behind the windows like he'd seen in the other towns. This empty town had an air of time having forgotten about it. If it hadn't been for the broken door and the ransacked sporting goods store, he would have been certain everyone in this town had just vanished, but then he supposed it could have been someone from outside of the town who had looted the store. He didn't know what had happened to the people of this town, where they had all gone, and he wasn't going to look for the answers either.

"It's so quiet," Rochelle whispered.

"Too quiet," Carl agreed.

"Maybe they were evacuated," John suggested. "I mean this town seems to be in relatively good shape, maybe they were taken somewhere else."

John was right about that. Some of the trees had toppled, and a few homes had been damaged by the quakes, but there wasn't the outright destruction here that they'd experienced in Massachusetts. The cities in Connecticut might not be as bad as Boston was, but he wasn't willing to risk trying to get through those cities in order to find out.

Carl drove past the front doors of the library and around to the side of the building. There was another parking lot for the building set down a gravelly hill. The tires crunched on the rocks as he drove down the hill and parked the truck outside of the glass side doors.

Stepping from the truck, he grabbed the keys and locked his door. He studied the two story building only slightly larger than a normal sized house. "I don't think they have a lot of books in there," John said.

Carl agreed with him, but he knew there would be plenty of places for something to hide within the building. The others gathered around him as he tried the side doors only to find them locked. Stepping back, he eyed the glass doors, but because of the noise it would make, the last thing he wanted to do was break them in order to get in.

"We'll check the front," Xander volunteered. Riley, Xander, and Bobby climbed up the side hill and around to the front of the building. Carl studied the darkening sky as he counted the seconds and waited for them to return.

Bobby reappeared and skidded down the path worn into the grass. "One of the front doors is open."

Relief filled Carl at the same time alarm trickled down his spine. It was such a disconcerting effect, he didn't know how to react to it at first.

They wouldn't have to break the glass of the doors, but there could be one of the sick humans inside; there could be *dozens* of them inside just waiting for unsuspecting people to enter. Both those thoughts warred incessantly inside of him as he tried to figure out what they should do. There were so many places to hide in a library, so many places those things could be slinking around, and far too many shelves they could climb on top of and leap off of.

There could also be answers inside; they might be able to find something that could help them or help the people affected by the sickness. There could also be hundreds of death traps just waiting to spring on them. He was still debating what to do when Riley and Xander appeared at the top of the hill. Xander slid down to meet them while Riley remained above.

"The front door was open, but the inner door is still locked," Xander informed them.

"Why is one door open and not the other?" Al asked.

"It looks like the lock on the outer door was broken, probably during one of the quakes. The inner door is glass; we can break through it and barricade the heavier outer door once inside. It looks like it will be safe or at least just as safe as anywhere else around here."

That much was true. Carl nodded and followed him back up the hill to join Riley before walking over to the front door. She pulled the heavy metal outer door open and walked over to the glass inner doors. "I can't see much inside, but it looks clear," she told them.

"So did the RV," John commented.

"True," she said as she flashed her beam into the building.

Carl stepped up to the glass doors and peered inside. The edges of the numerous stacks appeared from the darkness. The building was small, but they had crammed more shelves than he had expected into it. He spotted the outline of books and a table with some chairs lining it. Riley's beam moved toward the ceiling, but other than some cobwebs he saw nothing amongst the wooden rafters of the old building.

"Let's just go inside," Peter said impatiently.

Carl's fingers slid over the grip of his gun as he turned toward the teacher. It seemed sleep hadn't helped the man as much as

Mary Ellen had expected. Carl forced a smile to his face as he gestured toward the doors. "After you."

Peter's gaze slid toward him. *No, sleep hadn't helped him at all,* Carl decided. Like a pit of snakes, Carl was certain something twisted around within his mind. Was the sickness maybe starting to take hold of him, or was this something else entirely? Was this a madness that had taken root with the loss of everything Peter had always known and the pressure of the constant fear of death?

Carl didn't much care about the answer; he cared more about trying to get the gun back from the teacher before he completely spiraled out of control.

John eyed Peter like he was a deadly scorpion as he turned sideways to get past the man and out the front door. Carl was unwilling to take his eyes off Peter until John returned with a rock the size of a man's head. "Stand back," John said as he pulled his arm back and heaved the rock at the door.

The glass spider webbed but held firm. Retrieving the rock, John heaved it forward again. Most of the glass fell inside the building, but a few pieces fell about John's feet. It crunched beneath him as he pulled out his flashlight and stepped through the door. Carl followed behind him.

The smell of books, worn, used, and comforting instantly brought Carl back to memories of his childhood, when he would go to the library with his mother. From the time he was able to read, he would go into the children's section and lose himself amongst the Berenstain Bears and later the Hardy Boys. Then, when he'd turned twelve, he'd finally been allowed into the adult section upstairs where he'd devoured Tolkien before discovering King and losing himself to fantasy and horror. He'd stopped reading as much when he'd hit his teens and discovered girls, drugs, and alcohol but the comfort of those younger years, and the solace he'd found amongst the stacks had stayed with him over the years.

Now, standing amongst the rows of the written word, with the familiar scent washing over him he didn't find comfort, he didn't see adventures, mysteries, and mystical lands just waiting to be discovered. He only saw hundreds of places for monsters to hide and stalk them from, hundreds of places from where eyes could be watching them right now.

John cursed as his beam played over the stacks, computers, and tables pushed to the side for reading. The librarian's desk was on their right hand side, a computer, and a few returned books were the only things cluttering the desk. "Desk first," Carl said.

He made his way over to the desk and crept around it. He bent over to look underneath it, but the only thing he saw were the wheels of the roller chair. The door of the office behind the desk was ajar, the blinds over the window drawn. He stood to the side as he pressed his fingers against the door.

"Nothing good comes from opening doors," John muttered behind him.

"I don't think we have a choice this time," Carl told him as he pushed the door open.

John stopped breathing, and Carl worried the kid might start shooting even if nothing exploded from the room. The door silently slid open to reveal a neatly organized room with piles of books stacked against the back wall and on the floor next to one of the desks. Carl hurried through the room, but he discovered nothing threatening within it, and nowhere for a ravenous human to hide.

He stepped back into the main room and closed the door behind him. Donald, Xander, and Bobby had carried a table and some chairs over to the front doors to barricade them against opening. They would have to get some rope out of the truck when they made it downstairs again to tie everything into place.

His eyes drifted over the thirty or so stacks filling the room and blocking the back half of the room from view. *If they made it downstairs again*, he thought with an inward groan.

"This is not going to be fun," John said from beside him.

"Not even a little bit," Carl agreed as Riley, Bobby, and Xander gathered around him. He glanced back at the door. He didn't like leaving the others with Peter, but they had little choice. Peter would become a threat, he became increasingly convinced of that, but there may be larger threats looming within the shadows of the building. "Let's get it over with."

He shifted the light in his hand and raised it to eye level as he moved cautiously into the first stack with John at his heels.

CHAPTER 17

Al

THOUGH HE DIDN'T much feel like walking into the stacks with them, he also refused to stand idly by as the others searched the library for any threat. "I'm going with them," he said to Mary Ellen.

She pushed back a strand of straggling brown hair from her eyes as she turned toward him. "Are you sure?"

"I'm sure," he told her.

"I'll go with you," Donald volunteered.

Al glanced back at the group still standing by the door before nodding. Though he understood Mary Ellen's concern for Peter earlier, he didn't think the man would become a threat. They were all more than a little on edge with everything going on. He turned away from the group and began to walk forward with Donald at his side.

"I'll go with Xander and Riley, if you'll join Carl and John," he suggested.

"Sounds good," Donald agreed as they split up to follow their separate groups.

Xander turned his head to look back at him, but Riley remained focused on the ceiling and the tops of the shelves as she searched for a threat from up above. They waited for him to catch up to them before continuing forward.

The hush of the library was something he'd always appreciated over the years, but now he found it oppressive. The familiar squeak of a library cart, or the muffled turning of pages was something he would have greatly appreciated right now. Instead, all he heard was the inhale and exhale of those closest to him as they moved out of the row and toward the left while Carl, John, and Donald went to the right.

The beams from the flashlights carried by the others as they moved farther away, was the only indication Al had they weren't completely alone within the disturbingly still building. It confirmed that the others within their group hadn't simply disappeared, as it seemed much of this town had.

It wasn't until they passed the next row of books that a strange sound began to penetrate the intense focus he'd had while searching each row. Xander stopped before him and tilted his head to the side to listen. Riley's brow furrowed; her mouth pursed as she turned toward them.

"What is that?" she whispered.

Al shook his head as Xander moved by her. Xander's flashlight bounced back and forth as he tried to locate the source of the noise. "It's coming from up ahead," Xander said as he continued onward.

Al and Riley stayed close on his heels as they continued to search through the stacks. Al kept expecting to come across the source of the noise, or some other threat, but each row they walked by revealed nothing. Al's certainty they were going to be attacked at any second grew as they moved down the rows and the noise became louder.

"Is that *water*?" Riley asked.

Al started to shake his head no, but now that she'd suggested the idea of water, he found himself agreeing it did sound like a running water faucet. Stepping around the last stack, he was finally able to spot where the sound was coming from as the men's and women's bathrooms came into view.

They moved cautiously as they approached the bathrooms. "It's coming from the men's room," Xander said.

Riley stepped to the side and lifted her gun as Xander pushed the door open with his left hand and flashed his light around the room. Al spotted a urinal inside, but it was difficult for him to see much more over Xander's shoulder. Al stuck his hand against the door to hold it open as Xander stepped further into the room. The glow of Xander's flashlight illuminated another urinal and a small stall as Al followed him into the room.

The small yellow sink, that had been ugly before it went out of style in the eighties, sat next to the urinal. Xander stepped forward and turned off the hot and cold water running into the basin. Xander's reflection was ashen, his eyes shadowed as he met Al's gaze in the mirror over the sink. No one spoke, but Al recognized the same realization in Xander's eyes stealing through him as well.

Someone was here.

Al's attention turned to the closed stall door as Xander knelt down and shone his flashlight under it. Riley looked at them before stepping forward and pushing against the door, it silently slid open to reveal the empty stall. The door clinked against the metal wall before creaking back toward them. Xander took a step back as

Riley's beam shot toward the ceiling, but there were no strange creatures lurking above them.

Al flashed the beam around the room and landed upon the window at the other end of it. He brushed past the others as he walked to the square window large enough for him to fit through. He grabbed hold of the latch on the unlocked window and lifted it up. Shining his flashlight up, he was able to make out what looked like a small alley and the brick wall of another building next to them.

He soundlessly closed the window and slid the latch into place. "Do you think they left?" Riley asked nervously.

"I don't know but we have to inform the others," Al told her.

"We should probably search the women's room first."

Leaving the men's room, Riley was the one to prop open the door of the women's room while Xander stood behind her with his gun raised. The beam of his light revealed two stalls in the bubblegum colored room. The two pink sinks were silent, and the wall at the end of the room was completely windowless. Walking inside, Al realized the first stall door was open and empty; Xander pushed open the second door to reveal another empty stall.

Al was really beginning to dislike bathrooms as they made their way out of the room and into the library. They hurried by the rows they had already searched and walked rapidly toward the other group. The others were just getting to the end of the stacks they had been searching. "Carl," Riley said in a low hiss.

Their flashlight beams swung up as they turned toward her. Al threw his hand up to protect his eyes, but it was already too late. All he could see for a few seconds were bright stars behind his closed lids. "What's wrong?" Carl demanded.

"There's someone in here, or at least there was," Riley told them in a rush. "The sink in the men's room was on, the window unlatched."

"Wonderful," John said as he turned away from them to search the shadows of the stairwell before him.

"Did you tell the others?" Carl asked.

Riley shook her head and glanced toward the front of the library. "I'll let them know," Donald volunteered. "Just finish searching the building, and be careful."

Al watched Donald until he disappeared amongst the rows of books. Taking a deep breath, Al turned to the stairway leading to the lower floor. If there was still someone in this building, there was only one place left for them to be hiding. Carl took the first step down and leaned over the stairway railing. He shone his flashlight onto the flight of stairs below the one he was standing on. Al leaned over the rail beside him and peered into the darkness, but he didn't see anything stirring below them.

Sneakers squeaked on the non-slip rubber mats lining the stairs as Carl led the way to the first floor. The open entryway they stepped into revealed the glass doors they had first peered through upon arriving at the library. He could see the outline of the vehicles in the parking lot, but the early night had completely descended already.

He turned his light in the other direction to explore the rest of the library. There was a handicapped bathroom directly in front of them, but the entry hall had a wall on their right and another on their left, instead of an open space like the one above. A half wall, with glass on top of it that reached to the ceiling, was on their right; the other wall was made of solid brick and had a closed door.

Shining his beam through the glass on the right hand wall, Al spotted beanbag chairs, tiny tables and chairs, stuffed animals, and scattered toys on a rainbow colored rug. Though he could see the outline of shelves, he didn't have to see the shelves to know they would be lined with children's and middle school aged books.

Xander went to the brick wall on their left and grabbed hold of the handle on the closed door. Pushing it down, he took a step back as he shoved the door open. Nothing came screaming out at them, but Xander approached the open door as if it were about to sprout legs and run at him. Al shone his light around the twenty or so desks gathered within, and the computers sitting on top of them.

There weren't as many hiding spots in this room, but the idea of bending down to check all the spaces beneath the desks was less than appealing to him. Taking a deep breath, he moved into the room behind Carl and John. Grabbing hold of one of the rolling chairs, he pulled it out of the way before kneeling down to peer beneath the first desk. Cobwebs lingered in the far corners, but there was nothing else to be found.

His knees popped as he pushed aside the chair of the second desk and looked underneath. Riley stayed close to him as they searched through the first row of desks. John got to the end of the line and rose back to standing after inspecting under the last desk. "There's no one here," he announced.

Relief filled Al when he escaped the room full of computers and desks for the more familiar and comforting smell of the books he knew so well. He waited by the door to the children's section as Xander and Carl checked the handicapped bathroom. Under normal conditions the toys, stuffed bears, and the colorful tiny chairs wouldn't have unnerved him to such a degree. Now it gave him a cold chill, and he found he dreaded stepping foot in there.

Al pushed down on the door handle as Carl and Xander joined him. The door slid open on well-oiled hinges to reveal the rest of the room beyond. He'd spent a lot of time in rooms just like this one when his children had been young. He and Nellie had often brought the kids to the library on Saturdays for story hour with the librarian. It had been a wonderful chance to impart his and his wife's love of reading to their children.

Memories of those long ago days assaulted him as the familiar scent of aged paper and ink washed over him. He could almost hear his children's laughter as they regaled him with some new adventure. Tears brimmed in his eyes as he recalled holding his children on his lap and bouncing them on his knee. He could almost smell their baby shampoo, almost feel their sticky fingers against his cheeks as they pushed his lips out into a fish face and giggled. There were many things he had missed over the years as his children had grown, but those special story hours had been near the top of the list.

He was torn from that distant time by Xander accidentally kicking one of the chairs. Xander cursed as it skittered a few inches into the dark recesses of the room. For one collective moment everyone held their breaths as they waited to see if the noise would draw the attention of some unwanted enemy.

Finally breathing a sigh of relief, Carl and John moved further into the shadows closer to the books, while he, Xander, and Riley moved towards the librarian's desk. Xander pulled the librarian's chair out of the way as he knelt to search beneath the desk. Rising back to his feet, he looked to Riley and shook his head. Their attention shifted to the office behind the desk. It was smaller than the office Carl and John had first searched upstairs.

Al stood to the side as he waited for Riley to open the door. He moved into the room, but the small space didn't allow for many hiding places as he crept through it. He turned sideways to move by the desk and caught the corner of a book resting on it. The clattering noise it created as it hit the floor caused the three of them to jump. Riley spun her gun in his direction but thankfully, she didn't shoot it.

Bending down, Al picked up the book and turned it over in his hand to inspect it. It was a copy of *Where the Red Fern Grows*, a book he knew well as he'd once read it with his oldest son for a school book report. Determined not to get lost in the memories again, Al placed the book back on the desk, tapped it with his finger, and left the room.

"There's no one in here. Maybe one of the quakes turned the water on," John suggested.

"It turned on only one sink in this whole place?" Carl inquired doubtfully.

John shrugged as his gaze drifted helplessly around the room. "I don't know, maybe whoever it was ran away when they heard us break-in?"

"That's a possibility," Xander said.

"No matter what it was, they're not here now, and that's all that matters," Al inserted.

"We should gather some supplies from the truck. We need to get back upstairs and let them know we're okay," Carl said.

"I'll go up and let them know," Al told them. "Besides I'd like to start looking for some reference books that might help us."

"We'll keep our fingers crossed," Riley said. "And I'll come up with you."

She stood on her tip toes to give Xander a kiss on the cheek before squeezing Al's arm and nodding toward the open doorway. She silently walked up the stairs beside him and into the main room. They had left the others gathered by the front door, but they had branched out already. Bobby still stood by the barricade, but he leaned against the wall with his gun before him. Josh and Donald looked asleep on their feet by the librarian's desk, and

Mary Ellen and Rochelle were already sitting at one of the long tables.

Mary Ellen rose to her feet when she spotted them, but Rochelle remained seated. "Where's Peter?" Riley asked.

"He went to use the bathroom," Mary Ellen told her. Riley nodded, but her brow furrowed as her gaze drifted toward where the bathrooms were located. "Is everything all clear?"

"We didn't find anyone," Al assured her.

"Are you sure?" Mary Ellen asked nervously.

"We searched the entire building. If someone was here, they're gone now."

Mary Ellen's shoulders slumped in relief. "Good."

"Let's say we get started on looking for some books. Where are the card catalogs?" Al inquired as he looked around the library. It had been awhile since he'd been inside a library, but he didn't think they could have changed much over the past ten years.

"A lot of libraries don't use card catalogs anymore," Riley answered.

Al wouldn't have been more staggered if she'd just told him the earth was indeed flat. "What do they use then?" he asked incredulously.

"Computers."

He stared at the now useless machines set up on the side of the room. "Lot of good that does us right now."

"I'm sure we can find the medical reference books," Mary Ellen said.

"It shouldn't be too hard," Donald said as he approached them. "We just have to get started."

Al wasn't quite as confident as they were as he followed them into the stacks. He played his light over the numerous book spines lining the shelves. After three more rows of endless books that weren't what he was looking for, Al began cursing computers, the internet, and anything remotely technological and requiring electricity. His eyes were beginning to cross from staring at the endless tomes, and though he knew it actually hadn't been, he felt as if hours were wasting away as they continued to get nowhere.

"They couldn't have just left the card catalogues as a backup plan, to add to the ambience, or something?" he muttered.

"They probably took them out to make room for the computers," Donald said.

He didn't mean to, but frustration was getting the best of him when he shot Donald a fierce look. The man did a double take and actually started to blush before returning his attention to the books before them. The beam of another flashlight alerted him to Mary Ellen and Riley's presences as they rounded the stacks and headed toward them. They each held a pile of books in their arms.

"We found the medical section," Mary Ellen said.

"Thank God," Al muttered. He'd started to feel like a hamster in his wheel, constantly moving forward but going nowhere.

"We grabbed what looked like the newest editions," Mary Ellen continued as she nodded at the books pressed against her chest. "There's more if you think we should get them too."

"This seems like a good place to start," Al told her as he took some of the books from her.

They made their way back into the main room and placed the books on one of the tables. Al tiredly slid into a chair. It was going to be another night with little sleep, but maybe this night would finally give them some answers. Mary Ellen pulled out the chair next to him and sat down, Riley sat across from him.

"What are we looking for?" Riley asked.

"Start with the symptoms," he answered. "Fever, exhaustion, sores."

"Uncontrollable hunger?"

"That too," he said as he grabbed hold of one of the books and pulled it over to him. Light from the stairwell across from him drew his attention as Carl, John, and Xander appeared at the top of the stairs. Their arms were full of supplies from the truck. His stomach rumbled in expectation of food from one of those bags, but he remained where he was.

He turned his attention back to the thick book before him as they began to dole out supplies and set up a sleeping area for the night. John handed him a power bar and a bag of trail mix as Xander plopped into the seat next to Riley and took hold of one of the books.

"I'm going to see if I can boil some water and try to make some coffee. Would you guys be interested in a cup if I can?" John asked.

"I'd absolutely love a cup," Al told him.

"I think we all would," Xander agreed.

"I'll see what I can do," John told them before wandering away.

Al rubbed absently at his temples as he strained to stay awake and focus on the words before him. He didn't know how much time had passed before John handed him a mug of coffee. "Heaven," Mary Ellen murmured as she sipped at hers.

Al had to agree as the coffee began to rejuvenate him. He turned back to the endless pages before him with renewed vigor. He felt almost human again as he picked at the trail mix. The muffled sound of pages turning, and people moving about, was comforting as life filled the library.

CHAPTER 18

Xander

"Did you ever wonder what the world would have been like if just *one* little thing had been different? Like what if The Big Bang had never occurred? What if fire hadn't been discovered or that first caveman hadn't carved a spear? Or what if God had decided he didn't want to create man, or what if he had *really* messed up and not created woman?"

That last part finally caught his attention and forced Xander out of his own thoughts. He turned his head to frown at Carol. "It would have been a much more peaceful world without women."

She grinned at him as she leaned against his side. "It would, but far more boring."

"Peaceful."

She playfully pinched his arm. "You would have missed us, or at least me. Plus, you guys wouldn't have survived without us."

"I'm certainly not about to have a baby," he retorted.

The smile slid from her face as she looked at the park spread out before them. "Do you ever think about it though? I mean what if Hitler had won the war?"

"Nothing good would have come of that," he told her. "Why are you getting all philosophical on me?"

She shrugged as she absently pulled at the grass beneath her and tossed it into the breeze drifting over them. A strand of hair, nearly the same color as his, blew across her face and she tucked it behind her ear. From their vantage point on the hill, he could clearly see Bobby and Lee as they walked across the soccer field toward them. Bobby's skateboard was tucked under his arm, and Lee was staring at his phone as he typed a reply.

A pang of longing pierced his heart as he looked at Lee, but for the life of him he couldn't figure out why. His friend was right there, within five minutes he would be standing beside him again, as close as Carol. Carol…

There it was again, that yearning as something tugged at his memory, but it was a memory he wasn't going to recall, not right now. Now he simply meant to enjoy the day.

They were supposed to be going to see a movie tonight, but he doubted they'd actually make it there. They rarely did, as someone always seemed to come up with a different plan before they stepped into the theatre. Bobby looked up and waved as he caught a glimpse of them on the hill. Lee remained engrossed in his phone.

"So do you?" Carol inquired.

"Do I what?"

"Do you ever wonder if one *small* thing made all the difference?"

"No, I've never really thought about it," he admitted.

"Do you think about it now that it's all come to an end?" she asked.

There it was; the forceful intrusion into this small moment of peace he'd found. He'd known it had been too good to be real, but he tried to stick to the chance this was more than just a dream. That he could somehow return to those days of simplicity. He knew, even before Lee and Bobby faded from view, and the lush grass they'd been sitting on withered beneath him, it was too good to be true.

"I think about you a lot more now," he admitted. "I don't think about what could have been different. I think it would only drive me crazy, it would only drive *all* of us crazy if we did. There was nothing we could have done to stop whatever triggered these events."

"No, maybe not," Carol agreed. "But what if it was one tiny thing, someone else did, that triggered it?"

"You really want to see me go insane?" he retorted.

She laughed as she leaned against his side again. "I think we're all a little insane right now, some more than others."

Xander frowned over her words. "You're not here anymore."

"I am here though." She pointed at his chest and tapped the place over his heart.

"You're so corny," he told her with a laugh.

"Yeah well, it was always one of the things you loved best about me."

"It was," he confirmed.

"You have to be careful Xander, there are dangerous things out there…"

"I know all about the danger out there now Carol. I've lost you and Lee already."

Her gaze drifted over the completely black and barren world

that had replaced the sunny day in the park. "There is also danger in here, with you. There are things that are *wrong*."

He frowned as he turned back toward her. "What are you talking about?"

"You know what I'm talking about," her words were only a whisper now.

Xander tried to grab hold of her, but as he reached for her, she faded further away from him. "Carol," he groaned but she'd completely vanished and left him alone in this now empty dream world.

Xander's eyes blinked open. He was struggling against the lingering heartache as he stared at the darkened stacks across from him and tried to remember where he was. Had he fallen asleep in the college library again? But he knew he was wrong as recent memories flooded over him.

He wiped at his mouth, embarrassed to realize he'd drooled onto the medical book he'd turned into his pillow. He didn't remember putting his head down. Had he simply fallen asleep in the middle of reading?

That seemed very plausible, he realized as he pushed himself away from the puddle he'd left. "Are you ok?" Riley asked.

He rubbed at his gritty eyes before turning to look at her. Though her eyelids were heavy, and her mouth was pinched, she was still beautiful. He'd lost Carol and Lee, but she was still here, Bobby was still here, and he was still alive. He had to focus on that as his sister's dream image continued to haunt him.

"I'm fine," he assured her as he ran a hand over the back of her hair and pulled her close to kiss her forehead.

Her hand fell onto his thigh and her fingers curled into his leg as she leaned into him. Memories of his dream caused him to reluctantly pull away from her to inspect the room. Mary Ellen,

Donald, Carl, John, and Al were still sitting at the table. Rochelle had retreated to one of the sleeping bags they'd set out and was lying next to Josh. He could see Bobby still standing by the front door. Peter was sitting in the librarian's chair, his feet propped up on the desk; his hands were folded in his lap as he watched them from narrowed eyes.

Was *he* who Carol had been talking about when she had warned of danger in here with them? Or was she perhaps talking about something, or someone, else still inside the building? Maybe even something inside of him? His gaze drifted down to his chest as if he could somehow see inside himself. It had been his own subconscious talking to him in the dream after all; maybe it had been trying to tell him there was something wrong with *him*.

It was a terrifying notion, one he strained to shake off as tried to focus on something else. *It was only a dream*, he told himself. It was just his overtired mind conjuring up the image of his dead sister and friend.

Riley kept her head on his shoulder as she began to flip through the pages of her book. There was a notepad next to her with some hastily scribbled writing in it. Xander leaned forward and rubbed his temples as the words in his book blurred in front of him. Riley's head rose off of his shoulder and she leaned forward. Her hand pressed flatter against the book; she pulled it and the notepad closer to her.

"I think I may have found something!" she blurted.

The others were slower to respond than he was, but eventually their heads turned toward her. Al was the first to fully register what she had said as he sat up straighter in his chair. "What did you find?"

"Meningitis."

"Meningitis?" Mary Ellen asked in confusion. "Meningitis doesn't make people go crazy."

"Wait. Just listen to me for a minute. Meningitis is a disease caused by the inflammation of the protective membranes covering the brain and spinal cord. These are known as the meninges." Her finger trailed over the lines in the book as she read from it. "The inflammation is typically caused by an infection of the fluid surrounding the brain and spinal cord. The inflammation may be caused by a virus or bacteria, but it can also be caused by physical injury, cancer or certain drugs.

"The most common symptoms of meningitis are headache, *neck stiffness*, fever, confusion. Other symptoms include vomiting, photophobia." Xander stiffened as he recalled those things outside of the garage. He leaned closer to peer over her shoulder as she continued to read from the book. "Phonophobia..."

"What is photophobia and phonophobia?" Donald interrupted.

"Hold on." Al flipped to the back of his book where there was a list of definitions of medical terms.

"Photophobia is an inability to tolerate light," Xander informed them. "Or a sensitivity to it."

"Jesus," Mary Ellen whispered as she leaned back in her chair and rubbed at the bridge of her nose.

"Phonophobia is the same thing, but for loud noises," Al said as his finger froze on a line in his book.

"Keep reading Riley," Carl said as he rose and paced over to the stacks. The flick of a lighter sounded; the red tip of his cigarette lit up as he inhaled deeply.

"A rash may also be present in some cases and can indicate a particular cause of meningitis."

She turned the book toward them to reveal a picture. It was of a simple rash, one he would have associated with poison ivy, or chicken pox, but the caption below it read, "Petechial Rash." She turned the page to reveal almost the same rash but with larger almost purplish red lesions on the skin.

"That's a mixed petechial/purpuric rash," Riley said. "and this is where things start to get ugly."

"Gross," Bobby said when she revealed the next page. Xander had been so absorbed in the book, and what Riley was telling them, he hadn't realized his friend had also been drawn forth by Riley's excited words.

The purplish/red lesions in the picture covered more of the human torso and arm; they had grown in size and were beginning to take over the body. Xander recognized the rash and had seen it on far too many faces recently. "This is widespread purpuric rash of septicaemia," Riley explained.

"That is, you're royally screwed. That's what that is," John muttered.

"It gets worse," Riley told him and flipped the page. The next photo was disgusting, but it had been far worse seeing it on some of the people now roaming the earth. "Purpuric blotches of septi-caemia that resembles blood blisters."

"My God," Mary Ellen whispered as her hand went to her mouth.

Riley flipped to the last page to reveal a leg entirely covered in the purplish rash. "Extensive purpuric areas are usually called purpura fulminans, if left untreated it can lead to gangrene," Riley said.

There was an extended moment of silence as they all digested the information she had just given them. "Ok, so meningitis has a lot of the same symptoms as the ones we are seeing in some of those people, but it doesn't make people attack other people," Xander finally said.

"I was just showing you all of this first, but there is more. Many of the symptoms of encephalitis are similar to meningitis. Fever, headache, confusion, and like meningitis it can be caused by a virus or bacteria. One of the viral forms is rabies..."

"But this isn't transmitted by a bite," Bobby interrupted. "Xander already proved that."

"Just bear with me for a minute," Riley said as she flipped through the pages of the notepad. "Besides there are *many* ways a virus can be transmitted from one person to another, it's not just a bite. Another form of encephalitis is encephalitis lethargica. The disease attacks the brain, leaving some victims speechless and motionless. It caused an epidemic from nineteen eighteen to nineteen thirty. The ones who survived sank into a semi-conscious state lasting for decades. The survivors were revived with L-Dopa in the nineteen sixties."

"I don't see what that has to do with anything," John said, but he still leaned forward, completely riveted on Riley's words.

"The Lost Souls," Al said in a voice filled with dawning realization. "That's what you think they might have."

"Something like it," Riley said. "There is an illness called meningoencephalitis that is a combination of meningitis and encephalitis, and I think that's what these people are suffering from. Not the common form, not what's written about in textbooks, but a mutated form that's causing them to turn into what amounts to different kinds of zombies."

Riley dropped her notepad as she leaned forward. "Do you remember what Lee said in the hotel room, about people who believed global warming may be releasing new viruses from the earth that have been trapped for thousands of years? There are some people who believed one of those ancient viruses could be the reason for the increase in autism?"

Xander glanced at the others as he waited for their answers. "I remember," Carl said as he reemerged from the stacks.

"It all makes sense." Al pierced Xander with his gaze. "We're not entirely sure if your leg was just infected, if you became sick, or if it was the bite that caused you to fall ill."

"What are you talking about?" Xander demanded as he sat up in his chair.

"When you guys left to try and get supplies from the grocery store, we were discussing it. I had completely forgotten about it until now, but Riley how do you treat meningitis?"

"Ah..." her hand was shaking a little as she pulled the book back over to her and began to flip through the pages. "A combination of broad spectrum antibiotics and steroids if caught early enough, otherwise things get ugly. Encephalitis is treated symptomatically, but corticosteroids are used to reduce swelling in the brain and inflammation."

"What are broad spectrum antibiotics?" John inquired.

Al held his finger up as he began to flip through his book again. "It is an antibiotic used to treat a greater range of bacteria than more specific antibiotics. Some types of broad spectrum antibiotics are penicillin, amoxicillin, ampicillin..."

Mary Ellen's sharp inhale stopped Al before he could go through the whole list of medicines. "We gave Xander a high dosage of ampicillin and prednisone, which is a steroid."

Riley's hand seized hold of his and squeezed it. He couldn't stop himself from looking down at his chest again as Carol's words drifted back to him. *Was* there something twisting around inside of him?

But that made no sense, he felt fine, and if it had been the sickness, or something that had entered him from the bite, they seemed to have given him the right combination of medications to knock out whatever it was. He began to doubt it had simply been the infection that had made him so sick, but he knew there was no sickness left inside of him, not anymore.

"So what you're saying is we could still become infected by a bite?" John asked.

"Yes," Al answered.

"But Lee would have been vaccinated against meningitis? I had to be before I could go to college," Xander said.

"I've been vaccinated too," Bobby said.

"Same here," John told them.

"Yes, but vaccines don't always work, and if this is some kind of super mutated form of meningoencephalitis that has been trapped for thousands of years, then there is no way to be vaccinated against it," Riley said.

"This has just been a barrel of fun," John muttered as he leaned back in his chair and folded his arms over his chest.

"There is some good news in this," Al told him. "We may be able to help some of the sick ones. I think some of them may be too far gone, their bodies too ravished, and their brains too rotten, but The Lost Souls, the ones just roaming aimlessly around may be savable. We have to find L-Dopa, and we are definitely going to need to try and stock up on these antibiotics and steroids. We can survive a bite, if it is transmitted that way, and we may be able to fend off the sickness if we get it. The others, the really sick ones, they may just die off, and they may start doing so soon."

Xander didn't like wishing for anyone to die, but he also didn't want to have to deal with those things ever again if he could help it. He wasn't entirely sure Al was right about them just dying off though. They looked gross, they acted completely inhuman, but their movements and their thought processes led him to believe they were far healthier than they appeared to be.

"Maybe," he said.

"*If* we find the medicine for it," Peter finally spoke. "and *if* we can find these medicines why would we share them with people we don't know?"

Xander frowned at Peter's words, he actually made a good point, but it wasn't one he agreed with. "I think we're safe from the initial wave of sickness. We must have a natural immunity to it, or our bodies have been able to fight it off. If we can reawaken The Lost Souls, we'll have more people, and we'll be better able to fight off the more rabid ones," Al said.

"We'll also have more people vying for our food," Peter said as his feet hit the floor. "If you somehow manage to save more people you're risking our limited food supply."

Something tickled at the edge of Xander's mind as he stared at the teacher. Shadows played over Peter's face in a way that reminded him of the creepy fortuneteller machines, with the fake wizard inside you could sometimes find at a county fair. The fevered gleam in Peter's eyes made the maniacal laugh the wizards emitted, upon spitting out their predictions, sound in his head.

Xander's gaze slid to Riley beside him. He pulled her a little closer as his other hand fell to the gun at his waist. "If there's something we can do for them, then we have to do it," John said.

"Do you honestly think there is anything you can *do* for those people?" Peter demanded. "Half of them are eating anything they can get their hands on, and the other half are eating their *own* hair and flesh. Do you think they *want* to be saved? Would *you*?"

It was a fair enough question, and Xander pondered it as once again the library became unnaturally still. "Yes," he finally answered as his thumb brushed over the back of Riley's knuckles. "Yes, if there was something that someone could do for me, I *would* choose to be saved. Life, no matter how difficult and awful, is something I would choose to have."

Peter's eyes seemed as empty as deep space as he pinned Xander with his gaze. "There is also survival of the fittest, and only the strong survive. Right now they're occupied with eating themselves or simply starving to death. If you succeeded in reviving them, you're creating more enemies for us; more people we will have to worry about and possibly fight with."

"But, they're people," Riley said softly.

"They're a threat."

"Ok wait," Al said as he rose to his feet. "First of all, there is no guarantee we'd be able to find any L-Dopa, let alone know if it would actually work. There is no reason to fight over a purely hypothetical situation. If an opportunity happens to arise in the future we can discuss it then, but it's pointless to do so now."

Peter's eyes darted over them before finally settling on Al again. "You're right, but let's keep it hypothetical," he muttered before retreating behind the desk.

Al remained standing for a minute before sliding into his chair once more. Xander wanted to say something, but he was aware Peter's eyes were still focused on them. He got the same impression from the others as they shifted awkwardly and ruffled some paper. Carl remained standing, his arms folded over his chest. Shadowed by the brim of his hat, his eyes were riveted upon Peter.

"We *will* help them," John said under his breath.

"Shh," Carl hushed him.

"Let's make a list of all the medicines that would work. That way if we run across them we'll know which ones to take," Al suggested as the extended silence began to stretch awkwardly.

"Sounds like a good idea," Riley said.

Riley switched to a new page in the notepad and began to write as Al listed the antibiotics. Xander tried not to be obvious about it, but his gaze was repeatedly drawn back to Peter as the teacher's eyes remained riveted upon them. He became increasingly convinced whatever was going on with Peter was what Carol had been trying to warn him about.

CHAPTER 19

John

JOHN PLACED the last of the books into the trunk of the Cadillac. He'd purposely set the first aid book on top of the pile, if recent events were any indication it was the one they would end up using the most. He stared at it, wondering if it would help them if something really bad were to happen again. He noiselessly closed the lid of the trunk and rested his fingers against it. He knew it wasn't a matter of *if* something bad were to happen again, but *when*.

His gaze drifted back to the propped open library door as Riley shuffled out with an armload of blankets. He hurried to help her before she tripped over the edge of the blanket and ended up needing the first aid book before they pulled out of the parking lot.

Xander and Carl were standing at the back of the truck keeping watch when John and Riley approached them with the blankets. "Almost ready to go?" Carl asked.

"Almost," Riley answered.

Al and Mary Ellen appeared in the doorway next with Rochelle close on Mary Ellen's heels. "Where's Peter?" Carl asked Al.

"Heading for the bathrooms with Bobby, Josh, and Donald the last time I saw him," Al answered.

"Maybe we should just leave him," John muttered.

Riley shot him a fierce look before she tossed the blankets into the back of the truck. "We're not leaving Bobby," she told him forcefully.

"No, of course not," John assured her. "But that guy is really starting to creep me out."

"Which is why he's probably attached himself to the others," Carl said. "I think he suspects some of us have become not so fond of him."

Al glanced between them before turning to look at the library. "Maybe he is a little more unstable than I'd originally thought," he said as he rubbed at the gray stubble lining his jaw.

"He's more unstable than all of the Looney Tunes combined," John told him.

Carl adjusted his stance to look over at the library doors. John searched the deserted town, but the only movement he saw was a scrap of newspaper blowing across the street before catching on a small elm tree beside the road. In his head he could hear really bad horror movie music playing as he studied the motionless windows of the buildings surrounding them. *Where had they all gone?*

"Are you going to continue to ride in the car with him?" Carl asked Mary Ellen.

"Rochelle, put this stuff in the car," Mary Ellen said as she handed her daughter a bag of food supplies.

Rochelle's face scrunched up, she hesitated as she glanced around at them, but when no one else spoke she turned and walked over to the car. "She's a tough kid," John said.

"I know she is," Mary Ellen told him as she turned back to the others. "And I'm sure she suspects, or knows, most of what went on between her father and I, but her father is dead, and I'm not about to say anything bad about him in front of her."

John frowned as he leaned against the truck. "What does her father have to do with anything?" Riley asked.

Mary Ellen glanced over her shoulder to make sure Rochelle was out of hearing before she turned back to them. "I spent all of my adult life afraid of Larry, and trying to figure out a way to escape him, but he's gone now. I refuse to be scared of anyone who isn't trying to eat me anymore, and I'm not going to back down from anyone."

John shifted uncomfortably and looked around at the others. He knew not all relationships were great, knew how awful some of them could be. Even his parents, who had been deeply in love with each other, had been tempted to kill each other a time or two. But his mother had never been frightened of his father; he would have put money on the fact his father had been more afraid of his mother when she was in a mood, but then John had been too. His mom had been as sweet as pie most of the time, but cross her and she was scarier than an ogre guarding a bridge.

"I'd still prefer if you rode in the truck," Carl said. "I don't trust him."

"I don't either," Mary Ellen admitted. "But no, I'm staying in the car. I'd like Rochelle to stay with you though."

"This isn't the same as Larry, Mary Ellen. This is a man who might very well be spiraling into madness due to what is going on around him," Al said.

"You're right it's not the same. Larry was an ass at heart, but Peter was a good man once, or at least he seemed to be when we first met him. Peter may be cracking under the pressure, or he may simply need some time to get his act together again. I'm not willing to give up on him though, not yet."

She was a better person then he was, John decided. He wouldn't ride in the car with that guy or be anywhere *near* him if he had the choice. After last night, he pretty much considered Peter a lost cause. He didn't know what was going to happen with Peter if they ever did find some L-Dopa. He did know *he* wasn't going to let people die if they might be able to save them.

"Can we at least agree if we find something that could help people we are going to use it?" John asked.

Carl stepped forward as Peter and Donald emerged from the library. His hand moved toward the gun at his side before dropping down again. "We'll do what we can," Carl said briskly.

"Yes, we will," Xander agreed and stepped in front of Riley as Peter approached them.

Josh and Bobby followed behind the other two and joined them at the back of the truck. John glanced at the serene streets again before hitting the side of the truck. "Let's get out of here," he said. "Maybe we can make it out of Connecticut today."

"That would be good," Riley said.

John couldn't take his gaze away from Peter as the man covered his eyes against the harsh sun. Sensitivity to light was one of the symptoms, but as he studied Peter's haggard features he didn't see any of the other symptoms on the man. It wasn't sickness affecting him, John was certain of that.

He tore his attention away from Peter as Rochelle arrived at his side. Grabbing the handle of the passenger door, he pulled it open and waited for her to hop inside. He climbed in beside her and slammed the door closed. He grabbed the bag of Twizzlers off the dash, pulled one out and bit into it. The familiar taste of the much loved licorice didn't relax him as he braced his foot on the dashboard.

"You guys really don't like Peter, do you?" Rochelle asked as she snatched the next Twizzler out of his hand.

John shot her a look but dug into the bag and grabbed another one. "We didn't say that."

"I'm not blind, and I'm certainly not stupid," she said. "There's a reason my mom doesn't want me in that car."

"Kid, you don't exactly smell like roses right now," John told her.

"I still smell better than you on your best day!" she retorted.

He grinned at her as he bit into his Twizzler. "You are a kid after my own heart."

She rolled her eyes at him. "You're not getting me off the topic."

"I didn't think I would. No, we're not very fond of Peter," he admitted to her.

Carl glanced over at him, but he didn't say anything as he drove around a tree blocking half the road. "Why not?" she asked.

John shrugged and looked to Carl for help, but Carl just shook his head. "This is all you."

"I'm not really sure; there's just something about him," he told her as he handed her another Twizzler. "He seemed like an ok guy in the beginning, but I think he may be a little off right now; it's probably just the pressure of everything going on."

"Yeah, I guess," she said. "I wish my mom wasn't in the car with him."

"She'll be fine," Carl assured her.

Rochelle didn't say anything more as she leaned back in the seat. Carl pulled into the parking lot of a small grocery store behind Xander and drove by the broken glass door. "What do you think?" Carl asked as he stopped the truck in front of one of the shattered windows.

"I'm not exactly a fan of grocery stores anymore," John said as he studied the glass littering the sidewalk and the shadowed interior of the store. *Is it worth it to go in there for a possible can of beans and some stale bread?* He wondered as he scanned the debris scattered across the sidewalk. There probably wasn't any beans or bread left anyway. "I doubt there's much we can get from in there."

"There could be something," Carl said.

There could be, it may only be a can of beans, but it was a can they didn't have. He was grabbing for the door when movement within the store froze his hand on the handle. A shadow flickered over the walls before moving with rapid speed toward the broken windows. Judging by the shadow, whatever was coming at them was on all fours as it ran forward. He really hoped it was a dog, but instinctively he already knew it wasn't.

His hand fell away from the handle as he reached up to lock the door. "There's someone inside."

Carl was shifting into drive as a person's head popped up over the window frame. His eyes were more bloodshot than an alcoholic on a bender for a month. His gaze searched over the vehicles before coming to a rest on the truck. "I think you had better drive," Rochelle said as she lowered her hands into her lap. "Now."

John couldn't agree more as mottled red hands, with broken fingernails, wrapped around the brick wall of the store. Blood seeped from the man's sliced palms as glass from the frame dug into them. The strange new human didn't seem to notice the blood as he lifted himself onto the wall and perched like a cat. That hideous rash had spread over the right side of his face, but the left side remained strangely untouched. It was like some sort of gruesome mask where one side displayed what had once been a healthy man, and the other revealed the monster he'd become.

The man's bloodshot eyes focused on him. For one prolonged minute, John was certain the Dr. Jekyll and Mr. Hyde across from him saw straight into his soul. That this man searched for something within John, for some answer John didn't have, or for some connection to his humanity that had been taken from him. John pressed his fingers against the window as he stared at the man across from him.

The man rose and leapt off of the wall. John's heart lurched into his throat as the man began to approach the truck at a loping run.

"Carl..." he started.

The truck surged forward as Carl finally hit the gas. Xander had already moved the car and was driving out of the parking lot when they caught up to him. John looked in the mirror at the Caddy Donald now drove. The man who had emerged from the grocery store charged at the car, but Donald managed to swerve around him. John winced as the man threw himself forward and bounced across the parking lot before rolling to his feet and continuing to chase after the car.

"Damn," John muttered as he bit into his Twizzler again. "They're definitely persistent lunatics."

"I really hope this cabin is going to be safe," Rochelle whispered. "It would be wonderful to simply just be for a little bit, to have a roof over our heads, and a place to lie down."

"That sounds better than sitting on a beach with a rum drink in my hand," John confirmed.

"I think I might make myself a rum drink when we get there," Carl said.

"Make that two," John told him. "With an umbrella."

Carl offered him a listless smile as he drove onto the sidewalk and down a few front lawns to avoid some toppled poles and wires. "Sounds yummy," Rochelle said.

"Stick to the Twizzlers kid," John told her as he handed her the bag.

She frowned at him but took the bag. "My teeth are going to fall out."

"It's a good possibility."

He leaned back in the seat to take in the passing scenery. It was nice not to see the complete destruction in this town that had been waged throughout Massachusetts. Smoke curled on the horizon, but it didn't look like it was a raging inferno, and they were heading in the opposite direction of the smoke. At first he was so focused on the blaze in the mirror, he didn't realize the scenery around them had begun to change. He frowned and sat up straighter as they turned onto another street in what had only minutes ago been a completely lifeless town.

They drove by the burnt remains of a few homes. What looked like a massive airplane engine was lying on top of one of the homes with its tail in the side yard. A few seats had been scattered across front yards and in the middle of the road. "Is that a plane?" Rochelle inquired.

"It was," he confirmed.

Rochelle shook her head and dropped the bag of candy on the dashboard. The neighborhood around them didn't have the same devastation wrought on a lot of the neighborhoods in Massachusetts, but the atmosphere had definitely changed since they'd left the library. The front doors on most of the homes were open, and the windows had been busted out of most of them. Blankets, shoes, clothes, some chairs, and a few TV's were scattered across the front yards in a haphazard manner.

"I'd say these homes have been picked through pretty thorough-ly," Carl said.

"Were we planning on stopping?" John asked.

"Not unless we have to."

John rested his head against the window as they passed by an old Victorian with a pile of photos tossed onto the porch. "It just seems so wrong," Rochelle said. "These were people's things."

"It is wrong," John agreed. "But then nothing much is right anymore."

John frowned at the baby doll and teddy bear lying in the middle of the front walk leading to a small colonial. A crib had been tossed out behind the toys. "Why did they throw all of the stuff outside?" she asked.

"I don't know," John answered.

"Do you think it was people searching for supplies, or those sick, rabid humans?"

"I don't know," John said again. Though he suspected it had been the sick humans. There was no reason why a normally func-tioning human being would cause this much destruction, or put so much effort into throwing everything outside. He didn't know why the sick ones would do this, what thought processes had driven them to this, and he didn't want to ever find out. He sensed anger here though, or frustration. Maybe they'd been missing what they'd once had and were taking it out on the possessions that had been a part of their everyday lives.

It all seemed so surreal, like he was looking at photos of some war zone, but this war zone was just outside his window. He stared at the porch roof of a farmhouse with a mattress sitting on it as Carl turned onto another street. More debris littered the sidewalks and yards, but there was more than just people's possessions scat-tered about now.

There was also people's blood.

"I don't like this," John said as Xander began to slow down in front of them.

"Neither do I," Carl admitted.

John scanned the houses as he searched for an answer amongst the darkened homes. The more he searched though, the more questions he had and the less answers he found. He almost asked where the remains of the people who had left so much blood behind were, but he kept his mouth shut as Rochelle shuddered against his side. The answer to that question was made obvious as they turned onto another road, and the remains were clearly displayed for all to see.

He'd never known the human body could be decimated in such a way. Body parts were scattered on the grass, all over the porches, and across the road. He found himself holding his breath, unwilling to breathe in the stench he knew had to exist outside of the truck. Flies buzzed over the remains of what had to be at least a hundred bodies. Some birds and coyotes lifted their heads to look at them, but they quickly returned to their meals. Most of the remains had been picked down to the bone, but some still had flesh attached to them. His stomach turned at the sinew still stubbornly adhering to the bones.

Rochelle let out a small squeak; she drew her legs up onto the seat as Carl came to a stop behind Xander. The car idled before them, and then Xander put it in reverse and pulled up next to them. "I don't think you should roll the window down," John said.

"I can't tap out Morse code on the glass," Carl told him.

He was right, but John watched him roll down the window with dread. His hand went to his nose as the humid, rot laden air poured into the truck. He'd smelled landfills in August that didn't smell as bad as the outside around them did right now. Rochelle groaned and pulled her shirt over her nose. John leaned over as Riley rolled down the passenger side window.

"Should we keep going?" Riley asked nervously. "Al said there's another route, but it goes through more populated areas."

Carl's fingers drummed on the steering wheel as the Caddy pulled up beside him. John braced himself for the wave of putrid air he knew was about to enter the truck before he rolled his window down. "What's going on?" Donald inquired.

"Al said there's another route, but it goes through more populated areas," John answered.

Donald glanced at the road before turning to look at him. "I don't know if that's a good idea," Mary Ellen said.

"Something did this to these people, most likely lots of someone's," John said.

Peter scowled at him but remained silent as Carl and Riley continued to speak. "I think we should try a different route," Donald said.

John agreed with him, but Carl was already rolling the driver's side window up. "We're going back," Carl said.

John wanted to feel relief at the opportunity to escape the mess before them, but he felt like a cornered dog, or worse, a herded sheep.

CHAPTER 20

Mary Ellen

DONALD WAS in the process of backing the car up when the truck came to an abrupt halt beside them. Donald seemed to have missed the fact the truck had stopped as he kept going for a few more feet. "What the hell?" Donald inquired as he stopped the car again.

The window rolled down; John's arm came out to wave them forward. On the other side of the truck, Xander began to move his car forward again too. Mary Ellen recoiled when Donald rolled his window down, but even with the window closed the stench of the air was enough to make her want to stop breathing.

"What's going on?" Donald asked.

John was pale as he looked down at them; sweat beaded across his brow and upper lip. "We're rethinking doubling back."

"Why?" Mary Ellen managed to choke out.

John glanced at the hideous scene before them before focusing on them again. "They set a trap in the grocery store. They waited for us, and they baited us, and then they almost killed us."

"What does that have to do with anything?" Peter asked as he sat forward.

He'd been staying relatively quiet and Mary Ellen far preferred it that way. "Doesn't it seem odd to you that we've discovered nothing until now, and there is only one other way for us to go? It's like we're being herded, like sheep," John answered. "They *know* most people wouldn't drive through what is in front of us."

"What if that area is where they're living, and that's why there are so many remains?" Mary Ellen asked.

John swallowed heavily and brought his gun forth to rest it on the dashboard. "They're smart," he said. "*Really* smart. I don't see them letting anyone know where they're staying. I really believe they're trying to herd us."

"So we're going to go in there on your *belief*?" Peter asked incredulously.

John's nostrils flared as his jaw clenched. Mary Ellen saw Carl's hand seize hold of John's arm, but she couldn't see Carl. John looked away from them; the words they exchanged were muffled and lost to her. When John looked back at them, the lines in his forehead had cleared and his teeth weren't clamped together anymore. "No, I think we should go in there on what we *know* about these things."

"Jesus," Mary Ellen whispered and looked back at the neighborhood before them. It looked as if a bomb had gone off. She would have assumed the bodies were from the burned remains of the plane, but none of them were charred. It wouldn't have surprised her if some of the bodies had been flung from the wreckage before the fire had claimed it, but not this many of them.

When she looked closer, something she really did *not* want to do, she saw *none* of the bodies had any burns on them.

"I'm almost certain if we go back we'll be doing exactly what they planned for us to do," John continued.

Mary Ellen liked John, she really did, but she wasn't sure she was willing to put her life, and her daughter's life, in his hands. But then, Carl and John had gotten Rochelle to her in the first place. That was more than she ever could have asked for, from anyone. "Ok," she said.

"Ok what?" Peter inquired from the back.

"Ok, let's go. I trust you, John."

"Are you out of your mind?" Peter demanded.

"No," Mary Ellen answered. "I think he's right. The bodies of the sick are deteriorating, or at least they appear to be, but they're still able to reason."

"It's twisted their minds as much as their bodies," Donald muttered.

"Exactly," Mary Ellen said.

"Onward then," John said.

"The others?" Josh asked.

John looked away from them and said something to Carl before turning back to them. "They're ready to go forward."

She bet they were as thrilled by this option as she was, but she didn't say anything as Donald pushed the window button up. The closed window did little to block the odor from outside. Mary Ellen pulled her shirt over her nose, but a hundred floral scented air fresheners wouldn't have stopped that aroma.

"I hope he's right," she said as Donald drove onto the sidewalk in order to avoid running over a torso lying in the road.

A shiver slid up her spine; her eyes closed as she briefly tried to block out the carnage surrounding them. Opening her eyes, she grabbed hold of the armrest and searched the homes for any sign of movement.

When she was seven she'd watched a horror movie that had the spider the size of a school bus in it. The spider had encased an entire town. The people of the town had been trapped inside as the spider's legs worked to spin its silken web around the people it gradually turned to liquid in order to feed off of them.

It had given her nightmares for weeks, and she still despised spiders because of it. Her parents had become fed up with being awoken in the middle of the night by her screams. For the last week she had stayed awake, alone and shaking in her bed, as no one came to make sure she was ok. It had been the first time she'd realized she couldn't always count on them, and over the years their aloofness to her had only served to reinforce that realization.

Driving through this town now, she could almost see it encased within a snow globe like structure with a giant tarantula perched over top of it. She knew it wasn't possible, but she was certain bits of web were going to start floating down to ensnare them all. A shudder rocked through her; she couldn't stop herself from wrapping her arms around her middle as she tilted her head back to look at the red sky.

She was certain those people were out there, biding their time, waiting to spring on them and drain them dry just like that spider.

Mary Ellen sat up and braced her hand on the dash as she placed her gun in her lap. She was tempted to stick it in the glove box; she was certain she would shoot at the first thing that jumped out at them, but she felt safer with it nearby. A house burned in the distance and when they got closer, Mary Ellen spotted a few bodies on the flames.

"Those people are absolutely crazy," Josh said.

"What if it wasn't the sick people?" Donald inquired.

"What do you mean?" Mary Ellen asked nervously.

"I mean John thought it was the sick people trying to divert us somewhere else, but we haven't seen *any* residents of this town."

"I think we're seeing some of them now," Peter retorted. "Or at least what's *left* of them."

Mary Ellen's hand tightened on the gun. "There are way more inhabitants of this town than the bodies we're seeing around us right now. I mean this is a fairly large town, with a lot of homes in it," Donald said.

"So you think normal people did this?" Mary Ellen felt nauseated by the thought.

"Maybe."

"Holy crap," Josh said as he sat back in his seat and folded his arms over his chest.

"Why would they?" Mary Ellen asked.

"As a deterrent to other humans, and as a food supply to keep those things occupied for a while," Donald answered.

Mary Ellen didn't mean to, but her head tilted back to search for a spider descending upon them. She shifted uncomfortably in her seat and pulled at the shirt hugging her damp skin. She'd kill for a cool pool, and a glass of iced tea right now, but all she thought she was actually going to get was pounced upon at any second.

She glanced nervously at the truck as she wondered how Rochelle was holding up. Maybe she'd made the wrong choice by separating from her daughter, but she'd meant what she'd said earlier, she wasn't going to back down from anyone ever again, including Peter.

The houses faded away as a large meadow, one the size of a couple of football fields, appeared on her right. An eight foot high, black wrought iron fence ran all the way around the property.

Three large brick buildings were in the center of the field. There were other smaller buildings set up on the estate, one of which was a greenhouse. It took her a second to realize the ivy covered brick buildings were a school, and some of the other buildings were the dorms. The gate in the center of the cobblestone road leading to the buildings was closed. Behind the gate, she spotted at least a hundred people patrolling the property with weapons at the ready. There were more people moving about by the school.

"Guess that answers the question of what happened to the townspeople," Donald said.

"Did they do that to those people back there?" Josh asked in disbelief.

Mary Ellen studied the men and women gathered behind the immense fence. Her eyes narrowed as she strained to read a plaque on the front of a large boulder. It read, *Camden Preparatory School established eighteen hundred ninety-six.*

"I don't think so," Mary Ellen said.

"What are they doing?" Peter demanded.

Mary Ellen tore her attention away from the people behind the gate to focus on the truck pulling into the drive. She sat straighter in her seat as a few guns swung in their direction from behind the gate. "I don't know," she whispered as the truck stopped before the gate. Xander backed the car up and pulled up beside them.

Riley started to roll down the window, but when Carl stepped out of the truck, Donald drove the car forward and parked beside the truck. Mary Ellen hastily rolled down the window. "What are you doing?" she demanded in a low hiss.

Carl's eyes were indecipherable beneath the rim of his battered hat. "Just going to ask some questions. They might know if we should go forward or turn back."

An uneasy feeling settled in her stomach as she opened the

door and climbed out. They'd gone out of their way to avoid people, but now Carl was going to walk right up to that gate and question them. She looked around but saw nothing other than the distant remains of the massacre they had just left behind. Riley and Xander stepped out of the car too. No one else moved as more guns swung in their direction.

Mary Ellen stayed close to the car as she surveyed the people approaching the gate. "We mean no harm," Carl said as he held his hands up at his sides.

"We're not taking in any stragglers," a man with a rifle pointed at Carl's chest informed him.

Mary Ellen's heart beat accelerated as she looked from the tip of the rifle, to Carl, and back again. It could all be over in a second, and they'd have no chance to defend themselves. She trusted Carl knew what he was doing as he continued to hold his hands out at his sides and stopped before the gate. She focused on the foot-long spikes sticking up from the fence and shuddered. All she could think of was Dracula impaling his victims, and she half expected to see bodies hanging from the wicked looking spikes.

"We're not looking to be taken in," Carl assured him. "I just have some questions."

The man seemed to relax a little, but he didn't move the gun away from Carl's chest. "Ask."

"What happened back there?" Carl inquired.

From within the crowd a woman began to weep. Mary Ellen's heart went out to her as another woman wrapped her arms around the crying woman and pulled her away from the gates. Mary Ellen's gaze drifted back to the street they had just left behind. The woman's reaction put an end to any questions that it may have been the townspeople who had slaughtered those people. The man shook his head; it was a middle-aged woman who answered the question.

"People, or at least at one time they were people. Now they're just monsters."

Carl nodded and gradually lowered his hands to his sides. "Are the sick people gone?"

"They're never gone," another woman answered. "They always come back."

"Sometimes they get back in," a young boy whispered from behind his father's back.

Mary Ellen wrapped her arms around herself. She wanted to hug Rochelle to her, but her daughter remained in the truck with John. "Are they ahead of us?" Carl asked.

"They're everywhere," another man said. "but we have no way of knowing exactly where."

Carl nodded. "Do you know anything, did anyone come through here? Like the military?"

"No," the man with the rifle answered and finally lowered it away from Carl's chest. "We've seen no one since the quakes started and the sickness spread."

"You don't have the same amount of damage we had in Massachusetts," Carl told him and lifted his hat to wipe the sweat from his brow. "It was just… it was a disaster through there."

The man nodded and glanced at the vehicles outside the gate. "I'm sorry to hear that. The sickness was the worst here. It took so many, so quickly, and what it turned them into…" his voice trailed off as his gaze drifted toward the mess down the street.

"I know, we've seen it too," Carl said. "Thank you."

Another man stepped forward and whispered something in the first man's ear. He nodded before focusing on Carl again. "If you'd like you can come in for a little bit, maybe stay the night."

Carl shook his head. "Thank you, but we should move on."

The man turned back to him. "Good luck out there."

"Good luck in there," Carl told him and moved away from the gate.

"Maybe we should stay," Mary Ellen said.

Carl shook his head and looked back toward the gates. "It's only a matter of time before the sick ones try to overrun them. It's probably better if we get into less populated areas if we can."

"He's right," Peter said. "Besides who do you think those people in there will feed to those things first the next time they break in? Their neighbors or the strangers they took in for the night?"

Mary Ellen shuddered at the thought as Donald turned to stare at Peter in disbelief. "You're very cynical."

"I'm practical," Peter retorted. "It would serve you all better if you were the same way."

Mary Ellen didn't know how to respond so she focused on Carl again. "Are we going to keep going?"

Carl tore his gaze away from Peter as he looked back at her. "I don't think we have any other choice. I really think John's right about them trying to herd us somewhere. You didn't see them in the grocery store; they're cunning. More cunning than us I think." That certainly wasn't a comforting realization. "Or at least we don't know how to think like cannibalistic madmen."

"Let's hope we never do either," Mary Ellen said before slipping back into the car.

She closed the door as Donald shifted into reverse and pulled out before the truck began to move. Peter sat back in his seat and folded his arms over his chest as he stared out the window. The homes gave way, the bodies became fewer and farther between as warehouses and stores rose up around them. She was beginning to feel a little claustrophobic as she stared at the brick buildings looming over them.

"This is bull, we should have gone back," Peter muttered from the backseat.

"We've managed to stay alive so far, I think we'll be ok," Mary Ellen said, but she wasn't sure she believed it as she said it.

Carl made a right onto another road leading them through more warehouses. She thought she saw some movement in one of the windows, but when she turned to look there was nothing there. That didn't mean anything; she'd seen how fast those things could move. Her hands fisted on her thighs as they drove across an overpass.

Beneath the overpass railroad tracks crisscrossed the land. When the car made it to the middle of the bridge, she spotted some of *those* people sitting on the tracks, picking at their skin and hair. Most of them didn't acknowledge the presence of the vehicles, but a girl, no older than six or seven, turned her head to look up at them. The shadows under her eyes made them appear twice as large as the girl idly pulled at her hair. Watching them, Mary Ellen knew why Al called them The Lost Souls; there seemed to be nothing within them anymore.

Mary Ellen didn't realize she was crying until Donald rested his hand on her arm. "Are you ok?"

She swallowed heavily and wiped at her eyes. "I'm fine."

He nodded and released her arm. Mary Ellen focused on the back of the truck as they passed by a new town sign lying on the side of the road. She couldn't read what it said, but then she doubted it mattered anymore as long as they kept moving forward. She unfolded her hands and wiped them on her jeans as sweat trickled continuously down her back.

Xander pulled into a gas station a few miles down the road and parked the car. Glass from the door lay on the sidewalk, and there were a couple of candy bars with chocolate oozing from their wrappers sitting on top of the ice machine. Mary Ellen stepped out of the car and eyed the building as she leaned against the door.

"Thought we could use a break," Xander said as he stretched.

Her bladder sure could use one she thought as she eyed the building. "I'm not going in there first," John said as he leaned against the truck.

"Absolutely not," Riley agreed.

Mary Ellen moved away from the car and cautiously approached the building close on Carl and Xander's heels. She stepped over a crushed bag of chips as she followed them into the shadowed interior of the store. Little remained inside; her eyes found the restroom almost immediately. It took all she had not to bolt for it, but she hung back as Carl and Xander went through the store.

Xander pushed the bathroom door open and shone his flashlight inside it. He nodded to her before continuing down another aisle. Mary Ellen hurried toward the bathroom and slipped inside. Her hand fumbled for the flashlight at her side and she turned it on. She hurried about the small, surprisingly clean room.

A small thud brought her head up; she stared at her reflection in the mirror above the sink as she strained to hear anything more. Another thud drew her attention to the left and the concrete wall at the back of the room. The sound of three loud raps on her right caused a small squeak to escape her as she jumped. Her flashlight spun around the white room as she accidentally knocked it from the sink.

She bent, grabbed the light from the floor and hastily retreated to the bathroom door. Rochelle was waiting impatiently on the other side as she danced from one foot to the other. She grabbed her daughter before she could go into the bathroom. "Wait," she said more harshly than she had intended.

John looked up from where he had been flipping through a magazine. "What is it?" he inquired.

"There's someone behind the building."

The others all turned to her before focusing on the wall behind her.

CHAPTER 21

Riley

RILEY STEPPED around the back of the garage with her gun raised. She'd been expecting to find some of the sick humans back there and was prepared to start shooting, but what she saw instead stopped her dead in her tracks. Her hand wavered on the gun. She'd gone through a hundred scenarios in her head about what would be waiting for them behind the building; none of them had prepared her for what was actually there.

A single man was hanging from a rope draped over the side of the building. His body was blowing in the breeze, bumping against the side of the building as he swung back and forth. Behind the body the words 'End of Days,' had been sprayed in red paint on the concrete wall. The sight of those words caused a cold sweat to break out on her body. Goose bumps slid over her skin as she took an instinctive step back from the building. A few feet away from the body was a stepladder knocked onto its side and a discarded spray paint can.

Riley lowered her gun as the body spun toward them again. Bits of cheekbone and skull could be seen through the skin already peeled away from the bone. The man looked as if he'd been dead for a week, but it had probably been less time than that. She walked wide of the man and the building, her eyes following the rope as it slid over the top of the wall and onto the roof. The top of the rope disappeared until the she spotted a satellite dish on the roof and noticed the other end of the rope tied to its base.

She cursed under her breath as she ran a hand through her hair and shook her head. Suicide was something she would never understand. "I'll go let the others know it's safe," Bobby said and promptly turned away from the man swaying back and forth like some kind of demented wind chime.

"I can't believe that satellite held up," John said as he turned to survey the landscape.

Riley opened her mouth to respond, but John let out a low curse as his breath hissed out of him. She spun to confront whatever threat might be coming at them. Instead, she was faced with a display even more bizarre than the body swaying in the breeze behind the building.

A field spread out behind the gas station. Brown fencing surrounded the field, creating a pasture for animals to graze in. Not entirely sure what she was doing, Riley took a step forward to survey the mound in the corner of the field. "What is that?" she inquired.

"Horses," Carl answered in a gravelly voice.

"Horses?" Xander asked in disbelief.

"Yes. We saw something like this before we met up with you guys."

"What happened to them?" Riley asked.

Carl shook his head as he fished out a cigarette. "I have no idea. I'd thought it was a onetime fluke thing, that maybe the quakes had scared them into running over top of each other." He paused as he lit his cigarette and inhaled deeply. "There were more of them then; it looks like there are only a few of them over there though."

Riley swallowed heavily and rubbed at the back of her neck as she studied the large animals. "They still could have been confused by the quakes. This area may not have been as badly affected, but there's still damage, and the ground still shook."

"I guess," John said.

The banging against the building increased as a breeze blew her hair forward. She tucked the loose strands behind her ear and tilted her head back to take in the towering black clouds rolling across the sky. Heat lightning zigzagged in a crazy pattern that lit the clouds and turned the red sky pink.

She took an instinctive step back as the hair on her arms stood on end from the electrical current in the air. "There's another storm coming in."

"Wonderful, just what we need." Carl pulled the cigarette from his mouth and stomped it into the ground. "We should check out the house; there may be supplies in there, and it will be a more comfortable place to stay than the gas station."

"We also don't know what may be hiding in it," John said.

"True, but do you want to sleep on the floor of a gas station with busted out windows and doors?"

"I *want* to sleep in my own bed; since that's not going to happen, I would definitely prefer someone else's over a store that will be difficult to defend."

"We'll get the others and drive across the field," Carl said as he turned back to the store.

It took only a few minutes to get everyone organized and into the vehicles. Riley forced herself not to look at the mound of dead animals as Bobby drove around the fences toward the red farmhouse just beyond the pasture. The clouds were closing in on them when she pulled up in front of the steps of the farmer's porch.

Riley climbed out of the car and rested her hand holding the gun on top of the roof. A cheerful yellow porch swing creaked as it swung back and forth in the steadily stronger wind blowing across the land. Riley couldn't tear her gaze away from the front door as the screen door rattled and bumped within its frame.

She approached the porch with Xander, John, Carl, and Donald. They had decided at the gas station the others would stay with the vehicles in case they had to make a fast retreat. Al was now behind the wheel of the truck; he was leaning forward to peer up at the sky as she walked past him. His watery blue eyes met hers, and for one surreal moment Riley felt as if the whole world slowed down. The air had become like a wet blanket around her, trying to hinder her progress as she attempted to move forward.

The wind whipping around her broke her free of the strange sensation as a loud bang rent the air. She jumped and swung her gun up as she braced herself for a bullet to hit her before she had a chance to find her prey. "Easy, it's just the swing," Xander told her.

Feeling like an idiot, she lowered the gun as the swing crashed against the side of the house again. Carl climbed onto the porch and grabbed hold of the swing. "Help me take this down; I'm not going to be distracted by this thing the entire time we're inside."

John stepped forward and held the swing as Carl stood on his tiptoes to pull the chain from the hook set in the roof of the porch. Xander pulled the other side free, and the three of them placed the swing onto the porch. Riley tried to peer into the downstairs window but all she could make out was the arm of a sofa and a small table with a lamp on it.

"What do we do if someone is in there?" she had to raise her voice to be heard over the growing wind.

"Try not to get shot," John, replied.

That was one of the least comforting statements she'd ever heard, but she followed him to the front door. Carl stepped forward and tugged at the screen door, but it remained locked. Carl looked toward the windows.

"The inner door is probably locked too. We can break open this screen door but we're going to have to bust down the other one; that will just leave us vulnerable again. Going through the window would be the better option."

"Whoever climbs through it will be vulnerable," Riley said.

Carl nodded. "I'll go through, it will be fine. I think if someone was in there they'd already be shouting at us to get away."

"Like we'd hear anything over this wind," John said.

Carl was already approaching the window. He turned his gun around and used the butt of it to smash out the glass. Riley stepped back from the shards falling around them as Carl pulled the remaining pieces free of the frame and tossed them aside. He flicked on his flashlight and peered into the home.

"I don't see anything," he said and exchanged the flashlight for his gun.

"Wait, I'll go," John said before Carl could climb inside. "I'm faster than you."

"You'll trip over the sill and shoot yourself," Carl told him. Riley had to bite her lip to keep from laughing. If the look on John's face was any indication, he seemed to be contemplating the idea of shoving Carl through the window. "I'll be fine."

"Hope you fall," John told him as he took a step back.

Carl flipped him the finger before he disappeared into the house. Riley held her breath as she hurried back to the front door and waited for it to open. The seconds seemed to tick by at an excruciatingly slow pace. It seemed like hours, but probably wasn't a full minute before the inner door swung open. Carl flipped the lock on the screen door and opened it for them.

Riley stepped into the foyer as a bolt of lightning lit the small hallway. Pictures, knickknacks, and a coat rack were briefly visible until the white light faded back to black. Carl's beam moved over the walls as Riley pulled her flashlight out too. They passed by the small living room Carl had broken into and moved down the hall. A photo on the wall showed a man and woman in their early thirties. They were smiling as they stood before a lake in their wedding clothes. Riley felt a pang in her heart as she stared at their smiling faces.

She pushed the door open on a small half bath and closed it again when she saw it was empty. They passed by another door on their right. When Carl opened it she saw the rickety stairs disappearing into the cellar below. The scent of mildew was heavy as it washed over her and caused her nose to wrinkle.

Carl closed the door and pushed the lock on the knob in. "We'll search the house before going down there."

She wasn't going to argue with that. The last thing she wanted was to be trapped down there if something, or someone, was in the house with them. She followed John down the hall to the kitchen. Riley flashed her light over the top of the cabinets first to make sure one of the sick people wasn't up there, but the space above the cabinets was only a three-inch gap. John pulled a few cabinets open and gave a brief nod and thumbs up before closing them again. Riley walked back to the doorway and peered into the hall as Carl disappeared into the pantry. John and Donald explored the back porch while Xander joined her.

Carl emerged from the pantry with cans of vegetables in his hands. He dropped them onto the table before lifting his head to look at them. "These people would have taken food with them if they'd still been in their right minds or if they just packed up and left here. They may have already left home by the time the quakes hit though."

Riley really hoped that was what had happened as her hand tightened on her gun, and she looked to the stairs ahead of them. If those people *were* still here, and they were normal, they would have come out already. Using the back of her arm, she wiped the sweat from her brow. "Let's go," Xander said.

She stayed close behind him, her back against the wall as they climbed the stairs to the second floor. She was so focused on straining to see into the hallway above them, she didn't see the photo until her shoulder bumped into it. It crashed to the ground, and the glass shattered out of it.

John released a low curse and bent to grab the picture as it landed by his foot. A loud thump from somewhere upstairs froze him in mid-bend though. Riley's heart leapt into her throat, she found it difficult to breathe as she strained to see or hear anything else. Another small thud followed the first as something heavy clattered to the floor and broke.

She counted the seconds as she listened for more, but nothing followed the last heavy thump. Her heart was pounding so fast she wasn't sure she'd be able to hear anything over the staccato beat of it in her ears anyway. She started to grab hold of Xander when he took another step up the stairs, but she knew they had to go up there.

"Be careful," she whispered to him.

He didn't glance back at her as he gave a brief nod and continued onward. The carved muscles in his back and arms flexed with every step he took. Riley grabbed hold of the railing as she followed him up the stairs to the second floor. There were four doors off of the main landing; three of them were closed, but the other was open to reveal a small blue bathroom with a seashell shower curtain.

Carl pointed to the door at the end of the hall before pointing at the other two and then at Xander and Riley. He pointed to Donald and then to the spot where Donald was already standing. Riley nodded and followed Xander to the two doors closest to them as Carl and John went in the opposite direction. She glanced over her shoulder as Xander stopped outside of the first door and grabbed hold of the knob. Donald remained in the middle of the hall keeping watch as Carl and John stopped at the other door.

"Ready?" Xander asked.

She nodded and took a step back while he turned the knob and pushed the door open. Riley held her gun out before her with both hands as she stepped through the doorway behind Xander. She was really beginning to feel like a bad version of Charlie's Angels as she pointed her gun around the room. There was a single queen sized mattress with a blue bedspread. The bureau across from the bed had a small TV on top. No pictures decorated the wall, and when she pulled open the closet door, the only thing tucked inside were old boxes. She tugged the cover off of one to reveal an assortment of pictures, most of which were old Polaroid pictures of a young girl. Riley recognized the girl as the woman from the photos below.

She dropped the lid back over the box and stepped away. Rain began to pelt the windows in a battering assault that made her wonder if the siding would still be on the house in the morning.

Xander rose from where he had been inspecting under the bed and met her gaze as another bolt of lightning tore across the sky. The brief illumination highlighted the haggardness of his handsome features as he ran a hand through his disheveled hair.

He followed her out of the room. John and Carl were still in the room at the end of the hall, she could see the beams of their flash-lights bouncing over the walls and the large king size bed. Donald watched them as they stopped in front of the final door and Xander grabbed the knob. Riley entered the room like she had the last one, except the smell of this one knocked her back a step.

It was a brutal assault on her olfactory senses, but she couldn't cover her nose in order to block the smell if she was going to keep two hands on her gun. She'd smelled some pretty hideous things recently, but the strong odor of ammonia in this room made her eyes water. She had no idea what could have possibly created such a hideous stench.

Her gaze scanned over the large oak desk with a computer and papers on top of it. The wall was lined with pictures of a man accepting awards, fishing, golfing, and surrounded by his family and friends. There were a few pictures of a woman riding horses and standing proudly with her awards and ribbons. Trophies lined the wall behind the desk. She spotted a small golden golf club from one that had broken when it toppled to the floor. Her gaze scanned over the shelves as she searched for whatever had knocked the trophy from the shelf.

Xander stepped before her as something slid through the shadows on her right. Riley spun in that direction, she held her breath as she waited for the imminent attack to occur. A cat burst from the darkness, it gave a plaintive mewl as it raced past her legs and into the hall. Donald released a startled cry as he jumped back from the cat's onward rush.

A relieved laugh escaped her as she finally placed the scent of the room with the source. Moving further into the study, she stepped over cat feces and spotted the empty bowls in the corner. It seemed odd to her they had set up food and water bowls in the office. *Had they locked the cat in here for some reason, or had they always had bowls set up for it in here?* She wondered.

"Poor thing," she said softly.

"Almost gave me a heart attack," Xander said.

She picked up one of the papers on the desk and frowned at the words on it. It appeared to be a bunch of legal terms. Dropping it back on the desk, she looked toward the window as rain beat loudly against it. "It looks like they had a nice life here," she said.

"They did," Xander agreed as he stopped beside her. His fingers rested on the papers as he examined them. She leaned into the warmth he emitted, finding comfort in his solid, reassuring presence. "Come on let's go see what the others found."

Riley gathered the bowls in the corner and carried them out of the room. John and Carl were approaching the room when they stepped back into the hall. "Anything?" Riley asked.

"Nothing," Carl said. "You?"

"Just a cat, it took off down the hall."

"It was still alive?" John blurted.

"Probably not for much longer."

Riley searched for the cat as they made their way downstairs, but it seemed to have disappeared. "They must not have been home when the quakes hit," Carl said.

"Doesn't seem like it," Riley agreed. "But we should still search the basement."

"We will."

"Just let me get the cat some food and water." She returned to the kitchen and hurried to the sink to fill the small water bowl. She

placed the bowl on the floor as Xander handed her a bag of cat food. Shaking it out, she filled the bowl and placed it beside the other. She thought she spotted the cat retreating into the shadows at the end of the hallway, but she couldn't be sure as she followed the others to the locked basement.

Carl grabbed the knob and froze. "What's wrong?" John asked when the color drained from Carl's face.

Carl pulled his hand away and turned his head to search the hall. "The door is unlocked." It felt as if someone had just doused her with cold water as she took an abrupt step into the wall behind her. "We're not alone."

Riley brought the gun in front of her as her head turned to where she thought she'd seen the cat. A flash of lightning illuminated a set of eyes watching them from the shadows.

CHAPTER 22

Carl

CARL'S HEAD instinctively snapped back, his flashlight and gun both pointed at the ceiling. He fully expected someone to be perched over them, braced against the walls of the hall with their feet and hands. It was the only place he could think of for one to be. Lightning illuminated the hall; a clap of thunder shook the house so forcefully a picture fell to the floor.

The noise caused Donald to jump beside him. The lightning revealed nothing hanging above him waiting to pounce and tear into his flesh like a starving grizzly on a salmon. From the corner of his eye he saw Riley spin to the left with her gun raised. Carl cursed as he realized he'd looked in the wrong direction first.

Riley didn't shoot her gun though as the cat, rattled by the thunder, bolted out of the shadows and screeched its way into the kitchen. John cursed loudly and jumped back from the fleeing

animal. "Where are they?" Xander hissed as he turned toward the stairs.

Lightning lit the house again; it was immediately followed by a clap of thunder. Carl strained to hear or see anything over the rolling noise and blasts of light that made him feel like he was tripping on acid in some kind of insane disco. Something moved to his right; he spun in that direction as the bathroom door swung open. John already had his gun pointed at the bathroom. A flash of lightning made Carl think John had fired the gun, but Rochelle was still standing there with her mouth hanging open and her hands in the air. She'd jumped back as three guns pointed at her; the color had drained from her face so fast Carl was amazed she was still on her feet.

"No!" Mary Ellen screamed from where Carl had seen something move on his right.

Relief filled him as he realized just how lucky they were no one had shot the young girl. They were all too hyped up on adrenaline, too tired, and too unprepared for these kind of stresses on their bodies to react reasonably and on something more than just instinct.

"What are you doing here?" John shouted at Rochelle. John had turned his gun away from her, as had Donald and Riley, but none of them lowered their weapons. Carl continued to scan the hallway and stairs as he searched for something hunting them.

"I... I didn't get a chance to pee at the gas station; with the rain I just couldn't hold it anymore," Rochelle stammered out.

Mary Ellen hurried down the hall toward them and held her hand out for her daughter. Rochelle grabbed hold of her hand and stepped through the doorway. "Did you unlock the basement door?" Carl asked Rochelle.

"I looked down there," Mary Ellen told him. "But I didn't go down."

"Thank God," Riley said as she lowered her gun.

"We thought someone else was here," Carl explained at Mary Ellen's questioning glance. "You can go get the others; we're just going to check out the basement."

"Ok," Mary Ellen said as she pulled Rochelle further back.

"There's a cat in the house," Riley told her in between thunder claps. "If you see something running around it's just the cat, and it's terrified, so let the others know."

Mary Ellen nodded and pulled Rochelle toward the front door with her. She grabbed a coat from the coat rack and tugged it over her head before hurrying out to the front porch. Rochelle remained inside while Mary Ellen began to wave at the others. Carl didn't wait to see the others enter before he opened the basement door and shone his flashlight into the stairwell. He was surrounded by walls on both sides as he crept down the stairs. They could only go down one at a time in the narrow stairwell. At the bottom of the stairs were two doors, one to the left and the other to the right of him, both were closed.

Carl shifted his gun as he wiped the sweat from his brow. "Would you like to Inney Minney Miney Moe this one?" he asked John.

John was pressed close against his back, too close in the stifling heat of the basement. "We could always do some hot potato?" John responded tiredly.

Carl nodded and turned to the door on his right. "I say we just go this way."

"That works too."

Carl turned the handle and thrust the door open to shine his light into the room. Nothing moved as he stepped into the lower

level of the basement and examined the corners of the room. He spotted a boiler, a water heater, some boxes, a stationary bike, and a treadmill. Other lights ran over the ceiling and into the corners of the room. No cobwebs hung from the ceiling, and there was very little dust amongst the boxes and exercise equipment.

They all pushed back into the hall and up the stairs so he could move out of the room and into the hall. Carl shifted the gun in his hand and opened the door on his left. His beam played over a TV that had to be at least eighty inches, a bar, a sectional sofa, and more DVD's than he was sure were in the media section of a Wal-Mart.

John let out a low whistle as he stepped into the room behind him. "What did this guy do for a living?"

"He was a lawyer, I think," Riley answered. "And what makes you think he was the one supporting them? She could have been the one making all the money."

"Ok what did this *couple* do for a living?" John stressed.

"I don't know what she did," Riley admitted.

Carl suppressed a laugh as John scowled at her and stepped further into the room. Carl moved cautiously around the sofa and towards the bar. He eyed the bottles on the shelf as he edged around the bar and examined the space behind it.

"He had some good taste in movies," John said from the cabinets he was standing in front of with Riley and Xander.

Carl glanced at him before moving around the bar and toward a closet set off on the side. Donald had followed him toward the bar and was watching as Carl pulled the closet open. Carl couldn't help but release a low whistle at the four kegs, numerous cases, and bottles stacked within the vast walk-in closet.

"This guy was serious about his movies and booze apparently," he said as he closed the door on the closet. "That's more than most people consume in a lifetime."

Another loud clap of thunder shook the house, but the sound was muffled down here. He could hear the sound of footsteps crossing the floor though as the others entered. "So a drunken lawyer, not a bad life I suppose," John said. "He has every one of my favorite movies."

Riley reached forward and tugged something from the shelf. "Willy Wonka," she said.

"You and that movie," Xander said.

A wistful smile tugged at her lips as she slid it back into the empty slot. "What can I say, my first crush was on an Oompa Loompa."

"I would have thought Charlie, but good to know you appreciate the fake orange spray tan."

"I do."

"You and Carol knew every word of that movie. It was torture listening to it over and over again."

"I still know every word. I can sing you the songs if you'd like?" she asked.

"Not even a little bit," John said as he pulled another movie from the shelf.

"What do you have?" she demanded.

He turned the movie around and showed it to her. "The Goonies."

"Definitely a goodie," she agreed.

Carl and Donald were drawn forward as Xander pulled another movie down. It was such a strange thing to be doing right now, but it was something almost normal on top of a whole lot of *not* normal.

"Top Gun," Xander said.

Riley rolled her eyes and shook her head. "We also had to suffer through that one, Goose."

"I am definitely Maverick," he informed her.

"I actually always preferred Ice Man," she told him.

"No taste," Donald said as he tugged a movie free.

"What do you have?" John asked.

"The Neverending Story."

"I've never heard of that one," Riley said as she took the case from him and examined it.

"You would have been in for a real treat with it. I spent many hours of my childhood watching it over and over again," Donald told her.

"You liked it that much?" Xander asked as he took the case from Riley.

"It was the only thing I had to watch," Donald said as he took the movie back.

Carl sensed something behind Donald's words, but he didn't question him as he stepped forward and tugged a movie from the shelf. "What do you have?" A lot of the care-freeness had gone out of Riley's voice as she turned toward him; apparently, he wasn't the only one who sensed something more behind Donald's words.

Carl flashed the box at them. "The Godfather."

"Good choice," Xander said as he stepped away from the cabinets. "We should probably get up there before Peter starts calling for a riot or some other crazy ass thing."

"I wish he'd chosen to go out on his own," Riley said.

"Mary Ellen deals with him well," Donald told them as he reluctantly returned the movie to the shelf.

"Maybe she can continue to do so," Carl said as he headed back toward the stairs.

He found the others gathered within the living room. The lightning still flashed but the thunder had lessened, as had the driving rain. The carpet squished beneath his boots as he made his way to the broken window and peered out. He could just barely make out the mound of animals in the pulses of light fading into the distance.

A shudder slid down his spine. Those mounds were some of the creepiest things he'd seen, and that was saying a lot. Stepping away from the window, he grabbed hold of the coffee table and propped it against the broken window. "It's a good place to stay for the night," he said. "I'll take the first watch, there are only two bedrooms upstairs, but there's a large sectional downstairs at least two people can sleep on."

John helped him brace a chair against the coffee table and wedge it into place. "I'll sit with you."

Carl nodded and made his way out the front door to the porch. The rain continued to fall in a steady stream that brought to mind a summer storm, but this one did nothing to cool the air off. Xander and Riley followed them onto the porch. Xander helped him to hang the swing back up. Riley settled onto the porch against the house and drew her knees up as she leaned against the building. Carl slid the chain back into place and gestured toward the swing for her to sit, but she shook her head.

"I'm fine where I am," she assured him.

Carl sank onto the swing and pushed back as John sat beside him. He kept his gaze averted from the pile at the edge of the field, but it was a constant presence he felt at the edge of his vision. "Are you sure you don't want to go inside?" Xander asked Riley.

"It's too hot in there; I much prefer to be out here," she told him.

A small bit of optimism filled Carl as he watched their hands entwine. It wasn't a completely crappy world, not yet anyway, he decided. He turned away from them as Riley rested her head on

Xander's shoulder and closed her eyes. "We're going to have to find more gas tomorrow," Carl said.

"We should probably check the barn in the morning too," Xander said.

Carl glanced at the small building set beside the house and nodded. His head turned as the screen door opened; Rochelle and Donald stepped out. Donald had the notebook tucked under his arm; he slid down the wall of the house on the other side of the door from Xander and Riley. Rochelle made her way toward them.

"I almost shot you earlier," John said grouchily.

"Sorry," she said. "It wasn't exactly my idea of a good time either."

She squished down on the other side of John, forcing him up against Carl. They both gave her a disgruntled look she chose to ignore as her feet swung happily back and forth. "You are a strange child," John informed her.

"So I've been told."

She rocked on the swing with them for a few minutes before rising to her feet and stretching her back. "I should probably get back inside."

Carl watched her walk into the house before turning his attention to the night once more. He fought to stay awake, but more times than not he found his chin drooping against his chest as sleep pulled at him. The faint sound of John's snores didn't help him any either.

"I'm going to stay awake if you would like to get some rest," Donald said.

Carl glanced over his shoulder to where Donald sat. Riley and Xander were both asleep with their heads bent close to each other. Donald had the notebook propped in his lap and a flashlight sitting beside him as the pen hovered over the page. Carl wondered what the man was writing, but the idea of asking a question right now just seemed far too tiring. He nodded instead and turned back to face the tranquil night.

Nothing stirred within the shadows, but he found himself fighting against the pull of sleep. He was petrified if he went to sleep he wouldn't wake up again, that he would simply cease to exist. Even still, his body finally succumbed to its desperate need for sleep. The sun was just beginning to peek over the horizon when he woke again.

Rising to his feet, his back and knees popped as he tried to work the knots out of his body. He rubbed at his twisted neck as he stretched it to the side and moved away from the swing that had almost crippled him over night. The sky lit with red, oranges, pinks, and yellows as the sun moved further upward.

"The sky is blue," he hadn't realized Riley was awake until she spoke.

His gaze drifted to the patch of blue sky on the horizon. It had been such a normal scene throughout most of his life, now it filled him with awe. Hope coursed through him as he kept his eye on that small patch of blue. "It is," he agreed.

"It's beautiful." He'd been so focused on the sky, he hadn't heard Riley approach. She stood beside him now.

"It is."

He kept his gaze on the sky as the sun rose higher, and the blue faded away to be replaced with the hideous red he'd become accustomed to. He glanced at Riley and was astonished to see tears running down her face. She looked bashfully at him and hastily wiped the tears away.

"That's a good sign," she said.

"Yes." He squeezed her arm reassuringly and nodded toward the barn. "I'm going to check it out before we leave."

"I'll come with you."

Carl nodded and made his way to the small barn next to the house. He grabbed hold of the door and slid it open as Riley braced herself with her gun. The scents of hay, straw, manure, animal, and leather drifted over him. It wasn't unpleasant, but it wasn't something he was overly familiar with either.

He tilted his head back to study the rafters. Thankfully there wasn't a loft in this barn, and he didn't see anything moving through the beams running across the ceiling either. Riley stepped to the side and peered into the first stall, while he moved to the one on the left. Hay and straw were stacked inside of it as well as at least fifteen bags of oats. He opened the small door next to the feed room to reveal a room filled with saddles and bridles.

Riley was at the end of the other row of stalls and was turning back toward him when he closed the door again. He lifted the lid on a trunk and peered inside at the brushes and blankets stacked neatly within. Riley appeared at his side as he closed the lid. "There are some oats we should probably take with us," he told her. "I'll go get the truck."

"Ok," she said as she lifted the lid on the trunk and peered inside.

Xander was making his way toward the barn when he went back outside. "She's inside," Carl told him.

"Thanks." Xander tugged tiredly at his disordered hair as he made his way by.

John climbed down the porch steps and hurried toward him. Donald must have already retreated inside as the porch was vacated. "Where you going?" John asked around a yawn.

"There are some oats in the barn we should take with us."

John looked at him as if he'd just informed him there were

hitchhiking aliens in the barn that he planned to drive to San Diego. "You want us to eat horse food?"

"No, but I also don't want us to starve. We're not exactly in the position to be choosy."

"True."

John hopped into the passenger seat. Carl drove over to the barn and backed the truck up to it. Riley and Xander had already pulled some bags out of the room and were waiting for them when Carl climbed out and opened the back doors on the rack body. John climbed into the back and began to push things to the side.

"Toss out some waters," Carl said to him.

John handed three bottles out to them and took hold of the first bag Xander dropped in the truck. A shadow fell over the front of the barn, drawing his attention toward where Mary Ellen stood with Rochelle at her side. "Do you need our help with anything?" she asked.

"You can start packing up the food inside; that would help," Carl told her as he tossed another bag into the back of the truck.

She nodded and turned Rochelle around with her to head back into the house. "The sky was blue this morning, briefly, but it was blue again," Riley said. Xander and John stopped moving to stare at her. "It was beautiful."

"It sounds like it," Xander said.

Carl glanced out at the red sky spread out before him. This farm was almost a trip back into normalcy, yet he couldn't wait to get on the road again. Something about this normalcy bothered him now. His gaze returned to the pile of horses in the corner; he planned to be as far from here as they could be by nightfall.

CHAPTER 23

Al

"Jesus," Al whispered.

"We're not going through that, are we?" Riley's voice sounded like she had a lump stuck in her throat. Her fingers had stopped their movement on the cat in her lap.

Xander shook his head. "I don't think it's possible."

The truck pulled up beside them. John already had his window down and was leaning out toward them. "Is there a way around it?"

Al stared at the river in front of them before dropping his head back to the map book in his lap. There was no river through the middle of this town in the book, but then the geography of this land was no longer the same. "How is that possible?" Bobby demanded from the backseat with Riley.

"The quakes, they opened up a pathway from another river or lake," Al muttered as he studied the roads in the book. "There are a

couple of back roads we can try, but if they don't work out we're going to have to get onto the highway again."

"They have to work," Riley said.

"Follow us," Al said to John who turned to speak with Carl.

Xander put the car in reverse and followed Al's directions as they drove parallel to the river for half a mile before turning into the heart of the town. The fire station and police station had crumbled; the signs outside of them were the only things identifying the remains of the brick buildings. A few stores had also crumbled, but the church and movie theatre in the center of town remained standing. He turned his attention back to the map as Xander made a right.

"People."

Al's head lifted at Xander's word. A tendril of dread twisted within his belly at the people shuffling aimlessly down the road. The Lost Souls barely turned to acknowledge the vehicles as they drove past. "So lost," Al murmured.

"There are so many," Bobby whispered. "Why are there so many more here than in Mass?"

"The sickness spread through here, but the quakes didn't cause as much damage, and they didn't kill as many people," Al answered.

The thud of a woman bouncing off the front of the car made him shudder. "They have to be eating and drinking something, they simply have to be," Riley said. "They'd be dead if they weren't."

"Their own hair," Bobby muttered.

"There's still thought enough there to keep themselves going," Riley said.

"There is," Al agreed. He knew she needed the possibility within those words, but he didn't agree with them. Maybe there was a chance they could save these people, but he wasn't going to

put much faith into that chance. He wondered if The Lost Souls would continue on, if they would inhabit this earth with them for the rest of existence, or if they would die out. He wondered if *they* would eventually die out too. They'd made it this far, but there was no guarantee, not anymore.

Al shook his head and turned away from the window. One thing he did know for sure was morose thoughts would get him absolutely nowhere. Every day he woke up was another battle won, and that was all that mattered now.

"Take your next left," Al instructed.

They were barely going five miles an hour; Xander had to nudge some of the wanderers out of the way with the nose of the car in order to make the turn. "Shit," Bobby said. "Just shit."

Al met the eyes of a woman beside the car, but though she stared straight at him there was no flicker of acknowledgement. He was staring into nothing, and nothing was staring straight back at him.

Was this what limbo was? Was that what these people were trapped in, a permanent state of limbo? Then what were he and the others trapped in, Hell? He tore his attention away from the woman at the thought.

"Where are the angrier ones?" Riley inquired.

"I don't know, but let's just be happy they're not here right now," Xander muttered as he nudged a young boy out of the way with the bumper of the car.

In the mirror Al saw a few people stagger in front of the truck. Carl braked abruptly and had to back up in order to maneuver around them before continuing. "If they show up now..." Bobby's voice trailed off.

There was no need to finish that statement; they all knew what would happen if those things showed up now. Xander drove

around another large group and the road opened up before them. Al breathed a sigh of relief as he turned his attention back to the map. "You're going to make your next right, and hopefully there's not a river in the middle of the road."

Riley's hand curled around the back of Al's seat as she sat forward; he could feel her breath on the nape of his neck, but instead of being put off by the sensation, he found it oddly comforting to have another human being so close to him. Without thinking, he rested his hand against hers as they turned onto another road blessedly clear of water.

"Keep going straight," Al instructed.

Riley squeezed his hand and settled back in her seat again. "Walmart," Xander said as they entered a more business district area.

Riley and Bobby sat forward again as Xander pulled into the parking lot of the immense store. There were at least a dozen cars still sitting in the lot, just waiting for owners who would most likely never return to them. "Do you think there's any food left in there?" Riley asked.

Unlike most of the other stores they'd encountered, the front windows remained intact, and the door was not hanging open. "Someone has to have raided the place by now," Bobby said.

"I'm sure they have," Al agreed. "They just didn't feel the need to destroy it after."

Xander pulled up next to a Jeep Cherokee and parked the car. "That would be a better ride if it still has the keys in it."

"What do you think the odds of that are?" Riley asked.

Xander shrugged and climbed out. "Slim to none, but hopefully no one has siphoned the gas from these vehicles."

Carl and John were climbing out of the truck when Al exited the car. He eyed the building as the others gathered the gas cans.

Xander tried for the door on the Jeep but it was locked. "So much for trading up," he muttered as he walked over to the gas can.

"Newer vehicle," Carl said. "It probably has an anti-siphoning feature anyway."

Xander scowled at the Jeep before turning away. Al had been steadily approaching the store, his gun in hand as he neared one of the windows. Riley stayed close by his side. "They usually have pharmacies in them," she whispered. "I bet no one would think to grab L-Dopa from it."

He glanced at her out of the corner of his eye. He hadn't realized just how much expectation she was putting on finding that medicine and trying to use it on someone. "It might not work," he said.

"I know, but it could."

Al started to tell her not to put so much confidence into it, but he closed his mouth. She had every right to cling to this, to look forward to it, to have something else to focus on and keep her going. Who was he to take that away from her?

He turned his attention back to the windows as he stepped up to the glass and shaded his eyes in order to look inside. He couldn't see anything beyond the glass. Stepping back, he blinked as he stared at the window. It took him a second to realize the windows were covered in something, most likely paint.

"What the..."

He grabbed Riley's arm and pressed his finger against his lips as he pulled her back a few steps. "They're living in there," he said. "Or at least someone is, probably a lot of someone's."

"How do we know they're still alive?" she asked as she eyed the windows.

"We don't, but do you propose to walk in there blind to find out?"

"No," she admitted. "Great place to hole up for a while though."

"Yeah, until someone else comes along and takes it from them." Al had been unaware Peter was listening to their conversation until he spoke.

"I don't think anyone is going to take that chance," Al said. Peter stared at him and then the gun in Al's hand.

"Well maybe not you..."

"You?" he interrupted sharply.

"I'll go in," Peter said flatly.

"If you want to kill yourself just put the gun to your head, but I don't think anyone else is going to be pulling that trigger with you," Al told him.

Carl lifted his head from where he had been sucking on the tubing he'd slipped inside the gas tank of a small Honda. Carl's eyebrows were drawn together over the top of his nose; he held the hose out to John and stepped around the car to approach them. His eyes remained on Peter as he stopped beside Al. "What's going on?" he asked.

"The windows are painted; we think there are people in there," Al told him.

Carl glanced at the store and then back at them. "We'll get the gas and get out of here."

"I think we should go in," Peter said.

Carl shook his head and pushed the brim of his hat up. "That would be a bad idea. We have no idea what they have for weapons. We could be killed before we make it two feet in the door. If they're holed up in there, I doubt there's anything they'd be willing to give us."

"So we'll take it from them."

"You won't make it in there," Carl said.

Riley stepped closer. A stone settled in Al's stomach before she spoke. "Maybe they'll give us something they don't want and is completely useless to them."

"Riley, we don't know if they have a pharmacy in there," Al said.

She pointed at the building. Al followed her finger to the word Pharmacy painted across the top of it. He scowled at the word written in large block letters; he knew it was crazy, but all he could think was the word was a traitor. "They'll give it to us, if we ask," she said softly.

She had more faith in the human race than he did, looking at her he couldn't help but hope maybe she was right. "I don't care if they're willing to give it to us or not," Peter said.

"We're not going to go in there looking for a fight," Riley said from between clenched teeth.

"Go in where?" Xander demanded as he and Bobby returned from searching the nearby vehicles.

"The store," Riley answered.

Xander glanced at the building. "Has it been raided?"

"We're pretty sure there are people living in there; they have painted over the windows to keep someone or something from seeing inside," Al told him. "Riley would like to try to get some L-Dopa from them if they have it, and Peter thinks we should try and take it over."

"That is a very bad idea," Bobby said as he tugged at his shaggy brown hair.

"I just want to ask them…"

"There is no asking," Peter broke in. "We could just shoot out the windows."

"If there are any of those things in the area, they'll be drawn here by the noise. Besides the people in there could have far more ammo and weapons than us. I'm not about to turn this parking lot into some kind of O.K. Corral shoot out," Carl said briskly. "No supply is worth that."

"We can't just ask them," Peter insisted.

"Yes, we can," Riley insisted in return. "and I'm going to do it. It's only a question. If they say no, they say no, but we can't walk away from here without trying." Al glanced back at the painted windows of the store. "*I* can't walk away from here without trying."

"What is it you're asking for?" Peter demanded.

Al's hand tightened on his gun as Riley unwaveringly met Peter's gaze. "L-Dopa."

The teacher's eyes widened, his gaze drifted over all of them before settling on her again. "Are you out of your mind?" he hissed.

"I think we may have all gone a little mad," she informed him. "but I'm still getting that drug."

A sinking sensation settled in Al's stomach; he wanted to pull Riley away from the teacher, but he thought Xander was the bigger threat. The young man eyed Peter as he brought his gun before him. "Back off," Xander said to Peter in a low voice.

Peter stared at him for a minute before glancing at the rest of them. He seemed to realize he was outnumbered as he took a step back. "You'll go in there for something that won't do anyone any good, but you won't take what it is we *need* from them?" Peter demanded.

"If we start having that attitude we'll be no better than the sick humans haunting this earth now," Riley told him.

"Your attitude will get you killed; you have to learn how to survive in this world," Peter told her before turning away. Mary

Ellen pulled Rochelle out of his path as Donald took a step closer to the rest of them.

"He's going to have to be dealt with," Carl muttered.

"He backed off, he may just continue to do so," Mary Ellen said.

Xander rubbed tiredly at his forehead before turning to Riley. "You're not going to be the one who asks them."

"I think they'd hesitate to kill a woman and be a little less distrustful of me than you."

"And you may be the only woman they've seen in a while or may see again for some time."

Riley folded her arms over her chest. "You could be putting us all at risk if you do this," Bobby said.

Riley's arms fell to her sides. "I don't want to do that."

Al had thought he would feel relief over her words, instead he felt as if he had just taken a toy away from a two year old. She was right; this was something they had to do, an answer they all had to find. "I'll go. They're less likely to shoot at an old man, and I doubt anyone desires this body."

Riley choked on a laugh as she shook her head. "I can't ask you to do that."

"You didn't ask, I volunteered. We all need an answer, especially you. This will haunt you until you know, and no one deserves to be haunted, especially not now. We'll get the rest of the gas and get everyone situated so if we have to make a quick retreat we can."

"What if you can't get out?" she asked.

"I've lived a longer life than most."

"I'll go with you."

"Xander's right, a woman shouldn't go in there first. It's not sexist, it simply is a fact," Al told her.

"Let's get the gas," Xander said.

"You don't have to do this," Riley said to Al when the others returned to what they had been doing.

Al squeezed her arm and led her toward the car. "I do. It will be fine."

Xander and John carried the full cans over to the cars and filled the vehicles with them. "Maybe we should just go," Riley said as she hovered by his side. "There will be other places where we can try and find it."

Al glanced at her and then back at the building. "That might be true, but this could also be our last chance. If I truly believed something was going to happen, I wouldn't do this."

He watched as they finished topping off the vehicles before Carl dropped the cans into the back of the truck. Carl closed the doors and turned to Al. "Do you still intend to do this?" he asked.

Al nodded. "Just keep Peter away. I think it will get pretty ugly if he attempts to go in there."

"He won't go anywhere near that building, even if I have to shoot him myself," Carl vowed.

Al didn't doubt Carl would shoot the man as his eyes turned toward the teacher standing beside the car. Things were going to get ugly within this group soon. The thought came unbidden to his mind, but once it was there he couldn't shake it as he glanced between Carl and Peter. There was only so far Carl would be pushed. Mary Ellen may think Peter would eventually mellow out again, but Al doubted it. He wondered who would come out on top when things finally hit a boiling point though.

"I'll be out soon," Al told them and placed his gun on the dashboard of the car.

Al waited till the others were settled into the vehicles before approaching the building again. Xander drove behind him and parked outside the front door. Xander leaned over and opened the passenger door and pushed it open for him in case he had to make a hasty retreat. He'd meant what he said about the people inside probably not seeing him as much of a threat, but he had to take a calming breath and wipe his sweaty palms on his pants before knocking on the door. The glass doors hadn't been painted over, but he was still surprised when a curtain was pulled abruptly back, and a man's face appeared.

The man was shorter than Al at about five foot and appeared to be in his fifties. He tilted his head to look up at him as he pressed the barrel of his gun against the door. "Get away from the door!" he commanded as he tapped the metal gun against the glass.

"I'm not here to take anything, I mean no harm," Al said as he held his hands up beside him. "I simply want something you don't even need,"

"Why would you want something we don't need?" the man demanded.

Al glanced toward the cars. "We think we may have a way to help the sick ones rambling aimlessly around. Not the cannibalistic ones, but the others. A medicine."

The man's lined face twisted as he eyed Al from head to toe. "We're not giving out any medicine."

"Wait!" Al said when the man went to turn away. "It's L-Dopa, it will do nothing for you, *nothing*. Please, just one bottle. We're not sure it will help, but if it does it's worth a try."

The man's head turned to the side; he said something to someone else before turning back to Al. "Where are your friends?"

"They're in the vehicles; they're not getting out."

"Do you have any weapons on you?" the man inquired.

"No."

The man craned his head to try and see around him. Al kept his hands raised as he stepped to the side so the man could get a better view of the vehicles. "You can come in," he said. "but if the others get out we will kill you."

"I'll be right back!" he called to Xander. "Whatever you do, *don't* get out of the vehicles."

Xander nodded, but he kept his hand on the passenger side door to keep it open. The click of a lock brought Al's attention back to the door as the man pushed it open. Al stepped into the darkened interior of the store. Huddled near the cash registers was a group of at least twenty people watching him with wary eyes. There were a few children with them, curled within the laps of what he could only assume were their mother's.

Two men and one woman were holding guns by the front windows blockaded with furniture, but he didn't see any other weapons. That was something he was going to keep to himself; he had no interest in taking what these people had from them. The windows had been painted over, but he saw a few peepholes through the paint allowing sunlight to filter through the furniture. Amongst the clothing racks he saw other people. He didn't get a sense of a lot of others within the cavernous building. Though he could smell spoiled food, it wasn't overwhelming. They must have taken all the rotten food into the back, or perhaps they'd eaten most of it before it went bad.

A woman appeared from around one of the cash registers. In her hand was a small bottle he could hear rattling as she walked. "Is this it?" she asked as she held it out to him.

He turned the bottle over in his hand to examine the word L-Dopa on it. "Yes, I think so."

"Do you really think it will work?" the woman asked.

Al lifted his head to meet her questioning eyes. "It's the only chance we have," he told her.

CHAPTER 24

Xander

XANDER'S FINGERS tapped on the steering wheel while he waited for Al to come out. His leg bounced up and down as he stared at the seemingly quiet store. "I should have gone with him," Riley murmured as she nervously watched the store.

"No, he was right," Xander told her, but it took everything he had not to get out of the car and go after Al.

"What if this medicine doesn't work?" Bobby asked.

Riley's eyes were haunted as she turned to him, but her jaw was set in determination. "Then it doesn't work, but what if it does?"

"Peter may just flip his nut and try to kill us all if it does work."

Riley turned stiffly away from Bobby, but her next words caused Xander's fingers to stop tapping on the dash. "I think Peter turning on us is inevitable, even if we don't try and save the others."

Her disturbing words caused Xander to turn toward her, but her gaze was focused on the store once more. "Really?" he asked.

"You don't?" She didn't turn to look at him when she asked the question.

Xander glanced at Bobby; his friend was staring at Riley as if he didn't know who she was. "You're being pretty cryptic there Ri, you ok?" Bobby asked.

She finally turned to look at them. "I'm not trying to be cryptic. I just don't think it matters what we say or do; Peter will lose it. It's too much on him and he can't handle this. He may have had some mental health issues before this; maybe he's supposed to be on medication or something. We don't know anything about most of these people, but I do know I feel as if we can trust them all, except for Peter."

Xander resumed tapping his fingers on the wheel as he leaned against the driver's side door. "I'm not so sure about Donald."

"He seems harmless enough to me," Bobby said.

"I have to agree, but we've known him for less time than Peter so who knows," Riley said with a shrug. "What is taking so long in there?"

"We'll know if something is wrong," Xander assured her.

"Would we?" she muttered.

"Why do you have doubts about Donald?" Bobby asked.

Xander shrugged; he took hold of Riley's hand as her fingers started tapping on her knee. She smiled at him as her fingers entwined with his. "I don't know," Xander admitted. "We just don't know him, and what is he writing all the time?"

"Maybe he's keeping a diary," Riley suggested.

"Who would want to write down all of this?" Bobby asked.

"Maybe he would just like the world to know," Riley said.

"Know what?"

She turned away from the store to look at Bobby. "That he was here, that *we* were here, even if it's only for a short time more."

Bobby closed his eyes as he rested his head against the window. "Yeah, I can see that."

"I'm going to go in there," Riley said.

Xander tugged her hand when she went to open the door. "He said to stay here. You could get him hurt, or you could get yourself hurt. Just wait."

"If something happens to him..."

"Nothing is going to happen to him, and he didn't have to do this. This was his choice, remember that."

He glanced at Bobby as his friend surreptitiously twisted his hand into the tail of Riley's shirt. She wouldn't be getting out of this car if either of them had anything to say about it. Fortunately though, he saw the billow of the curtain as the door opened again, and Al stepped out. Bobby released Riley's shirt as she opened her door, but Al waved her back.

"Stay in the car," he called to her.

Xander leaned forward and held the door of the car open for him, Al slid into the passenger seat. "Are you ok?" Riley demanded before Al had settled in.

"Perfectly fine," Al assured her.

"What about the people in there?"

"They all seem to be in good health," Al answered as he closed his door. "They don't have much for weapons, but they've barricaded themselves in there, and they should be able to make a stand for a while. They'll be ok."

"Did they..."

The bottle Al held up rattled in his hand as he showed it to them before handing it over to Riley. "L-Dopa pills."

Riley twisted the bottle in her hand as she examined it. "I was expecting something injectable."

"So was I," Al admitted.

"How do you plan on doing this?" Xander asked as he pulled out of the parking lot. "Kidnap one of those things and bring them with us?"

"Is it considered kidnapping if they have no knowledge of it?" Bobby inquired.

"Who knows," Riley murmured. "If we do that, Peter may try and stop us."

"I don't think there's any way to keep this hidden from him, not if you decide to follow through with it," Al said.

"You went in there to get this; we will be following through on it," Riley said decisively. Her fingers ran over the cat's neck as she stared thoughtfully at the bottle. "I'm just not exactly sure how. We don't know how much time it would take to have an effect on them. It could be days before we see any results."

Xander followed Al's directions as he drove out of the business area of the town and back into a more rural area speckled with farms. He spotted another mound in the distance, but as they passed a cattle farm he was amazed to realize some of the animals were still alive. The cows roamed the pastures, and though they didn't look as if they were going to make it much longer, they were *alive*.

"I'll be," he breathed as he unknowingly slowed the car to take them in.

"Too bad we couldn't take some of them with us," Bobby said.

"It's difficult enough to maneuver through these streets without adding a trailer and some livestock to the mix," Al said. "But it's pretty rural where we're going, so there's a good chance we'll come across livestock that is still alive."

"Let's hope so," Riley said. She rotated the bottle in her hand one more time before slipping it into the pouch on the back of Al's seat. "We'll talk to the others before we decide what we're going to do."

"I'm not sure how comfortable I'll feel hauling one of those people around with us," Bobby said.

Xander glanced at Riley in the rearview mirror; she didn't say anything as she turned to look out the window. "We'll talk with the others," Xander said and focused on the road again as Al led them onward.

Though they drove by endless farms, they didn't pass by many businesses again until they entered another town. "How far are we from the border?" he asked as he drove around a streetlight lying across the road.

From the corner of his eye, he spotted something moving behind the buildings, but when he turned to look there was nothing amongst the lengthening shadows. The fact it was so much easier to drive through these streets was a relief, but Al was right; the lack of quakes in this area had left a higher human population he didn't want to deal with.

"About fifty miles."

"How much more rural is it where we're heading than here?"

Something in his tone must have caught Al's attention as his head came up from the map. He turned to look out the window before focusing on Xander. "There will be less people there," he assured him.

Xander was glad to hear that as he spotted a growing number of creatures moving through the backyards. "It's going to be getting dark soon," Riley said. "But maybe we can make it out of this state tomorrow."

She hadn't noticed the sick people following them yet, Xander realized as he searched the houses lining the roads. They had to get out of this area before nightfall. There just weren't many options right now.

"Al..." he started.

"I see them."

"Can you get us out of here?"

"I'm going to try," Al promised.

Xander went to make another right, but a tree lying across the middle of the road stopped him before he could complete the turn. Beginning to feel like a rat in a maze, Xander was able to pull a U-turn and drive out of the road before they became trapped within it. "They're smart," he whispered. "Al..."

"Turn around," Al said. "This isn't going to end well."

Xander didn't argue with him as he drove the car onto the sidewalk and turned back the way they had come. He caught a glimpse of Carl before he drove by the truck. Carl nodded to him and pulled the truck onto a front yard as he turned to follow them. Within the shadows of the woods, he saw the figures hesitating; one jumped up and down and shook its fists at them. Xander would have laughed at the almost comical action, but there was no humor here.

"You think they're laying a trap?" Bobby asked.

"I'd put money on it," Al said.

Xander wiped the sweat trickling down the back of his neck away as those things began to move through the trees with them again. He continued to search the homes they drove by, but though he felt vulnerable in the car, he knew they would never be able to defend themselves from within one of the homes. His knuckles were white as he twisted his hands on the wheel and glanced at the other vehicles in the rearview. The increased thump of his heart against his ribs was becoming almost uncomfortable as he shifted in his seat.

"Take your next right," Al said.

Xander didn't want to go anywhere he thought those people might have set a trap, but as he made the turn he realized it was a road they'd traveled before. They were backtracking but at least they knew the way was clear. They were almost to Walmart again when the people faded away and he was finally able to take his first easy breath in a while as they drove away from the store once more.

Al gave him directions down a separate area of the town. Every turn he took, he kept expecting to come up across some sort of blockade within the road, some trap set so those things could pounce upon them and devour them. He glanced at Riley in the rearview; her gun was in her lap with the cat, her gaze on the outside world.

Bobby remained unmoving with his head against the window. "Did you ever think it would be like this? I mean did you ever really think the world as we knew it would come to an end?" Bobby inquired.

"No," Riley answered. "I never thought it would really happen. I'd thought about the zombie apocalypse, but I certainly didn't expect cannibalistic humans to be running around trying to eat us."

"I never thought about it," Al said. "It just wasn't something that ever truly crossed my mind."

"I used to think about it, every once in a while," Bobby said. "I read the comic books, I watched the movies, and TV shows, but truth be told I never really thought it would happen. I didn't think I'd survive it either."

"Glad you were wrong about that," Riley said.

"So far."

Xander glanced at his friend but refrained from commenting. So far was right. He didn't like to think about it, but he knew it was true. He made another turn onto a road lined with hundred-year-old maples. Their lengthy branches touched each other over the top of the shadowed road. The mansions tucked behind the maples now seemed to stand barren to the world as nothing moved behind the windows. The flashing of lights from the truck caught his attention, and he pulled over to the side of the road.

He took his gun off the dashboard before opening the door. Carl was already halfway to them by the time he was out of the car. "What's going on?" Xander inquired.

"Night is coming; we haven't seen those things in a while." Carl gestured toward the large homes surrounding them. "These all look empty. There may be a fair amount of food in them. We might not find better before the night sets in."

Xander examined the massive homes and nodded. "There could be people in them."

"There could *always* be people in them," Carl said.

"True," Xander admitted. Riley still held the cat in her arms when she climbed out, but she put the animal back inside the car and closed the door. "Where do we start?"

Carl nodded toward the house behind him. "We should probably split up, it will go faster."

"What about Peter?"

"What about him?" Carl inquired.

Xander's attention turned to Peter as he climbed out of the car. "I brought him into the group, so I should probably be the one to go with him."

Carl lit a cigarette and studied Xander through the haze of smoke puffing up around his face. "Riley will probably go with you if you try to do that."

Xander glanced over at Riley as she spoke with Al. "I don't want her anywhere near him, and I'm staying with her."

"I know. I think if Peter is with Josh and agrees with this course of action he'll be fine, for now," Carl said. "Here they come."

Xander stepped closer to Riley as the others approached them. Carl told them of his plan to search through the homes. Thankfully, Peter didn't argue with them. He seemed pleased with the idea as he studied the homes surrounding them. "We should search the homes with the people we drove here with. It will be the easiest way to split us up," Peter suggested.

Xander was about to protest this when Mary Ellen spoke, "That will work."

He stared at her, wishing she would meet his gaze, but she remained focused on the home to their left. He understood her desire not to back down, but there was no reason to continue to put herself in jeopardy if she didn't have to. He took a step closer to speak with her, but she shook her head at him and turned away.

She grabbed hold of Rochelle's shoulders. "Stay with Carl and John, and do whatever they tell you to do."

"Mom…"

"It's better if you stay with them; they're going to need an extra set of eyes. Please don't argue about this."

"I can switch with you," John offered.

Mary Ellen shook her head and glanced over at Peter before speaking with them again. "It will be fine."

She kissed Rochelle on the forehead and walked over to join Peter, Josh, and Donald. Riley was peering in the back window at the cat curled up on the seat when Xander joined her. "We're going to have to let her out soon," Riley muttered.

Xander wrapped his hand around her shoulder and pulled her

away from the window she had cracked open. Even with the window open, the cat wouldn't be able to stay in there for long. He glanced at the sky and then back at the cat. "Maybe we should let her out now."

"She'll take off."

"It's better she runs away instead of dies from the heat. You never know; she might stick around."

Riley glanced at the sky again and nodded. "You're right."

She walked around the car, opened the front door, and popped the trunk. From the trunk she pulled out the bowls and filled one with food while she placed some water in the other. Opening the door she placed both bowls on the floor of the car and left the door ajar. The gray cat yawned and stretched before jumping out of the vehicle. The cat didn't wander far as she explored the front yard and watched them with her ears perked forward.

"She'll stick around," Riley said.

"I'm sure she will." Xander prayed the cat didn't take off as he pulled Riley away from the car.

"Try not to shoot your guns unless you absolutely have to," Carl told them.

"We won't," Xander said.

Xander watched the cat as they made their way toward the black front door of a house easily five times the size of the one he had grown up in. He kept hold of Riley's hand as he peered into the windows with Bobby and Al. Riley kept an eye on the street, but when Xander turned to look with her, he saw nothing moving amongst the homes surrounding them.

He turned back to the windows and peered in on a room the size of his old house. The room was floor to ceiling bookcases, there wasn't an inch of space on any of the hundreds of shelves as they were filled with books. A sense of awe filled him as he looked over the room. Carol and his mother would have spent weeks, if not months curled up in that room, lost within the pages of all those books. He may just lose Riley to it when they finally got in there.

"There's a lot of places to hide in this beast," Bobby said as he stepped away from the window and tilted his head to look up at the porch roof above them.

"We really don't have many options and there could be a good amount of food in there," Xander said.

"And weapons," Al said as he examined the front door.

Xander glanced over at Carl, John, and Rochelle gathered on the porch of the house beside them. They were only a hundred or so feet away, but it seemed like a thousand as Bobby grabbed the doorknob. Xander had expected the door to be locked, but it creaked as it swung open. He didn't look back before stepping into the darkened interior of the home.

CHAPTER 25

John

JOHN REMAINED behind Carl as his friend slid his hand through the window he'd broken out of the door, and pushed it open. "What do you think these people did for a living?" John inquired as he took in the airy, spotless interior of what could only be described as a foyer, though he'd never been in a foyer like this one before.

"Something neither of us was ever going to do," Carl answered as he stepped into the house.

"Something none of us have probably *heard* of," Rochelle said.

His gaze fell on the security panel next to the door. All of the lights were off on it, but he still couldn't shake the feeling the cops would be pulling up with the sirens blaring at any second.

Their steps, echoing on the marble floor beneath them, caused John to wince as they walked toward the doublewide staircase in the center of the room. Halfway to the second floor, the staircase split and went in two separate directions to the hallway above.

He'd never been so happy to step on a rug as they finally made it to the blue oriental in the middle of the floor that silenced their steps.

"We'll start on the right," Carl said and nodded at the room across from them. "Rochelle, stay in the doorway, and keep an eye out for anything coming this way. Just scream if you see something, don't try and take it on."

Rochelle nodded and shifted nervously. Carl pulled a gun from the waistband of his jeans and handed it to her. Her eyes were troubled as Carl closed her hand around it. "Do *not* use this unless you absolutely have to, and then you just point, shoot, and run. Do you understand me?"

"Yes."

"Rochelle…"

"I'll be fine, go on."

"What about those doors?" John asked as he nodded toward the three doors in the foyer.

"We'll check them when we get back," Carl answered. "She'll be able to see if something opens one of these doors; we can't see if something is stalking us from the other rooms right now though. If one of those doors starts to open you get out of here."

John didn't know how many rooms there were beyond the sliding door on their right, but he didn't like the idea of leaving her here by herself. "If you hear us scream, if you hear any gunfire, or *anything* else you run out of this house, and don't look back. If you feel spooked for any reason, you leave this house," John told her.

"I'll be fine," she said again and waved her hand at the rooms. "Go, just go."

John wasn't at all certain she would do what she said she would, but he didn't have time to argue with her over it as he turned away. He braced himself as they stepped into what he could only describe as a sitting room. In his mind's eye, he could picture little old women sitting on the delicate sofas, drinking tea as they ate crumpets and gossiped about men. He shook his head to clear the image, but the scent of the tea his mother used to boil in the morning was stuck in his nose.

Carl glanced back at him as he approached a set of closed double doors. He gestured for John to open the doors while he stood in front of them with his gun at the ready. John flung the doors open and jumped to the side. He waited for something to charge out of whatever room lay beyond, but nothing stirred. John leaned around the door and peered into the dining room.

An oak table with eight chairs around it was within the room. Flies buzzed around the remains of the three breakfast plates sitting on the table. Though John didn't want to look any closer at the bug-infested plates, he noticed the occupants of the house were eating bacon and eggs when the world had gone to hell. Not a bad last meal he decided, if it had been their last meal, bacon was definitely one of his favorites.

He was now fairly certain he would never eat bacon again. It had nothing to do with the fact he wasn't willing to slaughter Wilbur in order to get the bacon, and everything to do with what was moving around on those plates right now. He kept his eyes diverted from the table as he examined the corners of the room and the hutch tucked against the far wall.

Carl was already moving toward the door to the left of him; he poked his head around the corner before disappearing. John hurried to follow him into the gigantic kitchen. He couldn't help but release a low whistle as he took in the white cabinets, blue granite countertops, and a stove and fridge that could have been straight from Star Trek. He moved around the island in the center of the room and glanced up at the copper pots hanging from a rack over the middle of it.

He wasn't a cook, but even he got the urge to crack and fry an egg in this place. Carl pushed open a swinging door on their right and took a step back from it. "Pantry," he whispered. "There's a fair amount of food in it."

John nodded and followed him around the corner of the room and into a breakfast nook area. A small table was set to the side, the sun's rays spilled across the table and the three chairs tucked under it. John followed Carl out of the kitchen and into what he assumed was a music room. A grand piano sat before an enormous fireplace. From middle school music class, he recalled the instrument sitting next to the piano was a cello.

Carl approached another set of closed doors; John grabbed hold of one of them and slid it open. Rochelle jumped and spun toward them, but she didn't lift the gun and point it at them. She brushed back a strand of her long brown hair before walking across the floor toward them.

"All clear?" she asked in a hushed voice.

"It is in these rooms," Carl assured her. "We'll check out those doors."

He nodded to the three doors set within the hall; two of them were behind the staircase, but the first one was only ten feet away from him. "Wait here," John told her and followed Carl to the first door. Carl opened it to reveal a downstairs bathroom.

Carl closed the door and hurried to one of the doors beneath the stairs. A small bedroom lay beyond; John searched the room as they stepped into it. Carl was grabbing hold of the closet door when John knelt next to the full sized bed. His hand curled around the edge of the comforter; his breath froze in his chest as he cautiously bent forward with his gun at the ready. He was certain something was going to grab hold of his ankle and rip him under the bed before tearing into his flesh. He didn't care if there was only a dust bunny under there, if it so much as moved he was going to shoot it into oblivion.

The trembling beam of his flashlight revealed nothing under the bed, not even a speck of dust. His breath rushed back into his lungs as he dropped the cover into place and sat up. He rested his hands on his knees as he met Carl's gaze across the room. "You ok?" Carl asked as he closed the closet door.

John took another steadying breath. "Yeah, just shaving some years off the life of my heart."

Carl snorted. "Know how you feel."

John pushed himself to his feet and walked far more calmly than he felt toward the door. Rochelle was peering around the stairs at them; he gave her a brief wave before turning toward the remaining door in the foyer. John readied himself as Carl pulled the door open to reveal a set of stairs disappearing into total darkness halfway down to the basement. Carl closed the door again; he pushed in the lock on the handle and threw the deadbolt on the door.

"They liked their security," John said.

"Good thing the batteries on the alarm are dead; the last thing we need to do is attract a horde of those things," Carl said as he turned away from the door and hurried back to where they had left Rochelle. "All clear."

She smiled as she followed them to the foot of the steps. John stared up the winding staircase to where it split off. "Stay on the stairs until we've searched up there," John told her. "Right or left?" he asked Carl.

"Left," Carl said and climbed up the set of stairs closest to him.

John stayed on his heels as they wound their way up to the hallway running in a circle around the second floor. He counted eight doors off of the main hallway as they stood at the top of the stairs. "This is going to take a while," he muttered.

Carl walked toward the door across from them, the only one opened to the hall. He nudged it open with his foot to reveal the study within. John remained in the hallway, trying to watch every door at once as his eyes bounced around the hall and then the study. Carl left the door open as he exited the study and moved on to the next room.

The search went faster than he'd expected as they moved through the house. They encountered four bedrooms and two bathrooms. He was certain he could have gone swimming in the bathtub of one of the bathrooms, but he wasn't going to get a chance to try it.

John's grasp on his gun had become slippery by the time they got to the final door. His heart raced so fast he could feel every beat of it in his throat. This house was so large; there were so many hiding places within it, and just one place left to look. Carl nodded to him, and thrust the door open for him. Carl went in low as he held his gun before him and pointed it around the only half bath in the house.

Finally able to take an easy breath, John took a step back. Carl left the door open as he exited the bathroom. John's head tilted back to examine the domed roof over the top of them. The chandelier hanging from the ceiling caused colors of light to dance over the marble floor beneath them in the fading rays of the day. The house was empty of all threats, or at least everything above the basement was, but he still couldn't shake the feeling something wasn't right.

Carl remained standing beside him, his shoulders against his. From their angle they could both see Rochelle on the stairs. She was looking toward the front door, but she didn't seem concerned as she remained leaning against the rail.

"Everything ok?" she inquired.

Carl smiled at her and nodded. "Everything's fine up here."

"Carl..." John started when Carl took a step forward.

Carl turned back to him. Words failed John as he glanced around the vast house once more. "What is it?"

"Nothing," John said with a shake of his head. "Nothing."

"Everything will be fine. We'll look in the basement. Judging by the rest of this place it's probably only full of some kind of fancy wine or something."

"Yeah," John muttered, but his feet felt heavy as he followed Carl down the stairs to where Rochelle stood.

She stepped away from the banister to meet them. "Just have the basement to go kid," John told her.

"Why don't we just keep it locked?" she suggested.

"We really don't need one of those things popping out at us," Carl said. "I don't think these people stuck around here after the quakes hit. I didn't see any cars in the drive, so the basement should be clear."

"The cars are probably in the garage," Rochelle said.

John stopped walking and turned to face Carl as he realized why he couldn't shake the awful certainty something was wrong. "We missed a door."

Carl frowned at him. "We searched the entire house."

"No, we missed something somewhere. I'm certain of it. Look around you Carl. I don't think these people walked outside in the rain to get to their cars."

"They probably had a driver bring it around for them," Carl said with a forced laugh. "We didn't miss a door; the garage isn't attached to the house. This place may have all the modern appliances, and the look of a newly built house, but it's easily a hundred years old."

"Are you sure?" John demanded as he tried to recall the setup of the outside of the property.

"I'm sure," Carl told him. "It was further up the drive, almost behind the house."

John glanced around the house and back toward the basement door. "Why don't we check the garage first," he suggested. Carl gave him a questioning look. John couldn't explain why he had to see it, he simply knew he did. "I just can't shake this bad feeling, the dishes on the table..." he shook his head as he rubbed at the bridge of his nose. "There's something not right, or something we're missing."

"We're not missing anything," Carl said. "but we'll check the garage first."

John knew Carl only agreed to this to ease his mind, but he felt relieved when they made their way to the backdoor. They stepped into what had probably been lush gardens, but the flowers had all wilted and died beneath the oppressive heat. Some of them were plastered to the flagstone walkway.

John stepped over a broken branch lying in the middle of the walk and moved around a toppled birdbath. "Must have been pretty once," Rochelle murmured.

"I'm sure it was," John agreed.

He spotted the double car garage as they rounded the privet hedge split down the middle by the small oak that had toppled onto it. The branches of the privet were going in every direction, except the right one. The garage was set back from the house, tucked neatly in between some drooping maples. Though it looked as if it had been built after the house, it was still smaller than he had expected.

He walked up to the windows in one of the garage bay doors and stood on his tiptoes to peer inside. A silver bumper gleamed on a car, but he saw little else of the inside. Carl led the way around the side of the building; he kicked aside a fallen trashcan and grabbed hold of the knob. Carl pushed the door open and recoiled instantly as a putrid wave of odor drifted from within the building.

John had just registered the stench of decay when Carl slammed the door shut on whatever lay beyond. Carl pressed his face to the glass in the door and shook his head. "I don't see anything," he whispered.

The second the words left his mouth, something slammed against the door. John jumped and barely managed to suppress a shout; Carl brought his gun up and pointed it at the window as he took an abrupt step back. Rochelle stumbled into John; she knocked him back before he was able to grasp hold of her shoulders and steady her.

"Easy," he calmed her. "Easy."

Rochelle's nostrils flared, her hands trembled before her on her gun. She remained where she was as John stepped around her and moved closer to Carl. Carl had his gun focused upon the man inside. He didn't pull the trigger as the man's disfigured face traveled over the glass. John's upper lip curled in a sneer at the sight of the man's lipless face. Every one of his teeth was exposed as the skin around his lips had been torn off or rotted away. The bone of his jawline was exposed almost to his ears. John had no idea how the man could possibly still be alive, but his eyes followed him as he moved.

"Dear God," John breathed. "Shoot him."

"The noise could bring more of them, and it doesn't seem as if he can get out of there," Carl said.

Even as he said the words, the knob began to rattle. Carl seized hold of it and jerked it closed before the man could get the door open. A disgruntled, gravelly noise escaped the man as he jerked more forcefully at the door, but Carl didn't release it. The man's pink, mottled tongue was revealed as he released a furious cry and smashed his hands against the glass with enough force to crack the window. John took a stumbling step away as the man pulled back again and beat his fists into the window. Glass sliced over his skin as the window broke away; blood swelled from the cuts, poured down the man's forearms, and splattered the concrete step. Rochelle let out a startled cry as the upper half of the man's body fell through the hole the broken glass had created in the door.

Carl tucked his gun away and pulled out his knife. The man was still hanging half out the window but he grabbed at Carl as he stepped closer. "Carl..."

"Stay back," his brusque command cut John off.

John grabbed hold of Rochelle and pulled her behind him as Carl dodged a swinging arm, seized hold of the man's hair, and lifted his head. Carl's face remained expressionless as he drove the knife through the underneath of the man's chin and into his head. Nausea twisted through John's stomach as the man's spastic movements finally, blessedly ceased.

Carl lifted his head to look at them. There had been no hesitation in his actions, but John saw the flicker of remorse in his eyes before he wiped the bloody knife on his pants and slipped it into its sheath. Carl stepped forward to peer into the garage. John was dreading seeing what was inside, but he wasn't going to leave Carl to do it on his own.

Stepping into the garage, he spotted the remains littering the floor behind the Range Rover. From a picture in the master bedroom, he knew it was a mother and daughter, but there was no other way to discern this, not anymore. The man must have been content to stay here and feed on these remains until they had stumbled upon him.

"We'll search the basement now, but I think it's going to be clear," Carl said.

John nodded his agreement and followed him into the house again. They had just returned to the foyer when the distant explosion of a gunshot pierced the air.

CHAPTER 26

Mary Ellen

MARY ELLEN CAST one last glance at Rochelle before stepping into the house behind Peter. She silently prayed she had made the right choice by staying with this group instead of joining her daughter. Carl and John would keep her safe, she was certain of that, but she still wished they were together. She didn't want Rochelle around Peter though, and she wasn't ready to walk away yet.

Maybe she was being stubborn, maybe she was being stupid, but she was staying with this group for now. Peter was not Larry, the man she would truly like to stand up to was already dead, but she was beginning to feel a growing strength within her she'd never experienced before. She should be afraid of the man she thought may be a walking time bomb across from her, she'd always been on edge around Larry, but she had no fear of Peter. She didn't know what she was going to do if Peter did explode, she wasn't going to shoot the man, but for once in her life she *would* stand up to someone.

Her gaze ran over the shadowed and narrow hall they'd entered. Given the size of the home, the hall had a surprisingly claustrophobic feel to it. Furniture had been crammed into every available space, so much so that some tables were actually stacked on top of others. She had to turn sideways in order to maneuver through what should have been a space about twenty feet wide in each direction.

"Crap," Donald muttered as he bumped into a table. The dozen or so china bells sitting on the table released a tinkling noise that set her teeth on edge. The last thing she liked hearing was any kind of bell tolling right now. Donald grabbed the table and steadied it before continuing past the boxes stacked against the wall.

"They must have been in the process of moving," Josh muttered.

Mary Ellen didn't know what they had been doing, but she didn't want to be here right now. Peter stopped in front of a set of sliding doors and pushed them open. Her mouth dropped when she spotted the thousands of newspapers stacked in ten-foot high rows throughout the entire room. The musty smell of the old newspapers drifted over her; it wasn't an entirely unpleasant odor.

"Holy shit," Donald breathed as he took a step away from the newspaper room.

"Hoarder," Mary Ellen muttered. Her gaze flitted over the stacks before she turned toward the stairs leading to the second floor. There were boxes on the stairs but she didn't see as much clutter on the second floor as there was down here. It didn't matter though; this place was a mammoth deathtrap just waiting to bury them beneath the mounds of stuff filling it. Never mind what could be lurking within the assorted mess. "Maybe we should go to a different house."

"We're already in here," Peter responded, but she couldn't see him as he'd turned a corner in the elaborate maze created through the newspapers. She eyed the stacks surrounding her as she stepped cautiously into the room. The stacks appeared sturdy enough, but she didn't trust them. *Some of these newspapers probably go back thirty or forty years*, she realized. "Plus, if they kept all this junk they probably kept food too, and lots of it."

"I don't know," Donald said from ahead of her. "I've seen those hoarding shows; I'm not so sure we should eat the food they may have here."

Mary Ellen had watched ten minutes of one of those hoarding shows, once, before her stomach had threatened to revolt, and she had hurriedly changed the channel. She thought Donald was probably right about the food situation.

Turning to the side, she was able to avoid knocking one of the piles over. There was something almost intricate about the design of the stacks, something deliberate. *Had the owners come in here to get lost in the labyrinth they'd created? Had this been some kind of escape for them?* She wondered as she tried not to touch anything. She was frightened she would set the stacks off like giant dominoes that would bury them beneath their crushing depths. The sick humans wouldn't be able to climb over top of the stacks toward them as most of the newspapers were crammed up against the ceiling, but they would never escape here if those things fell on them.

She heard another door sliding open, but she still couldn't see Peter as she edged her way around a sharp turn. She almost bumped into Donald as she rounded the corner, but she caught herself before she plowed into him. Holding her hand behind her, she was able to keep Josh from walking into her back. Donald shook his head and muttered a curse as he peered into the room beyond. Mary Ellen still didn't smell anything overly unpleasant, but she was worried they'd just found the room where these people had kept all of their cats, or every bit of garbage they'd ever accumulated.

"What is it?" she asked nervously.

Donald glanced over his shoulder at her. "My version of Hell."

Her eyebrows shot up as she tried to see around his back, but it was impossible with all of the papers in the way. She glanced back at Josh, it was just as impossible to see behind him as it was to see in front of Donald. It was becoming increasingly difficult to breathe in the stifling house. She could feel the beat of her pulse in her temples, and had to fight the impulse to rub them as her head began to throb.

She started, and nearly screamed, as she caught the shifting black robes of what she swore was the Grim Reaper amongst the stacks. There were people who had stared down the throats of lions that hadn't felt as frightened as she did right then. She shook her head in order to clear it of the image of the reaper stalking them with his scythe at the ready. She thought she heard the rattle of his bones as an ominous laugh escaped him. They were trapped within this room, unable to flee from the steady pursuit of death.

When she opened her eyes and looked at the area again, she realized the robes were only a piece of a mostly buried curtain blowing in the breeze created by an open window. Mary Ellen pressed her fingers briefly against her forehead as she tried to calm the thunderous beat of her heart.

Grabbing hold of Josh's arm, she was able to step aside enough to maneuver the young boy in front of her. If those sick people did get into the house, or were already in here, they might not be able to climb over the stacks to get at them, but they could most certainly move through the stacks toward them. She wasn't going to let them get at the boy first. She nudged Josh forward when the curtain billowed again.

Josh's step faltered as he walked into the room beyond. Mary Ellen braced herself for rotten food, feces, dead animals or some other horror. Even prepared for all of those awful things, she still stopped dead when she entered the next room. She almost bolted across the room and out the opposite door at the same time she fought the urge to spin and flee back into the maze. Her paralysis broke, the step she took back nearly made her bump against one of the hundreds of porcelain dolls filling every inch of the dozens of shelves, tables, and curio cabinets in the room.

Eyes, there were eyes *everywhere* and *every* one of them was following her as she turned to shut the doors behind her. They may not be able to see if those sick humans were coming up behind them, but they'd be able to hear them opening the doors at least. She tried not to look at the dolls, however her gaze was irresistibly drawn to them over and over again.

She swore the doll's heads swiveled to watch them as they looped their way through the tables and shelves holding them. There were Victorian dolls, china dolls, some dressed in vivid colors, and others with plumes in their hair and sticking up from their outfits. Others were in costumes such as chefs, astronauts, racecar drivers, artists, pilots, and clowns. There were *hundreds* of clowns all smiling at them.

Mary Ellen shuddered as the black, blue, green, brown, and yellow eyes watched her walk through the room. She almost believed they were silently communicating a plan with each other to get up and attack them. Dolls had never bothered her before, but now they creeped her out worse than those pictures she'd seen where some kind of ghostly figure or strange face was lurking unsuspectedly in the background. Those pictures had never failed to make her skin crawl. She was certain there was something lurking within this room.

She hated those dolls, but she couldn't tear her gaze away from them as she searched for a human face within the mass, just trying to blend in until they could rise and pounce on her back. She felt as jumpy as a cat on a pound of catnip as her eyes bounced around the room.

She heard another set of doors slide open and then a muffled curse from Peter. She wasn't sure she wanted to know what waited ahead. So far, everything had been crowded but astonishingly clean for the amount of junk in this house. She couldn't help but think it was only a matter of time before they came across something worse.

Please no bugs, she pleaded silently as she followed Josh into another room. It wasn't until she spotted the oven beneath the containers piled on top of it she realized they were in the kitchen. Taking a deep breath, she turned to close the doors before she really began to inspect the room they'd just entered.

Thankfully, there were no bugs, but she doubted there was any food either as the large Tupperware containers sitting on the floor were stacked all the way to the counters. More of the containers were on top of the counters and piled to the ceiling. Looking through the clear containers, she could see they were filled with an assortment of collectibles from small silver spoons to beer steins. Colorful vases were stacked within at least five other containers, and though she couldn't be certain, they appeared to be antiques. She spotted some Precious Moments figurines mingled in with what appeared to be the entire Hummel collection. Face after smiling face stared out at her from behind the clear plastic of the bins they had been stored in. She began to agree with Donald's assessment of this place as she became certain they'd just entered another circle of Hell.

She couldn't begin to imagine how much money was stored within these containers, within this *house*. She'd never seen anything like it, and she was certain there were museums that would have liked to get their hands on some of the things being held here. Moving around the island packed with more containers, she spotted a trashcan by the backdoor. Empty Chinese food containers poked out the top of it; pizza boxes were wedged against the wall behind it.

"That doesn't bode well for food," Mary Ellen muttered as she looked toward what she assumed was the pantry. She wasn't going to bother looking in the cabinets; she doubted any of the containers sitting in front of them had moved much since they'd been placed there.

Peter pulled open the pantry door; they all craned their heads to peer into it. Containers were stacked so completely inside they reached the ceiling and were only an inch away from the door. Cobwebs danced in the breeze the opening of the door had created. It was the first sign of uncleanliness she'd seen in the house.

"Couldn't they have hoarded food?" Donald muttered as Peter shut the door. "Or at least something useful."

Mary Ellen didn't think they were going to find anything useful in this place, but she followed them through the kitchen to another set of sliding doors. Though she knew nothing could be behind her, she still glanced nervously back as she waited to see what the next room would reveal. Peter's breath hissed out of him on a harsh curse. Donald said something unintelligible, but the tone of his voice caught her attention.

Mary Ellen froze when she stepped through the next door.

She'd thought the doll room had been bad, but it was nothing compared to *this* room. No matter how hard she tried to stabilize them, her hands were trembling when she turned to close the doors again.

Taking a deep breath, she forced herself to turn back to what she could only describe as a trophy room. A trophy room she'd never thought she would see unless it was in a nightmare or haunted house. Dead and stuffed animals covered nearly every inch of the walls, there were so many she couldn't tell what color the walls had been. Deer, elk, moose, bears, wolves, marlins, and swordfish all stared at her as she took a step forward. Mixed in with the larger animals were squirrels, raccoons, crows, hawks, foxes, coyotes, and turkeys decorating the floor and branches from the fake trees placed around the room. The musky scent of preserved and mounted animals filled the room and caused her nose to wrinkle.

A cat perched on the armrest of a sofa; the sofa was the first place in the house she'd seen to sit on. Across from the sofa was a TV with two ravens perched on each end of it. She'd thought the dolls eyes had been following her, but she couldn't shake the irrational *conviction* the gold, brown, black, and hazel eyes surrounding her now knew exactly where she was. Though all the animals were now missing their bellies, she was convinced they were hungry.

She stepped to the side to avoid a beaver perched on a log as she rounded the back of the sofa. The coffee table came into view, sitting on top of it was a small plate. There was nothing on the plate, but the glass sitting next to it was still half filled with water. "This is the room they spent most of their time in."

"That's more disturbing than the fact they actually collected all these things," Donald said as he stopped beside the sofa. His fingers brushed over a book that was open and lying face down on the cushion. "I think they lived here alone."

"Would you live with this nut job?" Josh inquired.

Mary Ellen didn't like calling anyone a nut job, but she had to admit she would *not* live with this person. She turned her head away from the eyes of a colorful pheasant and came face to face with the substantial fangs of a snarling wolf. There was no winning in this room, nowhere safe to look, even when she kept her head down she was still confronted with stuffed animal after stuffed animal lining the dark hardwood floor.

"I can't believe they were able to keep this place so clean," Mary Ellen said. "I can't begin to imagine how much time it would take to dust this place without all this stuff in it, but at least there wasn't much vacuuming."

"That's looking on the bright side," Donald agreed.

Peter had made it to another set of sliding doors. Mary Ellen braced herself for whatever lay beyond, but the doors slid open to reveal the cramped main hall. They shuffled back into the foyer and she slid the doors closed again.

"I don't see any reason to check upstairs," Peter said. "I imagine it's only more of the same."

"I certainly don't plan on spending the night here. If those things find us and decide to come in here, we would be sitting ducks," Josh said. "It appears whoever lived here survived on take-out so I doubt there's any food up there anyway."

"What about weapons?" Mary Ellen suggested though the last thing she wanted was to spend another minute in this suffocating place. "Perhaps they have a room full of them stashed somewhere. Something had to kill all of those animals."

It wasn't an overwhelming possibility, but she wouldn't feel right walking out of here without looking first. "Maybe they weren't the hunter," Josh suggested.

"Most likely they weren't," Mary Ellen agreed. "I doubt whoever lived here got out much, but we should still look."

"Let's go quickly," Peter said.

Mary Ellen wasn't going to argue with that. She found herself able to breathe easier as the clutter within the house eased by the time they hit the top of the stairs. They went through two bedrooms and two bathrooms rapidly. The rooms had little to nothing within them, including furniture.

"Strangest place I've ever been in," Donald muttered beside her as he ran a hand through his disordered hair.

She had to agree as they stopped in front of the last door. Peter grabbed hold of the handle and thrust it open. Mary Ellen's hand flew to her nose; she took an abrupt step back. The stench wafting out of the room caused her eyes to water and her throat to burn. Josh turned and wretched in the hall, but Mary Ellen found her gaze riveted upon the set of legs poking out from beneath the covers on the bed. The image of the Wicked Witch of the East's feet poking out from beneath Dorothy's house blazed through her mind at the sight of those legs.

She didn't know if it was the events that had just transpired that had killed the person within, or if they had passed away before the quakes had hit. She suspected they had died before the quakes, but no one had come looking for them. Her heart ached for the loneliness this house represented, and the body, as she hastily turned away from the room.

Peter's face was expressionless as he closed the door. An uneasy feeling settled in the pit of her stomach at the hollow look within his eyes. There seemed to be nothing behind them, not anymore. She exchanged a pointed glance with Donald, but Josh didn't seem to have noticed as he leaned against the wall and wiped at his mouth with the back of his hand.

"We should go," Mary Ellen said.

She was halfway down the stairs, almost caught up to Peter, when the first gunshot shattered the tranquil day.

CHAPTER 27

Riley

RILEY FOUND her feet planted in place as she gazed in awe at the books lining the shelves. Some of them were so old she wouldn't dare touch them, even if she'd had gloves on. "I think that's a first edition Grapes of Wrath," she whispered. "And look at how old the Merchant of Venice appears to be. I don't want to breathe on one of them."

"We can be concerned about breathing on them after we check the house," Xander said.

She couldn't turn her head to look at him as her gaze remained riveted upon the books before her. "I wonder if those Harry Potter books are signed," she pondered as her fingers twitched to take one of them down from the shelf. She'd spent hours with Carol reading through series, discussing what was going to happen. They'd both spilled more than a few tears over those pages.

"We'll find out later," Xander assured her.

Al lingered beside her, his gaze traveled longingly over the spines as Bobby and Xander left the library and walked to the French doors on the other side of the cavernous front hall. Riley threw one last glance over her shoulder before hurrying to join the others.

Xander and Bobby got ready to open the other set of doors. Riley and Al lifted their guns and prepared to take on anything that might leap out at them. Bobby and Xander simultaneously pulled the doors open and stepped to the side. Nothing moved in the room beyond but they proceeded cautiously as they crept closer to the doors.

Riley poked her head in to find ten chairs set around a rectangular dining room table. Three white candles still sat in their silver candlesticks. Without thinking, she ran her hand over the oak table. It was grainy beneath her fingertips; she could feel the dips and swirls within the wood as she walked down the length of it.

"Beautiful home," she murmured as she glanced over the paintings hanging on the dark wood paneled walls. "Outdated, but beautiful."

A massive stone fireplace took up most of the right hand wall. She'd never seen one so big before, and she could almost picture a woman standing over it, cooking dinner for her family. Riley tore her attention away from the beautiful room as they approached another room in the back. They stepped into a small den with a computer and papers scattered across the top of the desk. A telescope was set up in front of the bay window. Curiosity caused her to bend down and place her eyes against the eyepiece; she was greeted with a view of the reddened sky.

"At least they weren't spying on their neighbors," she said as she took a step back.

She followed the others into the dining room and through

another set of open doors. They stepped into a yellow kitchen so cheerful she was certain Big Bird would blend in with the background. "It looks like a daisy threw up in here," Bobby muttered and Riley couldn't help but agree.

Riley studied the ceiling, but there was nowhere someone could be lurking above them. She leaned over the black marble countertop and opened one of the white cabinets. She'd been hoping for some food, instead she was greeted with shelves full of cookbooks. She closed the cabinet and moved on to the next one. There were more cookbooks in that one.

"What is going on?" she muttered but as she focused on the spines, she realized they were all written by a Darla Bates. Riley had never heard of the author before, but judging by the sheer number of books, she'd been popular.

"Apparently she only wrote the recipes but didn't practice cooking them," Xander said.

Most of the cookbooks were for baking, and as Riley closed the cabinet doors, she understood what was going on. "She most likely had her own bakery somewhere else where she tested the recipes and sold them. Is there a pantry?"

"I don't see one," Bobby answered from the other side of the kitchen. "But we do have some boxes of spaghetti, spaghetti sauce, canned veggies, and potato chips."

She turned to find Bobby standing in front of a floor to ceiling cabinet with Lazy Susan-like shelves inside. "We also have some flour, sugar, vanilla, and anything else you need to bake with," Xander said as he shut a cabinet like Bobby's but on the opposite side of the fridge.

"We'll grab the spaghetti and stuff later," Al said as he moved on toward a room off of the kitchen.

Riley followed behind him and wasn't at all surprised to find a few tables pushed against the walls and covered with assorted pots and pans. The small rectangular room ran across the back of the library, but there was no doorway to get into the library from here. *It's an addition*, she realized as Xander walked to the glass door at the end of the room. He peered through the door before pulling it open.

She stepped into the greenhouse behind him. It had once been a thriving world of plants, and judging by the tempting scent causing her stomach to rumble, herbs. Her nose twitched at the scent of chives as she was drawn to one of the brown plants dangling over the sides of their pots. She lifted the wilted chive and let it drop down before turning to inspect the rest of the ruined plants. A few cactuses were still alive, but for the most part everything within the room was dead.

Beyond the glass was a garden with flowers and plants wilting along the white seashell pathways. For one brief second she was back on her porch as her mother sang while deadheading her roses and weeding her perennials. Her mother had possessed an amazing green thumb; she probably could have saved these plants if she'd been given enough time. The memory was so intense Riley could almost feel the mug of coffee in her hands and smell the heady scent of the roses. Her mother may have had a way with plants, but her singing could scare away the bravest of people; it had never scared Riley or her father away. It had been their joke that her mother was tone deaf, but they were going to go deaf after years of listening to her.

Riley hadn't realized her fingers were pressed against the glass of the building until the memory full of color and love faded away, and she was left with the brownness of the plants surrounding her. She dropped her hand away before the tears burning her eyes could fall. Turning away from the garden, she stepped out of the greenhouse and back into the room with all the pots and pans.

Leaning against one of the tables, she tapped her foot as she waited for the others to join her. Xander stepped beside her and wrapped his arm around her waist; she went willingly into his arms and rested her head against his chest. Inhaling deeply, she took in the scent of sweat, dirt, and earth clinging to him. Just a short time ago it wouldn't have been a pleasant scent, but right now she thought it was the best one in the world.

"I love you," she whispered.

His hands tightened on her arms; his breath tickled her ear as his lips brushed against her skin. "I love you too."

Her fingers curled into his back before she took a step away from him and examined the room again. Xander's hand slid into hers as he walked with her through the kitchen, dining room, and into the main hallway once more. She released his hand as he approached the door tucked against the side of the staircase. He opened the door and peered inside the closet before closing it again.

Riley adjusted her hold on her gun and kept her back against the railing as they made their way cautiously up the stairs to the second floor. Xander stayed in front of her while Al and Bobby brought up the rear.

The sun was sinking lower in the sky when they stepped off the stairs and into the hallway running the length of the second floor. Three of the seven doors were open, and across the way she could see a bubblegum colored bathroom that made her nose wrinkle. The woman may have been a successful baker, but she'd had *no* taste in colors.

Xander nudged the door open with the toe of his shoe; it didn't get any better when the nearly neon pink shower curtain, and watermelon colored toilet seat cover were exposed. "Dear Lord," Bobby muttered and shook his head. "I don't want to know what this woman's bedroom looks like."

Riley wholeheartedly agreed as she turned away from the room and looked up and down the hall. She moved onto the next room and pushed the door open. The walls of the room beyond were lined with mirrors reflecting the exercise bike, elliptical machine, yoga mat, and weights lined against the back wall.

"Wow," Al said in a low whisper.

That about summed it up, Riley decided as she closed the door. Bobby stopped in front of the next room; the first closed door they had come across. He took hold of the knob and pushed the door open. At first Riley thought the room had been painted robin's egg blue and splashed with red and black paint, and then the smell hit her. She took a step back as her gag reflex kicked in.

Her brain was still trying to process what it was she was seeing, when something burst from the room with a shrieking sound that could have shattered glass. Riley already had her gun raised, but she didn't have time to pull the trigger before the screeching thing slammed into her and knocked her into the railing. Shouts filled the hall; Riley barely heard them as she battled to keep the woman who had been hiding somewhere in the room, off of her. Fetid breath washed over her as hands slapped and tore at her. Fingers curled into her hair; her scalp screamed in protest as strands of her hair were torn free.

The banister pressed against her back; she was nearly bent over it as the woman continued to beat at her. Riley caught a glimpse of the floor of the main hall beneath her, panic slammed into her at the thought of plummeting to the hardwood floor below. The woman's screaming abruptly cut off as her fingers curled into the flesh of Riley's upper arms. The noises coming from the woman made Riley think of apes in the zoo, and she suddenly understood the theory of evolution in a whole new way.

Blood covered the woman's face, but Riley didn't think any of it was actually the woman's as her teeth snapped with a loud clacking that caused Riley to wince. She was certain the woman's teeth were going to shatter from the force of her biting. Terror caused her to fight the woman with more strength than she'd thought she could possess, but the muscles in her arms were beginning to protest having to hold the weight of the woman off.

It had probably only been seconds since the woman had burst from the room, but it seemed an eternity had passed before a sickening thud resonated within the hall. The woman released a loud grunt, her eyes rolled back in her head before her weight eased from Riley, and she slumped to the floor. Riley's eyes met Xander's; he was holding his gun by the barrel, the butt of it was covered in the woman's blood as he twisted it within his hand and slid it into the waistband of his jeans.

"Are you ok?" he demanded as he stepped over the woman and took hold of her brutalized arms.

"I'm fine," she murmured as she strived to catch her breath. His hazel eyes burned into hers as he leaned closer and examined her from under his curling, dark blonde lashes. "She didn't hurt me."

The muscles in his forearms and biceps flexed as he turned her hands over before him and examined the scratches and gashes on her arms. His thumb briefly stroked over her skin before he released her and took a step away. "Is she dead?" she asked as Xander knelt by the woman's side and pressed his fingers against her throat.

"Yes," he said flatly.

Kill or be killed, she reminded herself as she looked down at the scratches marring her arms. Blood trickled down steadily and dripped from her fingertips onto the floor. It wouldn't be the last time any of them would kill. She would be more upset if she stopped feeling any regret over it; she wouldn't be able to recognize the person she would be if that ever happened.

Xander rose and gently took hold of her hand. "Let's get you cleaned up."

"We should finish checking the rest of the house first. Where there's one..." Her voice trailed off, there was no reason to finish the sentence, they already knew.

Xander nodded; he took hold of her wrist as he turned back to the bedroom the woman had come from. She took a cautious step inside, but didn't make it far as the blood and bones littering the room were overwhelming. Her foot brushed against something she assumed was a femur judging by the size of it. Her stomach was beginning to feel like she'd just ridden on the spinning teacups for two hours straight.

"She must have been bringing people back here," Bobby said as he took a couple of steps to the side.

Riley spotted three skulls in the corner, one of which was far too small for her liking. "I've seen enough," she said and left the room.

They went rapidly through the rest of the rooms, but no one commented on the neon green bathroom or black bedroom. Riley had ceased to find any humor in the woman's color choices. Xander led her into the green bathroom and sat her on the toilet cover while Al and Bobby remained outside the door.

Xander opened and closed the medicine cabinet before bending down to look under the sink. He pulled out a bottle of peroxide and some bandages. "How does your leg feel?" she inquired.

He glanced up at her as he placed the peroxide on the sink.

"Fine." Her gaze slid to the scratches on her arms as she took a deep breath and closed her eyes. "How are you?"

"Good. I'm good."

He dropped a couple of towels next to her and turned her arms over to pour some peroxide on the scratches. The bubbles fizzed as the liquid ran over her skin. He wet a towel before wiping the blood and peroxide away.

"Xander." At first he didn't look at her, but when she said his name again his attention turned to her. "Thank you."

He clasped her cheeks in his hands as he rose up and pressed a kiss against her forehead. She thought he was going to pull away from her, instead his mouth brushed over her cheek before settling over hers. A small sigh escaped Riley as she wrapped her hands around his forearms and melted into the heat his mouth created against hers.

There was a minute when the rest of the world slid away and she was filled with him and *only* him. A minute when everything was right, and she had found where she belonged. A groan of regret escaped her when Xander pulled away and rested his forehead against hers.

"There isn't anything I wouldn't do for you," he whispered against her mouth.

A smile tugged at her lips as she kissed him again. "I could say the same to you."

He sat back on his heels again and took hold of her wrists. "Good."

He finished wiping the scratches off, but when he reached for the bandages she seized hold of his hand. "I don't think those are necessary."

"Are you sure?"

She nodded and released his arm. "The scratches aren't that deep, and I'm ready to get out of this freak show of a bathroom."

"Green not your color?"

"I don't think the Muppets would like this color."

"Probably not," Xander agreed and helped pull her to her feet.

Al and Bobby turned to look at them when they exited the room. "We'll get the food and find the others," Al said.

Riley didn't look at the woman again as she stepped over the body and made her way downstairs. She glanced at the library, but she didn't return to it; the room had lost all the luster it had held for her upon first entering the house. Stepping back into the kitchen, she searched through the cabinets under the sink for some garbage bags.

She heard a door open and turned as Bobby looked into the basement. "Found them," he said and pulled a box of trash bags from the top step.

Al took a bag from him and opened it up for Xander to drop the spaghetti, sauce, canned food and chips into it. Riley stepped next to Bobby and peered down the stairs to the basement. "Should we go down there?" she asked.

"I don't think there's anything down there we have to see," Bobby answered.

"There could be supplies down there," Xander said.

She knew that was doubtful, but if there was a small chance there was something useful in the basement, then they couldn't leave here without looking first. She pulled her flashlight free and clicked it on as she took the first step down.

Shining the beam around the room, she searched for any hint of danger, but all it revealed were stacks of boxes against the wall. Riley crept down the rest of the stairs and turned to search underneath them. Bobby remained close by her side as they moved through the shadows hugging the walls and boxes. She didn't bother to open the boxes as they were all labeled, most of them with the words pots and pans, Christmas, or photos. A jumble of stuffed animals in the corner caught and held her attention; she'd had the same exact pink Care Bear sitting in her closet at home.

It was a disconcerting realization, but she didn't feel a pang of homesickness with it. There was no home to return to; she'd accepted that now. She would grieve her losses for the rest of her days, but she had to move on. She simply didn't have any other choice, if she was going to keep on living.

"Riley." She turned to find Xander standing at the bottom of the stairs.

"It's all clear down here," she told him.

"We're ready to go."

She and Bobby followed him up the stairs and into the kitchen. Stepping out of the stairwell, Riley froze as she spotted Al standing by the kitchen sink. The color had vanished from Al's lined face; he appeared to have aged ten years as he turned to look at them. The feeling of a trap door opening beneath her feet descended over her as all the blood seemed to drain from her head. She had the disconcerting feeling she was falling as the world around her focused on one central thing...

The four hideous faces within the doorway that led to the room with all the pots and pans.

It was impossible to tell what sex the people were as their blisters and sores had caused their skin to peel off of their distorted features. She didn't know how they had managed to get in here, but she wasn't about to investigate it either. Her gaze slid to Al, only four feet away from where the intruders stood in the doorway.

"Run." Xander grabbed hold of her arm and pushed her toward the dining room.

"No," she refused as she pulled her arm free of his grasp.

Lifting her gun, she aimed at the one closest to Al as it lurched toward the older man. The other three people rushed at them. Al tried to scramble out of the way, but he wasn't fast enough to escape the person lunging at him. She should avoid firing the gun, but she had no other choice as the first person seized hold of Al's arms and opened its mouth wide.

CHAPTER 28

Carl

CARL HAD JUST STEPPED out the front door of the house when the second shot pierced the air. His gaze went rapidly back and forth between the two houses the others had entered in order to search. He couldn't pinpoint the source of the gunfire until Mary Ellen and the others emerged from the house on the other side of the one in the middle.

"Get in the truck!" Carl barked at Rochelle.

"But..."

"No buts; get in the truck!"

Panic drove him as he ran across the porch; bypassing the steps, he leapt over them to the sidewalk. John grabbed hold of the rail on the side of the porch and launched himself over top of it. Carl had expected him to break his ankle, it must have jarred his ribs, but John barely missed a step as he raced across the yard. John was ahead of Carl when they got to the porch of the middle house and lunged up the stairs toward the door. From the corner of his eye, he spotted Mary Ellen running at them, but he waved her back.

"Stay with Rochelle!" he yelled at her as John grabbed hold of the knob and thrust the door open.

The third shot was much louder as it reverberated through the home. He glanced toward the room on his right, but he couldn't see anyone amongst the shelves of books. John was already moving to the left when two more shots rent the air. Carl tried to catch John before he could enter the other room, but his youth made him faster and more impetuous.

"John!" he shouted as his friend disappeared. "Let them know you're coming!"

John didn't glance back at him as Carl entered the dining room, but he eased in his rush toward the room at the end. "I'm here!" John yelled. "I'm coming from the dining room!"

Carl glanced at the study to his right, but again he saw nothing moving within. He finally caught up to John before he plunged into what Carl assumed was the kitchen. "Don't shoot at us!" Carl called. He kept his gun raised before him as he tried to see into the other room without exposing too much of himself.

He wasn't sure if the others had heard them as another shot echoed through the house, and loud grunts came from the room. The potent scent of blood and gunpowder filled the house and burned his nostrils. Adrenaline coursed through his body as concern for his friends made him yearn to plunge recklessly into the room. Common sense kept him where he was until he had a better idea of what was going on though.

He could still hear noises coming from the room, but he didn't hear any words from the others. A pain filled cry filled the air as something clattered and bounced across the floor. John was pressed against the other side of the door when Carl gestured for John to follow him. He stayed low as he swept into the kitchen with his gun raised and ready. The blood splattering the canary colored walls seemed completely out of place in the hideously vibrant room. Cookbooks and a garbage bag were tossed amongst the mess littering the white tiled floor.

Two bodies were sprawled face down on the floor; a growing puddle of blood seeped out around them. For a second his heart leapt into his throat at the thought that one of those bodies was one of his friends. The tattered clothing on the bodies, and their dirt streaked, purplish red skin made him realize neither of them were his friends.

His attention moved from the bodies to the doorway on the other side of the room. Riley was watching him from the other side of the archway, beyond her seemed to be a room full of tables. Her lips were compressed into a thin line as she met his gaze. "There's still two of them," she whispered. "I have to stay here to make sure they don't try and circle around behind us."

"Stay with her," Carl instructed John as they stepped over the debris on the floor.

John nodded as he walked over to the door and positioned himself across from Riley. Carl didn't look back at them as he cautiously approached Xander and Bobby. They were standing by a door that went into what appeared to be a greenhouse. Carl stopped beside Al standing against a wall in the middle of the room. Al's hair was spiked up and Carl could already see murky bruises forming on his upper arms but he appeared otherwise unharmed.

"We don't know where they went," Xander said in a low voice.

Carl glanced over the tables lined with pots and pans and then at the doorway beyond. "The noise might have frightened them off," Carl suggested.

"We should retreat. We can't stay here, not anymore. There's no reason to go after them and risk getting injured," Al said.

"He's right," Carl said. "And we should get out of here before more come. They might not like loud noises, but they know *we're* the ones making them."

Bobby and Xander stepped away from the doorway and edged cautiously toward him and Al. Even as they began to retreat a sound from the greenhouse froze all of them in place. It took Carl only a second to recognize the increasingly familiar sound of breaking glass. It was followed by what sounded like the scrambling sounds of one of those things trying to flee the building.

"Let's go," Carl said.

A sense of growing urgency was beginning to fill him as he took another step toward the kitchen. Those things had just been a little too loud for his liking. He knew how stealthy they could be, how covert. He couldn't shake the feeling the creatures were simply toying with them. Holding his hand up, he gestured for the others to stop as he strained to hear anything more. Riley and John moved closer, but he waved them back.

Raising the gun, he spun back toward the pots and pans room as one of the sick humans burst into the room from the greenhouse. Carl tried to follow it with his gun. As he tracked it, it scooted underneath one of the tables and into the shadows. Fear caused the hair on the nape of his neck to stand up as a strange hiss issued from beneath the table.

He wasn't so much worried about that one, at least he knew where it was, but the other *sneakier* one was of far more concern to him. Carl gestured to the rest of the group to fall back. He wasn't going to get caught in a bottleneck if they all tried to get through the doors at the same time.

Grabbing hold of the handle on the door, he pulled it closed behind them. Riley snagged the garbage bag from the floor and kept hold of it as she backed toward the dining room. Donald was already in the dining room when they entered it. His gaze darted between them and the front door as they edged toward him.

"We have to get out of here," John informed him briskly.

Donald nodded and moved toward the door. Carl couldn't tear his gaze away from what he could still see of the kitchen as he walked backward through the room. He was almost past the dining room table when a head poked around the corner of the doorframe. Cracked and bloody lips skimmed back to reveal gaps between the remaining teeth. Carl didn't have a chance to squeeze the trigger before the head pulled away from the doorway, and feet pounded over the tile floor of the kitchen.

His heart raced like a runaway locomotive in his chest as his mouth went completely dry. All of this just seemed so wrong, like they were the mice being batted around by a cat. These things were taunting them, or perhaps getting ready to bat them around in order to tenderize their meat. His gaze went past the kitchen to the windows in the backdoor, he saw nothing out there, but he knew they were coming.

"Run," he breathed.

"What?" John asked in a choked voice.

"Run!" Carl shouted as he turned toward them.

They were already rushing through the dining room door when he broke into a run after them. He glanced behind him and almost fired a warning shot, but there was nothing pursuing them and he couldn't waste the bullet. The echoing slap of their feet resonating through the front hall caused Carl to wince. The noise they were making would cover the sound of any possible pursuit, but there was no helping it.

Riley slipped through the front door first, but Donald and Bobby got caught up on each other. John was unable to stop his forward momentum in time to stop himself from plowing into them. The force of John's body knocked the other two through the doorway and onto the porch. Bobby was able to catch himself before falling over, but Donald wasn't as lucky as he sprawled on the porch in an inelegant heap. Bobby grabbed hold of his arm and helped to pull him back to his feet. Xander and Al were still ahead of him, but Xander held back in order to let Al through the door without incident.

Rochelle, Mary Ellen, Josh, and Peter stood in the front yard near the Cadillac. Carl's anger spiked when he spotted the teacher. The man loved to run his mouth, and argue about everything, but he was never anywhere to be found when help was needed.

"Get in the vehicles!" he called.

"Is everyone ok?" Mary Ellen demanded.

Carl didn't answer her as he glanced back at the house. Even as his attention turned toward the building, his eyes were settling on the yards behind the homes. There were plenty of times when he'd been afraid, most of those times had occurred within the past couple of weeks, but they all paled in comparison to right now. His heart seemed to stop beating as he caught sight of what was coming toward them from behind the houses.

A low curse escaped him; he hadn't realized his legs could move as fast as they did now as at least two dozen of those sick humans honed in on them. The people were still a good hundred feet away, but it was far too close for Carl's liking as the vehicles were almost a hundred feet away from *them*.

"Get in the vehicles!" he shouted at the other four again.

Rochelle pulled away from Mary Ellen and ran toward the truck. Mary Ellen followed behind her though, staying close on her heels until Rochelle was in the truck. Slamming the door closed behind her daughter, she turned to go back to the car but Carl waved her back. Mary Ellen did a strange little stutter step before opening the door again and jumping into the truck beside her daughter.

"You'll have to get in the back," Carl panted to John. He labored to catch his breath as they ran. He swore he would quit smoking after this, but he knew that wouldn't happen.

"On it," John assured him.

Something streaked across the yard with more speed than any of them could have exhibited. For a disconcerting second, Carl had no idea what it was and thought some monstrous new threat had been unleashed upon them. Then he recognized the cat as it bounded into the still open backseat of the car. The loud blaring of a horn sounded from the truck as Mary Ellen leaned across the front seat to press on it relentlessly. Some of the people let out a squeal and stumbled back with their hands over their ears, but it didn't deter the others.

Carl wanted to yell at her to stop, the noise would only bring more, but he didn't think they had enough time for all of them to make it to the vehicles without those people catching up to them. They could fight off some of them, but they wouldn't be able to fight off *all* of them.

Carl lifted his gun and shot at the one closest to him. The shot hit the ground two feet before the approaching... man? But it didn't deter him. Taking the time to turn and steady himself, Carl fired again, this time it hit the man in the shoulder and knocked him back a few feet. More gunshots exploded around him, but more of the bullets missed their intended targets than actually hit the mark.

Another one of the sick people went down. Carl grabbed hold of Al's arm when the older man faltered and nearly fell beside him. He kept hold of Al's arm as he rushed him toward the vehicles. Carl didn't think Al had enough left in him to make it all the way to the car in front of the truck.

"Open the back doors!" he shouted at John.

John skid to a halt behind the truck, his hands fumbled over the lock on the doors before he flung them open and lifted himself into the bed. A startled cry from behind him caused Carl to turn before they made it to the truck.

"Bobby!" Riley screamed as she spun away from the car she was only feet away from.

Carl swore as he spotted Bobby sprawled across the lawn. Donald grabbed hold of Bobby's arm and tried to propel him to his feet. Bobby started to rise as one of those things descended upon him. "Bobby!" Riley shrieked again.

Xander turned back and ran toward his friend, but Carl didn't think he was going to be able to get to him in time. Carl heard Riley's footsteps behind him; releasing Al, he swung to grab her before she could throw herself back into the fray. "Get in the car!" he commanded.

Riley struggled within his grasp, but he pushed her backward. Al grabbed hold of her arms and pulled her away from Carl. "Easy," Al said soothingly. "The best way for you to help them is to get the car started. It's the only way we'll all get out of here."

Riley's eyes were turbulent, her nostrils flared, but Al's reasoning seemed to reach her as she gave a brief nod and spun away. Carl raised his gun as Donald was knocked aside by the human clinging to Bobby, and another one of the sick ones honed in on Xander. The person on Bobby tore at the back of Bobby's shirt as it sought to get at the tender flesh below. Xander spun and shot at another person bearing down on him; he was close enough he was able to hit the woman in the forehead. The woman's head snapped back as she was knocked onto her back beside the car.

Carl took up a stance and carefully aimed at the person still tearing at Bobby's back. An awful howl escaped Bobby as the person bent down and sank their teeth into Bobby's shoulder. Bobby slapped at the person over his back, but they grabbed hold of Bobby's head and bounced it off the sidewalk. The loud crack of Bobby's skull against concrete reverberated through the air. Carl found he much preferred the howling to the silence following the violent blow.

Carl had a clear view of the person attacking Bobby as they sat up again. He never would have taken the shot, even with the training he'd received at the academy, but Bobby's blood already stained the ground. Carl took a steadying breath before squeezing the trigger.

Though he knew the world around him was filled with far more noise and chaos than he'd experienced since the start of the quakes, the only sound he heard was the bullet erupting from his gun. A silent prayer ran through his mind that he didn't kill a man he'd come to consider an ally and friend.

The bullet struck the person in the chest. They released an inhuman squeal, as they were lifted up and flung from Bobby's back by the force of the impact. Donald grabbed hold of Bobby's arm and attempted to lift him to his feet but Bobby was a deadweight pulling Donald down with him. Carl put his gun back in his waistband. He'd managed to dislodge the person from Bobby, but he didn't see how they were going to get him to safety before the entire horde surged over them.

He'd been so absorbed on firing the gun, and trying to defend Bobby, he hadn't heard the truck start up until it went flying past him across the lawn. He caught a brief glimpse of Al in the bed of the truck before he was driven out of view. The doors smashed against the metal sides of the truck with a loud clang as John came to an abrupt halt.

"Get in!" Mary Ellen screamed from the passenger side as John continued to blare the horn from the driver's side.

Carl burst into motion as he spotted the car coming across the lawn toward them. Xander and Donald were scrambling to get Bobby to the truck when Carl got to them. Grass and dirt skidded up around the car as Riley screeched to a halt beside them.

Peter leaned out the passenger side window of the Cadillac and fired at the people continuing to stalk them. *At least he was finally doing something,* Carl thought.

"Get in the car," he told Xander as he took Bobby's arm from around Xander's shoulders.

"Bobby..."

"Someone has to ride with Riley; the map is in there, and we have to have some idea of where we're going. We'll take care of him," Carl promised.

Xander hesitated before he released Bobby's hand and helped Donald and Carl to maneuver Bobby into the back of the truck. Casting one last glance at Bobby, Xander turned away from them. He released a few shots to scare back a few of their enemies as he ran around the car to the passenger side. Riley threw the car into reverse as soon as Xander was settled and hit another person who had been closing in on them.

Donald scrambled into the back of the truck as the car shot past them again. Carl hefted himself into the back of the truck; he was rolling away from the doors when a hand seized hold of his ankle and jerked him back. His fingers scrabbled over the truck bed; splinters bit into his skin as wood dug beneath his nails. He ferociously kicked at the hand holding him as he scrambled for purchase on the bed. No matter what he did though, he continued his slide out of the truck as another hand seized his calf.

With the sinking realization of a man who was coming to the end of his life, he knew he wasn't going to be able to maintain his hold, and the others couldn't stay. Not if they were going to escape the things pursuing them.

John and Mary Ellen wouldn't be able to see him, not with the doors open. "Go, we're good! *Drive*!" Carl bellowed.

His legs slid out the back of the truck when John hit the gas.

CHAPTER 29

Al

"WAIT NO!" Al shouted but it was impossible to be heard over the commotion raging around them. He lurched toward the metal blocking him from the cab of the truck in an attempt to get John to stop, but the acceleration of the truck threw him back again. He managed to catch himself before he plummeted out of the truck and into the street.

Donald dove forward and grabbed hold of Carl's wrists as his waist slipped over the back of the truck. Donald was jerked forward, but he stopped himself from falling out the open doors by catching his foot on the metal siding. Al was almost hit by a case of water as he strained to right himself over the incessant bouncing of the truck.

"The supplies," Carl protested. "You *need* the supplies, let me go."

"We need you more," Donald said as a case of water slid past him, it fell out the open doors and splattered on the roadway.

Al's heart sank as Donald continued to try and pull Carl into the truck. Donald had been right when he'd said they needed Carl more than the supplies, but they had to get those doors shut before they lost everything. A bag of oats slid by him; Al lunged forward and managed to grab it before it was lost. Throwing the bag behind him, he was able to get close enough to grab Carl's left wrist with both of his hands. Donald released it and seized hold of Carl's right wrist with both of his hands. Al's arms protested the weight of Carl, and the person still clinging to his legs, but he refused to release him.

"Hold on," Donald insisted.

One of Donald's hands released Carl's wrists; he reached back and grabbed hold of a jug of water sliding around the back of the truck. He leaned forward and smashed the jug off the face of the man almost at Carl's waist now. Blood poured from the nose and lips broken open by the force of the blow as the man slipped. Before the man could regain his firm grasp on Carl, Donald raised the jug and slammed it into his face again. Plastic split open, water poured out, but the man finally lost his grip on Carl. Josh had to swerve the car to avoid hitting the body tumbling away from the truck.

One of the open doors swung toward them. Donald and Al pulled back with all of their might; they lifted Carl into the truck as the door clanged shut with a thunderous crash. More supplies spilled out the remaining open door as they pulled Carl further away from the edge of the truck bed.

Al could feel Carl's heaving breaths against his arm, but as Al struggled to catch his breath, Carl regained his feet. Carl leapt forward and grabbed hold of the closed door before it could swing open again.

"Hold this!" he barked at Donald and scurried to the other side of the truck.

Grasping the side of the truck, Carl leaned out to grab the other door. His muscles bulged; his face became florid as he fought to pull the door closed. The entire truck shook from the force of the door crashing back into position. Carl kept one white knuckled hand wrapped around the side of the truck and the other on the door as he turned to survey the supplies still in the truck.

"You should have let me go," he said gruffly.

"No," Al said firmly. "Even if we'd lost everything we had, we never should have let you go. Donald is right, we need you."

Carl shook his head. "Not more than you needed all the things we just lost."

Al sat back on his heels to stare at the stubborn man before him. "I am too old to lead, Donald is too new to the group, John, Riley, Bobby, and Xander are too young, Mary Ellen is not the type, not yet, and Peter is too unstable. So yes, we *do* need you. Even Donald sees that," Al told him.

Donald didn't say anything as he glanced between the two of them, but he gave a brief bow of his head to Al. Carl's jaw was locked, his gray eyes unrelenting as they met Al's. "I'm not a leader."

"Maybe not before, but you have no choice now."

Before Carl could protest further, Al decided to let those words sink in and turned away from him. He focused on Bobby's unconscious form near the front of the truck. The young man's breathing was shallow; his head was turned to the side to reveal the jagged bite mark on his shoulder. Muscle and skin had been torn away; Al could see the white of Bobby's shoulder bone through the blood oozing from the wound. A feeling of doom settled over him as he leaned forward and pressed his palm against the bite mark. Even still, the blood seeped around his fingers, and a growing pool of it spread beneath Bobby.

Al glanced at the others for help, but if they were going to keep the doors shut, they had to remain at the back of the truck. Al's hand pressed more firmly against the young man's neck as he gently turned Bobby's head toward him. His heart dropped when he spotted the large egg, already turning purple in the center of the boy's forehead. Blood seeped from the cut that had split Bobby's forehead, but it wasn't as profuse as the bite on his shoulder. Al could slow the bleeding on his shoulder until they were able to find something to sew the bite wound shut with, but there was nothing he could do for a head injury.

He pressed at the edges of the ugly looking bump. His prodding should have been painful but Bobby didn't stir. Helplessness filled him as he realized there was no way for them to know the extent of the damage done. Bobby could have a concussion or a contusion, perhaps even a fractured skull and brain damage.

Al took a deep breath as he decided to focus on the things he *could* help to fix right now. "Are they still following us?" he demanded.

"They're out there," Carl confirmed. "How is he?"

Al shook his head, and keeping his fingers pressed against Bobby's neck, he leaned forward to grab hold of one of the bags closest to him. There were medical supplies somewhere back here, but trying to find them was going to be a difficult task in the bouncing truck. If the medical supplies weren't some of the things that had gone out the back...

"Al...?"

"Don't let go of the doors," he commanded briskly.

Carl hiked an eyebrow up as he stared at him. "I don't think your age should count. Not if you're capable of leading."

Al chose to ignore him as he shoved aside a bag full of batteries and motor oil. The next bag he grabbed contained food, a welcome sight, but a useless one right now. He shoved it aside and tore through two more bags before locating one with bandages, antiseptics, ointments, and Band-Aids.

Pawing through the supplies with his free hand, he tugged out some packages of bandages. The bite had to be cleaned, but he was more concerned with getting the bleeding stopped first. Using his teeth, he tore open the packaging and pulled the cloth free. He pressed it firmly against the wound and grabbed the tape. Tearing the tape awkwardly with his teeth, he was able to pull enough free to secure the cloth in place. It wasn't the best-looking bandage, but it would do for now.

Trying to hold Bobby's head as steady as possible, Al was able to turn him enough to get a look at the crisscrossing gashes marring his back. Al winced and looked at his own hand pressed against a small, unmarred section of Bobby's skin. The burns on his palm were far better, but it was still reddened, and the blistered skin had begun to peel away. What had been done to his hand was nothing compared to the flesh stripped from Bobby's back.

Al hadn't felt this powerless since Nellie had been dying, and though Bobby was still alive, Al was fighting against the grief trying to take him over. Turning back to the bag of supplies, he hesitated a second before pulling out more. It may not look good for Bobby right now, but the young man was still breathing. The gashes on his back were vicious looking; they weren't as threatening as the one on his shoulder. He poured some peroxide on the gashes before wiping away the blood. He took off his shirt and placed it under Bobby to keep him off of the grass stained wooden truck bed. Relief filled him at the shallow rise and fall of Bobby's chest as he settled Bobby onto his back again.

Digging into the bag again, he was dismayed to realize none of the antibiotics or steroids were inside. Then he recalled they'd been placed in the trunk of the car to keep them safe from the rain. They must have missed this bag when they'd been moving the supplies around. A low curse escaped him; his gaze traveled to the still bleeding bite mark on Bobby's shoulder.

The bandages were already soaked through with blood; he leaned forward, pulled out more cloth and folded it in half. He refused to acknowledge the dwindling supplies as he placed the bandage against Bobby's neck and pressed down hard. Al knew there were times in life when difficult decisions had to be made, perhaps this was one of those times, but he couldn't bring himself to acknowledge that. No, he was not a leader, but he didn't think Carl would have made a different decision right now either.

Peter would have.

That realization sent a shiver down his spine. If Peter had his way, Al was certain he would kill him off for being too old. Perhaps he would even kill some of the others in order to conserve their supplies. No, he and Carl weren't ready to make the difficult decisions, not yet anyway, but they were still far better at making decisions than Peter was. Perhaps one day he would be able to walk away from Bobby, or Carl would, but today was not that day.

The wind blowing over the back of the truck tickled against Al's bared flesh but he barely felt it as he looked toward the others. Their hands, on the sideboards and backdoors, had turned white as they strained to keep them closed. Al taped the second set of bandages to Bobby and used the side of the truck to help himself up.

He held on as he looked over roads completely unfamiliar to

him. He had no idea where they would end up by the time they came to a stop, but he'd figure it out when he had a chance. For now, he was mostly concerned with what might still be following them.

"I haven't seen any other people in a few minutes," Donald said in response to his unasked question.

Al nodded and held onto the side of the truck as he shuffled toward the front of it. He pounded heavily against the board blocking him from the cab of the truck. He felt the truck decelerating before it pulled to the side of the road. Al kept a wary eye on the woods as he walked toward the back with the others. Carl fisted and un-fisted his hands before bending to grab some of the bags gathered near the doors. He moved them to the front again before kneeling at Bobby's side.

Carl examined the young man before turning to Al. He looked about to ask Al a question when the backdoors flew open again. The doors were barely out of the way before Riley and Xander appeared. Riley scrambled into the back of the truck with Xander close behind. "How is he?" Riley demanded.

"Not good," Al said. She barely glanced at him before rushing to her friend. Al stopped Xander before he could go any further. "You have to get him some medicine; we have to know exactly what it was Mary Ellen gave to you, and we need to find some needle and thread to stitch him up."

Xander glanced worriedly toward Riley and Bobby, but he jumped back to the ground. Al didn't see where Xander disappeared to as Carl dropped down in front of him and turned to offer him a hand. Pride made him want to wave Carl's hand away, but he eyed the three-and-a-half-foot distance to the ground warily. He was holding up fairly well, but that drop was not something he was eager to tackle. He refused Carl's hand and sat at the edge of the truck before easing himself onto the ground.

He spotted Mary Ellen and Xander at the trunk of the Cadillac, pawing through the supplies as they sought what it was Bobby required. Mary Ellen and Xander came toward them with a bag in Xander's hand. As she moved past the car, Peter opened the driver's side door and stepped out.

"If he isn't going to make it..." Peter started.

"*Don't* finish that statement," Xander interrupted crisply. He tossed the bag into the back of the truck and climbed in behind it. Al watched as he approached Riley and knelt at Bobby's side.

"I'll help them," Mary Ellen said before scrambling into the back of the truck.

Peter closed the door of the car and began to approach them. "You know I'm right."

Perhaps he was, but it wasn't something Al was willing to admit. "I don't know that," Al told him. "If we find a needle and thread, and get him the medicine, he has a chance of making it."

"A chance?" Peter demanded.

"There is no guarantee, not anymore. Not for anyone," Al told him.

"Cutting our losses..."

"He's not a loss, not yet," Carl inserted.

Peter shook his head as he folded his arms over his chest. "He's not an asset anymore either."

"He could be again," Carl retorted. "Is this what you would expect us to do if you were to get hurt one day, maybe even today? Do you want us to count you out as a loss? Because if that's what you want I'll be more than happy to do it when the time comes."

Al straightened away from the truck, his breath caught in his chest as Peter took a threatening step toward Carl. *This was it*, Al thought as his eyes darted between the two men staring at each other like two alpha wolves circling a deer. Al could almost picture them snarling at each other with their hackles raised.

Al knew Peter's meltdown was imminent, and he suspected the big blowout would be with Carl, but it couldn't happen now. "This isn't the time," he said quietly as he tried to step in between them. Peter nudged him out of the way though as he moved closer to Carl.

"You're an asshole," Peter grated.

"You have no idea just how much of an asshole I can be," Carl assured him. "But you keep pushing me and you'll find out."

John appeared from around the back of the truck; his mouth was moving as he began to speak, but Al didn't catch his words before John came to an abrupt halt, and his mouth clamped shut. His hand went to the gun at his side but Carl waved his hand away. The silence stretched onward until Al was certain it would never end.

It wasn't one of them who spoke first, but Riley. "There's no need to fight."

Al was uneasy about tearing his eyes away from the two men, but he couldn't resist as something in her tone had caught his attention. Tears shimmered in her vivid blue eyes, but only one slid through the dirt on her cheeks. Xander remained kneeling beside Bobby, his head bowed and his arm resting upon his knee. Al couldn't see Xander's face, but the small tremor of his shoulders gave away his sorrow.

"There's no need for anything, not for Bobby, not anymore. Some of us only make it so far." Riley's lower lip trembled as more tears spilled from her eyes.

Al realized her words echoed the haunting conversation she and Bobby had shared in the car. *"I didn't think I'd survive it either," Bobby had told them. "Glad you were wrong about that," Riley had said. "So far," Bobby had replied.*

Tears burned Al's eyes as he turned away from the boy's broken body. Had Bobby somehow known, or at least suspected, his time was coming to an end? It was a disconcerting notion; one he couldn't shake as that conversation continued to replay in his mind.

Carl cursed, his hand slammed down on the bed of the truck with enough force to rattle the sideboards. Riley jumped at the action and wrapped her arms around her middle as a small sob escaped her. Carl spun away from the truck and paced a few feet away. Al didn't know what to say as Riley straightened herself up and wiped the tears away. She was trying to appear strong, but the broken air surrounding her made Al long to hug her. Mary Ellen didn't say a word as she walked over to embrace a silently crying Rochelle.

"We should get him out of the back of the truck," Peter stated. "We can put him…"

"I'm not leaving him," Riley whispered.

The last thing Al wanted was to side with Peter, but the man was right. "We can't keep a dead body with the supplies, Riley," he said kindly.

"I know that." She met his gaze. "But I can't just *leave* another one of my friends in the middle of nowhere. Bobby deserves better."

Xander rose to his feet and approached them. His eyes were bloodshot, but he had wiped the tears away from his face. "You mean to dig a grave with what? Our *hands*?" Peter inquired.

Al was even tempted to shoot Peter over that comment. "Shut up," Riley snarled at him. "Just shut up for once! We are not leaving him on the side of the road like a piece of garbage!"

Xander rested his hands on her shoulders and pulled her against his chest. Carl stepped forward as Peter seemed to be gearing up for more protests. "She's right." Carl held up his hand to forestall any further argument. "We'll find somewhere to put him, somewhere better than this. He deserves better; we will *all* deserve better when our time comes. He can't stay back there for long though."

"He won't," Xander promised.

"We should get on the road," Carl said.

Carl closed and locked the doors after Riley, Mary Ellen, and Xander jumped down from the truck. Al rubbed at his chest in an attempt to ease the ache deep within his heart. A single tear slid free as he walked toward the car that would now only be carrying the three of them.

CHAPTER 30

Xander

XANDER SAT FORWARD with his hand on Riley's shoulder as she followed Al's directions down the road. She had insisted upon driving, and Xander hadn't been in the mood to argue with her, not right now. Every breath he took was a struggle as he fought against the constriction in his chest threatening to choke the air from his lungs. He looked at the map over Al's shoulder in an attempt to distract himself, but it did nothing to ease his sorrow.

He couldn't shake the memory of that dream he'd had with Carol now. The image of Bobby and Lee walking along the pathway and Carol sitting beside him haunted him. Had he suspected Bobby's time was coming to an end or had it simply been his subconscious at work? He didn't think there would ever be an answer to that question, but he was extremely grateful no one else had been in the dream.

Night had been approaching before they'd started entering the houses, now little illumination pierced through the thickening clouds overhead. Under normal conditions, the headlights would be on, but Riley had kept them off. Her eyes were narrowed, her shoulders hunched as she leaned over the steering wheel. In the side mirror, he could see the running lights of the truck and the dim beams of the Cadillac that had turned on automatically.

"I can barely see the map anymore," Al muttered. Xander hadn't spotted any of those things in a while but he couldn't see much in the woods beside them, not anymore. "We're going to have to find a place to stay soon."

She eased her foot off the gas as they rounded a turn and an extensive stonewall came into view. It was like so many of the other stacked gray and blue stonewalls seen throughout the Northeast. The different sizes, colors, and the amount of time it must have taken for people to stack them, had always fascinated him. He found no fascination in the wall now as only an odd emptiness resided within him.

"We can camp on the side of the road for all I care. I'm not much in the mood for searching another house today," Riley said as the road became obscured by the encroaching night in such a way it reminded Xander of the fog rolling in off the ocean.

"I think it may be our only option," Al said.

Riley stopped the car as they came to a break within the rock wall. "Is this cemetery on the map?" Riley inquired.

Xander craned his head to look up at the wrought iron sign arcing over the road to the cemetery. *Peaceful Meadows* was intricately spelled out in the iron. "It is," Al answered.

"Is there another way out of it?"

The map was almost touching Al's nose; he lifted his glasses as he squinted at it. "Two others," he said.

"Then I think we've found our place for the night and a place for..." her voice broke, she hitched in a shuddery breath. "For Bobby. It may not be the safest place to sleep, but if we stay close to the vehicles..."

Al wrapped his hand around her forearm and squeezed it. "I think it's the best place for us tonight, and it will be a wonderful resting place for Bobby."

That awful tightness constricted Xander's chest again. He struggled to fill his lungs with air. "Maybe one day we'd be able to come back and find him, to do it right," Riley whispered.

"Maybe one day," Al assured her.

Riley eased off the brake and turned into the cemetery. The road split in two directions as they drove beneath the archway. Riley kept to the road on the right. She drove past a large building that had once been the old cemetery keeper's residence, but Xander assumed it was probably used for storage now. He thought they might be able to stay in there tonight, but he found he actually preferred the idea of being out in the open.

The road wound up a hill past thousands of headstones neatly set up in rows. Most of the older stones, and a few of the new ones had toppled over, but for the most part the cemetery had held up well beneath the onslaught of the quakes. A pond came into view when they broke over the top of the hill. Riley drove toward it and pulled onto the grass ten feet away from the pond. Though there were a few benches set up before the pond, there weren't any headstones on this side of the road.

"This is it," she said softly.

Xander stared at the still surface of the water before he opened the door and climbed out beside Riley. Carl, John, and Rochelle stepped out of the truck. He couldn't see the others in the car behind it. "This will be a good place for Bobby," Al explained as he walked over to join the group by the truck. Xander was grateful for his words; he wasn't up to speaking right now. He wrapped his arm around Riley's waist and pulled her against his side. Though his grief didn't ease, the feel of her gave him some comfort as she rested her head and hand against his chest. "And we're not going to find anywhere else to stay."

"You want to stay *in* the cemetery?" John inquired as he nervously glanced around.

Carl elbowed him in the side sharply. John grunted and rubbed his ribs, but he didn't say anything more. "This is a perfect spot," Carl agreed.

"I'll be back," Riley pat Xander's chest and slipped away from his grasp.

He watched as she hurried to one of the gravestones and bent down to tug a fake flower from a bouquet. She rested her hand briefly upon the stone, bowed her head, and whispered something he couldn't hear. When she returned to him, she was clutching a faded red rose in her hand.

Carl and John already had the doors of the truck open when he took hold of Riley's hand and walked over to join them. Carl was in the bed of the truck; Peter, Mary Ellen, Al, Donald, Josh, and Rochelle were standing by the Cadillac. John went to jump into the truck but Xander grabbed hold of his arm and shook his head. "I'll do this."

"Are you sure?" John asked in surprise.

Xander nodded and climbed up to join Carl. Bobby's arms were still warm when he slid his hands under his friend's armpits and lifted him from the bed. Bobby's head fell back, his shaggy brown hair fell across his pale face, and his half-open brown eyes seemed to meet Xander's in the night.

Memories of their childhood crashed through his mind. In vivid detail he recalled the first day they'd met; they'd been so young and carefree. He recalled the first drink they'd shared at Lee's house in the ninth grade. He remembered all the nights they'd snuck out of their homes to go to the stadium. He could hear Bobby's voice as they talked about comic books, movies, sports, and video games before talk of girls had taken up most of their time. There had been so many laughs over the years, some tears, a few fights, and a couple of punches, but they'd come out of it all stronger and closer.

They'd grown apart when he'd gone away to college, but he'd always known that no matter what, Bobby would have his back. He'd always known when they sat down together again the ease of their friendship would flow effortlessly between them. Bobby had always been there for him; Xander should have been there to stop this from happening.

A garbled sound escaped him. Carl lifted his hand as he took a step toward him but Xander shook his head. Tears burned his eyes; he found it increasingly difficult to keep hold of Bobby's body, but he was able to regain control of himself. He'd done everything he could to save his friend, and to second-guess himself now would only open up a bottomless abyss of despair. That was an abyss he wasn't willing to crawl into, not now, not ever.

He walked with Carl to the edge of the truck. John took Bobby's arms from him and Riley took his feet from Carl. Xander jumped out of the truck and reclaimed his hold on Bobby. Carl went to take his feet back but Riley shook her head and kept hold of Bobby's lower body.

Taking a step back, Carl relented to her, but he stayed beside her as she walked toward a bench facing the pond. "I wish we could bury him," she murmured.

"He would like this," Xander assured her.

"The animals..."

"Riley, don't. There might not be many animals left around here."

Night had completely descended, but he could clearly see the blue of her eyes as they met his. She didn't have to speak for him to know the next thought running through her mind, the *people*. He didn't think the people were going to be a worry either; from what he'd seen, they preferred their meals on the run, but he wasn't going to tell her that right now.

Riley stopped behind the bench and lowered Bobby's feet to the ground. Xander gradually placed his shoulders down; his hands lingered upon Bobby's lifeless form. His eyes were still half-open; Xander stretched his hand forward and slid the lids the rest of the way closed. Mary Ellen handed him a blanket taken from the RV. Riley stepped beside him as Xander draped it over his body.

"Goodbye friend," he whispered before covering his face.

Riley bent beside Bobby and placed the flower on top of him. "Maybe we could put his name on something."

Xander glanced around the cemetery. He might be able to scratch Bobby's name into a piece of wood, or a stone, or *something*. He was at least going to give it a try. "I'll see what I can do about that," he promised her.

"Should we say something?" Rochelle asked quietly.

There were hundreds of words running through his head, but Xander didn't know what to say. "You were a great friend who made me laugh every day, and made me a better person. You will be missed... so much," Riley choked out.

Xander slid his arm around Riley's waist and pulled her against his side. Al stepped forward and made the sign of the cross. "Rest in peace, friend."

Xander shuddered at the finality of those words. Rochelle had tears streaking down her cheeks when she stepped forward and placed a fake white rose on the blanket. Some of the others stepped forward to drop a colorful array of flowers upon the blanket. Peter was the first to retreat back to the Caddy, the farthest vehicle from the body. The others drifted away as time went by, but he and Riley remained standing at Bobby's side well into the night.

"We're going to make it for Bobby, for Carol and Lee, for our parents. We're going to make it and people will *know* their names," Riley said forcefully.

Xander turned his head into her hair and kissed her tenderly. The scent of her wasn't fruity and sweet anymore but as sweaty and dirty as the rest of them. It didn't matter though; he would never get enough of her. "Come on, I'm going to make something for him before we leave."

Her feet remained planted, but he was able to nudge her away from the body and toward the others. "Where are Peter, Josh, and Rochelle?" he asked.

The remaining group, gathered around two flashlights, looked up at him. Carl and John froze in the middle of passing a water bottle between them. There were two small piles of food set up in the empty spaces between John and Donald. Xander settled in beside Donald and Riley beside him and then John. Riley bit into her bottom lip, grabbed for the food, and then pulled her hand back. He was about to say something when she took hold of a package of peanut butter crackers and opened it. Xander knew how she felt, the last thing he felt like doing was eating, but not eating would only make them weaker. The cracker tasted like sawdust in his mouth, but he continued to chew it.

"Peter and Josh are asleep in the car, Rochelle's in the truck," Al answered.

Xander swallowed heavily and fished another cracker out of the package. Before he had finished eating, Carl approached him with a piece of tree and a screwdriver. The tree was a sliver of oak left behind from a tree that had been cut down. "I found it in the woods," he explained. "I thought you could carve his name into it."

"Thank you." Xander took the sliver and the screwdriver from him and set it on the ground beside him. He didn't know what he was going to write, but then he thought he'd only be able to fit *Bobby* onto the piece of wood anyway. Though he wished he could say more, just having Bobby's name to mark him was important.

Xander managed to force the rest of the food down his throat before he picked up the log and screwdriver. Twisting it in his hands, he stared at the now browning piece of wood. Beside him, Donald opened up the notebook and began to write again.

The only sounds filling the night were the scratch of the screwdriver against the wood, and the pen as it moved rapidly over the paper. Xander found the sounds, and the work, strangely comforting as the night progressed. The screwdriver slipped, Xander swore as he stuck his finger in his mouth to stop the flow of blood. His gaze settled on Donald as he continued to write at a pace that made Xander think he raced a clock.

Then again, perhaps he was.

Xander continued to watch him as he sucked on his offended finger. Curiosity finally drove him to ask what he knew they were all thinking. "What are you writing?" Donald didn't answer him; Xander didn't think it was because he was being rude, but rather because Donald was so engrossed in his words he hadn't heard him. "Donald?"

The man continued to write a few more lines before Xander's words finally seemed to pierce his concentration. Donald blinked as he looked around the circle, and then at him. "Did you say something?"

"I asked what you were writing?"

Donald glanced at the notebook and shrugged. "All of it."

Xander frowned at him. "All of what?"

"Everything, everything we've been through. Our story," Donald answered.

Riley had been right in her guess, Xander realized. "We're in the story?"

"I think the story started when I met you guys."

"But *your* story began before us," Riley said.

Donald placed his finger in the notebook and closed it to look at her. "My story wasn't all that interesting," he replied nonchalantly.

"But wouldn't you want people to know about you before all of this happened? Wouldn't you want them to know..."

"No," Donald interrupted her, though his tone hadn't been abrupt. "They wouldn't want to know about me, and there's not much about my life I'd like to recall."

The word sorry formed on the tip of Xander's tongue, but he didn't utter it. Donald wasn't looking for sympathy, he was certain. Xander didn't know what this man had been through, or what it was he was trying to forget, but it was obvious he didn't want to talk about it, and Xander wasn't going to pry.

"I'll tell what you went through when all of this started, if you would like?" Donald asked hesitatingly.

Xander didn't know how to feel about that. He saw the same uncertainty in the faces of those surrounding him. He glanced down at the slab of wood in his hand. His blood had stained the bottom half of the third B a deep mahogany color. That blood may be one of the few marks he left upon this earth by the time this was all over. This log may be one of the only things left of Bobby. There was already nothing left of Lee, or Carol and his parents, other than his memories. Even if no one ever saw what Donald wrote, he'd like to tell what had happened.

People will know their names, Riley had said. This may be the best way for them to do so, Xander realized. Perhaps it would help him to heal, help *all* of them to heal in some way.

"We're not that interesting either," Mary Ellen said.

"More so than me," Donald assured her.

"I was at work," John started and then glanced around at the others. "When it started, Carl and I were at work."

Donald opened the notebook again. "What about before then?"

John frowned thoughtfully before shaking his head. "Before was a different life. I'll tell you about my family, they should be remembered, but I'm not going to live in the time before. I'd prefer to tell how we survived until now. The others might like to tell you more, but not me."

"He's right," Mary Ellen murmured. "*Before* was someone else."

Donald stared at them before bowing his head in acceptance. "I'll write whatever you're willing to tell."

"We were at work," John started again as he began to pick at the browning grass beneath him. "When the first quake hit."

Xander continued to work on Bobby's grave marker as John began his story. When his voice trailed off, Mary Ellen started speaking and then Riley. Xander listened to them as the screwdriver scraped over the wood. When his time came, he took a deep breath before picking up where Riley had left off on their story.

He finished carving the wood and placed it down to listen as John picked up his tale again, and so it went around the circle. Xander glanced over at Donald as he placed the pen down and stretched out his cramped fingers. For the first time Xander noticed Donald's loose fitting shirt had long sleeves as he watched Donald push them up. It was such a strange thing in this heat, but then Xander's gaze fell to the marks on his arm. The marks were faded and appeared to be more like scars marring his fair skin, but Xander recognized some of them as needle marks. He'd seen them on a few of his college classmates. Donald rolled his sleeves back down when he caught Xander's gaze on his arms.

"I told you, mine's not a very interesting story," Donald said so quietly Xander knew no one else had heard him.

"We all have ghosts," Xander whispered.

"Some of them are uglier than others."

"Some humans are uglier than others too."

Donald gave a low chuckle. "I suppose we are."

"The sun will be rising soon," Riley murmured.

"We can pick this up again later," Donald said as he closed the notebook.

"Do you think that man at the church was right?" John asked, drawing Xander's attention away from Donald. "The one who said God has forsaken us?"

"No," Al answered as he stood up and stretched his back. "No one has forsaken us. We're still here, we're still surviving, and that's enough for me to know we haven't been forgotten. It's times like this when you learn who you are. Some of us will fall, and I'm not talking about the people who have been lost, like Bobby and Lee. We must all succumb to death one day." His gaze went to the car Peter and Josh were in before focusing on the group surrounding him. "Some of us will rise up and become something more, maybe something better. *None* of us have been forsaken, and I don't care what anyone else says about that."

They were all struck speechless by Al's passionate words. Looking to break the lengthy silence, Xander took hold of the log before he rose to his feet. "We should probably get back on the road. Just let me put this with Bobby."

Riley yawned as she rose beside him and slipped her hand into his. He caught a glimpse of the notebook in Donald's lap. Scrawled across the top were the words, *The Survivor Chronicles*. He lifted an eyebrow at the title. "Is that what you're calling it?"

Donald glanced at the notebook and nodded. "I think it's fitting."

"So do I," Xander agreed.

He walked with Riley over to Bobby's final resting place and stood for a minute before bending to place the log by Bobby's head. "Goodbye friend," he whispered. "Thank you for allowing me to be a part of your life."

Riley wiped at her eyes as he kissed the top of her head before turning her toward the car. It was going to be an exhausting day, but he was eager to get the final leg of their journey started as he slid behind the wheel and started the car.

Al was right; he knew that in his heart. Bobby had not been forsaken, none of them had. What lay ahead of them was a road of their own choosing. A road they would all have to travel as they learned who was going to rise, and who was going to fall.

~

**The fourth and final book, *The Risen*,
is now available at your favorite ebook retailer:
ericastevensauthor.com/Riwb**

**Stay in touch on updates and other new releases from the
author by joining the mailing list.**

Mailing list for Brenda K. Davies and Erica Stevens Updates:
brendakdavies.com/ESBKDNews

**Join the Erica Stevens/Brenda K. Davies book club on
Facebook for exclusive giveaways, to discuss books, and join in
the fun with the author and fellow readers!**
Book Club: brendakdavies.com/ESBKDBookClub

FIND THE AUTHOR

Erica Stevens/Brenda K. Davies Mailing List:
ericastevensauthor.com/ESBKDNews

Facebook page: ericastevensauthor.com/ESfb

Erica Stevens/Brenda K. Davies Book Club:
ericastevensauthor.com/ESBKDBookClub

Instagram: ericastevensauthor.com/ESinsta
Twitter: ericastevensauthor.com/EStw
Website: ericastevensauthor.com
Blog: ericastevensauthor.com/ESblog
BookBub: ericastevensauthor.com/ESbkbb

ABOUT THE AUTHOR

Erica Stevens is the author of the Captive Series, Coven Series, Kindred Series, Fire & Ice Series, Ravening Series, and the Survivor Chronicles. She enjoys writing young adult, new adult, romance, horror, and science fiction. She also writes adult paranormal romance and historical romance under the pen name, Brenda K. Davies. When not out with friends and family, she is at home with her husband, son, dog, cat, and horse.

ALSO FROM THE AUTHOR

Books written under the pen name

Erica Stevens

The Coven Series

Nightmares (Book 1)

The Maze (Book 2)

Dream Walker (Book 3)

The Captive Series

Captured (Book 1)

Renegade (Book 2)

Refugee (Book 3)

Salvation (Book 4)

Redemption (Book 5)

Broken (The Captive Series Prequel)

Vengeance (Book 6)

Unbound (Book 7)

The Kindred Series

Kindred (Book 1)

Ashes (Book 2)

Kindled (Book 3)

Inferno (Book 4)

Phoenix Rising (Book 5)

The Fire & Ice Series

Frost Burn (Book 1)

Arctic Fire (Book 2)

Scorched Ice (Book 3)

The Ravening Series

The Ravening (Book 1)

Taken Over (Book 2)

Reclamation (Book 3)

The Survivor Chronicles

The Upheaval (Book 1)

The Divide (Book 2)

The Forsaken (Book 3)

The Risen (Book 4)

Books written under the pen name

Brenda K. Davies

The Vampire Awakenings Series

Awakened (Book 1)

Destined (Book 2)

Untamed (Book 3)

Enraptured (Book 4)

Undone (Book 5)

Fractured (Book 6)

Ravaged (Book 7)

Consumed (Book 8)

Unforeseen (Book 9)

Forsaken (Book 10)

Relentless (Book 11)

Coming Fall 2020

The Alliance Series

Eternally Bound (Book 1)

Bound by Vengeance (Book 2)

Bound by Darkness (Book 3)

Bound by Passion (Book 4)

Bound by Torment (Book 5)

The Road to Hell Series

Good Intentions (Book 1)

Carved (Book 2)

The Road (Book 3)

Into Hell (Book 4)

Hell on Earth Series

Hell on Earth (Book 1)

Into the Abyss (Book 2)

Kiss of Death (Book 3)

The Edge of the Darkness

Coming Summer 2020